BONES NEVER LIE

As a forensic anthropologist to the province of Quebec, Canada, Kathy Reichs has often said that she works *with* the dead, but *for* the living.

Forensics are an integral part of her world, with cases constantly coming in to her lab. And yet her chosen profession is, she says, like any other job. However, though you may get used to what's happening around you, and to the sounds and smells and sights of death, this doesn't mean you become immune to it.

Each of her books is based loosely on the cases she's worked on, or an experience she's had. She believes that her stories remain fresh because they originate from her being enmeshed and engaged in forensic work on a regular basis.

Kathy Reichs is one of only eighty-two forensic anthropologists ever certified by the American Board of Forensic Anthropology. She served on the Board of Directors and as Vice President of both the American Academy of Forensic Sciences and the American Board of Forensic Anthropology, and is currently a member of the National Police Services Advisory Council in Canada. She is a Professor in the Department at the University of North Carolina–Charlotte. She is a native of Chicago, where she received her PhD at Northwestern. She now divides her time between Charlotte, NC and Montreal, Quebec.

www.kathyreichs.com
facebook.com/kathyreichsbooks
twitter.com/kathyreichs

Praise for Kathy Reichs

'Reichs' real-life expertise gives her novels an
authenticity that most other crime novelists
would kill for'
Daily Express

'Reichs is the queen of pathology thrillers'
Independent

'Completely engrossing ... drags the reader into a different world
where dialogue is tense, dead men tell the best tales and the ice
will freeze the bones. Read this and you'll know why the word
"thriller" was invented'
Frances Fyfield

'Reichs has proved that she is now up there with the best'
Marcel Berlins, *The Times*

'The forensic detail is harrowing, the pace relentless and the
prose assured. Kathy Reichs just gets better and better and
is now the Alpha female of the genre'
Irish Independent

'A long way from your standard forensic thriller:
all the excitement you crave, indefatigably expert.
But conscience-generated and compassionate too'
Literary Review

'A brilliant novel ... fascinating science and dead-on
psychological portrayals, not to mention a whirlwind of a
plot ... a must-read'
Jeffery Deaver

'Tempe Brennan ... is smart, resourceful and likeable ...
an investigator to follow'
Daily Telegraph

'It's becoming apparent that Reichs is not just "as good as"
Cornwell, she has become the finer writer ...
the ever-accelerating unfolding of the plot has all the
élan of Kathy Reichs at her most adroit'
Daily Express

Also available by Kathy Reichs

The Virals Series
with Brendan Reichs

Kathy
REICHS

BONES
NEVER
LIE

arrow books

Published by Arrow Books in 2015

2 4 6 8 10 9 7 5 3

First published in Great Britain in 2014 by William Heinemann

Arrow Books
The Random House Group Limited
20 Vauxhall Bridge Road, London, SW1V 2SA

www.randomhouse.co.uk

Addresses for companies within The Random House Group Limited can be
found at: www.randomhouse.co.uk/offices.htm

The Random House Group Limited Reg. No. 954009

A CIP catalogue record for this book
is available from the British Library

ISBN 9780099558071
ISBN 9780099558088 (export)

Typeset in Palatino by SX Composing DTP, Rayleigh, Essex
Printed and bound by CPI Group (UK) Ltd, Croydon, CR0 4YY

MIX
Paper from
responsible sources
FSC
www.fsc.org   FSC® C018179

Penguin Random House is committed to a sustainable future
for our business, our readers and our planet. This book is
made from Forest Stewardship Council® certified paper.

For
Alice Taylor Reichs
born August 3, 2012
and
Miles Aivars Mixon
born August 11, 2012

Part One

1

I received the message first thing Monday morning. Honor Barrow needed me at an unscheduled meeting.

Not what I wanted, with cold germs rolling up their sleeves in my head.

Nevertheless, coming off a weekend of Sudafed, Afrin, and lemon-honey tea, instead of finishing a report on a putrefied biker, I joined a billion others slogging uptown in rush-hour traffic.

By seven-forty-five, I was parked at the back of the Law Enforcement Center. The air was cool and smelled of sun-dried leaves—I assumed. My nose was so clogged, I couldn't sniff out the difference between a tulip and a trash can.

The Democrats had held their quadrennial soirée in Charlotte in 2012. Tens of thousands came to praise or protest and to nominate a candidate. The city had spent $50 million on security, and as a result, the ground floor of the Law Enforcement Center, once an open lobby, now looked like the bridge of the starship *Enterprise*. Circular wooden barrier. Bulletproof glass. Monitors displaying the building's every scar and pimple, inside and out.

After signing the register, I swiped my security card and rode to the second floor.

Barrow was passing as the elevator hummed to a stop and opened. Beyond him, through the door he was entering, arrows on a green background directed *Crimes Against Property* to the left, *Crimes Against Persons* to the right. Above the arrows, the hornet's-nest symbol of the Charlotte-Mecklenburg Police Department.

"Thanks for coming in." Barrow barely broke stride.

"No problem." Except for the kettledrums in my head and the fire in my throat.

I followed Barrow through the door, and we both turned right.

Detectives crowded the corridor in both directions, most in shirtsleeves and ties, one in khaki pants and a navy golf shirt featuring the intrepid wasp logo. Each carried coffee and a whole lot of firepower.

Barrow disappeared into a room on the left marked by a second green sign: *2220: Violent Crimes Division.* Homicide and assault with a deadly.

I continued straight, past a trio of interview rooms. From the nearest, a baritone bellowed indignation in strikingly inharmonious terms.

Ten yards down I entered a room identified as *2101: Homicide Cold Case Unit.*

A gray table and six chairs took up most of the square footage. A copy machine. File cabinets. White erasable board and brown corkboards on the walls. In the rear, a low-rise divider set off a desk holding the usual phone, mug, withered plant, and overfilled in- and out-baskets. A window threw rectangles of sunlight across the blotter.

Not a soul in sight. I glanced at the wall clock. 7:58.

Seriously? Only I had arrived on time?

Head pounding and slightly peeved, I dropped into a chair and placed my shoulder bag at my feet.

On the table were a laptop, a cardboard carton, and a plastic tub. Both containers bore numbers on their covers. The ones on the tub were in a format familiar to me: 090430070901. The file dated to April 30, 2009. A single call had come in at 7:09 A.M.

The numbering system on the carton was different. I assumed the case was from another jurisdiction.

A bit of background.

The Charlotte-Mecklenburg Police Department had roughly five hundred unsolved murders dating back to 1970. Recognizing that this was a lot of bodies and a lot of folks waiting for justice, in 2003 the CMPD established a cold case unit.

Honor Barrow, twenty years at the murder table, had run the CCU since its inception. The other full-timers included a police sergeant and an FBI agent. A volunteer review team composed of three retired FBI agents, a retired NYPD cop, a civilian academic, and a civilian engineer provided support in the form of pre-investigation triage and analysis. The cold case unit regulars gathered monthly.

As a forensic anthropologist, I work with the not so recently dead. No secret why I was sometimes invited to the dance. But I usually got a heads-up about why my presence was being requested. A query concerning a set of remains. A question about bones, trauma, or decomposition.

Not this time.

Impatient, and curious why I'd been summoned, I drew the tub to me and pried off the lid. Inside were hundreds of pages separated by dividers. I knew the headings on each of the tabs. Victimology. Summary of the Crime. Crime Scene Report. Evidence/Property Recovered/Analyzed. Medical Examiner's Report. Witnesses. Related Investigation. Potential Suspects. Recommended Follow-up.

Lying across the files was a case review summary written by Claire Melani, a criminologist and colleague at the University of North Carolina at Charlotte. I flipped to the first section of her report. And felt my neck muscles tense.

Before I could read further, voices sounded in the hall. Moments later, Barrow appeared with a guy looking like something off the cover of a survivalist manual. Washed-out jeans. Faded army jacket over long-sleeved red tee. Dark hair curling from below a neon-orange cap.

I replaced the report in its tub. "Everyone stuck in traffic?"

"I didn't invite the volunteer team."

Though that surprised me, I said nothing.

Barrow noticed my gaze shift to the survivalist and introduced him. "Detective Rodas is down from Vermont."

"Umparo. Umpie to my friends." Self-deprecating smile. "Both of them."

Rodas extended a hand. I took it. Umpie's grip matched his appearance, rough and strong.

As Barrow and Rodas took seats, a familiar figure framed up in the doorway. Erskine "Skinny" Slidell, cop legend in his own mind.

Can't say Slidell's presence thrilled me. Since Skinny works homicide, and I work the morgue, we are often thrown together. Over the years our relationship has had more ups and downs than a polygraph chart. His manner is often grating, but the man clears cases.

Slidell stretched both hands in a "What gives?" gesture and drew in one wrist to look at his watch. Subtle.

"Glad you could pry yourself free from the computer porn." Smiling, Barrow hooked a chair free from the table with one foot.

"That sister of yours does love a camera." Cushions *hoof*ed as Slidell deposited his substantial derrière.

Barrow partnered with Slidell back in the eighties

7

and, unlike most, claimed to have enjoyed the experience. Probably their shared concept of witty repartee.

Barrow had just introduced Rodas and Slidell to each other when the door swung out. A man I didn't recognize entered the room. He had a weak chin and a too-long nose and, standing ramrod, matched me in height. His polyester shirt, tie, and off-the-rack suit suggested midlevel management. His demeanor screamed cop. The four of us watched as polyester man took a place at the table.

"Agent Tinker is SBI." Barrow's reference to the State Bureau of Investigation conveyed zero warmth.

I'd heard of Beau Tinker. Intel had him as a narrow thinker with a mile-wide ego. And a player with the ladies.

"Don't seem like such a long drive was warranted." Slidell spoke without looking up from the fingers laced on his belly.

Tinker regarded Slidell with eyes as gray and bland as unpolished pewter. "I'm right up the road at the Harrisburg field office."

Slidell's jaw muscles bulged, but he said nothing.

Like everywhere else on the planet, North Carolina has its share of interagency rivalries. Sheriff's, campus, airport, and port police versus local PD's. The state versus the city boys. The feds versus the world.

Except for some offenses in which it's required—

such as drug trafficking, arson, gambling, and election fraud—SBI involvement in criminal investigations was usually at the request of local departments. The chill coming from Barrow and Slidell suggested no such invite had been issued.

Was Rodas the draw? If so, why the interest in Raleigh about a case from Vermont?

Slidell considers himself a hot property in the homicide squad. Too hot to gasbag around a table, as he'd once put it. I also wondered why he was here.

I remembered the file in the plastic tub.

I glanced over at Slidell. His gaze was up now, aimed at Tinker with the kind of expression normally reserved for pedophiles and mold.

Did the hostility go beyond turf issues? Did Slidell share history with Tinker? Or was Skinny just being Skinny?

Barrow's voice cut into my thoughts. "I'm going to let Detective Rodas start off."

Barrow leaned back and repositioned the neck chain holding his badge. He often reminded me of a large leathery turtle. Skin dark and crinkled as that on a shrunken head, eyes wide-set and bulgy above a pointed little nose.

Rodas opened the carton, withdrew a stack of reports, and slid one to each of us. "Sorry if my style's less formal than yours." His voice was deep and gruff, the kind you associate with white cheddar and the Green Mountain Boys. "I'll give you the rundown, then take questions on anything that's unclear."

I started flipping through pages. Heard Tinker and Slidell doing the same.

"Between two-thirty and three P.M., on October 18, 2007, a twelve-year-old white female named Nellie Gower disappeared while riding her bicycle home from school. Six hours later, the bike was found on a rural two-lane a quarter mile from the Gower farm."

A nuance in tone caused me to look up. Rodas's Adam's apple made a round-trip before he continued. "Nellie's body was discovered eight days later at a granite quarry four miles outside town."

I noted that Rodas was using the child's name, not depersonalizing, as cops often do—the kid, the vic. It didn't take Freud to recognize that Rodas was emotionally invested in the case.

"The ME found no signs of trauma or sexual assault. The child was fully clothed. Manner of death went down as homicide, cause as unknown. The scene yielded nothing. Ditto the body. No tire tracks, no trace, no blood or saliva, no forensics at all.

"The usual persons were interviewed—registered sex offenders, parents and relatives, friends, friends' families, neighbors, babysitters, a Girl Scout leader, those working at the school, the church, the community center. Anyone with even the remotest link to the victim."

Rodas dug spirals of bound three-by-fives from the tub and winged them around the table croupier-style. Went silent as each of us viewed the grim cards we'd been dealt.

The first several prints showed the quarry. A leaden sky overhung an expanse of rock and soil bereft of trees. On the left, a gravel road climbed from the foreground toward a ragged horizon.

Temporary barricades had been set up along the road. Parked behind them were cars, pickups, and media vans. Drivers and passengers stood in twos and threes. Some conversing, others staring across the sawhorses or looking at the ground. A number wore T-shirts printed with the words *Find Nellie* above the face of a smiling adolescent.

I knew the players. Samaritans who'd devoted hours to searching and to answering phones. Gawkers eager for a glimpse of a body bag. Journalists seeking the best slant on another human tragedy.

Inside the barrier were cruisers, a crime scene truck, a coroner's van, and a pair of unmarked cars, each angled as though suddenly frozen in flight. I recognized the usual responders. Evidence and coroner's techs. A woman in a windbreaker with *Medical Examiner* printed in yellow block letters on the back. Cops in uniform, one with his head cocked to speak into a shoulder radio.

A canopy had been erected at center stage. Below the blue plastic, yellow tape stretched from pole to pole, forming a rough rectangle. Enclosed in the rectangle was a painfully small mound. Rodas squatted beside it, face grim, notepad in hand.

The next series focused on the child. Nellie Gower lay on her back, legs straight, arms tight to her torso. Her red wool jacket was zipped to her chin. Her sneaker laces were looped in symmetrical bows. The bottom of a polka-dot blouse was neatly tucked into bright pink jeans.

Several photos framed the face printed on the tees. No smile now.

Nellie's hair covered her shoulders in long chocolate waves. I noted that it was parted down the center of her scalp and evenly draped, as though combed and arranged.

Eight days of exposure had wrought the inevitable. The child's features were bloated, her skin mottled purple and green. A maggot mass filled her mouth and each of her nostrils.

The last three shots were close-ups of the child's right hand. Dotting the palm were traces of a filmy white substance.

"What's that?" I asked.

"CSS bagged both hands. The ME swabbed her skin and scraped under her nails. The trace guys thought it might have been remnants of a tissue."

I nodded, still staring at the photos. Synapses were firing in my brain. I remembered another child. Another set of heartbreaking photos.

I knew why I'd been called. Why Skinny was here. "Sonofabitch."

Rodas ignored Slidell's outburst. "We got a few leads, phone tips, a witness saying a teacher showed unusual interest in Nellie, a neighbor claiming he saw her in a truck with a bearded man. Nothing panned out. Eventually, the case went cold. We're a small department. I had to move on. You know how it is."

Rodas looked at Slidell, then Barrow. Met eyes that knew only too well. "But it ate at me. Kid like that. Whenever I had spare time, I'd pull the file, hoping to spot something I missed."

Again, the Adam's-apple bob. "According to all accounts, Nellie was timid. Careful. Not likely to go with a stranger. We all believed the perp was local. Someone she knew. I guess we got channeled on that.

"Last year I figured what the hell. Think outside the box. I tried VICAP."

Rodas was referring to the FBI's Violent Criminal Apprehension Program, a national database maintained to collect and analyze information about homicides, sexual assaults, missing persons, and other violent crimes. The repository contains approximately 150,000 open and closed investigations submitted by some 3,800 state and local agencies, and includes cold cases dating as far back as the 1950s.

"I entered what we had, MO, signature aspects, crime scene descriptors and photos, victim details. Took weeks to get a response. Then damned if our profile didn't match an unsolved here in Charlotte."

"The Nance kid." Slidell spoke through barely parted lips.

"Never got a collar on that one." Tinker's first words since telling Slidell he was posted locally.

Slidell opened his mouth to reply. Apparently reconsidered and closed it.

I glanced at the tub. 090430070901. Lizzie Nance. Skinny's own gut-eating failure.

On April 17, 2009, Elizabeth Ellen "Lizzie" Nance left a ballet class, heading for her mother's apartment three blocks away. She never made it home. Media coverage was massive. Hundreds turned out to answer tip lines, post flyers, and search the woods and ponds near Lizzie's complex. To no avail.

Two weeks after Lizzie's disappearance, a decomposed body was found at a nature preserve northwest of Charlotte. The corpse lay supine with feet together, arms tucked to its sides. A black leotard, tights, and pink cotton underwear still wrapped the putrefied flesh. Bright blue Crocs still covered the feet. Residue found under a thumbnail was identified later as common facial tissue.

Slidell led the homicide investigation. I analyzed the bones.

Though I spent days bending over a scope, I spotted not a single nick, cut, or fracture anywhere on the skeleton. Tim Larabee, the Mecklenburg County medical examiner, was unable to establish definitively whether sexual assault had occurred. Manner of death went down as homicide, cause as unknown.

Lizzie Nance died when she was eleven years old.

"Fortunately, Honor had also entered his unsolved. The system picked up the similarities." Rodas raised both hands. "So here I am."

A moment of silence filled the room. Tinker broke it. "That's it? Two girls roughly the same age? Still wearing their clothes?"

No one responded.

"Wasn't the Nance kid too far gone to exclude rape?"

Palming the table, Slidell leaned toward Tinker. I cut him off.

"The autopsy report noted complicating factors. But the child's clothing was in place, and Dr. Larabee was confident in concluding there'd been no rape."

Tinker shrugged, not realizing or not caring that his cavalier attitude was offending everyone. "Seems weak."

"It's not just the VICAP profile that brings me to Charlotte," Rodas continued. "By the time we found Nellie, her body had been rained on for a day and a half. Her clothes were saturated with a mixture of water and decomp runoff. Though not optimistic, I submitted everything to our forensics lab up in Waterbury for testing. To my surprise, some DNA had survived."

"All hers," Slidell guessed.

"Yes." Rodas placed his forearms on the table and leaned in. "Eighteen months ago, I went over the file yet again. This time I caught something I thought could be a break. The residue from Nellie's hand hadn't been submitted with her clothing. I phoned the ME; she found the scrapings taken at autopsy by her predecessor. Knowing it was a long shot, I had her send them up to Waterbury."

Rodas looked straight at me.

I looked straight back.

"The material contained DNA not belonging to Nellie."

"You sent the profile through the system?" Tinker asked the unnecessary question.

Rodas chin-cocked the report in my hands. "Take a look at the section marked 'Updated DNA Results,' Dr. Brennan."

Curious why I'd been singled out, I did as instructed.

Read a name.

Felt the flutter of adrenaline hitting my gut.

2

The report was short, printed in both French and English.

Struggling to make sense of it, I reread the closing paragraph. In both languages.

A match was obtained on DNA sample 7426 to Canadian national number 64899, identified as Anique Pomerleau, W/F, DOB: 12/10/75. The subject is currently not in custody.

Anique Pomerleau.

My eyes rose to Rodas. His were still fixed on me. "You can imagine how amped I was. Years of nothing, then I get word they've sequenced DNA that isn't Nellie's. I told the analyst to shoot the profile through CODIS."

Like VICAP, the Combined DNA Index System is a database maintained by the FBI. CODIS stores DNA profiles and uses two indexes to generate investigative leads.

The convicted offender index contains profiles of individuals convicted of crimes ranging from misdemeanors to sexual assault and murder. The forensic index contains profiles obtained from crime scene evidence, such as semen, saliva, or blood. When a detective or analyst enters an unknown profile, the CODIS software electronically searches both indexes for a potential match.

A match within the forensic index links crimes to one another, possibly identifying serial offenders. Based on a "forensic hit," police in multiple jurisdictions can coordinate their investigations and share leads. A match between the forensic index and the convicted offender index provides investigators with an "offender hit." A suspect. A name.

Anique Pomerleau.

"She's not American." Lame, but that's what I said. What I meant was, how did Rodas get a match to a Canadian citizen? Our neighbors above the forty-ninth use the CODIS software but maintain their own national repository of DNA data.

"We came up blank in the U.S., so I decided to send the profile north. It's not uncommon. Hardwick is less than an hour's drive from the border." Rodas pointed at the report I was holding. "That's from the Canadian National DNA Data Bank."

I knew that. In the course of my work at the

Laboratoire de sciences judiciaires et de médecine légale in Montreal, I'd seen dozens of these reports. The pseudoephedrine and oxymetazoline I'd taken for my cold were short-circuiting my ability to articulate clearly. "How did you make the connection to me?" I clarified.

"The hit was in Canada, so it seemed logical to start there. I have a buddy at the Royal Canadian Mounted Police. He ran the name and found an Anique Pomerleau who fit the identifiers. Pomerleau is wanted by the Sûreté du Québec on a warrant dating to 2004."

"Hold on. You're saying that five years after the Canadians are looking for this chick, she leaves DNA on a dead kid in Vermont?" Tinker, king of compassion.

"The lead detective still works there, but apparently, he went AWOL recently." Rodas gave a wry smile. "I got the feeling that was a story in itself."

I felt a soft pulsing in my wrist. Stared at the delicate blue vein worming under my skin.

"No one remembered much about the perp or the case. But a coroner hooked me up with a pathologist who's been around forever. Pierre LaManche.

"LaManche told me Pomerleau was a suspect in the deaths of several young girls. Said her accomplice was a guy named Neal Wesley Catts. Back in '04, Catts either shot himself or Pomerleau killed him. Then she vanished.

"I told LaManche about the DNA found on Nellie Gower's hand and about the VICAP match to your unsolved here in Charlotte. He advised me to contact Dr. Brennan."

Anique Pomerleau.

The monster.

The only one who ever got away.

I kept my face blank. My eyes focused on the vessel snaking my flesh.

"You're thinking Pomerleau did both Gower and the Nance kid." Tinker, again stating the obvious.

"I think it's a possibility."

"Where's she been all this time?"

"We sent out a BOLO." Be on the lookout. "So did the SQ, though I didn't feel a lot of love there. Can't really blame them. It's been ten years. Pomerleau's maybe dead, maybe using an alias, and the only pic they have dates to 1989."

I remembered. It was the only photo we had. Taken when Pomerleau was around fifteen.

"So. After Montreal, Pomerleau goes to ground for three years, then resurfaces and grabs a kid in Vermont." From his tone, I knew Slidell was rolling the theory past his own ears.

"Last I checked, North Carolina's a few miles from the tundra," Tinker said. "How'd Pomerleau end up here?" When no one responded, he pressed on. "DNA links this Pomerleau to the Gower kid. But what links Gower to Nance? I said it before, and I'll say it again. It's sad, but kids are murdered every day. What makes you so sure we're looking at one doer?"

The pressure in my sinuses suddenly felt explosive. Discreetly, I pressed a hand to one cheek. My skin was fiery hot. Was the virus upping the ante? Or was it the shock of what I was hearing?

As I reached for a tissue to blow my nose, Rodas ticked off points, beginning with his right thumb. "Both victims were female. Both were eleven to fourteen years of age. Both vanished during daylight from a public road—a highway, a city street. Both were left on the surface in an unprotected setting—a quarry, a field. Both bodies were lying faceup, with arms and legs straight, hair carefully arranged."

"Posed," Barrow said.

"Definitely."

Rodas shifted to his left hand. "Both victims were clothed. Both had remnants of tissue on their fingers. Neither showed evidence of trauma. Neither showed evidence of sexual assault." He withdrew a plastic sleeve from his carton and put it on the table. Inside was a white-bordered five-by-seven color print.

Barrow dug a similar print from the tub and placed it beside Rodas's. As one, we leaned forward to view them.

The photos were undoubtedly school portraits. The kind we all sat for as kids. The kind kids still take home every year. The backgrounds differed. A tree trunk versus rippled red velvet. But each subject looked straight at the camera with the same awkward smile.

21

"I got to admit," Tinker admitted, "they are of a type."

"Of a type?" Slidell pooched air through his lips. "They look like friggin' clones."

"Both victims were roughly the same height and weight," Rodas said. "No bangs. No glasses. No braces, which I'd guess are fairly common in that age group."

It was true. Both girls had fair skin, fine features, and long dark hair center-parted and drawn back from the face. Gower had hers tucked behind her ears.

I looked at Lizzie Nance. At the face I'd studied a thousand times. Noted the dusting of caramel freckles. The red plastic bow at the end of each braid. The hint of mischief in the wide green eyes.

And felt the same sorrow. The same frustration. But new emotions were stirring the mix.

Unbidden, images genied up in my mind. An emaciated body curled fetal on a makeshift bench. Yellow-orange flames dancing on a wall. Blood-spattered crystal casting slow-turning shadows across a dimly lit parlor.

My gaze drifted past Slidell toward the back of the room.

Though I couldn't see the view from where I was seated, I knew the window looked out over the parking lot. And the buildings of uptown. And the interstate snaking through the power grids of the Northeast. And the far distant Canadian border. And a dead-end street beside an abandoned railroad yard. Rue de Sébastopol.

The sound of silence brought me back to the present.

"You need a break?" Barrow was studying me with an odd expression. They all were.

I nodded, rose quickly, and left the room.

As I hurried up the hall, more images popped. A dog collar circling a willowy neck. Dark refugee eyes, round and terrified in a morgue-white face.

I locked the lavatory door, crossed to the sink, and held my hands under the faucet. Watched and didn't watch as water ran over them. A full minute.

Then I cupped my fingers and drank.

Finally, I straightened and looked in the mirror. A woman looked back, knuckles white as the porcelain she was clutching.

I studied the face. Not young, not old. Hair ash blond but showing gray feelers. Eyes emerald green. Revealing what? Grief? Rage? Congestion and fever?

"Pull yourself together." The reflected lips mouthed the words. "Do your job. Nail the bitch."

I shut off the tap. Yanked paper towels from the dispenser and dried my face. Blew my nose.

Returned to the CCU squad room.

"—just saying it's unusual to find no sexual component." Tinker sounded steamed.

I resumed my seat.

"Who knows what's sexual to these fuckwads."

Kathy Reichs

Slidell slumped back in his chair, dragging a balled
fist across the tabletop.

"If the perp's female, we could be looking at a whole
different ball game," Tinker said.

"Yeah, well, it's *our* ball game," Slidell snapped.
After a pause, "Gower was 2007."

"So?"

Slidell slid Tinker a withering look. "Gower was
2007. So there's a three-year gap between Vermont and
what went down earlier in Montreal. Another year
and a half goes by and Nance is grabbed here."

"What's your point?"

"Time line, you dumb shit." Slidell shot to his feet
before Tinker could fire off a cutting retort. "I'm done
here."

"Let's call it a morning." Barrow, trying to defuse
what was escalating toward open combat. "We'll
reconvene when Detective Slidell and the doc have
reviewed the Nance file."

A look passed between Barrow and Slidell. Then
Skinny was gone.

"Send in the clowns." Giving a tight shake of his
head, Tinker pushed up from his chair.

Rodas watched Tinker disappear through the door
before eyebrowing a question at Barrow. Barrow
gestured at him to stay put. Rodas settled back. So did
I.

Slidell reappeared minutes later, a manila folder in
one hand. Attached to the folder was a snapshot.

Dropping into the closest chair, Slidell thumbed off the paper clip and placed the photo beside the two school portraits.

I felt adrenaline flutter anew.

The girl had brown eyes and light olive skin. Her long chestnut hair was center-parted and drawn up in combs. I guessed her age at twelve to thirteen.

"Michelle Leal. Goes by Shelly," Slidell said. "Thirteen. Lives with her parents and two siblings in Plaza-Midwood. Last Friday afternoon the mother sent her to a convenience store at Central and Morningside. She bought milk and M&M's around four-fifteen. Never made it home."

I'd spent most of the weekend zoned out on cold meds, drifting off quickly every time I turned on the TV. I recalled vague fragments of news reports on a missing child, video of a search team, a mother's teary appeal.

Now I was seeing that little girl's face.

"She hasn't turned up?" I swallowed.

"No," Slidell said.

"You think it's related."

"Look at her. And the MO fits."

I glanced up. Met Barrow's eyes. "You think I'm the draw," I said evenly.

Barrow tried a comforting smile. It didn't work out.

"You think Pomerleau learned where I live, came here, and killed Lizzie Nance. And now she's taken Shelly Leal."

"We have to consider the possibility," Barrow said quietly.

"That's why you asked me here this morning."

"That's one reason." Barrow paused. "With cold cases, we've got all the time in the world. No pressure from the public, the media, the guys up the pay scale. That won't be the situation with Shelly Leal."

I nodded.

"Maybe the kid's already dead," Slidell said. "Maybe not. Gower was found eight days after she was snatched. If Leal is alive, we may be looking at a real narrow window."

Barrow jumped back in. "You're familiar with Pomerleau's thinking, her way of operating."

"I'm an anthropologist, not a psychologist."

Barrow raised both palms. "Understood. But you were there. That's one reason we need your help."

"And the other?"

"A detective named Andrew Ryan was lead on the Pomerleau investigation. Word is you know the guy personally."

Heat rushed my face. I hadn't seen that one coming.

"We want you to find him."

3

"I do not keep track of Detective Ryan's whereabouts."

My heart was still sending blood to my cheeks. I hated it. Hated that I was so easy to read.

Barrow had a habit of clearing his throat. He did it now. "You've worked with this Ryan a long time, right?"

I nodded.

"Do you know why he dropped off the grid?"

"His daughter died."

"Suddenly?"

"Yes." OD'd in a heroin den.

"Age?"

"Twenty."

"That would knock anyone off the rails."

I glanced down at my watch. Reflex. I knew the time.

"It's been almost two months, and no one has a clue where this Ryan has gone."

I said nothing.

"He ever talk about favorite getaways? Places he wanted to visit? Places he'd gone on vacation?"

"Ryan is not the vacationing type."

"The guy has quite a reputation." Rodas grinned. "Way they *parlez-vous* up there, he's cleared every homicide since the Black Dahlia."

"Elizabeth Short was killed in L.A."

The burn of embarrassment also colored Rodas's cheeks. Or something did.

"Ryan worked Pomerleau," Barrow said. "We could really use his input."

"Good luck." Testy, but I don't respond well to pressure.

"LaManche had the impression that you and Ryan were close."

I managed to curb my impulse to get up and leave.

"Sorry. That came out wrong."

No, Detective Rodas, that came out right. Ryan and I share more than murder. We share memories, affection. We once shared a bed.

"What I meant was, LaManche thought if anyone could find Ryan, it would be you."

"Bring him in from the cold?"

"Yeah."

"That only happens in books."

Original files never leave the CCU squad room. After telling Slidell, Barrow, and Rodas everything I could remember about Anique Pomerleau, I set about photocopying the contents of the plastic tub.

Slidell went to take a call. He never came back.

Shortly before one, my mobile rang. Tim Larabee wanted me to examine remains found in the trunk of a Subaru at an auto salvage yard.

My head felt like lead, my throat like hot gravel. And I was about to pass out from toner fumes.

Screw it.

I delivered a duplicate of the Nance file to Slidell's desk. Then I got a box, loaded my own copy, and left.

Instead of heading to the ME facility west of uptown, I called Larabee to beg off, citing plague as an excuse. Then I pointed my Mazda toward an enclave of overpriced homes set beneath trees so large, their summer foliage turned the streets into tunnels. Myers Park. My 'hood.

In minutes, I turned off Queens Road onto a circular drive that swooped up to the pompous brick Georgian reigning over Sharon Hall. My complex.

I continued past the carriage house to a tiny two-story structure tucked in one corner of the grounds. The "annex," date of birth and original purpose unknown. My home.

I let myself in and called out, "Hey, Bird."

No cat.

I thumped the box on the counter and looked around the kitchen. The shutters were angled down, casting long golden slashes across the oak floor.

The refrigerator hummed. Otherwise, the place was quiet as a crypt.

I pushed through a swinging door, crossed the dining room, and climbed to the second floor.

Birdie was curled on my bed. He lifted his head from his paws at the sound of movement. Looked startled. Maybe irked. Hard to tell with felines.

I tossed my purse to the chair, then my clothes. After pulling on sweats, I downed two decongestant tabs and slipped under the covers.

Eyes closed, I listened to familiar sounds, trying not to think about Anique Pomerleau. Trying not to think about Andrew Ryan. The steady *dip dip dip* of the bathroom faucet. The soft *scree scree* of a magnolia branch scraping the screen. The rhythmic *prrrrr* of air flowing past Birdie's vocal cords.

Journey burst into song. "Don't stop believin' . . ."

My lids flew open.

The room was dim. A thin rectangle of gray outlined the shade.

"Hold on . . ."

I rolled to my side. The glowing orange digits on the clock said 4:45.

I groaned.

The music ended abruptly. I stumbled to my purse, yanked out my iPhone, and checked caller ID.

Groaned again.

Dropping onto the edge of the bed, I hit callback.

Slidell picked up right away. Background noise suggested he was in a car. "Yo."

"You phoned."

"Tell me this ain't some new epidemic?"

My drug-clogged brain could do nothing with that.

"First Ryan takes a powder, then you."

Seriously? "You're welcome for the photocopies," I said.

Slidell made a noise I took to mean thanks.

"You pulled your own disappearing act." I yanked a tissue from the box and held it to my nose.

"Had to check out a lead on the Leal thing."

"What lead?"

"Guy walking on Morningside Friday afternoon spotted a kid getting into a car. Said she looked upset."

"Meaning?"

"Meaning the moron's got the IQ of lentil soup. But the time line fits, and the guy's sketch of the kid skews right."

"Did he get the license?"

"Two digits. What the hell's wrong with your voice?"

"It could be a break."

"Or it could be the toad's hallucinating."

"What's with you and Tinker?"

"Guy's like something crawled out of a saucer at Roswell."

Slidell's negativity didn't surprise me. His knowledge of the alleged UFO incident did.

"Is it just that Tinker's state?"

"It's all bullshit."

"What do you mean?"

"The SBI's taken a real hosing in the press lately. Now some asshole in Raleigh's decided a clear on a serial involving kids is just the spit shine they need."

Beginning in 2010, the SBI had been rocked by a scandal involving the serology and bloodstain units in its forensics lab. The North Carolina attorney general commissioned an investigation, and the conclusions were blistering. Faulty lab reports. Failure to report contradictory results. A unit director who lied about his training, perhaps perjured himself. Prosecutorial bias up the wazoo.

Defense attorneys throughout the state did the happy dance.

Appeals were submitted. Convictions were overturned. The ensuing avalanche of litigation was expected to cost North Carolina millions.

The media went batshit.

In the end, heads rolled, including that of the lab director. The legislature enacted a number of reforms. Procedures and policies were revamped. The accreditation process was changed. The SBI was still battling to restore credibility.

Was Slidell right? Was the bureau inserting itself into our investigation in an attempt to rehab its image?

"You think Tinker was sent to this morning's meeting because of politics?"

"Nah. I think he likes the pickles they serve downstairs."

"Nance has been cold for years. Isn't it risky for the SBI to insist on involvement in such an old unsolved?"

"The public sees a clear, they're heroes. They don't, we're the dumb rubes who screwed up."

I had to admit, that made some sense. "SBI input isn't necessarily a bad thing. Maybe Tinker can help. You know, bring a different perspective."

"The fuckstick's already on my back."

"Meaning?"

"Meaning I'm topping his speed dial."

"Perhaps he has something useful to tell you."

"He's trying to slime into my case."

Sensing further discussion of Tinker would be unproductive, I changed tack. "What's your take on Rodas?"

"Lose the cap. It ain't bear season."

"Actually, it is. In some counties."

"Guy seems okay."

"His first name is Umpie."

"No shit."

"No shit."

"I may have to rethink my view. Look, while I'm tied up with Leal, what say you go back over Nance. See if anything jumps out at you."

"Sure." I closed my eyes for a moment. Rebunched the tissue. "You think you'll find her alive?"

"I gotta get back on the street."

Three beeps, then dead air.

Birdie was in the kitchen staring at his dish. I filled it.

No appetite, but I forced myself to eat. Tuna on toast. Gourmet.

When I was finished, I took the Nance file to the dining room and spread the folders on the table. I started with the case review I'd glanced at earlier.

The cold meds were still jamming my wiring. And the morning's retelling of the horror had me on edge. Instead of Lizzie Nance, I kept seeing the old house on rue de Sébastopol. The dank cellar where Pomerleau and Catts had caged their victims.

The case had started quietly enough. Many do. A pizza-by-the-slice joint. Leaky pipes. A long forgotten staircase.

Who knew why the plumber ventured into the basement. How he spotted the human femur sticking out of the dirt.

The proprietor called the cops. The cops called me.

I excavated three partial skeletons, one in a box, two buried naked in shallow graves. I brought them to my lab for analysis. Young girls.

Foul play? No one thought so at first. The bones were probably ancient, like the rat-infested building under which they lay.

Radioactive isotopes proved that theory wrong.

Ryan worked the case also. And a city cop named Luc Claudel.

In the end we learned the names of the dead. The names of their killers.

But questions remained.

The bones provided no clue as to cause of death. Did the girls die of starvation? Abuse? Loss of will to live another day in hell?

We learned of one captive from a journal entry. Never found her remains. Kimberly Harris. Hamilton. Hawking. Where was this young woman whose name I couldn't remember? Did she lie somewhere in an unmarked grave? Did others?

One victim had survived, and I'd thought of her from time to time ever since. Asked myself: Is recovery possible after years of torture and isolation? After a childhood stolen by madness?

Andrew Ryan also invaded my thoughts. More fragmented images.

Ryan's features gouged from darkness by the soft yellow of my porch light.

Ryan's tears as he talked of Lily's death. His embarrassment at having shed them.

Ryan's back receding into the night.

Ryan didn't inform his superiors, didn't take leave. He told no one his destination or when he'd return. *If* he'd return.

That no one included me.

I'd numbed the pain by blocking Ryan from my thoughts.

Now, as I tried to focus, it all crashed back.

35

Murdered children in Montreal. Murdered children in Vermont, possibly Charlotte. The unthinkable. The horrific possibility that Anique Pomerleau was active again.

Pressure to locate a man I'd forced myself to forget. To persuade him to reenter a world he'd abandoned.

And waves of fever rolling over me.

At nine I gave up.

After a hot, steamy shower, I downed two more tabs and dropped back into bed.

I'd been there only moments when the landline rang.

The voice blindsided my overwrought, overmedicated brain.

4

I love the Carolina mountains. Love driving the narrow two lanes that worm like twisty black ribbons through the humpty-back giants.

That morning the beauty was wasted on me. I hadn't the time. Or the mindset for a Blue Ridge outing.

The dashboard clock said 7:44 A.M. I'd been up two hours, on the road ninety minutes. Surprisingly, I felt good. Or at least better. God bless chemistry.

Just before Marion, I turned east off Highway 226. The sun floated above the horizon, a yellow-orange ball winking on and off as I rounded curve after curve. Long slanted rays sparked mist still lingering in low spots between the ridges.

I passed a field with a chocolate mare grazing side by side with her colt. Both raised their heads and ears, mildly curious, then resumed eating.

Within minutes a sign peeked from the foliage on my right. Wrought-iron script announced the entrance to Heatherhill Farm. Discreetly. If you don't know we're here, just keep on motoring.

I turned onto an unmarked strip of asphalt arrowing through enormous azaleas and rhododendron. When I cracked the window, a post-dawn mix scented the car's interior. Pine, wet leaves, damp earth.

Soon I passed buildings, some small, some large, each looking like a set straight out of *Christmas in Connecticut*. Ivy-covered chimneys, long porches, white siding, black shutters.

I knew Heatherhill's forty acres contained multiple structures. A chronic-pain center. A gym. A library. A computer lab. Amenities for the well heeled with issues.

Knew only too well.

Beyond the four-story main hospital, I split off onto a tributary road, passed a low-rise building housing business and admissions offices, and made another left. The tiny lane ended fifty yards later in a rectangle of gravel enclosed by a white picket fence.

I parked, grabbed my jacket and purse, and got out.

Through a gate in the fence, a flagstone path led to a small bungalow. Above its door, a sign said *River House*. One calming breath, then I started toward it.

On the inside, River House could have been anyone's mountain cottage. Anyone with a predilection for antique reproductions and a whole lot of bucks.

The floors were wide plank and covered with Oushaks and Sarouks that cost more than my house.

The upholstery involved shades a decorator probably called mushroom and moss. The wooden pieces were stained and distressed to look old.

I wound through the living room, past gas-fed flames dancing in a stacked stone fireplace, and exited double glass doors at the back of the house. The deck held a teak table and matching chairs, several tubs planted with pansies and marigolds, and four chaise lounges with bright melon cushions.

The farthest chaise had been displaced several feet and angled away from the others. On it was a woman with white hair cut pixie-short. Before her, on the porch rail, sat a thick ceramic mug. The woman wore khaki slacks and an Irish sweater that hung to the middle of her thighs. On her feet were ballet flats, two-tone, the leather on the toes a perfect match for the pants.

I watched a moment. The woman sat motionless, hands clasped, eyes fixed on a forest thick with morning shadows.

I approached, my bootfalls loud in the stillness.

The woman didn't turn.

"Sorry I couldn't make it last night." Cheerful as Mickey's Marching Band.

No response.

I dragged a chaise close and positioned it parallel. Sat sideways, oriented toward the woman. "I like your new haircut."

Nothing.

"The drive was good. I made it in under two hours."

Still no acknowledgment of my presence.

"You sounded upset last night. Are you feeling better?"

A bird landed on the rail. A nuthatch, maybe a waxwing.

"Are you angry with me?"

The bird cocked its head and regarded me with one shiny black eye. The woman crossed her ankles. The bird startled and took flight.

"I was planning to come for Thanksgiving." Still speaking to her profile. "That's next Thursday."

"I'm aware of the date. I'm not an idiot."

"Of course you're not."

A fly dropped onto the rim of the mug. I watched it test its way around the perimeter, feelers and front legs working the substrate. Tentative. Unsure what to expect. I felt total empathy.

"Did you know that Carrauntoohil is Ireland's highest mountain?" The woman unclasped her hands and laid them on the armrests. The skin was liver-spotted, the nails perfect ovals painted dusty rose.

"I didn't."

"It's in County Kerry. Rises thirty-four hundred feet above sea level. Not much of a mountain, if you ask me."

I reached out and placed my hand on hers. The bones felt fragile beneath my palm. "How are you?" I asked.

One cable-knit shoulder lifted ever so slightly.

"You said you have something you want to share."

The woman's free hand floated up, held, as though unsure of its purpose in rising. Dropped.

"Are you unwell?"

Again the shoulder.

"Mama?"

Deep gusty sigh.

They say a daughter becomes some variation of her mother. A different reading of an old script. A new interpretation of an existing character.

I studied the face so vigilantly preserved by creams and lifts and injections. By wide-brimmed hats in summer and long cashmere scarves in winter. The flesh was looser, the wrinkles deeper, the lids a bit droopy. Otherwise, it was the mirrored reflection I'd seen at the CMPD. The green eyes, the set jaw.

The air of tension. Of guardedness.

I knew I resembled my mother physically. But I'd always believed the similarity ended there. That I was an exception. A contradiction to the rule.

I was not my mother. I never would be.

Physicians, psychiatrists, psychologists. So many diagnoses. Bipolar. Schizoaffective. Schizobipolar. Disorder of the moment. Choose your favorite.

Lithium. Carbamazepine. Lamotrigine. Diazepam. Lorazepam.

No medication ever worked for long. No treatment ever stuck. For weeks my mother would be the warm, vibrant person I loved, a woman who brought

Kathy Reichs

sunshine into every room she entered. Happy, funny, clever. Then the demons would claim her again.

Bottom line: my mother is as loony as a bag of squirrels.

Throughout my childhood, each time the blackness descended, Mama would pack her Louis Vuittons; kiss my sister, Harry, and me; and disappear in the old Buick with Daddy at the wheel. Later Gran.

But there were no public hospitals for Daisy Brennan, née Katherine Daessee Lee. Over the years Mama visited dozens of private facilities, each with a name that promised healing in the bosom of nature. Silver Birch. Whispering Oaks. Sunny Valley.

Mama never made an encore appearance. Always something was lacking. The food. The room. The attentiveness of the staff.

Until Heatherhill. Here the menu suited, and she had her own room and bath. And after so many visits, she was now welcome to stay as long as she liked. As long as the Lee family trust ponied up.

Mama spoke without meeting my eyes, voice low and honeyed as Charleston in August. " 'In that other room I shall be able to see.' "

The quote sent cold rippling across my chest. "Helen Keller." Mama loved Keller's story, retold it often when Harry and I were kids.

Mama nodded.

"She was speaking of death."

"I'm old, darlin'. It happens to all of us."

Was this a ruse? A new ploy to gain my attention? A delusion?

"Look at me, Mama." More stern than I'd intended.

For the first time she rotated to face me. Her expression was serene, her gaze clear and composed. The sunshine Mama.

When I was younger, I'd have tried to force an explanation. I knew better now. "I'll speak to Dr. Finch."

"That's an excellent idea." The manicured hand slipped free of mine and patted my knee. "No sense spoiling the little time we have together."

Behind us, the glass door opened. Closed again.

"How about you, darlin'? What's on your plate these days?"

"Nothing extraordinary." Murdered children. A depraved killer I'd hoped to never encounter again.

"Are you still seeing your young man?"

That threw me. "What young man?"

"Your French-Canadian detective. Are you two still an item?"

The million-dollar question. But how did Mama know?

"Did Harry tell you I was dating?" Really? Dating? Did that term even apply to the complex rituals of those over forty?

" 'Course she did. Your sister and I have no secrets."

"Harry could use a bit of discretion."

43

"Harry is fine."

If four husbands, obsessive overindulgence, and an insatiable need for male attention classifies as fine.

Mama leaned close and did something with her eyebrows meant to encourage shared intimacy.

There was no point denying her. "I haven't seen him recently."

"Oh, dear. Did he dump you?"

"His daughter died. He needs to be alone for a while."

"Died?" The perfectly plucked brows arched up.

"She was ill." True enough.

"Oh, how very, very sad."

"Yes."

"Do you still hear from— What's this gentleman's name?"

"Andrew Ryan."

"That's a lovely name. Have you communicated with him since his child's passing?"

"One visit and one email."

"My, my. That's hardly devotion."

"Mmm."

"Did he tell you where he was going?"

"He told no one." Defensive.

"Others are looking for him?"

There's no slipping anything past Mama. "Some detectives would like his help on a case."

"Is it something just too wretched for words?"

Mama had always shown keen interest in my work.

In my "poor lost souls," as she called the unnamed dead.

Seeing no harm, I described the cold case investigations involving Vermont and Charlotte. Anique Pomerleau and Montreal. I said nothing about Shelly Leal.

Mama asked her usual questions: who, when, where. Then she settled back on the chaise and recrossed her ankles. I waited. After a full minute she said, "These other detectives think your Andrew Ryan can catch this dreadful woman?"

"Yes."

"Do you?"

"Maybe." If he hadn't fried his brain with booze. Fried himself with grief and self-loathing.

"Then we shall find him."

I snorted.

Mama's jaw tightened.

"I'm sorry. I just know you have other things on your mind. You need to focus on recovery. I don't doubt you can find him."

I didn't.

When she was fifty-eight and emerging from a particularly cavernous funk, I bought my mother her first computer, an iMac that cost much more than I could afford. I held little hope that she'd find the cyber world attractive, but I was desperate for something to occupy her attention. Something other than me.

I showed her how to use email, word processers,

spreadsheets, the Internet. Explained about browsers and search engines. To my surprise, she was fascinated. Mama took class after class. Learned about iTunes, Myspace, Facebook, Twitter, Photoshop. Eventually, as was typical, her mastery of the new sport was way beyond mine.

I wouldn't call my mother a hacker. She has no interest in the secrets of the DOD or NASA. Doesn't collect credit card or ATM numbers. Nevertheless. When she's on her game, there's nothing she can't tease from the World Wide Web.

"Do you still have his email?" Mama asked.

"I suppose I could find it. But all he said was—"

"I'll be right back."

Before I could object, she was up and into the house. Moments later, she returned with a Mac the size of a fashion magazine.

"You use Gmail, don't you, darlin'?" Lifting the lid and tapping a sequence of keys.

I nodded.

She patted a spot to her right. When I shifted to her chaise, she placed the laptop on my knees. "Pull it up."

I logged in to my service provider and entered an identifier I thought might work. Seconds later, Ryan's email appeared on the screen. I opened it.

Doing well. Miss you. AR.

I passed the computer to Mama. She clicked on a tiny triangle to the right of the reply arrow. From a drop-down menu, she chose the command "Show Original."

A block of data appeared. The font looked like something produced by the old mainframe I used as an undergrad.

Mama pointed to a line about halfway down. The header said "Received." Embedded in the gibberish was a string of four numbers divided by periods. "Every email has an IP address. It does basically the same thing a street address does for snail mail. That's our sweet baby there."

She highlighted and copied the numbers to the clipboard. Then she logged out of Gmail and entered a site called ipTRACKERonline.com. "Now we do what's called geolocation."

After pasting the string of numbers into a box in the middle of the screen, she hit enter. In seconds, a Google Earth satellite image appeared. On it was a red circle with its root stuck into the ground.

Below the map was information organized into three categories: Provider info. Country info. Time info.

I skimmed the center column. Country. Region. City. Postal code. I looked at Mama. "It's that easy?"

"It's that easy."

She closed the laptop, turned, and hugged me. Her arms felt frail inside their thick woolen sleeves. "Now, my sweet girl, you go find your Andrew Ryan."

"If I do, I may not be able to visit on Thursday."

"We can have turkey any ole time. You go."

Before leaving River House, I detoured down a carpeted corridor accessed from one side of the dining room. Dr. Finch's office door was cracked, allowing a partial view of her seated behind an ornately carved desk. A plaque shared the fact that her first name was Luna.

I knocked softly, then entered.

Dr. Finch looked up. A moment of surprise, then she gestured to one of two chairs opposite her.

As I sat, Dr. Finch leaned back and steepled her fingertips. She was short and round, but not too short and round. Her hair was curly, dyed brown, and blunt-cut just below her ears.

"Her spirits are up," I said.

"Yes."

I smiled, and Dr. Finch smiled back.

"She thinks she is dying."

A pause, then, "Your mother has cancer."

My heart froze in my chest. "She just learned this?"

"She's been seeing an oncologist for several months."

"And I wasn't informed?"

"We are not your mother's primary physicians. We attend to her mental well-being."

"Can the two be separated?"

"Upon arrival, your mother informed us of her condition and requested confidentiality. She is an adult. We must respect her wishes. Now she feels it is time we talk to you."

"Go on."

"Go on?"

"Tell me the rest."

"The cancer is spreading."

"Of course it is. That's what cancer does. How is it being treated?"

Luna Finch regarded me with eyes that answered my question.

Yes, I thought. *No hair loss and wigs for Mama.*

"Would chemo help?" I asked.

"It might."

I swallowed. "And if she continues to refuse?"

Again the eyes.

I looked down at my hands. My right thumb was red and swollen. Itchy. A mosquito, I diagnosed.

"What now?"

"Your mother has chosen to stay at Heatherhill Farm as long as she can."

"And how long will that be?"

"Perhaps a good while."

I nodded.

"Is the number we have on file for you still current? In case we need to reach you?"

"Yes." I rose.

"I'm very sorry," she said.

Outside, the mist had burned off. High above, a white vapor trail streaked a cloudless blue sky.

Mama couldn't be dying.

Yet Luna Finch said it was so.

49

5

I don't sleep well on planes. Believe me, I try.

It was midafternoon by the time I got back to Charlotte. Eight when I finished a prelim on Larabee's car trunk case. Ten when I finally found and booked a flight and room.

After arranging for cat care with my neighbor, I packed a carry-on, took a shower, and fell into bed.

My mind kept churning, offering up outtakes, unedited, lacking chronology.

Childhood memories of my mother.

Happy times. Reading to Harry and me on the garden swing. Quoting Shakespeare, Milton, other long-dead strangers we didn't understand. Driving the Buick on illicit après-bedtime ice cream sorties.

Sad times. Listening outside Mama's bedroom door. Confused by the tears, the breaking glass. Terrified she'd come out. Terrified she wouldn't.

Memories of Andrew Ryan. Happy times. Skiing

at Mont Tremblant in the Laurentian Mountains. Celebrating successes at Hurley's Irish pub. Laughing at our shared cockatiel Charlie's bawdy quips.

Sad times. The day Ryan was shot. The plane crash that took the life of his partner. The night we ended our relationship.

Doubts about my upcoming excursion. Was it futile? Ryan's email was almost a month old. Had he moved on?

No. Barrow had nailed it when he'd asked if I could think of a spot Ryan had mentioned. I remembered comments. Ryan loved the place. It was where he'd go to hide out. To drop out.

Doubts about my decision not to tell my daughter about Mama. No. That decision was sound. Katy was serving in Afghanistan. She had enough on her mind.

All night I tossed and turned, questions skittering up and down my neural pathways. Doubts. Uncertainties.

Certainties. Luna Finch. Rogue cells multiplying out of control.

The last time check occurred at 2:54. The alarm screamed at five.

The flight to Atlanta was short, the layover just a little over an hour. Not bad. But this leg was torture.

I tried reading. *Life*. Maybe Keith Richards's problems could make mine seem small. No go.

I closed the book and my eyes.

Something brushed my arm. I raised my lids. My chin from my shoulder.

51

The passenger beside me was steadying the plastic cup holding the remains of my cranberry juice. He was tall, with faded red hair and eyes the color of smoked glass.

"We are about to land." They were the first words he'd spoken since takeoff, four hours earlier.

"Sorry." I took the cup and returned my tray to its upright position. My seat.

"You are on vacation?" the man asked in softly accented English.

What the hell. The guy had prevented a spill. "I'm trying to find someone."

"In Liberia?"

"Playa Samara."

"Ah. My destination also."

"Mmm."

"I own property there."

The man withdrew a card from his wallet and handed it to me. His name was Nils Vanderleer. He sold irrigation systems for a company headquartered in Atlanta. Or so his card claimed.

I managed a smile. I thought.

"Perhaps I could be of assistance?" Vanderleer asked.

"I'm good. Thanks."

"Yes, you are."

The plane banked and we both glanced toward the window. Vanderleer could see out. I could not.

Moments later, the wheels engaged. Vanderleer

turned back to me. "Might I buy you dinner one evening?"

"I'm hoping to be in Samara only one night."

"That's a shame. Costa Rica is a magical place."

The line at passport control took thirty minutes. I exited the terminal perspiring, headachey, and cranky as hell.

Vanderleer was on the sidewalk, frowning and pacing. I had no choice but to pass him. When he saw me, he put up his hands in a "What can you do?" gesture.

"I booked a car, but of course it has not arrived on time. The driver is now ten minutes out. If you don't mind a short wait, I am happy to take you to Samara."

"Thanks for the offer. My hotel has ordered a taxi."

Three hours after wheels down, I finally passed under a white stone arch rising from a wall thick with some sort of flowering vine. A wooden sign announced my arrival at Villas Katerina.

The place looked as advertised online. Palm trees. Woven hammocks. Villas with yellow stucco walls, white trim, and red tile roofs circling an amoeba-shaped pool.

The woman at reception was small and bubbly and had a bad case of acne. She took my credit card, all smiles, then led me to a villa set apart from the others. Smaller. Overlooking a garden lush with tropical vegetation.

I entered, wheeled my bag to a carved wooden chair beside one window, opened the drapes, and looked out. Nothing but foliage.

I turned and surveyed my surroundings—buttery walls, orange trim, orange bedspread and drapes. Native art, crude, probably local. Tiny kitchenette. Tiled bath, jarringly blue coming off the carroty bedroom.

Suddenly, I felt exhausted. Kicking off my shoes, I stretched out on the bed to consider options. Nap? No way. The sooner I found Ryan, the sooner I could leave.

Where was I, exactly? Samara Beach. Playa Samara. On the Pacific coast of a peninsula curling down from the northwest corner of Costa Rica, not far from its border with Nicaragua.

The night before, I'd done some research. Costa Rica is a small country, just a hair over fifty thousand square kilometers. A country known for its biodiversity. For its rain forests, cloud forests, woodlands, and wetlands. A country with a quarter of its territory protected as national parks and refuges.

Somewhere in it was Andrew Ryan. I hoped.

The IP address had placed Ryan in Samara four weeks earlier. The town was small, less popular with tourists than the upmarket sands of Tamarindo and Flamingo. That would work in my favor.

I pulled out the map I'd downloaded and studied the small tangle of streets. Noted a church, a laundromat, a number of shops, hotels, bars, and restaurants. A couple of Internet cafés.

Ryan is many things. Witty, generous, a crack detective. When it comes to communication, he is a Luddite. Sure, he has a smartphone. And he knows how to use the tools available to cops. CODIS, AFIS, CPIC, the lot. But that's it. When off duty, Ryan prefers to call. He never texts, rarely emails.

And he doesn't own a laptop. Says he wants to keep his personal life personal.

I got to my feet, undressed, and went into the shower. After toweling off, I put on sandals, jeans, and a T-shirt. Then I popped two Sudafed, shouldered my purse, and headed out.

The acne-faced woman was sweeping dead blossoms from the stone decking surrounding the pool. On a whim, I crossed to her and spoke in Spanish. Flashed a picture of Ryan.

The woman's name was Estella. She knew of no Canadian living in Samara. She remembered a foursome who visited briefly from Edmonton. Both men were short and bald. When I asked, she cheerfully provided directions.

The walk along the beach took only minutes. I passed a restaurant, a surf school, a police station the size of a soap dish.

Samara's main drag was a jog in the highway cutting through town. I reached it by heading straight up from the water.

Two horses grazed a patch of grass at the first corner I reached. A few cars and motorcycles were parked on either side. Power lines crisscrossed the air above.

The nearest Internet café was jammed between a souvenir shop and a small grocery. Its front was stucco, done in the same lemon and tangerine theme as my room. Lettering on the window offered international calls, Internet service, computer and iPhone repair.

The interior, considerably more drab than the exterior, held a counter, a soda vending machine, and six computer stations. At one station a confused-looking young woman studied a Lonely Planet guidebook, backpack at her feet. I assumed the other services were offered through the door at the far end of the shop.

A kid manned the register, back against the wall, front legs of his stool raised off the floor. He was maybe sixteen, with pasty skin and ratty blond dreads gathered high on his head. The dreads bobbed as he talked into a cellphone.

I approached.

The kid continued his conversation.

I cleared my throat.

The kid pointed to the computers but didn't disconnect.

I placed a photo on the counter and slid it toward him.

The kid righted the stool and glanced at the image. Up at me. Something flickered in his eyes, was gone.

"I'll call you back." East Coast accent, maybe New York. To me, "So?"

"Have you seen him?"

"What makes you think that?"

"He may have come here to use the Internet."

"Yeah, lady. That's what people do."

"You'd notice him. He has sandy hair and stands over six feet tall."

"In his moccasins?"

I hadn't a clue what he meant by that.

"I'll be damned, Natty Bumppo right here in Samara."

Okay. The kid read James Fenimore Cooper. Maybe he wasn't a total loss.

"It's important that I find him."

"What's he done?"

"He's a cop. His input is needed on an investigation."

The kid glanced toward the door, the Lonely Planet girl. Then he leaned forward on his elbows and whispered, "Could be I've seen him."

"Here?"

"I'm having a little trouble remembering." His brows flicked up, dropped. "You catch my meaning?"

I did. I dug my wallet from my purse and teased free a twenty.

The kid's hand shot forward. I held the bill out of his reach.

"Take the highway west from town. Beyond where the Arriba Pathway T's in, past the Las Brisas del

57

Pacifico, down on the beach. Got a blue awning. Watch for a road cuts inland on the left. There's a guy named Blackbird rents out a couple of tree houses up there. Your guy's in one of them."

"He's still here?"

"He's still here."

Our eyes locked for a moment, then I let him snatch the money.

As I hurried back down toward the water, my pulse was racing. Could it be this simple? Walk into one café and score?

Or had I been played? Was the kid now laughing on his cellphone, describing the dumb gringo he'd just scammed?

But he knew I'd come back if I'd been conned. Right. Come back and do what?

Again I considered options. Which seemed few. Hurry there now? Wait until later, when Ryan might be in bed? How much later? Sleep, then strike at sunrise?

My stomach growled.

That decided it. Dinner first, then I'd set off.

I unfolded and checked my TripAdvisor printouts. El Lagarto was just up the beach. A lot of people liked it. What's not to like about a joint with a slow-dancing gator couple as its logo?

I located the entrance and followed a lantern-lit walkway to a very long bar. Beyond the bar, a man tended steaks, fish, and plantains on a huge grill. The smell set my stomach whining again.

A woman wearing an embroidered cotton top seated me in an open area filled with tables and chairs that looked made of fossilized wood. Already half were occupied. Overhead, lanterns and colored lights twinkled softly. At ground level, candles flickered inside dozens of glass hurricane chimneys. In the gathering dusk, across the sand, the ocean boomed softly.

I ordered the seafood platter. Ate it. Felt sluggish as blood diverted to my gut.

I was on my second coffee, idly scanning my fellow diners, when my brain snapped back to attention.

Across the restaurant, a man stood talking to the bartender, his back to me. He wore a black T-shirt with a neon-green surf logo, faded denim shorts, and boat shoes. The hair was blonder and shaggier than the last time I'd seen it. But I knew the jawline, the shoulders, the long ropy limbs.

As I stared, heart pounding, the man flicked a quick one-finger wave at the bartender, turned, and walked out.

I dug money from my purse. Too much. I didn't care.

Slapping *colones* on the table, I bolted for the door.

6

In the atmospheric but ineffective lantern light, I saw a neon-green surfboard near the end of the walkway. It disappeared as its wearer turned right.

Ryan was ten yards ahead when I hit the beach road. He wasn't walking fast, yet I had to quicken my pace to keep up.

After going north a few blocks, he headed west along the highway. That fit with the dreadlocked kid's account.

The tourists thinned as we moved farther from the center of town. With fewer rival noises, the ocean sounded louder. The sky, now fully black, was starting to show points of twinkling white light.

Fifteen minutes out, Ryan stopped abruptly. I froze, certain he'd seen me. Uncertain how my intrusion into his new life would be received.

Ryan's shoulders rounded and his hands rose. A match flared. A tiny orange dot lit his face briefly. Then he straightened and turned left.

I let the distance between us increase, then I followed.

The road was narrow and paved only with gravel. Vegetation packed both sides, dark and dense in the moonless night.

Mosquitoes whined. Fearful of discovery, I fought the urge to slap them away.

Ryan's footsteps continued another fifty, maybe sixty yards. Then a door opened, banged shut. Seconds later, light filtered through slivers in the tightly packed flora.

I held back a full minute, then moved forward.

It was a Tarzan arrangement of sorts, a crude cabin on stilts within the branches of a tree. I crept close and peered through the wood-latticed screening.

The lower level contained a very basic kitchen whose centerpiece was a wooden table with two blue plastic chairs. In one corner, an open door revealed a bath with stone-covered walls. In another, slatted stairs angled steeply to an upper floor. The wan illumination was seeping from above.

I stood a moment, breath frozen. What if I was wrong? What if the man wasn't Ryan?

It was Ryan.

Moving gingerly, I eased open the screen door, tiptoed across the tile and up the stairs. I was on the second tread from the top when he spoke. "What do you want?"

The voice sounded hoarse, weary. Angry? I couldn't tell.

"It's Tempe," I said.

There was no response. I swallowed. Tried to recall the words I'd practiced in my head.

"Why are you following me?"

"I located you through your email."

"Congratulations."

"It wasn't hard."

Shit. Was I trying to make him feel bad?

"Actually, I had help."

"So I have been found. Now leave me alone."

"May I come up?"

Silence.

"Don't you want to know why I'm here?"

"No. I don't."

I stepped onto the top riser.

Ryan was sitting on an unmade bed, knees raised, back to the wall. A single bulb oozed light through a paper-covered fixture above his left shoulder. A fan rotated slowly overhead. A book lay spread on his chest.

An open bottle of Scotch sat on a table made of sticks to the right of the bed. An empty bottle rested at the base of one wall, abandoned where it had rolled to a stop. The smells of old booze and soiled clothing overrode the jungle bouquet coming through the screening that formed the upper half of the walls.

"You look good," I said.

Partially true. Ryan's skin was tanned, his hair bleached by hours in the sun. But he'd lost weight. His cheeks were gaunt below the stubble of beard. The shadowing of ribs and hollow spaces rippled his T-shirt.

"I look like shit," he said.

I launched into the speech I'd practiced. "You're needed. It's time to come home."

Nothing.

Screw it. I cut to the quick. "Anique Pomerleau."

Ryan's eyes flicked in my direction. He seemed about to speak, instead reopened the book.

"It's her, Ryan. She's killing again. A girl was murdered in Vermont in 2007. Her body was posed. The cold case detective—"

"Past life." His eyes returned to the book.

"Pomerleau's DNA was found on the kid."

Ryan's gaze remained fixed on the page. But a changed tension in his neck and shoulders told me he was listening.

"You tracked Pomerleau. You caught her. You know how she thinks."

"I'm no longer in the show." Still not looking up.

"She's resurfaced, Ryan. She got away from us on rue de Sébastopol, and now she's back at it."

Finally, his eyes rolled up to mine. A spiderweb of red surrounded each neon-blue iris.

"A girl was murdered in Charlotte in 2009. The

victimology and crime scene signature parallel the case in Vermont."

"Including Pomerleau's DNA?"

"That's being confirmed."

"Sounds weak."

"It's her."

Ryan's eyes held mine for a very long moment, then dropped back to the page he wasn't reading.

"Another girl has now gone missing. Same physical type. Same MO."

"No."

"Undoubtedly, there were others in between."

"Leave me alone."

"We need you. We have to shut her down."

"Do you know the way back to your hotel?"

"This isn't you, Ryan. You can't turn your back on these kids, knowing there will likely be more. More murders of young girls."

Ryan reached up and killed the light.

Above the whine of insects and the gentle ticking of wind-tossed leaves, I heard him turn away from me.

Back at Villas Katerina, my iPhone picked up a signal, and messages pinged in.

Slidell had called three times.

Of the past forty-eight hours, I'd slept maybe two. Nevertheless, I phoned him. As was his style, Slidell launched in without greeting. "Where the hell are you?"

"Costa Rica."

"Long way to go for a taco."

"I'm talking to Ryan." No point in discussing distinctions of ethnic cuisine.

"Yeah? How's that going?"

"It's not."

"Just tell the bastard to get his ass home."

"Never thought of that. Why did you phone?"

"When Barrow got the call from Rodas, he set up a cold case review on Nance."

I knew that.

"First thing he did was resubmit the kid's clothing and the shit stuck to her hand."

"Thinking technology has improved since '09?" I stifled a yawn.

"Yeah. And go figure. It has."

Suddenly I was wide awake. "The lab found DNA that didn't belong to Nance?"

"Guess the happy donor."

"Pomerleau."

"None other."

"Holy crap."

The speed of the report didn't surprise me. The CMPD has its own DNA capability, and turnaround averages two weeks. What shocked me was the fact that the link was now real. Undeniable. Anique Pomerleau had abducted and killed a child in my town.

"What about Shelly Leal?"

Kathy Reichs

"Still out of pocket. But we might have caught a break there. Kid had her own laptop. I had the computer guys take a run at it. The thing was wiped."

"When?"

"Around three on Friday afternoon."

"Right before she disappeared."

"Eeyuh."

"What was erased?"

"The browser history and the email. Clean. Not one friggin' message. Not one friggin' page."

"Isn't there an option to clear the history at specified intervals? Or every time you log off?"

"The guy said that's what clued him. When he checked, the browser wasn't set to do that. So he did whatever voodoo it is they do, found that someone had manually deleted the stuff. Emptied whatever it is archives your email on Mars."

"Anything else?"

"Photos, music, documents, those files are all there. Hadn't been touched since Friday morning. The only thing nuked was the online stuff."

"Unlikely a middle-schooler would know how to do that."

"Mom said the kid wasn't a techie."

"Clearly, she was coached."

"Eeyuh."

"You're thinking she met Pomerleau online?"

"I'm thinking I'm damn sure gonna find out."

"Can your guy retrieve any of the deleted files?"

"He's working on it, no promises."

"Did you roll this past Rodas?"

"The kid in Vermont didn't own a computer."

"Mobile phones? Other devices?"

"Gower didn't own a cell. Leal did, but the thing's missing. And the record search turned up shit."

"How about Nance?"

"That's why I called. You see any mention of a phone in the CCU file?"

"I'll check as soon as I get back."

"When's that?"

"Tomorrow."

"Good. I want this bitch in bracelets before she drops another kid."

After disconnecting, I rewound my conversation with Ryan. Felt anger and resentment at his refusal to help. Then I thought beyond tonight back into the past.

Ryan was one of the good ones. He'd had a few rough years, made a few false starts. But since his rocky youth, he'd done everything right. Played it straight as a cop. Tried hard as a father.

Sure, his loss was unthinkable. But the time for wallowing was over.

I had an idea. Was it callous?

Nope. Enough self-pity.

Decision made, I dug out my Mac, logged on, and went to the US Airways site. When finished, I sat a moment, attempting to calm my frazzled nerves.

Outside, late-night swimmers splashed in the pool. High in the palms, a howler monkey grunt-barked an end-of-day message. Another answered. A small creature, perhaps a gecko, skittered across my window screen.

My thoughts turned to a river cabin shaded by trees soft with moss.

On a whim, I dialed Mama. Got voicemail. I left a rambling message about Samara and fresh seafood and beaches and meeting with Ryan. Said good night. Told her I loved her.

In the moments before sleep came, memories of Ryan again bombarded my mind. His body shielding mine during a biker shoot-out in a Montreal cemetery. Stretched out on a beach in Honolulu. Lying beside me in a hammock in Guatemala.

I dreamed about a cellar beside a rail yard covered in snow.

7

By six, I was chugging along the beach road again.

The sky was thinning from black to gray. The ocean had calmed overnight. Its surface was rippling yellow-pink in a triangle announcing the return of *el sol*.

A few vendors were already setting out their wares. Gulls were throwing a party out on the beach. The occasional car or motorcycle passed, now and then a battered pickup. Mostly, I had the pavement to myself.

Ryan was downstairs in one of the blue kitchen chairs, dressed in the same T-shirt and shorts he'd worn the night before. He glanced up when I opened the screen door, then continued spooning Cheerios into his mouth. His face registered nothing.

"Why Costa Rica?" I asked.

"Birds."

"Over eight hundred species," I said.

"Eight hundred and ninety-four."

"Charlie would feel right at home." I was referring to the pet cockatiel we shared.

"Charlie's peeps come from down under. Hungry?"

As I settled into the other chair, Ryan retrieved a bowl and spoon from the counter behind us. His face was sallow and baggy-eyed. His sweat smelled of booze. I wondered if he'd finished the entire bottle of Scotch.

I poured myself cereal. Added milk, tamping the urge to check the expiration date.

"There are half a million animal species in this country." Ryan spoke without looking at me.

"Three hundred thousand of those are insects."

"Bugs gotta live."

"What's your plan?"

"Find every one."

"How's that going?"

"Place has something else in its favor."

I floated a brow. Focused on his O's, Ryan missed it.

"Thousands of miles between here and Quebec."

"That's it? Distance and fauna?"

"Booze is cheap." Ryan pointed his spoon at me. "And Cheerios can be had by the savvy consumer."

"This isn't you, Ryan."

He feigned looking over his shoulder. "Who is it?"

"I can't imagine losing a child, and I don't presume to understand your pain. But wallowing in self-pity, numbing yourself with alcohol, turning your back on life? That's not you."

"I thought about keeping a journal." Spoken with a full mouth. "Like Darwin in the Galápagos."

"What happened?"

"Can't draw."

"I mean what happened to you."

Ryan's spoon rattled as it hit the empty bowl. He snagged a pack of cigarettes from the table, tapped one out, drew matches from the cellophane, and lit up. One drag, then his eyes finally met mine. "You found me. Let's hoist you on our shoulders and march you around the room."

"Grow a pair, Ryan. Come with me. Do what you do. What *we've* done together for almost two decades. We catch the bad guys. We take freaks like Pomerleau off the streets."

"Go back and tell your buddies I'm not the guy you need."

I accessed the flight itinerary and slid my iPhone to him. Ryan studied the screen. "Who paid for this?"

"That's irrelevant."

"No way the CMPD's footing the bill to fly me stateside."

"Do you have your passport?"

Ryan drew smoke deep into his lungs, exhaled through his nose.

"They want you there," I said.

"Hope for your sake the fare is refundable."

"I got a call last night. Skinny Slidell."

Ryan knew Slidell from a case we'd all worked together years earlier in Charlotte. He said nothing.

"The lab lifted DNA from Lizzie Nance's clothing."

Ryan questioned me with bloodshot eyes.

I nodded.

Ryan stubbed out his cigarette with one sharp jab. Slumped back and folded his arms.

"Also, Slidell thinks he may have caught a break in the Leal case."

As I explained the erased files, the shadows and contours of Ryan's face seemed to deepen.

"If Pomerleau has taken Leal, she's stepped up her game," I said. "She's now stalking her prey online. One other thing—why Charlotte? I think I know. She's learned I'm there and she's taunting me. Sending a message that I can't beat her."

I settled back. Waited.

Ryan gave me the long stare.

"Suit yourself." I snatched up my mobile and dropped it into my purse.

I was outside when his voice came through the screening. "What time is the flight?"

"We need to leave Samara by ten." Masking my surprise. "I can wait while you shower and pack."

"I have to see someone before I go."

"No problem." Now masking pain. Irrational. The "someone" could be his landlord. His Cheerios source. And Ryan and I had agreed we didn't work as a couple. Still, the thought stung. Another woman in Ryan's life? We'd meant so much to each other for so long.

"Where are you staying?"

"Villas Katerina."

"I'll meet you there at nine-thirty."

I hesitated. Did I trust him?

What choice did I have?

My watch said 9:40. I hadn't given up, but I was close.

9:50.

Of course he wouldn't show. The bastard was probably halfway to San Jose.

I knew Ryan was wounded, but I'd underestimated the extent of the damage. I wondered if he could ever be whole again. Nevertheless, I was hurt more than I'd expected by the fact that he'd leave me to face Pomerleau by myself.

Once, Ryan would have worried about my safety. About the impact of a case on me as well as on the victims. His paternalism had both annoyed and warmed me. Seeing him made me realize how much I missed that.

A horn honked on the street beyond the wall.

Five past ten.

I wheeled my carry-on through the door and up the path. Estella waved from behind the window as I passed reception.

The driver was leaning on the hood of his taxi. He smiled, took my bag, and placed it in the trunk.

I was climbing in, thinking about the long trip back, about what I would say to Slidell and Barrow, when I spotted Ryan weaving through sunscreen-slicked tourists heading for the beach. He'd shaved and changed into a black polo and jeans. An overstuffed backpack hung from one shoulder.

"Thanks," I said.

"Out of Cheerios," he replied.

We passed the next two hours in silence. At Daniel Oduber Quirós International, we checked in, made our way through security, handed in our boarding passes, finally took our seats, and buckled in. Not a word.

I had the window this time, watched as Costa Rica disappeared beneath us. When I could take the silence no longer, "Wonder what the weather's like in Charlotte."

"Continued dark overnight, widely scattered light by morning."

Recognizing the George Carlin quote, I smiled to myself. The old Ryan was still in there somewhere.

Then I was out.

I awoke to the captain announcing our landing. And wishing his passengers and crew a happy Thanksgiving.

As we wound down the ramp from the airport parking deck, I offered Ryan the guest room.

"A hotel close to the law enforcement center will be fine."

I wasn't surprised. So why the hollow feeling? Relief? Resignation? Sadness that at last I had full confirmation?

Yes. Definitely sadness.

I said nothing.

"It's better this way." In response to my silence.

"I'm good with it," I said.

"I'm not the same person, Tempe. Not the man I was."

I dropped him at the Holiday Inn on College.

It was after ten when I hit the annex. The place seemed incomplete without Birdie. After downing the takeout burritos I'd grabbed en route home, I phoned Barrow.

He was impressed that I'd bagged my quarry. And pleased. Suggested a meet at eight the next morning. Said he'd call Rodas and Slidell.

After disconnecting, I dialed the Holiday Inn. Asked for Ryan. Shocker—they connected me. He'd actually checked in.

I offered a ride in the morning. Ryan said he'd find his own way to the CCU. *Or back to the airport*, I thought cynically.

That was all I could handle.

Exhausted, I fell into bed.

"Wish I could say you look good." Slidell was eyeing Ryan with an expression of amusement.

Ryan shrugged.

"What the fuck's with your hair?"

"Been touring with Shaggy."

The reggae reference was lost on Slidell, whose musical taste ran to C&W and sixties rock and roll.

Barrow cleared his throat. "The sooner we start, the sooner we get home to leftover turkey."

"Or back on the street," Slidell said.

"This will be short. There's nothing new on Pomerleau. Leal is still missing; Detective Slidell says so far, the tech boys have recovered nothing from her Mac. They're still at it."

"The computer's not out there." This was Slidell's way of saying, "Don't discuss it with the press."

"Right," Barrow affirmed. "The media's starting to turn ugly. Mainly, I wanted to get us all face-to-face—"

"Without that fuckwad Tinker."

Barrow slid a look to Slidell before continuing. "I wanted Detective Ryan to meet Detective Rodas."

The men nodded at each other, acknowledging earlier introductions.

"Dr. Brennan has briefed Detective Ryan on details of the Vermont and Charlotte cases." Question, not statement.

"Yes." I'd done it with zero feedback on the drive from the airport to Ryan's hotel.

"I'm only here as an observer." Ryan favored me with a sideways glance. "And to appease Dr. Stalker."

Hurt and anger reared up in equal proportions. I fought both down.

"Two murders," Barrow said. "And Shelly Leal is missing one week today."

"Still, the link is weak." Ryan often played devil's advocate.

"DNA connects Gower to Nance and both to Pomerleau. The MO for Leal is identical."

Ryan rubbed a thumbnail along the edge of the table. Thinking about long-ago girls in a cellar? His dead daughter? A bottle of Scotch he'd left in his room?

"Ryan—" I started.

"I'll be no good to you."

"You know Pomerleau," I said.

"I'm a mess."

Slidell snorted. "Should take the heat off my ass."

"I'm sorry." Ryan wagged his head. "I'm done with cracked skulls and slit throats and cigarette burns. No more dead kids."

"What about live ones?"

Ryan's thumb continued its slow back-and-forth. I wanted to slap him, to shake him to his senses. Instead I kept my voice even and neutral. "Pomerleau's thrill didn't come from killing. You know that. She fed her victims just enough to keep them alive so she could torture and rape them. She and her twisted sidekick."

"Neal Wesley Catts," Rodas tossed in. "Aka Stephen Menard."

"Leal could be alive," I continued. "But if Nance and Gower are indicative, it's not like the old days.

Pomerleau's pattern has changed. Leal won't last long."

Still Ryan said nothing.

Rodas placed a palm on the cardboard box holding his case notes. "I have to head north in the morning. Would you at least skim the file?"

Ryan closed his eyes.

I looked at Slidell. He shrugged.

A very long moment passed.

Ryan ran a hand over his jaw. Sighed. Then his eyes rose to mine. "One day."

He looked at his wrist. Which bore no watch.

"Twenty-four hours."

8

Ryan and I got coffee before plunging into the Nance file. We wouldn't drink it. The stuff tasted like liquefied dung. It was a ritual, like sharpening a pencil or straightening a blotter. Meaningless action as prelude to the real show.

We started with a section titled *Summary of the Crime*.

On April 17, 2009, at 1620 hours, Elizabeth Ellen "Lizzie" Nance, eleven, left the Isabelle Dumas School of Dance, located in the Park Road Shopping Center, heading for the Charlotte Woods apartment complex on East Woodlawn. A motorist reported seeing a child matching Lizzie's description at the intersection of Park and Woodlawn roads at approximately 1630 hours.

Lizzie lived with her mother, Cynthia Pridmore, thirty-three, and sister, Rebecca Pridmore, nine. Cynthia Pridmore reported her daughter missing, by phone, at 1930 hours. She reported having contacted the school, several of Lizzie's classmates, and her former husband, Lionel Nance, thirty-nine. Pridmore said she and Nance repeatedly drove the route between the school and the home. Said her daughter could not be a runaway. An MP file was opened, with Detective Marjorie Washington as lead investigator.

On April 30, 2009, a groundskeeper, Cody Steuben, twenty-four, found a child's decomposed body at the Latta Plantation nature preserve, northwest of Charlotte. Medical examiner Timothy Larabee identified the remains as those of Lizzie Nance. The case was transferred to the homicide unit, with Detective Erskine Slidell as lead investigator.

Lizzie Nance was a sixth-grade student with no history of drug, alcohol, or mental issues. A low-risk victim. Cynthia Pridmore was a legal secretary, twice divorced. The second former husband, John Pridmore, thirty-nine, sold real estate. Lionel Nance was an electrician, unemployed at the time of his daughter's disappearance.

Neither of the Pridmores had an arrest record. Lionel Nance had a 2001 arrest for public drunkenness.

Witnesses who knew the victim all stated that the person responsible had to be someone she knew or someone she trusted. Witnesses all doubted Nance or either of the Pridmores was involved.

We skimmed a few newspaper articles. It was the usual bloodlust frenzy. The disappearance. The search.

The angelic little face with the long brown hair. The headline screaming that the child was dead.

I was still reading when Ryan leaned back in his chair. I laid down the page. "You okay?"

"Rosy."

"Move on to crime scene?"

"Sure."

I exchanged the folder we had for the crime scene search report.

CSS arrived at 0931 hours, 4/30/09. The site was an open field surrounded by woods, an unsecured area, but one not normally visited by the public. The body had been left fifteen feet north of a small access road.

The victim lay faceup, clothed, with feet together, arms straight at the sides. There was little damage attributable to animal activity. Some debris had accumulated on the remains (leaves, twigs, et cetera, collected by CSS), but no attempt had been made at concealment or burial.

Fingerprinting was impossible due to decomposition, but both hands were bagged. Photographs were taken of the victim and the surroundings.

The detailed report of each crime scene tech followed. Leaving those to Ryan, I moved on to the section labeled *Evidence/Property Recovered/Analyzed*.

Each article had been entered into a grid. The five columns were headed: *Control #. Item. Location. Type of Collection. Results.*

The rows contained pitifully few entries. Photographs, forty-five. A soda can. Leaves. Bark chips. A rusty battery. Hair. A weathered sneaker, woman's size ten. The hair was Lizzie's. The can, battery, and shoe were negative for DNA or latent prints.

I must have made a sound. Or Ryan caught something in my face. "What?"

"Katy took ballet when she was a kid." I was referring to my daughter. "She carried her slippers in a bag and wore street shoes to and from class."

Ryan cocked a brow. I rotated the property log so he could read it. When he'd finished, "Where are the kid's dance shoes?"

"Exactly."

"None of the CSS techs refer to shoes. Nothing on a bag or backpack." Ryan rolled his head, trying to release tension in his neck.

"How about you take the witnesses and I take the autopsy report?" I suggested.

"You don't have to protect me."

"I'm not." I was. "Interviewing is closer to your skill set."

The section labeled *Witnesses* was ten pages long. Standard. When a child was murdered, the cops talked to everyone who ever intersected the kid's life.

The interviews were listed in chronological order. The first was that of the groundskeeper who discovered the body. He'd been questioned by Slidell.

I turned to the section labeled *Medical Examiner's Report.*

Elizabeth Ellen Nance. Victim is described as an 11-year-old white female, 57.5" in height, slender build, brown hair. Autopsy conducted on 5/1. Remains are partially skeletal with putrefied tissue remaining on the cranial posterior, torso, limbs, and feet.

The body is clothed in a green wool jacket, black leotard, black tights, pink cotton underwear, and blue plastic shoes. The panties appear to be in place. All clothing is heavily soiled. No bloodstaining is observed.

The body shows no evidence of sharp or blunt force trauma.

There is no fracturing of the skull, internally or externally. The skull base is intact. The facial bones are intact. The dentition is present and intact except for two right maxillary incisors that appear to have been lost postmortem.

The hyoid wings are not fused to the body. What remains of the laryngeal and tracheal cartilages is intact. Observation of aspirated blood in the upper airway or bronchi is not possible. Observation of obstruction of the airways or bronchi is not possible.

Parallel grooving on two right medial hand phalanges is consistent with rodent scavenging.

Two right distal hand phalanges are missing. Neither hand shows trauma consistent with defensive wounding.

A number of fine hairs and/or fibers are observed on the ventral aspect of the right forearm. A sampling of these was taken by the crime lab.

Decomposition makes it impossible to determine if there is trauma of the external genitalia or fluid deposit or any other extraneous material around the genitalia or in the pubic area. The flesh of the lower torso in the area of the lower abdomen and thighs and legs is putrefied, but the bones show no fractures or other trauma.

Submitted for evidence:

1. scalp hair
2. bags removed from right and left hands
3. right- and left-hand fingernail remnants
4. clothing and evidence sheet in which the body was wrapped
5. hair/fibers collected from the right forearm

Blood ethanol and carbon monoxide levels: undetermined
Manner of death: homicide
Cause of death: undetermined

Such a pitifully small amount of information.

The clock said 1:10. Ryan was still wading through interviews.

"Anything?" I asked.

"Kid's uncle sounds like a punk, but no."

"Grab some lunch?"

We rode in silence to the basement. I got a salad. Ryan went for a pizza slice that had been waiting awhile for a buyer. We took our trays to a table by the back wall.

"This civilian review system is good." My attempt to open conversation.

"Seems so."

"The investigation was thorough enough. The cops just had nothing to work with."

"Not unusual with stranger abductions."

"A stranger abduction but no sexual assault?"

"That's what the ME concluded?"

"He left it undetermined. But the clothes were undisturbed, so he felt pretty strongly there'd been no rape. Cause of death was also undetermined."

We ate without speaking for a few moments.

"Pomerleau's MO was to kidnap kids and keep them alive for her sick little fantasies. Why change that?" I'd been asking myself that since learning about the DNA hit.

"When torture's no longer enough, these sickos up the ante."

Something else had been bothering me. "That last night on de Sébastopol. Pomerleau set the house on fire." And left me in it to die. I didn't say that. "She escaped before Claudel could arrest her. Why was her DNA in the Canadian system?"

"Couple of years ago some counties in California started collecting DNA from violent offenders who'd died before authorities got their genetic profiles."

"Using what?"

"Old court exhibits, blood or saliva from a vic or a crime scene. They've been comparing those profiles to genetic profiles obtained from unsolveds."

"Cases with DNA from unidentified perps."

"Right."

"Will that hold up in court?"

"Doubtful. But they've managed to close some cold cases."

"So Canada's doing the same thing?"

"I've been out of the loop. But I'm guessing it's something similar. When we first found Pomerleau, she went to Montreal General, right?"

Flashbulb image. Deathly white bodies in a pitch-black cell. I nodded.

"Doctors probably took blood from Pomerleau when she was admitted. Crime scene collected biological material from the house on de Sébastopol. The profiles matched. When Pomerleau became a suspect in the homicides, she went into the NDDB."

"That tracks."

Back upstairs, Ryan continued reading the witness interviews while I turned to the next folder: *Related*

Investigations. I'd been at it an hour, and was well into a section headed *Investigators' Notes,* when an entry caused me to sit up straighter.

The note was described as handwritten, dated 5/2/2009. There was no name to indicate who had made it.

Forensics computer tech F. G. Ferrara called to advise that the Dell Inspiron 1525 laptop computer collected from the victim's bedroom had yielded no useful information. Email and browser history empty.

I raced through the rest of the page. The next. Found no further reference to the computer or to Ferrara. "Ryan."

He looked up. I rotated the page and jabbed the entry with my finger. While he read, I dialed Slidell.

My call rolled to voicemail. I left a message: "Phone me."

I dialed Barrow. Asked him to come back to the CCU. He was there in under a minute. "What's up?"

I showed him the entry.

"What's Slidell say?"

"He's not answering. Is Ferrara still up on four?"

"Hold on." Barrow stepped out, returned moments later.

"Frank Ferrara moved to Ohio in 2010."

"Pay was too high here, hours too short." The old Ryan wit.

"Something like that."

"What's the chance that PC is still around?" I asked.

"Was it logged as evidence?"

"No."

"Five years?" Barrow wagged his head slowly.

"Does Cynthia Pridmore still live in Charlotte?"

"Oh, yeah. She calls every few months asking for updates. Mainly to keep us thinking about Lizzie."

"Give her a buzz?"

Barrow hesitated. "I hate to raise hopes."

Ryan and I waited.

"Let me see what I can do."

Barrow was back in twenty minutes. His face spoke of a painful conversation. Of a woman's days again haunted by guilt and grief. Of her nights again filled with dread of what lay within sleep.

"Pridmore remembers a cop collecting the Dell, along with other items from her daughter's room. Recalls questioning about Lizzie's use of email and the Net. That's it."

"Where's the laptop now?" I asked.

"Pridmore got it back. Two years later used it to trade up to a newer model."

"Did you ask if Lizzie's other files were saved first?"

Barrow nodded. "They were. Pridmore copied the photos and Word docs to disk before wiping the drive for resale. Remembers a school report on ER nursing. The assignment was to research a career—that's what the kid wanted to be. After reading it, she couldn't bear to look at anything else."

"We should get those disks."

"I'll give it a go."

"Any chance of tracking the laptop?"

Barrow spread his palms in a "Who knows?" gesture.

"Either no one paid attention to Ferrara's report, or no one realized the significance of an eleven-year-old kid selectively clearing her own history," Ryan said.

"So Pomerleau may have been finding victims online as far back as 2009," I said.

"Let's get through this." Ryan flipped a page in the interview file.

In the end, it wasn't Pomerleau's cyberstalking that changed Ryan's mind about staying.

It was the call that came in at half past nine.

9

Ryan and I kept with it until well after seven. Uncovered nothing else of interest.

As we were leaving, I suggested dinner. He agreed. With a remarkable lack of enthusiasm.

We walked to the Epicentre, a two-story extravaganza of shops, theaters, bowling alleys, bars, and restaurants commanding an entire square block of uptown acreage.

The place was packed. We decided on Mortimer's. No reason except seating was immediately available.

I ordered the Asian chicken wrap. Ryan chose the Panthers pita. His looked better than mine.

When finished, we did our usual grab for the check. Our fingers brushed, and I felt heat sear my skin. Jerked my hand back. *Down, Brennan. It's over.*

But I'd scored a rare victory. Ryan was definitely not on his game.

We were exiting onto College Street when my phone

vibrated to tell me I had voicemail. I pulled it from my purse, expecting a message from Slidell.

Area code 828. I felt a zap of apprehension. Heatherhill Farm had called at eight-fifteen. I clicked on to listen. "Dr. Brennan. It's Luna Finch. I thought you should know. Your mother—she didn't come to dinner. When we checked her room, she wasn't there. We've searched the house and grounds, will do so again, then move on to other parts of the facility. I'm sure it's nothing, but if you know where she might have gone, could you please give us a ring? Thank you."

"Damn!" I hit redial. "Freakin' damn!"

Ryan had paused when I stopped walking. "Problem?"

"I just need a minute to clear something up."

Far away in the mountains, Finch's phone rang. Rang again.

"Dr. Finch."

"It's Temperance Brennan." I turned my back, a not-so-subtle hint.

Ryan moved off a few paces to allow me privacy. In the corner of my eye, I saw him shake free a cigarette and light it.

"We found her. I'm sorry to have bothered you. But she failed to sign out. She's never done that before."

"Where was she?"

"In the computer center, on the floor of a carrel. She'd placed a cart across the entrance and hidden behind it. That's why we didn't see her on the first sweep."

"She has her own laptop." This didn't make sense. "Why go there?"

"The Wi-Fi was down in River House. You know how it is in the mountains."

"She couldn't wait until service was restored?"

I heard a long sigh. "Daisy feels she is intentionally being kept offline."

"Was that the reason for the cart?"

"I'm afraid so. She feels she's being watched."

"She's crashed since I saw her on Wednesday."

"No, actually, she's seemed quite happy. A bit distracted, perhaps. Introspective. Like she has something on her mind."

"Where is she now?"

"Taking a bath. I'm sure she'll be fine."

Jesus Christ. Fine was the last thing she'd be. The woman was dying.

"Shall I try to speak to her?" I was pleased with my tone. Not a hint of the fear churning inside me.

After a slight pause, "Wait an hour. She'll have a snack, then settle into bed with her journal."

I disconnected. Turned on the ringer, then dropped the phone into my purse. Stood a moment, steadying my nerves.

Mama was journaling. Always a prelude to the downward spiral.

Ryan was ten feet up the walk. In the glow of the

Epicentre's copious neon, his face looked eroded down to orange and green bone.

I wormed toward him through the throng of Friday-night revelers.

"Everything okay?" Crushing the cigarette with his heel.

"Dandy."

An awkward beat, then, "Buy you a sarsaparilla, ma'am?" Bad cowboy drawl.

We both tried to smile at the old shtick. Didn't really pull it off.

"I'd better get home," I said.

Ryan nodded.

That was when the call came in. Thinking it was Finch again, and fearing a crisis, I clicked on.

"It's Slidell."

Skinny never opened by identifying himself. I waited.

"We've got her."

It took a moment. Then terrible realization. "Shelly Leal?"

"A guy collecting weeds or seeds or some shit stumbled across her body about seven-fifteen." Tight.

"Where?"

"Lower McAlpine Creek Greenway, under the I-485 overpass." In the background I could hear voices, the hum of traffic. Guessed Slidell was at the scene.

"Has Larabee arrived?"

"Yeah."

"Does he need me?" Leal had been missing a week. Depending on how long she'd been there and the severity of animal scavenging, body parts could be dragged and scattered.

"Doc says he's got it covered. Just wanted you to have a heads-up that he'll be doing the post first thing tomorrow. Says he wouldn't mind you being present."

"Of course." I was silent a moment as I thought about what to ask. "The weed collector. Does he seem solid?"

"Hasn't stopped crying and puking since I been here. I doubt he's in play."

"Same MO?"

"Clothed and posed." Clipped.

"Does Tinker know?"

"Oh, yeah. The asshole's acting all mind-hunter, pissing everyone off."

"He's not a profiler."

"Try telling him that. Is Ryan with you?"

"Yes."

"Loop him in."

"I will."

I heard a staticky radio voice. "Gotta go," Slidell said.

"You'll attend the autopsy tomorrow?"

"Wearing bells."

I disconnected.

"The child is dead?" Ryan asked.

I nodded, not trusting myself to speak.

"They want us to join them?"

I shook my head.

"Larabee's doing the autopsy tomorrow?"

I nodded again.

People flowed in two directions around us. A girl passed, maybe twelve or thirteen, a parent at each elbow. All three were eating chocolate ice cream cones. I pictured lights rippling blue and red across a small, still body on filthy concrete. I watched the girl melt into the crowd, my stomach clamped into a hard, cold lump.

Suddenly, my hands began to tremble. I pressed them to my thighs. Looked down at my feet. Noted a lone weed growing from a crack in the pavement.

Shelly Leal. Mama. Ryan. Or maybe it was the tail end of the cold. Or simply lack of sleep. I had no energy left to block the despair.

Tears welled. Broke free. I backhanded fat salty drops from my cheeks.

"I'll walk you to your car," Ryan said. No questions about Leal. About the call from Finch. I appreciated that.

"I'm a big girl." Not looking up. "Go on to your hotel."

Music swelled as a door opened in the colossus behind us. Receded. Somewhere, a truck beeped rhythmically, backing up.

Ryan reached out and took both my hands in his. Clamped tight to stop the shaking.

95

"I'll pick you up in the morning," I said.

Ryan's gaze burned the top of my head. "Look at me."

I did. The irises were too bright against the backdrop of bloodshot. Electric blue. Startling.

"When a child is killed, something inside us dies." Ryan's tone was gentle, meant to calm. "But an investigation doesn't normally throw you like this. It's me, isn't it?"

I took a second and a breath to make sure I'd say nothing I'd later regret. "Life's not always about you, Ryan."

"No. It's not."

I pulled my hands free and wrapped my arms around my ribs. Lowered my eyes.

"I can't explain why I needed to go away. To grieve alone. To see if anything remained of me worth salvaging. My leaving was selfish, but I can't undo it."

I focused on the green wisp struggling for life at my feet. Said nothing.

"Please know I never meant to hurt you."

I wanted to smash Ryan with my fists. I wanted to press my cheek to his chest. To allow him to pull me close.

Ryan had walked out of his life with barely a backward glance at me. One quick visit. One email. His daughter's death had been an unimaginable blow. But could I forgive the insensitivity? Would forgiveness just set me up for more pain?

I studied the brave little weed. Felt oddly buoyed. Such optimism in the face of impossible odds.

I had no obligation to explain myself to Ryan. To ever trust him again. Yet the words came out. "My mother is here in North Carolina."

I could sense Ryan's surprise. I'd never spoken to him of Mama.

"She's dying." A sliver of a whisper.

Ryan remained still, allowing me to continue or not.

Snapshots formed in my mind. Mama's hand in mine in the dark when she couldn't sleep. Mama's face flushed with delight after a binge at the mall. Mama's suitcase packed with silk scarves, satin nighties, and Godiva cocoa mix.

Mama hunkered with her laptop behind a cart.

The weed blurred into a wavery green thread. A ragged breath juddered up my chest.

No.

I palmed the new tears, squared my shoulders, and raised my chin.

Ryan's neon-etched face was right above mine.

I managed a weak smile. "How about that sarsaparilla?"

At the annex, Ryan brewed coffee while I went to the study to phone my mother. She sounded tranquil and lucid. She'd gone to the computer center to continue her research. No big deal.

I wasn't fooled. Even when the demons slipped

their leash, Mama was able to coat her actions in wholly believable rationalizations. To convincingly lay on others the blame for overreaction. It may have been the most disturbing aspect of her madness.

"Are you making progress on your end?" A fizz of excitement below her calm.

"Progress?" I was lost.

"With your poor dead girls."

"Listen, Mama. I—"

"I'm doing everything I can on mine." Her voice dropped to a conspiratorial whisper. "They're trying to stop me, but it won't work."

"No one is trying to stop you. The Internet went down."

"There are more, you know."

"More?"

"Poor lost souls."

Jesus. "Are you taking your meds, Mama?"

"The minute you left, I began pulling up old newspaper stories from Charlotte and the surrounding area. The Vermont girl was killed in 2007, so I started with that year."

Jesus bouncing Christ.

"I've found at least three." Again, the spy-versus-spy whisper.

I had two options. The smart one, shut her down and call Finch. The easy one, hear her out. It was late, I was exhausted. I opted for easy. Or perhaps I hoped enough of her brain was functioning logically to have actually produced something.

"Three?" I asked.

"I'm putting it all in my journal. In case anything happens to me." I could hear the gleam in her eye. "But I've sent you the names, dates, and locations. In separate emails, of course."

"This isn't necessary, Mama."

"What about your young man?"

"Ryan has agreed to help."

"I'm glad. If my brilliant baby likes him, this gentleman must be very clever."

"I'll visit as soon as I can."

"You'll do no such thing. You be dogged until you catch this horrible creature."

I found Ryan in the kitchen discussing baseball with Birdie. Over coffee and quinoa-cranberry cookies, I gave him the basics.

10

When I was eight, following the loss of my father to an auto crash and my baby brother to leukemia, my grandmother relocated Mama, Harry, and me from Chicago to the Lee family home at Pawleys Island, South Carolina. Years later, after Harry and I had each married and moved on, Gran died at the overripe age of ninety-six.

A week after Gran's funeral, Mama disappeared. Four years later, we learned she was living in Paris with a maid/nurse named Cécile Gosselin, whom she called Goose.

When I was thirty-five, Mama and Goose returned to the States. Since then they'd migrated between the Pawleys Island house and a sprawling condo on Manhattan's Upper East Side.

Throughout the years, if Mama felt the darkness closing in, or if Goose noted the telltale signs, they'd make their way to whatever facility had caught my mother's attention most recently. While Daisy reassembled herself, Goose would return to France to revisit whatever life she'd lived pre–Katherine Daessee Lee Brennan.

It was midnight by the time I'd explained Mama to Ryan. Her beauty. Her charm. Her madness. Her cancer. By then we'd ingested sufficient caffeine to barefoot the entire Appalachian Trail.

"She's smart as hell. And kick-ass on the Net. You want something, Mama will find it." Perhaps needing to emphasize the positive. "She helped me find you."

"Sounds like your mother should work for the NSA."

"My mother should be shot straight back into treatment."

We looked at each other, both knowing the time for therapy was past.

"Check her emails?" Ryan suggested.

"Sure."

There were nine in all, sent to my Gmail, AOL, and university accounts. Coded, to indicate what linked to what.

"She is cautious," Ryan said.

"She's batty," I said. Immediately regretted it.

We opened the lot, and I copied the information into a Word document.

Avery Koseluk, age thirteen, went missing in

Kannapolis, North Carolina, on September 8, 2011. The child's father, Al Menniti, vanished at the same time.

Tia Estrada, age fourteen, went missing in Salisbury, North Carolina, on December 2, 2012. Her body was found in a rural area of Anson County four days later.

Colleen Donovan, age sixteen, had been reported missing in Charlotte the previous February.

"I remember Donovan," I said. "She was a high school dropout living on the streets. I think a prossie filed the missing persons report."

"Cops probably wrote her off as a runaway. And she was older, so she didn't fit Rodas's profile," Ryan said. "Koseluk would have been treated as a noncustodial parent abduction."

"Estrada was Latina, so she wouldn't have matched Rodas's profile, either." I'd just said that when my phone pinged three times, signaling incoming texts. Mama had sent photos of the girls, undoubtedly copied and pasted from the archived articles she'd found.

Ryan put his head close to mine as I tapped to enlarge each image. I had to work to keep breathing normally.

Each girl had fair skin and long center-parted brown hair. Each was at that child-woman phase typical of adolescence, limbs gangly, chests showing the first blush of breasts.

Donovan didn't look sixteen. Estrada didn't look Latina. It didn't need stating.

"Slidell can contact Salisbury tomorrow," Ryan said.

I nodded in his direction, not really seeing him. We knew what the police and autopsy reports would say. The article on Tia Estrada reported that she was found in the open, dressed and supine. Cause of death undetermined. No arrest made.

"Until then, we could both use some sleep."

"Yeah." I didn't move.

"Tempe."

I brought Ryan's face back into focus. His eyes made me think of cool blue fire.

"You solid?"

"As a Russian tanker."

"Would you prefer that I stay here tonight?"

Yes.

I shrugged.

"Go on up." Ryan's voice sounded strange. "I know where you keep the bedding."

I awoke to the feeling that something was wrong.

Birdie was gone. Sunlight was knifing in through the shutters.

My eyes whipped to the clock: 8:10. I'd slept through my alarm. I never do that. Larabee may have already started the Leal autopsy.

I shot out of bed, threw on clothes, no shower. Pulled my hair into a pony and brushed my teeth. Thundered down the stairs.

Ryan was in the kitchen, pouring Raisin Bran into bowls. The cat was asleep on top of the fridge.

"Jesus, Ryan. Why didn't you ring me? Or holler up?"

"I figured you were tired." Adding milk to the cereal. "Eat."

"We need to go."

"Eat."

"I'm not hungry."

"You have to eat."

"No. I don't."

"I do."

Ryan filled two travel mugs with coffee, added cream to mine. Then he sat and began spooning flakes into his mouth.

Eyes rolling, I sat and emptied my bowl. "Can we leave now?"

"Yes, ma'am." Salute to the brim of his cap. Which was purple and said *This is not your father's hat* in Spanish.

The drive took only minutes. An advantage to crossing uptown on a Saturday morning.

I swiped us in at the MCME. We passed through the lobby and biovestibule, then followed the sound of muted voices to autopsy room one.

The wave hit as soon as I pushed through the door.

Sulfur-saturated gas produced by bacterial action and the breakdown of red blood cells. The stench of putrefaction.

Larabee was viewing X-rays on wall-mounted illuminators. He wore scrubs and had a mask hanging below his jaw. A half-dozen crime scene photos lay on the counter.

Slidell was beside Larabee, looking like hell. Dark stubble, baggy eyes, skin the color of old grout. I wondered if he'd been up all night. Or if it was the odor. Or the grim show he was about to witness.

An autopsy assaults not just the nose but all senses. The sight of the fast-slash Y incision. The sound of pruning shears crunching through ribs. The *schlop* of organs hitting the scale. The acrid scorch of the saw buzzing through bone. The *pop* of the skullcap snapping free. The *frrpp* of the scalp and face stripping off.

Pathologists aren't surgeons. They're not concerned with vital signs, bleeding, or pain. They don't repair or overhaul. They search for clues. They need to be objective and observant. They don't need to be gentle.

The autopsy of a child always seems more brutal. Children look so innocent. So soft and freckled and pink. Brand-new and ready for all life has to offer.

Such was not the case with Shelly Leal.

Leal lay naked on a stainless steel table in the center of the room, chest and abdomen bloated and green.

Her skin was sloughing, pale and translucent as rice paper, from her fingers and toes. Her eyes, half open, were dull and darkened by opaque films.

I steeled myself. Kicked into scientist mode.

It was November. The weather had been cool. Insect activity would have been minimal. The changes were consistent with a postmortem interval of one week or less.

I crossed to the counter and glanced at the scene photos. Saw the familiar faceup straight-armed body position.

We watched as Larabee did his external exam, checking the contours of the belly and buttocks, the limbs, the fingers and toes, the scalp, the orifices. At one point he tweezed several long hairs from far back in the child's mouth.

"They look a little blond to be hers?" Slidell asked.

"Not necessarily. Decomp and stomach fluids can cause bleaching." Larabee dropped the hairs into a vial, sealed and marked the lid.

Finally, the Y-cut.

There was no chatter throughout the slicing and weighing and measuring and sketching. None of the dark humor used to lessen morgue tension.

Slidell mostly kept his gaze fixed on things other than the table. Now and then he'd give me a long stare. Shift his feet. Reclasp his hands.

Ryan observed in grim silence.

Ninety minutes after starting, Larabee straightened.

There was no need to recap his findings. We'd heard him dictate every detail into a hanging mike.

The victim was a healthy thirteen-year-old female of average height and weight. She had no congenital malformations, abnormalities, or signs of disease. She'd eaten a hot dog and an apple less than six hours before her death.

The child's body had no healed or healing fractures, scars, or cigarette burns. No bruising or abrasion in the area of the anus or genitalia. None of the hideous indicators of physical or sexual abuse.

Shelly Leal had been nurtured and loved until a maniac decided it was time she should die. And there was nothing to verify how that had happened.

"No petechiae?" I was asking about tiny red spots that appear in the eyes due to the bursting of blood vessels.

"No. Though the sclera is toast."

"What's that?" Slidell.

"Petechial hemorrhage is suggestive of asphyxiation," I said.

"The lips are badly swollen and discolored, but I saw no surface or subdermal hemorrhage. No cuts or tooth impressions."

"So, what? You thinking smothering? Strangulation?" Slidell said.

"I'm thinking I can't determine cause of death, Detective." Larabee's voice carried a slight edge. He'd just dictated that conclusion.

Slidell's cheeks reddened through the pallor. "We done here, then?"

"I'll go over her with an ALS. Recheck the clothes. Not sure there's much point, given the decomp, but I'll try to get samples to send off for tox screening."

Slidell nodded. Made a move toward the door.

"Ryan and I think we've found evidence of other victims." No way I'd mention Mama.

"Yeah?" The pouchy eyes shot to Ryan. "You planning to share that?"

"We're sharing it now."

Slidell drew a long breath through his nose. Exhaled with a dry whistling sound. "I gotta explain this to the parents." Flapping an arm at the table. "Ryan, you want to ride along, lay it all out on the way? Then we brief Barrow."

"You're the boss," Ryan said.

When Slidell and Ryan were gone, Larabee and I got out the alternate light source kit, donned goggles, and killed the overheads. As we ran the wand over Leal's body, I told him about Koseluk, Estrada, and Donovan. He listened without comment.

We found no latent prints, no hairs or fibers, no body fluids. No surprise but worth a shot.

Leal's clothing hung on a rack by the side counter, stained and mud-stiffened. Yellow hooded nylon jacket, plaid shirt, red jeans, cotton panties, black and yellow Nikes, white socks.

We started with the jacket. Got nothing on the front. Flipped it.

"What's that?" I pointed to a bat-shaped luminescence on one edge of the hood.

Larabee bent close but said nothing.

"I'll bet the farm that's a lip print," I said. "Look at the shape. And the wiggly vertical stripes."

"How's a lip print survive a week in the elements?" Still studying the vaguely lustrous smear.

"Maybe it's gloss? Or ChapStick?"

Our eyes met. Wordlessly, we crossed to Leal. Under our light, the bloated little lips showed not the faintest glimmer to indicate makeup or balm. Larabee wiped them and sealed the swab in a vial. "You thinking cheiloscopic ID?" Some researchers believe the patterning of a lip's surface furrows is as unique to an individual as the lines and ridges on a fingerprint. Larabee was referring to the science of analyzing them.

"No. Well, maybe. Mostly, I'm thinking DNA. If there's saliva and the lip print's not hers . . ." I let the thought hang.

"Son of a biscuit. Could we get that lucky?" Larabee placed the jacket in an evidence bag and scribbled case info on the outside.

The rest of the clothes yielded zilch.

As Larabee and I removed our aprons, gloves, goggles, and masks, I mentioned an idea that had been percolating since I'd read Mama's emails.

"Gower was abducted in Vermont in 2007. Nance

was killed here in Charlotte in 2009. Koseluk was 2011, Estrada 2012, Donovan late 2013 or early 2014."

"Now there's Shelly Leal." Larabee balled and dropped his gear into the biohazard bin. "An annual kill since the action moved to North Carolina." The lid clanged shut. "With one gap."

"I'm going to pull a file from 2010," I said.

Larabee turned to me, face glum. He also remembered.

11

I logged on to my computer and pulled up the file. Scanned the contents. As I feared, case number ME107-10 fit the pattern.

The skull had been found by hikers off South New Hope Road, near the town of Belmont, just west of Charlotte and just north of the South Carolina border. It lay in a gulley across from the entrance to the Daniel Stowe Botanical Garden.

The facial bones and mandible had been missing, and the calvarium gnawed and weathered. Remnants of brain matter had adhered to the endocranial surface, suggesting a PMI of less than a year.

I'd led a recovery team. For a full day we'd worked a grid shoulder to shoulder, poking under rocks and fallen trees, sifting through vines, leaves, and brushy undergrowth. Though we found a fair number of bones, much of the skeleton had been lost to scavenging animals.

I was able to determine that the remains were those of a twelve- to fourteen-year-old child. What was left of the cranium suggested European ancestry.

Gender determination based on skeletal indicators is unreliable prior to puberty. But articles of clothing found in association with several bone clusters suggested the victim was female.

A search of MP files turned up no match in North or South Carolina. Ditto when we ran the profile through NamUS and the Doe Network, national and international data banks for missing and unidentified persons.

So the child remained nameless, ME107-10. The bones were archived on a shelf down the hall.

I pushed from my desk and walked to the storage room, boot heels echoing in the quiet of the empty building.

After locating the correct label, I pulled the box and carried it to autopsy room one. Larabee's closed office door told me he'd already left. The autopsy table was empty. Its small occupant had been stitched, zipped into her body bag, and rolled to the cooler.

I thought of the heartrending conversation Slidell was having with Shelly Leal's grieving parents. Receiving autopsy results is never easy. Nor is delivering them. I felt empathy for all three.

Deep breath. Only a faint trace of odor lingered in the air.

After gloving, I lifted the lid.

The skeleton was as I remembered, stained tea brown by contact with the vegetation in which it had lain. And woefully incomplete.

Still psyched about finding the lip print, I spread paper sheeting on the table and placed all the bones and bone fragments on it.

The skull's outer surface was scored by tooth marks, and the orbital ridges and mastoids were chewed. Most of the vertebrae and ribs were crushed. The one pelvic half had several canine punctures. Each of the five long bones was truncated and cracked at both ends.

I examined everything first with a magnifying lens, then with the ALS. Spotted no hairs or fibers snagged on or embedded in the bones. Detected not the faintest suggestion of a glimmer.

I was repacking the skeleton when my eyes fell on a bag tucked into one corner of the box. Odd. Had the clothing never left the MCME? Had it gone to the CMPD lab and come back? I'd noted no report in the electronic file.

I opened the bag, withdrew the contents, and placed everything on the sheet.

One lavender sandal, size marking abraded by wear.

One pair of purple polyester shorts, girls' size twelve.

One T-shirt saying *100% Princess*, size medium.

One pink polyester bra, size 32AA.

One elastic band from a pair of girls' panties, label faded and unreadable.

I repeated the process with the lens and the ALS.

Except for a few short black hairs, obviously animal, I got the same disappointing result.

Discouraged, I reshelved the box, then returned to my office. Thinking perhaps an error had occurred and a report hadn't been entered, I pulled my own file on ME107-10. I still keep hard copy. Old habits die hard.

Data entry omission. The clothing had been submitted, examined, and, for some strange reason, returned to us. The lab had gotten zilch.

I was dialing Slidell when my iPhone rang. He and Ryan were going to the Penguin. The junkie inside me rolled over and opened an eye.

What the hell. I was done here.

I cleaned up and headed out.

Larabee's car was gone from the lot. But two vans sat outside the security fence. One had *WSOC* written on the side panel, the other *News 14 Carolina*.

Crap.

As I crossed to my Mazda, each van's doors thunked open and a two-person crew leaped out. One member of each pair held a mike, the other a shoulder-propped camera.

I hurried to my car, jumped in, and palmed down the locks. Gunning through the gate, I lowered a window and waved a message that needed no clarification.

I knew the media had picked up on transmissions

concerning the discovery of Leal's body, and that the reporters sitting vigil at the morgue were just doing their jobs. I also knew that dozens more were swarming elsewhere—the underpass, the convenience store, the Leal home—salivating for an inside line to pipe to their editors.

My gesture was unfair. Definitely inelegant. But I refused to provide fodder for voyeurs wanting a peek into the heartbreak of others.

The Penguin drive-in is a clogged artery waiting to take you out. Featuring a menu with caloric levels very possibly illegal, the place has been a Charlotte institution since before I was born. I crave its burgers and fries like an addict craves dope.

The restaurant was close to the convenience store where Shelly Leal was last seen. Where she'd bought milk and candy and it had cost her life.

Pulling from Commonwealth into a spot by the entrance, I could see Ryan and Slidell through the double lens of my windshield and a tinted front window. The look on Skinny's face almost made me regret my decision to come.

Though it was nearly two P.M., the place was crowded. And noisy with the hubbub of conversation emanating from fat-glutted brains.

The men looked up when I drew close. Ryan scooched left to make space for me in the booth.

Slidell was eating a sandwich that almost defied

description. Blackened bologna on Texas toast with lettuce, tomato, and mayo. The Dr. Devil. One of the few offerings I'd never sampled. Ryan was working on a hot dog barely visible under a layer of queso and onion rings. Both were drinking sodas the size of oil drums. The iconic flightless bird grinned from each plastic cup.

I slid in and Ryan handed me a menu. No, thanks. I knew what I wanted.

The waitress appeared and queried my health in a syrupy drawl. I assured her I was swell and ordered the Penguin burger, a heart-stopper topped with pimento cheese and fried pickles.

While waiting for my food, I told Ryan and Slidell about the possible lip print.

"It could be Leal's." Ryan sounded skeptical.

"Yes," I said. "Or it could have been left by her attacker. Maybe Leal fought and was pulled close, to pin her arms. Or maybe her body slipped while being carried to the underpass. There are lots of reasons her abductor's face might have come in contact with the jacket."

"You think DNA's gonna last that long?" Slidell outdid Ryan at dubious.

"I'm hoping so." I was. And that the match would send Pomerleau straight to hell.

My drink was delivered. Sugary tea, not the unsweetened I'd ordered. While sipping it, I shared my thoughts on the gap year, 2010. And described ME107-10.

The men listened, chewing and wiping grease from their chins. Though he hadn't been involved, Slidell remembered the case.

I mentioned the media ambush at the MCME. Slidell delivered his usual rant. His suggestions for curtailing the power of the fifth estate did not involve amending the constitution.

By the time my food arrived, Slidell had finished his. He bunched and tossed his napkin and leaned back. "I'm convinced the parents are clear. Co-workers place the old man at the body shop when the kid went missing. Mother's barely holding it together. Says she was home with the other two, waiting for the milk. It feels right to me."

Ryan nodded agreement.

"How did they take the news?" I spoke through a mouthful of ground beef and pickle.

Shoulder shrug. You know.

I did. Though it wasn't a frequent part of my job, I'd participated in the notification of next of kin. In that moment when lives changed forever. I'd seen people faint, lash out, cry, go catatonic. I'd heard them berate, accuse, beg for retraction, for reassurance that it was all a mistake. No matter how often I partook, the task was always heartbreaking.

"Mother wondered about a ring the kid always wore. Silver, shaped like a seashell. You got something like that?" Slidell asked.

"I didn't see any jewelry in the autopsy room, but

I'll check," I said. "Maybe Larabee bagged it before I arrived." And separated it from the clothing? I doubted he'd do that. Didn't say so.

"We did some poking into your other vics. Koseluk and Donovan are still missing. Both files are inactive, since no one's been pressing."

Ryan excused himself. I stood and watched him walk to the door. Knew he was going outside to smoke.

As I sat back down, Slidell freed a toothpick from its cellophane and began mining a molar. The action didn't stop the flow of his narrative. "Lead on the Koseluk girl is a guy named Spero. Kannapolis PD. He's okay. Worked with him once. Gangbanger got capped—"

"What's his take?"

"He's still liking the ex."

"Al Menniti?"

Slidell nodded.

"Has he surfaced?"

"No." Slidell withdrew the toothpick and inspected something on the tip. "Talked to the mother. She says the dumb fuck couldn't hide his own ass, much less a kid. Says he didn't give two shits about fatherhood. Her words."

"Lyrical. What about Colleen Donovan?"

"Parents both dead, lived with an aunt, Laura Lonergan, who spends her time frying her brains on meth. And there ain't much to fry. That conversation was a treat."

I gestured for Slidell to skip the character analysis. "Does Colleen have a jacket?"

Slidell nodded. "Juvie, so we'll need a warrant to unseal it."

I raised my brows in question.

"Yeah, yeah. I'm writing something up." Slidell paused, as though debating whether to make the next comment.

"What?" I urged.

"One weird thing. According to the file, Donovan was entered into a national database for missing kids."

"By whom?"

"MP investigator name of Pat Tasat."

"What's weird about that?"

"I checked for the hell of it. Six months out, the kid was removed from the system."

"Did Tasat say why?"

"No. And he won't." Tight. "Poor schmuck drowned in Lake Norman last Labor Day weekend."

"I'm sorry. Did you know him?"

Slidell nodded. "Jimmy B and Jet Skis don't mix."

I thought a moment. "Isn't it standard to enter a reason when removing a name from the database?"

"Yeah. That's what's weird. No reason was given."

"Who removed her?"

"That wasn't there, either."

I gnawed on that, wondering what it could mean. If anything. "And Estrada?" I asked.

"Kid vanished in Salisbury—that's Rowan County

—turned up in Anson, so they caught the file. The investigation went nowhere, eventually landed with a ballbuster at the sheriff's department name of Henrietta Hull. That's who I talked to. Goes by Cock. You believe that?"

Hen. Cock. I was sure fellow cops had crafted the nickname. Doubted she went by it. "Was the problem lack of interjurisdictional sharing?" I asked.

"Partly that. Partly the Anson County Sheriff's Office was busy mucking out its own barn."

"Meaning?"

"Couple of their superstars got nailed for taking bribes."

I remembered now. Both deputies had gone to jail.

"Partly it was timing. The initial lead retired some months into it. That's when the case bounced to Hull. Mostly it was the fact that no one found dick. No physical evidence, no eyewitnesses, no cause of death."

"Who did the post?"

"Some hack who didn't bother to visit the scene."

I wasn't surprised. The *Charlotte Observer* had done more than one exposé on the failings of the North Carolina medical examiner system. A scathing series ran in 2013 after an elderly couple and an eleven-year-old boy died three months apart in the same motel room in Boone, and it turned out the culprit was carbon monoxide. The local ME had neither visited the motel nor filed a timely report after the first deaths. Another series shocked the public in 2014. Murders classified as accidental deaths, accidents as suicides, misidentified bodies delivered to the wrong funeral homes.

When interviewed, the state's new chief ME attributed problems in the system to inadequate funding. No kidding. Except for Mecklenburg County, local medical examiners were paid a hundred dollars per case. And since the state didn't require it, many had little or no training in forensic pathology. Some weren't even physicians. The new boss was trying to bring about change, but without increased financial support, her chance of success was unlikely.

"No one kept pushing?" I asked.

"Estrada's mother got deported to Mexico shortly after the kid vanished. There was no *señor* in the picture."

I finished my burger and thought about Mama's three girls, Koseluk, Estrada, and Donovan. One dead, two missing. Files ignored because no one was pushing.

Ryan rejoined us, carrying a hint of cigarette smoke into the booth.

"Tinker was at the scene last night?" I asked.

Slidell snorted loudly, then went back to working his gums.

"The SBI's taking the position that the investigation will benefit from sharing information and resources at the state level." Ryan's first spoken contribution.

"There's no way the SB-fucking-I will share piss-all." Slidell jammed the toothpick into the remains of his slaw. "They think a clear on these cases is their ticket to a makeover. And that don't include us."

"What does Tinker think about these other three vics?" I asked.

"That asshat couldn't think his way through a fart without coaching." Slidell's outburst caused several patrons to glance our way.

"He's not convinced they're related," Ryan said.

"Leal?"

"That one he's saying maybe."

"What happens now?"

"I kicked what we got up the COC." Slidell was using shorthand for "chain of command." "Now we wait."

We were returning to our cars when Slidell's mobile sounded. He answered, and as he listened, his face grew red. Finally, "A couple extra whiteboards ain't gonna clear this thing."

Disconnecting with a furious one-finger jab, Slidell turned to us. "We're screwed."

12

The ruling was that the Leal homicide would continue to be viewed as a one-off, so there would be no task force. Slidell was getting space but not extra personnel. He was to cooperate with Tinker and use Ryan ex-officio. If the investigation tossed up stronger links to the other cases, the situation would be reassessed.

While Ryan and a seething Slidell headed back to the law enforcement center, I returned to the ME facility. The press vans were gone, in search of bloodier pastures.

Leal's ring wasn't in autopsy room one or lying in a Ziploc on Larabee's desk. A quick scan of his paperwork turned up no mention of jewelry.

I thought a moment, then gloved, went to the cooler, and checked every inch of Leal's body bag. Found twigs, leaves, some gravel, but no ring.

I phoned Larabee. Got voicemail and left a message.

Out of ideas, I drove to the LEC. Slidell wasn't at

the CCU or in his cubicle in the homicide squad. Ryan was nowhere in sight, either. A few detectives were talking on phones. A guy named Porter was discussing footprint impressions with a guy I didn't know. He directed me to the conference room.

The scene looked like a setup in a low-budget cop show. A phone and computer sat, unstaffed, on a desk in one corner. Erasable boards stretched the length of the back wall, most used, two empty.

The large oak table still filled the center of the room. On it were the two MP and four homicide files. Those for Gower and Nance were hefty, a box and a tub, thanks to the work of Rodas and Barrow's CCU team. The others were meager enough to fit into brown corrugated files secured with elasticized binders.

Ryan was trolling through Rodas's box. Slidell was beside him, studying a printout. Neither looked up when I entered.

I crossed to the boards. Topping six of the seven were victim photos. A name was penned below each in large block letters. A last-seen-alive location and date.

NELLIE GOWER, HARDWICK, VERMONT, 2007
LIZZIE NANCE, CHARLOTTE, 2009
AVERY KOSELUK, KANNAPOLIS, 2011
TIA ESTRADA, SALISBURY, 2012
COLLEEN DONOVAN, CHARLOTTE, 2013–2014
SHELLY LEAL, CHARLOTTE, 2014

Each LSA date marked the beginning of a time line

tracing that child's movements backward from the moment of her disappearance. Few items had been entered on any chronology. Posted on the Gower, Nance, Estrada, and Leal boards were CSS photos. I stepped up to inspect the Estrada pics, which I hadn't seen.

Like the others, Tia Estrada lay faceup, fully dressed, with her arms at her sides. Beneath her were brown grass and dead leaves, above her gray sky. In the background I could see a picnic table and what looked like the base of a gazebo.

A soupçon of Brylcreem told me Slidell had closed in.

"Is it a campground?" I asked.

Slidell nodded. "By the Pee Dee wildlife refuge. You know, for the boat and bug spray crowd. Has a couple docks, tent and trailer sites, latrines so the fam can take a dump with the birds."

Nice.

"Was she found inside the grounds?"

"Eeyuh."

"And no one saw anything?"

"It was winter. The place was deserted."

"Were the neighbors questioned?"

"We're talking the boonies."

"Where people take notice." Curt. "No one remembered selling gas to a stranger? No one saw an unfamiliar car pass by on the road? Parked on the shoulder?"

125

Slidell looked at me without blinking. "You know why these douchebags don't acknowledge we got a serial here?"

Though I shared Skinny's opinion that his superiors were wearing blinders, I had no desire to hear his latest conspiracy theory.

"I didn't find Leal's ring," I said. "Could it be downstairs in the property room?"

Slidell gave an "I don't think so" twist of his mouth. Then, "I'll pull the CSS report, see if a ring turned up in their sweep."

"And ask the mother to look around at home."

Slidell nodded.

"Nance should have been carrying ballet gear, at least shoes. Nothing was listed in the file."

Another nod.

"We should query Hull, see if anything was missing with Estrada. Maybe give Rodas a call about Gower."

Slidell knew what I was thinking. Souvenirs. Reminders of the kills. He strode over to Ryan. Explained. Ryan nodded. Pulled out his phone.

As I moved to the last board, Slidell rejoined me.

"Did Ryan fill you in on Anique Pomerleau?" I asked. A decade had passed, and still I could barely say the name.

"Yeah."

"Good."

"Before we started setting up in here, he gave

a yodel to the home folk. I don't par-lay-voo, but it sounded like he had some 'splaining to do."

I wondered how that had gone.

"He says he learned dick about Pomerleau. But I'm guessing he blew fire up some Canadian arses about needing to fix that."

For a moment I concentrated on my breathing. My pulse. Then I looked at the photo.

It was a mug shot, taken years before the horror in Montreal. Pomerleau's face was softer, an embryonic version of the one forever etched in my brain. I recognized the heavy brows slashing across the deep-set eyes. The pinched nose, the full lips, the jarringly square chin.

"She was, what, sixteen?" Slidell asked.

"Fifteen. A store owner in Mascouche nabbed her for shoplifting in 1990. Insisted on pressing charges. This was the only picture we had back in '04."

"Ryan couldn't dig up something less vintage?"

"Pomerleau's parents lost all their belongings in a fire in '92. By then she was out of the house, raising hell in Montreal."

"Five-finger discounting?"

"And some petty stuff I don't remember."

"So her prints are on file?"

I nodded.

"Fifteen? Mom and Dad didn't drag her back to the old homestead?"

"They were in their forties when Anique was born.

127

By the time she bagged school to hit the big city, they were exhausted and tired of dealing with her crap."

Slidell pooched out his lips and rubbed the back of his neck. "So she enters the States sometime between '04, when you and Ryan bust her in Montreal, and '07, when she leaves DNA on the Gower kid." He squinted as he did some math. "She's thirty-nine now, surely using an alias. And I'm guessing she's street-savvy?"

"Pomerleau is vicious and delusional but smart as hell."

"And her only surviving pic's got more than two decades on it. No wonder she's managed to fly under the radar."

Sudden thought. I shifted to Leal's board. On it was a black-and-white printout of a child's face showing a reasonable though lifeless resemblance to the school portrait on top. I guessed the image had been generated by software such as SketchCop, FACES, or Identi-Kit, in which interchangeable templates of features were selected based on an individual's memory of an actual face. I assumed Slidell's eyewitness from Morningside had given the input.

"Who did the composite?" I asked.

"We get 'em done through an FBI liaison."

"Could he do an age progression on Pomerleau's mug shot?" As I said it, I was surprised none had been done before. Or had I missed that? I made a note to check.

Slidell smiled. I think. "Not bad, Doc."

"Rodas says Gower was wearing a house key on a chain around her neck." Ryan spoke from across the room. "They never found it."

Slidell and I crossed to him. "What about Estrada?" I asked.

"There's no mention in the file." Ryan gestured at the papers fanned out before him. "Hull knew nothing about missing effects. Said she'd check in to it."

I met Ryan's eyes. He gave me a straight look, then went back to reading interviews.

"I'll call over about that sketch." Slidell turned and chugged from the room.

I dropped into a chair. Trolled through the Estrada file until I found what I wanted.

Estrada's autopsy report consisted of a single page of text and four pages of scanned color photos. It was signed by Perry L. Bullsbridge, MD.

Slidell was right. Considering a child had been murdered, Bullsbridge had done a piss-poor job of documenting the postmortem. Considering *anyone* had been murdered.

I read the section on physical descriptors and condition of the body. The brief remarks on health, hygiene, and nutrition. The one-sentence statement regarding absence of trauma.

I skimmed the organ weights. I was scanning the list of items submitted as evidence when an entry jumped out at me.

"They pulled two hairs from Estrada's trachea."

"And?" Ryan didn't look up.

"Larabee pulled two hairs from Leal's trachea."

"He thought they were probably hers."

"He said it was odd to find hair so far down the throat."

Ryan's eyes met mine. "What are you saying?"

"I don't know." I didn't. "Coincidence?"

"You don't believe in coincidence."

"No," I said. "I don't."

That night Ryan came over to my place and we got carryout sushi from Baku. We ate in the kitchen, under Birdie's steadfast gaze. Every few minutes Ryan would slip the cat raw fish. I'd scold them both. The cycle would repeat.

We were clearing the table when Slidell phoned. By reflex, I checked the time. Nine-forty and he was still working. Impressive. His update was not.

The possible Leal witness from the convenience store whom he'd interviewed a week earlier had provided car descriptors and two digits from the license. The pairing had generated over twelve hundred possibilities. Someone was making calls.

Leal's ring was neither listed on the CSS inventory nor in the property room. It appeared in none of the photos.

The IT guys had yet to recover any of the browser history deleted from Leal's laptop. They were still trying.

The FBI's sketch artist had agreed to age-progress Pomerleau's mug shot. When he could.

Hot damn. We were on fire.

"I plan to visit my mother tomorrow," I said to Ryan, rinsing rice and soy sauce from a plate.

"I'll hang here, go through the rest of the files, and push harder on tracking Pomerleau."

"Sounds good."

"Shouldn't you give Daisy a heads-up?"

"Like she won't be there?" Turning off the tap.

"She is a known flight risk."

"Funny."

Actually, it was. Sort of.

I took my mobile to the study and settled on the couch. Ryan's backpack now hung from the arm of the desk chair. His phone charger jutted from a socket. Inexplicably, seeing his belongings amid mine calmed me. And filled me with sadness.

I was glad Ryan had agreed to relocate to my guest room. It was nice having him under my roof. A friend now, nothing more. Still, I was glad he was here.

I dialed. The first ring was cut short.

"I am so glad you phoned." Mama's voice had the intensity of a pit bull signaling a break-in. "I was about to phone you."

"Mama—"

"I wanted to be sure."

"I'm coming to see you tomorrow."

"I was hitting a lot of dead ends. 'Daisy,' I said

131

to myself, 'the devil's in the details. Focus on the details.'"

When Mama's round the bend, her listening skills are not at their best.

"I'll be there by noon."

"Are you hearing me, Tempe?"

"Yes, Mama." I knew that trying to interrupt would only crank her up further.

"I've learned something dreadful."

I felt a tickle of unease. "Dreadful?"

"Another little girl is going to die."

13

"Dates, Tempe. Dates." Almost breathless. "I was out of ideas so I ran a matrix on the dates."

"What dates?"

"Some you gave me, most I found through online news reports."

"I'm not following you, Mama."

"The dates the children were taken. I don't have all of them, of course. But I have enough."

"What children?" I kept my voice even.

"The ones in Montreal. And the later ones. Do you have something to write with?" Dramatic stage whisper. "It's unsafe to transmit this information electronically."

I relocated to the desk and got pen and paper. Then I pressed a button and set the phone down.

"What was that? Am I on speaker?"

"It's okay, Mama."

"Are you alone?"

"Yes."

Ryan appeared in the doorway. I gestured for him to be quiet but to come closer so he could hear.

"I located a great deal of information on the situation in Montreal."

"How?"

"I started with names—Anique Pomerleau, Andrew Ryan, Temperance Brennan. I paired the names with key words such as 'SQ,' 'Montreal,' 'skeletons.' One loop led to another and another. That's always the case. Coverage was quite extensive, you know, in both French and English."

That was an understatement.

"Have I told you how very proud I am—"

"Where are you going with this, Mama?"

A beat, then, "You identified three girls from their skeletal remains in the cellar: Angela Robinson, Marie-Joëlle Bastien, and Manon Violette. Correct?"

"Yes."

"Write down those names."

I did.

"Angela Robinson went missing on December 9, 1985. Marie-Joëlle Bastien on April 24, 1994. Manon Violette on October 25, 1994."

I scribbled each date beside the appropriate name.

"Did you write that?"

"I did."

"Were there any others?"

"A girl's name was written in a journal found at Pomerleau's house. But we learned nothing about her, and no remains were ever found."

"Do I have your full attention?"

"You do."

Ryan and I exchanged glances, both at a loss.

"Nellie Gower was abducted in Vermont on October 18, 2007. Lizzie Nance in Charlotte on April 17, 2009. Tia Estrada in Salisbury on December 2, 2012. Add that to your notes."

I started another two-column list.

"Now read what you've written."

Ryan and I got it in the same instant.

"Sonofabitch." I couldn't help myself.

"There's never call to be vulgar, sweetheart. But I think you understand what I'm saying."

"Each of the later victims disappeared exactly one week before the date on which an earlier victim was taken."

"Yes." Breathy.

"You're suggesting Pomerleau is reenacting previous abductions?"

"I have no idea of her motivation. Or why she's now killing these poor little lambs."

"Mama, I—"

"There was one survivor, a girl held five years in the cellar. Is that correct?"

"Yes."

"She was a minor, so her identity was to remain secret. But it wasn't hard to find the name." Pause. "Tawny McGee."

I said nothing.

"By tracking backward, I was able to establish the date of her disappearance. February 13, 1999."

I looked at Ryan. He nodded confirmation.

A muffled voice buzzed in the background. Mama shushed someone, probably her nurse.

"Listen, Mama. I'll see you tomorrow, and we can discuss—"

"You'll do nothing of the sort. You'll continue your pursuit."

The voice buzzed again. The air went thick, as though the phone had been covered with a palm or pressed to a chest. Then three beeps told me the call had ended.

I looked up at Ryan. He was staring at the tablet.

I read the scribbled names and dates. Pictured the skeletons arranged on the tables in my Montreal lab.

Angela Robinson had been Neal Wesley Catts's first victim, taken in California in 1985, well before his deadly partnership with Anique Pomerleau. Catts had transported Robinson's remains to the East Coast, buried them in Vermont, then dug them up and reburied them, eventually, in the pizza parlor basement in Montreal.

Marie-Joëlle Bastien, an Acadian from New Brunswick, was sixteen when she traveled to Montreal to celebrate spring break. She disappeared from rue Sainte-Catherine, on the city's east side, following a movie and dinner with cousins. My skeletal analysis suggested she'd died soon after her abduction.

Manon Violette was fifteen when she was last seen in *la ville souterraine*, Montreal's underground city. She bought boots, ate poutine, called her mother, then vanished. Her bones suggested she'd survived several years.

Tawny McGee was the only captive alive at the time of the 2004 raid. She'd been taken in 1999 at the age of twelve.

McGee visited me once following her rescue. Though reluctant, a social services psychiatrist had agreed to McGee's request to come to my office.

I pictured the serious little face under the crooked beret. The clenched hands and somber voice. Managed not to wince at the memory.

"You're not kidding. Your mom is good." Ryan's voice cut into my thoughts.

"You think the connections are real?"

"Three matches would be one hell of a coincidence."

"Shelly Leal vanished on November twenty-first. If Mama is right, is Pomerleau memorializing some kid we don't even know about?"

Ryan looked equally troubled by the thought.

"According to a statement Pomerleau gave the ER doctors in '04, Catts grabbed her when she was fifteen," I said.

"She was living on her own and not reported missing, so we may never know the exact date she was taken."

"Ditto for Colleen Donovan. And my Jane Doe skeleton, ME107-10."

"Any progress on that?"

I shook my head. "I sent the descriptors back through the usual data banks. Got no hits."

"It always blows my mind. A kid that young, and no one's looking."

"Do the ages bother you?" I asked.

"What do you mean?"

"Pomerleau and Catts preyed on girls in their mid- to late teens. These recent victims skew younger. Or look younger, in the case of Donovan."

"Psychoses can evolve over time."

Birdie chose that moment to hop onto the desk and roll to his back. I scratched his belly. He began to purr.

"You think we should tell Slidell?" I asked.

Ryan's eyes gave me his answer.

I did go to Heatherhill Farm on Sunday. My guilt for staying away trumped my guilt for time lost on the investigation.

I found Mama sitting cross-legged on her bed, the Lilliputian laptop lighting her face. Her door was closed, and the TV was blasting.

After delivering the expected chastisement, Mama sighed and admitted she was delighted I'd come. Since the day was cold and overcast, which ruled out the deck, she insisted we stay in her room.

Mama was intense, restless. As we talked, she repeatedly scurried over to press her ear to the door.

Knowing the source of her agitation, I tried to steer

our conversation toward lighter topics. Mama, as always, proved unsteerable.

Sadly, or happily, she'd found no new information on the abductions or murders. I told her she could stand down. Made comments suggesting greater progress than was actually occurring.

She demanded a full update. I gave a vague overview of developments on my end.

She asked about Ryan. I outdid myself at vague.

When I broached the subject of chemo, my questions were rebuffed. When I asked about Goose, Mama rolled her eyes and flapped a dismissive hand.

Ryan had stayed in Charlotte and reviewed the files he hadn't tackled on Saturday. Slidell had hit pawnshops in search of Leal's ring.

I arrived home around nine. Over Ben & Jerry's chocolate nougat crunch, Ryan filled me in on his day.

He'd focused on the investigation chronologies, the time-ordered outlines of actions taken by detectives and calls and inquiries received from the public. He looked and sounded discouraged. "With Donovan and Koseluk, there was little to review. Within weeks of each disappearance, nothing was happening and no one was calling. I gave up on those."

Other bodies hit the morgue. The cops moved on. I didn't say it.

"With Estrada, the investigation was more thorough. Interviews were conducted in Salisbury and Anson

County—registered sex offenders, friends and family, teachers, the campground owners, residents along the highway."

He could have been talking about Nance or Gower. About the investigation of any murdered child. I didn't say that, either.

"A few interviews triggered follow-ups. None yielded a serious suspect."

"Everyone had an alibi?"

Ryan nodded. "There was the usual flurry of phone tips following the discovery of Estrada's body. A sporting goods store owner was accused, a kid who drove his Harley too loud and too fast, a farmer who shot his collie."

"Bike hater, dog lover."

"You've got it. The calls thinned, stopped within a month."

"There was the scandal, then the lead detective retired. Hull ultimately inherited the file," I said.

"The final call came from a reporter at the *Salisbury Post*. She phoned six months after Estrada disappeared."

"And that was it."

Ryan set down his bowl and spoon. Patted his chest. Remembered where he was and dropped his hands.

"It's okay to smoke." It wasn't. I hate the smell of cigarettes in my house.

"Uh-huh." A corner of his mouth twisted up ever so slightly. A few moments passed before Ryan spoke again. "It wasn't that the cops didn't want to solve these cases. They had nothing to go with. There was no ex-con working at a kid's home, no psycho teacher, no parent with a history of violence. The vics were too young to have angry boyfriends. Donovan was high-risk, but not the others."

"And Donovan and Estrada weren't the type the media bothers to cover." I couldn't help but sound bitter.

"When the bodies turned up, there were no witnesses or forensics."

"Nothing to suggest a suspect."

"Until Rodas got a DNA hit."

I flashed on a dark figure darting through flames with a five-gallon can in her hands. The memory brought with it the smell of kerosene and my own burning hair. The terror of waking in a house that was burning down around me. Anger grabbed me like a muscle cramp. "Pomerleau despises me," I said.

"She hates us both."

"It's because of me that she's here." I knew it was melodramatic, said it anyway. "I let her escape. She wants to remind me, to taunt me."

"We all let her escape."

"It's because we failed that children are dead. That another may die soon."

Two stormy blue eyes locked on to mine. "This time the moth has flown too close to the flame."

"She. Will. Burn."

Silly, but we smacked a high five.

The next morning our confidence was blown to hell.

14

My bedroom window overlooks the patio. When I opened the shutters the next morning, I saw Ryan below on one of the wrought-iron benches. He was sitting forward, elbows on knees. I figured he was smoking. As I watched, Ryan's head dropped, and his shoulders began rising and falling in jagged little hops.

I felt my insides sucked out. I also felt like a voyeur, and quickly withdrew.

After a hasty morning toilette, I dressed and hurried down to the kitchen.

Coffee was perking. Birdie was eating. The TV was running with the sound on mute.

I glanced at the screen. An anchor with flawless hair and unnaturally white teeth was talking beside footage of a jackknifed truck, projecting a well-rehearsed mix of shock and concern.

I was eating yogurt and granola when the back door opened. I looked up from the morning's *Observer*.

Ryan seemed composed, though a red puffiness in the eyes gave him away.

"Good brew." I raised my mug.

Ryan joined me at the table.

"You saw?" I displayed the headline. Below the fold, but still front-page. *No Arrest in Shelly Leal Murder.*

"Slidell will be livid," Ryan said.

"The article makes it sound like Tinker and the SBI are driving the train."

"Do you know this"—Ryan squinted to read the byline—"Leighton Siler?"

"No. He must be new on the crime beat." I cocked my chin toward Miss Hair and Dentition. "Any TV coverage?"

"Daisy would disapprove of the vulgarity."

Great. A camera had caught me flipping the bird while leaving the MCME.

"Have at the files some more today?" I asked.

Ryan nodded. "There's nothing obvious linking these kids. No common medical providers, libraries, classes, hobbies, summer camps, pageants, teachers, pastors, priests, pet stores, allergies, or rashes. We're still batting zero with online info for Nance and Leal. I'm going to focus on minutiae, see if there's any detail that might have been overlooked or underappreciated. There's got to be something connecting one vic to another."

Ryan once described to me what he called the "big bang break": the one clue or insight that suddenly sets an investigation barreling in the right direction. That one synapsey moment when realization explodes and the search hurtles forward on the right trajectory. Ryan believed at least one big bang lurked in every case. And despite his personal pain, he was determined to find one for the "poor little lambs." His commitment buoyed my spirits.

I was rinsing my bowl and mug when the phone rang. Larabee was calling to remind me of a meeting that morning. A prosecutor was coming to the MCME to review our findings for an upcoming deposition. Larabee was on at eight, I was on at nine.

The case involved the death of an L.A. actor who'd flown to Charlotte to play the part of a rabbit in a feature film. After two days of shooting, the man had failed to reappear on-set. He was found four weeks later in a culvert by the tracks in Chantilly. His sometime boyfriend had been arrested and charged with murder one.

As Larabee and I wrapped up, Ryan caught my eye and pointed upstairs. I nodded, distracted. And annoyed. Wet-nursing a lawyer was not in my plan for the day.

Ten minutes later, Ryan returned, hair wet and slicked back below the Costa Rican cap. He wore jeans and a short-sleeved polo over a long-sleeved tee.

We talked little in the car. Which, thanks to my passenger, smelled of my pricey Egyptian musk black soap.

I dropped Ryan at the LEC and continued on to the MCME. I was reviewing my file on Mr. Bunny when Larabee came through my door. "How was your weekend?" he asked.

"Good. Yours?"

"Can't complain. I hear Ryan's hanging in."

"Mmm." I wondered who'd told him. Figured it was Slidell.

"You'll never guess what was waiting on my voicemail this morning." Larabee loved making me predict what he had to say. I found the game tiresome.

"A giant sea slug."

"Hilarious."

"And she's playing here all week."

"Marty Parent called."

It took a moment for the name to register. "The new DNA analyst at the CMPD lab."

"She's a go-getter. And an early riser. Left a message at 7:04, asking that I call her back."

I waited him out.

"Which I will do as soon as I'm done with Vinny Gambini in there." Tipping his head toward the small conference room.

"Who is it?"

"Connie Rossi."

Constantin Rossi had been with the DA's office for as long as I could recall. He was shrewd and organized and didn't waste your time. Or try to push you beyond conclusions allowed by the facts.

"Rossi's okay," I said.

"He is."

I was finished at eleven and went in search of Larabee. Found him in autopsy room one, slicing a brain.

"What did Parent say?" I asked.

Larabee looked at me, knife in one hand, apron and gloves speckled with blood. "I'm not sure if it's good news or bad." Spoken through three-ply paper hooked over his ears.

I wiggled my fingers in a "Give it to me" gesture.

Larabee laid down the knife and lowered the mask. "Parent spent all weekend analyzing the smear on Leal's jacket."

"You're kidding."

"She's divorced, and her kid was away with the ex."

"Still."

"The kid's a daughter. Ten years old."

"Right." When Katy was younger, I'd have done the same if a maniac had been targeting girls her age.

"You nailed it. What the ALS picked up was a lip print. Our swab contained beeswax, sunflower oil, coconut oil, soybean oil—"

"Lip balm."

"Yes, ma'am."

"Saliva?" I felt my pulse kick up slightly.

Larabee smiled the answer.

"Holy shit. Tell me she got DNA."

146

"She got DNA."

"Yes!" I actually did that pump-action thing with one arm.

"She'll send it through the system today."

"And up to Canada."

"Maybe."

"What do you mean, maybe? It'll come back to Pomerleau." I was totally jazzed. It was Ryan's big bang. Slidell would get his task force.

"Are you familiar with amelogenin?"

Larabee was referring to a group of proteins involved in enamel development, a process called amelogenesis. Amelogenins are thought to be critical in dental formation.

The amelogenin genes, AMELX and AMELY, are located on the sex chromosomes, the version on X differing slightly from the version on Y. Since human females are XX and human males are XY, this difference is useful in gender determination. Two peaks, your unknown is a gent. One peak, your perp is of the fairer sex.

"Yes?" My rising inflection indicated puzzlement at Larabee's question.

"Amelogenin indicated the saliva was left by a male."

"Is Parent sure?" Of course she was. She wouldn't have called on a whim.

"Yes."

"Isn't amelogenin occasionally wrong?"

"There have been some cases of false-positive female readings. Probably because the Y chromosome–specific allele was deleted. But I've never heard of an error going the other way."

I knew that. The shock was causing me to blurt dumb questions.

Larabee rehooked his mask and took up his blade. "I'll let you know if Parent gets any hits locally or with CODIS."

I returned to my office. Sat and listened to the silence. Stunned. Disappointed. Mostly confused.

Were Slidell's bosses correct? Was Leal's murder unrelated to that of Gower and Nance? To the others'? Was her killer a man?

But the patterning in victimology and MO. The similar ages and physical traits. The broad-daylight abductions. The posing and lack of concealment of the bodies.

It had to be one doer. It had to be Pomerleau.

The name triggered another neural flare. Blood oozing from a dime-sized hole, across a hairline, a temple, a cheek. Brain matter splattering a dim parlor wall.

Sweet Jesus. Could that be it?

I called Ryan.

"Oui."

I relayed what Larabee had said.

"It could be nothing. Someone's face accidentally brushed the jacket."

"The print had clean edges."

"Meaning?"

"It wasn't created by a casual swipe."

"We have no idea how long it was there. Could have been weeks, months."

"On nylon? Outside? No way. There was too much detail. Contact happened close to the time Leal was killed."

Ryan was silent a long moment. I knew his thoughts were traveling the same path mine had.

"You're thinking she has an accomplice," he said.

"Another sick twist like Catts."

Again, there was a long pause. I could hear male voices in the room. Sharp.

"What about the hairs Larabee found in Leal's throat?" Ryan cut off my question about the background row.

"He didn't mention it." And I'd been too channeled on amelogenin to ask.

"Slidell's going to shit his shorts," Ryan said.

"Where is he?"

"Here. His license plate search generated twelve hundred hits. He just finished re-interviewing the wit who saw the kid on Morningside."

"Hoping for what?"

"Maybe nail down digit order, vehicle color, four-door versus two-door, that kind of thing. To get a sense which hits are good."

"How did it go?"

"The car was blue or black. And the seven on the tag might have been a one."

"Skinny's not happy."

"That's an understatement. Then Tinker showed up. They've been locked in a dick-measuring contest ever since."

"What's Tinker doing?"

"Going through the Leal file and answering the hotline."

"Any interesting calls?"

"The usual wingnuts. A teacher wanting to discuss the immodest dress habits of today's youth. A man ranting about Muslims. A woman pointing the finger at declining church attendance."

"Awesome. How's your search going?"

"I finished with Gower. That Rodas is one thorough guy."

"Umpie."

"What?"

"His name is Umpie."

"Then I worked through Koseluk and Estrada. Reports, statements, phone messages, tips. Nothing. I left Donovan for you."

"Now what?"

"I'm turning the heat up on Pomerleau, following up queries I sent to Quebec, Vermont, and statewide here. This time I'm requesting they run possible aliases. I made a list of names."

"How?"

"People aren't all that creative. They tend to use something that's easy, usually a variation on their own name or initials. Ann Pomer. Ana Proleau. That sort of thing."

"It's worth a try."

"Next I'll work the DMV, social security records, tax rolls. It's a long shot, but what the hell."

"A long shot is better than no shot at all." How often had Ryan and I said that over the years?

The background squabble grew more heated. A door slammed. I wondered whether Slidell or Tinker had stormed out.

Ryan ignored the spat. "When Pomerleau slipped the net in '04, we sent her picture out over the continent."

"Right." I actually snorted. "A mug shot taken when she was fifteen."

"Granted. But the image generated dozens of calls."

I remembered. Pomerleau had been sighted in Sherbrooke, Albany, Tampa, Thunder Bay.

"Your point?" I asked.

"We're running out of road here."

"And?"

"Maybe there's something there."

I nodded. Pointless. Ryan couldn't see me.

"We need to go to Montreal."

15

I checked with Larabee. He had no problem with my being away for a few days.

Before leaving the office, I booked two seats on the 8:25 nonstop to Pierre-Elliott-Trudeau. Then I phoned to arrange for cat care.

My neighbor was unavailable but suggested her granddaughter, Mary Louise Marcus, who lived just blocks from Sharon Hall. I called. Mary Louise was available, at a whopping ten bucks a day. She promised to come by at seven to meet me and Birdie.

On my way across uptown, I stopped at Bojangles', Slidell's favorite, and bought enough food for a family of six.

It was after two when I arrived at the LEC. Slidell was at the computer, lips pressed to his teeth, head wagging slowly from side to side. Tinker was sticking pins into a map of North Carolina spread on a corkboard that hadn't been there before. Today he looked like someone sponsored by Wiseguys R Us. Black jacket, black shirt, shiny lavender tie.

Ryan was speaking on his mobile. I heard the name Manon, guessed he was trying to locate the Violette family. His quiet French rode on air brittle with suppressed hostility.

I tossed my jacket on a chair and waited. After concluding his call, Ryan briefed me.

Slidell had made zero progress with his license plate search. The guy in IT had recovered only snatches of data from Leal's computer, none of it useful. Barrow was having no luck locating Nance's laptop. The age-progressed image of Pomerleau wouldn't be ready for days, maybe a week. Ditto DNA sequencing from the hair found in Leal's trachea. The tox screen was going nowhere.

I placed my bags on the table. "How did Slidell react to the amelogenin shocker?"

"His commentary was unconstructive."

"Lunch," I announced.

Slidell's eyes rolled up to peer at me over the screen. I could almost see the smell of deep-fried grease hit his olfactory lobes.

As I began spreading paper plates, plastic utensils, and cardboard cartons of chicken and sides, Slidell heaved to his feet. Behind me, I heard Tinker cross the room, keys jangling in a pocket or on a belt loop.

"We need to think about highways." Tinker spooned mashed potatoes onto his plate, added gravy, slaw, and a biscuit. "Nance was dumped at Latta Plantation, not far off I-485." To Slidell, "You gonna paw every piece?"

Slidell continued digging through the chicken, maybe even slowed, eventually emerged with two legs and two thighs.

Tinker stepped up and helped himself to a breast. Took a bite before continuing with his train of thought. "Gower was left just off a state highway, Vermont 14, I think Rodas said."

"Pure genius." Spoken through masticated drumstick. "We've determined that vics are transported by car. We can forget tossing all those choppers and yachts."

I ignored Slidell's sarcasm. "Koseluk was abducted in Kannapolis, Estrada in Salisbury. Both lie along the I-85 corridor."

Tinker looked at me with his flat little eyes. Swallowed. "I'm having a hard time putting those two in the show."

"Leal was found under I-485," I added.

"Amelogenin says she's not in there, either."

"Not necessarily."

Tinker did something that combined a shrug with a "Give it to me" finger curl.

"Pomerleau could have an accomplice. Or—"

Slidell cut me off, voice dripping with scorn as he addressed Tinker. "Low number of vics make it easier to tie the bow? Buff up the image?"

"Or perhaps you're projecting, Detective. Talking about yourself," shot back Tinker.

I feared the smart-ass tone would goad Slidell to smash Tinker's plate up into his face, Stooges-style. I glanced at Skinny. His lower lids were crimped and twitching, sparkling grease coating his upper lip and chin.

"What the fuck are you talking about?" Now Slidell was the recipient of Tinker's flat-eyed stare. For a moment their gazes locked. Skinny turned away first. "That's it. I ain't working with this troll." Wrapping his poultry in a napkin, Slidell strode from the room.

Tinker finished eating, wiped his hands digit by digit, and returned to his map.

I raised my brows at Ryan. He raised his at me.

I pointed at the chicken.

Ryan shook his head.

Realizing I'd never answered Slidell's question about a cellphone for Nance, I asked Ryan if he'd come across any mention of one in the file. He had not.

While clearing the lunch debris, I told Ryan about our flight reservations. He hesitated a moment, then thanked me. Asked how much time we had. I suggested we leave the LEC by six. He nodded, grabbed his phone, and started punching digits.

Ryan hadn't been back to Montreal since Lily's death. I wondered what storm was swirling inside him. Didn't ask.

After positioning one of the empty boards between

Nance and Koseluk, I pulled the ME107-10 file from my purse and began posting information. Biological profile. Estimated time of death. Date of discovery. Location. Scene photos of the skeleton and associated articles.

Tinker abandoned his pushpins to eyeball my display. Which was meager. "Seriously?"

"Clothing was still in place on some of the bone clusters. Missing articles were probably dragged off by scavengers."

Tinker nodded, noncommittal.

"A lot fits the pattern."

"Where was this kid?"

I showed Tinker on his map. He stuck in a yellow pin, indulging me.

It took a moment to decipher his coding system. Green marked the intersection where Nance was last seen alive, red the place her body was found. Stoplight colors for a murder solidly connected to another by DNA.

Blue indicated LSA sites for girls "not in the show," yellow the places Estrada and Leal were found.

The rainbow pins flowed north along I-85, circled Charlotte on the I-485 beltway, and dropped south toward the South Carolina border. One red and two blue pins marked inner-city locations.

One yellow pin sat off to the southeast by itself.

Tinker read my thoughts. "Estrada's body wasn't anywhere near I-85."

"It wasn't far from NC-52." I studied the configuration, willing a pattern to make itself known. "Estrada was at a campground near the Pee Dee National Wildlife Refuge. Nance was at Latta Plantation." I was juggling aloud, twisting and turning pieces to make them connect. "ME107-10, my Jane Doe, was at the Daniel Stowe Botanical Garden. Gower was at a quarry."

"Break out the champagne. We got us a nature lover."

Smiling coolly at Tinker's smarmy cynicism, I resumed posting ME107-10.

We worked the next couple of hours without saying much. After finishing my Jane Doe board, I began with the other girl about whom we knew almost nothing.

Ryan was right. Little effort had gone into finding Colleen Donovan. And paperwork wasn't Pat Tasat's strong suit.

I went through the interview summaries. The aunt, Laura Lonergan, a tweaker and sometime prostitute. The director of a homeless shelter. A dozen street kids. A hooker named Sarah Merikoski, aka Crystal Rose, who'd filed the MP report.

At some point I heard Slidell slouch in and settle at the computer. I continued reading.

It seemed a cliché. But clichés become what they are due to constant validation. A case either broke quickly and was solved in the first frantic days when witness memories were vivid, evidence was fresh, and theories abounded, or it lingered, dried up, inevitably grew cold. The longer the drought, the deeper the freeze.

Such was not the case with Colleen Donovan. Twenty-four hours. Forty-eight. A year and a half. It wouldn't have mattered. Right out of the gate, there was nothing to indicate what had happened to her or why. Or when.

If anything *had* happened to her. No proof of a crime existed. No blood spatter on a hotel room wall. No treasured belonging left behind in a shelter. No wallet or purse recovered from a trash can. No whispered fears about a john or pimp.

One thread ran through every witness statement. Life on the street is harsh and unpredictable. Kids come, kids go. Everyone but Merikoski, an old-style streetwalker and Donovan's self-appointed tutor on the workings of the sex trade, felt Colleen had taken off on her own. Even Merikoski had misgivings.

A lack of evidence meant no narrative. No narrative meant no suspect.

No big bang break.

As I worked through the chronology, I was vaguely aware of Slidell leaving his keyboard. Of raised voices by the corkboard.

A few calls had come in from the public, not many. A kid named Jon Sapuppo reported seeing Donovan on a bus on Wilkinson Boulevard two weeks after

Merikoski walked into the LEC to file her report. A clerk claimed he'd sold Donovan cigarettes at a gas station on Freedom Drive.

It registered in my brain that the scrum by the corkboard was gaining in volume. Still I ignored it.

The calls tapered off, stopped by the end of February. In August the aunt called to ask where the case stood. That was it.

". . . questioning my integrity?"

"I'm questioning your effort."

Slidell and Tinker were at it again.

"You stick to the cold ones," Slidell snapped. "Leave Leal to me."

"Once burned, twice shy, eh, Skinny?"

"What the hell does that mean?"

I turned in my chair. Slidell was glaring at Tinker, arms down, hands balled into fists.

"Don't push too hard? Play it careful?"

"I'm pushing full-out. There ain't much to push."

"You background the guy who spotted that car?"

"He's got cataracts and a prostate the size of a squash."

"How's that computer search going?"

"It's going." Slidell's tone sounded dangerous.

"You get Donovan's juvie file?"

"Yeah. She lifted a watch at Kmart. Got caught in a sweep with an ounce of weed in her purse. Oh, and her big one. She fell while shitfaced and had to have her head stitched."

That stilled Tinker a moment. "This Pomerleau. She works your turf, what, five years, and you can't roust her?"

"I'm following every lead, you worthless piece of—"

"Are you?"

"What are you suggesting?"

"I'm just wondering. It took a while to put that other thing behind you. Maybe you decide to play it safe on this one. You don't screw up, everyone forgets. Pretty soon you're a rock star again."

"You're a fucking moron."

"Or is your beef something else?" Tinker's mouth curled in an oily little grin. "Something more personal."

Slidell gave Tinker a long, hard stare, his face so red it was almost purple.

"You had to know Verlene would eventually trade up." Tinker jumped his eyebrows, Groucho-style.

"Bloody hell!"

I shot to my feet. "Do I have to turn a hose on you two?"

Slidell looked at me. Shook his head in disgust to say I didn't get it. "I'm filing a complaint on this asshole." He pivoted and stomped from the room.

I checked my watch. Ryan had reviewed all the other files. Was now focused on Montreal.

I crossed to the boards. Slowly worked my way down the row. I was looking at Shelly Leal's school portrait when something said *pssst* in my head.

What?

I'd seen no pattern in Tinker's pins. No geo-profile to suggest a terrain-motivated course of action.

Mama thought the LSA dates were significant. Was my unconscious telling me there was something more there?

Leal had gone missing ten days earlier, on Friday, November 21. I got my iPhone and pulled up a calendar for 2009. Felt a jolt of excitement. Nance had also disappeared on a Friday.

I checked 2007. The jolt fizzled. Gower's LSA date was a Thursday. But so was Koseluk's. Estrada had vanished on a Sunday.

I jotted the dates, returned to the table, and studied the list.

The *pssst* called out louder.

On a whim, I did some math.

For a moment I sat very still, staring at the numbers I'd generated. Feeling a lump at the base of my throat.

"Ryan."

He looked up.

"Gower disappeared on October 18, 2007. Nance on April 17, 2009."

He nodded, clearly puzzled by the chill in my voice.

"There's an eighteen-month interval between the two abductions."

Ryan nodded again.

"A little over two and a half years go by between Nance and Koseluk."

Ryan ran the numbers in his head. "Twenty-nine months."

"But if you slot in ME107-10, my Jane Doe skeleton, the intervals are cut to roughly fifteen months." Ryan started to speak. I cut him off. "Koseluk vanished on September 8, 2011. Estrada on December 2, 2012."

He saw where I was going. "Fifteen months in between."

"Merikoski reported Donovan missing on February 1, 2014."

"According to her statement, she hadn't seen the kid in weeks."

"Leal vanishes nine months later."

"Remember Mama's theory?"

"Each recent LSA links to the LSA of a vic in Montreal."

We'd accepted the idea of the linked dates. But Mama had grasped the full significance of the pattern. Because Ryan and I hadn't done the math that day, we hadn't seen it. Or perhaps we'd gotten channeled on the difference in ages between the earlier and the more recent victims.

As one, we now had the same terrible thought.

"The intervals are decreasing," I said. "The next child could be taken *this* February sixth. That's roughly two months off."

Part II

16

We left the law enforcement center twenty minutes late. Fortunately, the girl who was going to catsit for me arrived at the annex precisely at seven. She was a gangly kid wearing the kind of cloche hat once favored by flappers. Birdie took to her right off. Ryan and I left them playing fetch with a red plaid mouse in the study.

I transit a lot of airports. Except for baggage retrieval, which takes longer than the average fall harvest, Charlotte Douglas is perhaps my favorite. Rocking chairs. Grand piano. Sushi bar. That night, forget it. We had barely enough time to grab takeout and dash to the gate.

The wheels left the tarmac right on the dot. Ryan and I had twelve hundred miles of East Coast to eat lukewarm barbecue and fries and plan our attack.

We knew we'd be on our own. The Service de police de la Ville de Montréal detectives who'd worked the case, Luc Claudel and Michel Charbonneau, were both unavailable. Claudel was in France, Charbonneau was on leave following knee surgery. Perhaps just as well. Given the jurisdictional rivalries between the provincial and city cops, we doubted much help would come from the latter on a ten-year-old file.

Angela Robinson was fourteen when she disappeared in Corning, California, in 1985. Hers had been one of the three skeletons unearthed in the pizza parlor basement in 2004. Stalled at every turn, Slidell had agreed to phone the Tehama County Sheriff's Department to try to churn the waters out there. With little optimism. Almost thirty years had passed since Robinson's abduction.

The other skeletons belonged to Manon Violette and Marie-Joëlle Bastien. The former was fifteen, the latter sixteen, when they vanished in 1994.

Ryan's phone queries concerning Bastien had turned up zilch. She was from Bouctouche, New Brunswick, and in the two decades since her disappearance, her nuclear family had dispersed, leaving only a few cousins in the area. No one recalled anything about Marie-Joëlle except that she'd been murdered. And that her remains were buried in the cimetière Saint-Jean-Baptiste.

Ryan had fared better with Violette. Manon's parents still lived at the same address on boulevard Édouard-Montpetit in Montreal. Though reluctant, they'd agreed to see us the next day.

In the morning, after reexamining our respective files, we would interview Mère and Père Violette. Then we'd work on locating Tawny McGee, the sole survivor of the Pomerleau-Catts reign of terror. We held little optimism that the visits would yield fruit. But what the hell. Nothing else was working.

Another aviation miracle. The flight landed early. The bookend punctuality made me mildly uneasy.

Exiting the airport, I was hit by a wind corkscrewing straight off the tundra. I admit it—I gasped. No matter how often it happens, I'm never prepared for that first frigid slap.

Ryan and I shared a taxi from Dorval. At his insistence, I was dropped first. I suppose it made sense. My condo is in Centreville. His is across the St. Lawrence in a concrete LEGO curiosity called Habitat 67.

Ryan offered to collect me in the morning. Happy to avoid the Métro, and frostbite, I accepted.

Digging for keys, I was aware of the taxi lingering at the curb, exhaust billowing like a small white cumulus in the red glow of the taillights. I was touched. Though I knew we had no future together, it meant something that he still cared about my safety.

My condo was cold and dark. Before removing my inadequate autumn-in-Dixie jacket, I thumbed the lever on the thermostat left. Way left. The hum of the furnace sounded loud in the stillness.

After a slapdash facial and dental effort, I threw on sweats and dropped into bed.

I dreamed about snow.

I awoke to bright sunlight leaking around the edges of the shade. Knew the day would be colder than crap.

The cupboard was bare, not even coffee. Rather than hike to the corner *dépanneur*, I skipped breakfast.

Ryan phoned at 7:55 as he was making the turn onto my street. I dug out my Kanuk jacket, mittens, and a scarf. Pulled on boots and set forth.

I was right. The air was so crisp, it felt like tiny crystals sliding in and out of my nose. The sun was a tight white ball hanging low in an immaculate blue sky.

I scurried to Ryan's Jeep and climbed in.

Ryan never tired of teasing about my inadequacy in dealing with polar climes. Today he said nothing. His skin looked gray, and a dark half-moon sculpted each lower lid.

Congealed blood marked a spot on Ryan's chin that he'd nicked while shaving. I wondered if he'd slept. If so, I guessed he'd dreamed about the Lily-shaped void now forever in his life.

I also wondered if he'd called ahead to his squad, or if he'd opted to appear unannounced. Either way, I suspected he was dreading the upcoming encounter.

You've got it. I asked about neither.

Traffic was surprisingly light across Centreville and through the Ville-Marie Tunnel. By eight-fifteen we were parked at the Édifice Wilfrid-Derome, a T-shaped high-rise in a working-class neighborhood just east of the city center.

Here's how the place works.

For almost twenty years I have served as forensic anthropologist for the Laboratoire de Sciences Judiciaires et de Médecine Légale, the central crime and medico-legal lab for the province of Quebec. Charlotte, North Carolina? Montreal? Right. The commute is a bitch. A story for another time.

The LSJML occupies the top two floors of Wilfrid-Derome, twelve and thirteen. The Bureau du coroner has ten and eleven. The morgue and autopsy suites are in the basement.

Ryan is a lieutenant-détective with the provincial police, the Sûreté du Québec. The SQ has the rest of the building.

After entering the front doors, we swiped our security cards and passed through *thunk-thunk* metal gates. Ryan took an elevator to the Service des enquêtes sur les crimes contre la personne, located on the second floor. I waited for the restricted LSJML/ Coroner elevator.

I ascended with a dozen others mumbling *"Bonjour"* and *"Comment ça va?"* At that hour, "Good morning" and "How's it going?" are equally perfunctory no matter the language.

A woman from ballistics asked if I'd just come from the Carolinas. I said I had. She queried the weather. When I answered, my fellow passengers groaned.

Kathy Reichs

Five of us exited on the twelfth floor. After crossing a marble-floored lobby, I swiped a different security card, then swiped it again to pass into the medico-legal wing. The board showed only two pathologists present, Jean Morin and Pierre LaManche, the chief. The others were testifying, teaching, or absent on personal leave.

Continuing along the corridor, I passed pathology and histology labs on my left, pathologists' offices on my right. Through observation windows and open doors, I could see secretaries booting up computers, techs flipping dials, scientists and analysts donning lab coats. All the world slamming down coffee.

The anthropology/odontology lab was last in the row. There I used an old-fashioned key to enter.

My previous visit had been almost a month earlier. My desk was mounded with letters, flyers, and ads. A packet of prints from a Division d'identité judiciaire photographer. A copy of *Voir Dire*, the LSJML gossip sheet. One *demande d'expertise en anthropologie* form.

After removing my copious outerwear, I skimmed the anthropology consult request. Bones had been found in a farmer's field near Saint-Chrysostome. If the remains were human, LaManche wanted a full bio-profile, estimated PMI, and trauma analysis.

Inwardly groaning, I walked to the side counter and opened a brown paper bag stamped with SQ identifiers. The contents included a partial tibia, a phalange, and one rib. Nothing human in the lot. That was why LaManche hadn't phoned me in Charlotte. He knew. But perfectionist that he was, the old man had held the bones for my evaluation.

After getting coffee, I returned to the lab and dug three dossiers from a gray metal filing cabinet around the corner from my desk. LSJML-38426, LSJML-38427, LSJML-38428. The numbering system was different, but the covers were the same neon yellow as at the MCME.

I began by studying the pictures. And circled straight to that cellar with its rats and refuse and reek of decay.

Manon Violette's bones were jumbled in a crate stamped with the words *Dr. Energy's Power Tonic.* Marie-Joëlle Bastien's skeleton lay naked in a shallow grave. Angela Robinson's was wrapped in a moldy leather shroud.

The images. My findings. Reports of the SQ and city cops. Lab results. The final positive IDs. The names of those responsible. Pomerleau. Catts, aka Menard.

At one point I lingered on a crime scene pic of the house on de Sébastopol. I thought of the original owners, Menard's grandparents, the Corneaus. Wondered if the crash in which they'd died had ever been investigated.

The file felt like a phone call from a decade ago.

Two hours later, I sat back in my chair, frustrated and discouraged. I'd found nothing I didn't already know. Except that Angela Robinson had broken her wrist in a fall from a swing at age eight. I'd forgotten that.

The wall clock said 10:40.

I wrote a brief report on the Saint-Chrysostome deceased. *Odocoileus virginianus.* White-tailed deer. Then I went to tell LaManche. He was not in his office. I left a note.

As agreed, I met Ryan in the lobby at eleven.

André and Marguerite Violette lived in Côte-des-Neiges, a neighborhood known for sprawling cemeteries and the Université de Montréal, not for architectural caprice. Like the Westmount of the well-heeled English, and the Outremont of their French counterparts, the quartier is up-mountain from Centreville, a mix of student, middle class, and blue collar, with enough rough spots to make it interesting.

Twenty minutes after leaving Wilfrid-Derome, Ryan pulled to the curb on a stretch of boulevard Édouard-Montpetit within spitting distance of the university campus. We both took a moment to look around.

Duplexes and low-rise apartments lined the street, red brick, plain, and functional. No turrets, no mansard roofs, no curlicue iron stairs. None of the whimsy that gives Montreal its charm.

The Violette building fit with the theme. The address was posted on a two-story brick box stuck to another two-story brick box, each accessed by a set of shotgun steps.

"Remind me," I said. "What did André do?"

"He was a pipe fitter. Still is."

"And Marguerite?"

"She irons his shorts."

"As I recall, he was difficult."

"The guy was a cocky little prick."

"Charming turn of phrase."

"What I have can't be taught."

Ryan and I got out and climbed to the door, footsteps clanging on the stiff metal risers.

When Ryan rang the bell, I heard a muffled double bong, then a voice barked once, like a Doberman firing a warning. Seconds later, locks rattled and the door opened inward.

André Violette looked smaller than I remembered, shorter and thinner. His hair was dyed now, dull and unrelentingly black. The pompadour styling was unchanged from 2004. So was the brash kiss-my-ass attitude.

"Perhaps you remember us. I'm Detective Ryan. This is Dr.—"

"I know who you are."

"Thank you for seeing us."

"Pfff. You give me a choice, me?"

Joual is a form of Quebecois French. Some speak it due to lack of education, others as a statement of francophone pride. André's accent was thicker than I recalled. His *moi* came out a nasal "moe"; his *toi* was "toe." I doubted his choice of lexicon was based on politics.

Kathy Reichs

"We're very sorry—"

André cut me off. "For my loss. I heard that speech ten years ago."

"We're still working to find the woman who hurt your daughter."

No reply.

"May we come in?" Ryan's tone said the request was clearly a formality.

André stepped back. We followed him down a short hall to a living room overfilled with bulky sofas, chairs, and carved mahogany pieces. A tasseled lamp occupied every table. A doily protected every seat back. Shelves on either side of a painted brick fireplace held bric-a-brac, religious statues, and framed photos.

André dropped into a chair and lifted an ankle onto a knee. The upraised foot looked unnaturally large inside its salt-stained boot.

As Ryan and I settled on opposite ends of the couch, a woman materialized in a doorway to our left. Her hair, once brown, was fast going gray. She was doing nothing to hide it. I liked her for that.

André's eyes cut to his wife. "Is it all right—?" she started.

André flicked an impatient hand. The woman scuttled to a chair, hands clutched to her chest.

I'd never met Marguerite Violette. Back in '04, André had been my sole point of contact. It was André who'd delivered antemortem records. André to whom I'd reported the ID.

174

I recalled his odd reaction. He hadn't cried, hadn't questioned, hadn't lashed out. He'd pulled a Mr. Goodbar from his pocket, eaten half the chocolate, risen, and walked from my office.

Seeing the Violettes together, I understood the dynamic.

"Would anyone like—?" Marguerite began.

"This ain't a social visit." To Ryan, "So, what? You finally caught this freak?"

"I'm sorry I can't report that. Yet. But there are new leads."

André shook his head. Marguerite slumped visibly.

"We have reason to believe that the woman involved in your daughter's abduction—"

"My daughter's murder." André's foot began winging on his knee.

"Yes, sir. We believe your daughter's abductor is now in the U.S."

"Anique Pomerleau." Marguerite's whisper was barely audible.

Ryan nodded. "Recently discovered evidence places Pomerleau in Vermont in '07, and in North Carolina this year."

"What evidence?" André asked.

"DNA."

Marguerite's eyes went wide. The irises were blue and flecked with caramel-colored points. "Has she hurt another child?"

"I'm sorry," Ryan said softly. "I can't discuss details of the investigation."

"So arrest the bitch," André snapped. "It's good she's in America. They can put her down."

"We are using every resource at our disposal to find her."

"That's it? Ten years and you tell us our kid's killer maybe left her spit in one place or another? Whoop-de-fucking-do." The last was delivered in English. "You guys are worthless. Next you'll say it's bonhomme Sept-Heures done it."

"You've had a lot of time to think," I said gently. "Perhaps one of you has remembered a detail that hadn't occurred to you back when Manon went missing. Or hadn't seemed important. Any bit of information could prove useful."

"Remember? Yeah, I remember. Every day." His face hardened, and venom infiltrated his voice. "I remember how my baby kicked off the covers and slept sideways on her bed. How she loved rainbow sherbet. How I patched up her knee when she fell off her bike. How her hair smelled like oranges after she washed it. How she got on the fucking Métro and never came home."

André's jaw clamped suddenly. His cheeks were aflame with ragged patches of red.

Ryan caught my eye. I got the message and didn't reply.

But neither Violette seemed compelled to fill the

awkward silence that followed the outburst. André remained mute. Marguerite's breathing went faster and shallower as a thousand emotions clearly vied for control of her face.

I studied André's eyes, his body language. Saw a man hiding pain behind macho bluster.

A full minute passed. Ryan spoke first. "Those are precisely the types of recollections that might prove useful."

"I got a recollection. I recall my knitting club meets today." André's foot was again dancing on his knee. "We're done."

"Mr. Violette—"

"I got a right to remain silent, yeah?"

"You are not a suspect, sir."

"I'm gonna do that anyway."

"Thank you for your time." Ryan rose. I followed. "And again, we are so sorry for your loss."

André remained seated, his thoughts obviously fixed on things other than needles and yarn.

Marguerite led us down the hall. At the door, she placed a hand on my shoulder. "Don't judge my husband harshly. He's a good man."

The sadness in the caramel-blue eyes seemed bottomless.

17

"What's bonhomme Sept-Heures?" I asked Ryan when we were back in the Jeep.

"*Excuse-moi?*"

"André used the phrase."

"Right. Bonhomme Sept-Heures is a Quebecois bogeyman who kidnaps kids up after seven P.M."

"What's his MO?"

Ryan snorted, sending vapor coning from each nostril. "He wears a mask, carries a bag, and hides under the balcony until the clock strikes seven."

"A myth to scare the kids into bed."

"Frightening when the myth hits home."

"Yes."

"This was a waste of time." Ryan slipped aviator shades onto his nose.

"At least the Violettes know we're not giving up."

"I'm sure they're popping the bubbly even as we speak."

"Did you have a bad night?"

Ryan activated his turn indicator.

"You look like you spent it somewhere dark and dank."

My attempt at humor drew no response. Ryan made a right, another, then a left. Loud and clear. The boy wanted distance.

Using a mitten to clear condensation from the glass, I looked out my window. Pedestrians streamed the sidewalks flanking Queen Mary and bunched at the intersections, impatient to cross. Students with backpacks. Shoppers with plastic or string-handled bags. Mothers with strollers. All wore clothing suited for Antarctica.

Undaunted, I tried again. "Did you locate Tawny McGee?"

"Working on it."

"Is her family still in Maniwaki?"

"No."

"The mother was on her own, right? Two kids?"

"Yes."

"Wasn't the sister somewhere out west?"

"Sandra Catherine. In Alberta."

"She still there?"

"No."

"What next?" When Ryan didn't elaborate.

"Sabine Pomerleau."

"Anique's mother is still alive?" Whipping sideways to look at him.

Sun glinted from the aviators as they swiveled my way, then recentered on the road.

I settled back. Of course my question was stupid. Though desperate, we obviously couldn't interview a corpse.

But Ryan's words surprised me. The Pomerleaus had married late, tried for years to conceive. After prolonged anguish and much priestly counsel, Anique, their miracle child, finally had been sent by God in 1975, when Mama was forty-three and Papa was forty-eight. Thus Sabine told the story of her daughter's birth.

I did the math. Sabine would be eighty-two now, her husband eighty-seven.

"Is Jacques still alive?"

"Kicked in '06."

I wondered if the miracle child's infamy had contributed to her daddy's demise. Kept the thought to myself.

We'd just parked in front of a two-story gray stone semi-detached in the Notre-Dame-de-Grâce neighborhood when my iPhone buzzed. As I dug it from my purse, Ryan pantomimed smoking by placing two fingers to his lips. He got out of the Jeep, and I clicked on. "Brennan."

"I coulda better spent the time flossing."

An image of Slidell working his teeth at a mirror was not one I welcomed. "You talked to Tehama County?"

Bones Never Lie

"The high sheriff himself. Willis Trout. The guy's got the brainpower—"

"Did Trout remember Angela Robinson?"

"I doubt he'd remember how to sneeze without prompting."

I waited.

"No. But once I convinced fish boy I wasn't a crank, he agreed to look for the file. I just got a callback. You're gonna love this." Slidell allowed another theatrical pause. "It's gone."

"Gone?"

"Robinson disappeared in '85. In those days everything was still on paper. When the case chilled, the file ended up in a basement. Which turns out to be real bad planning, since the Sacramento River gets frisky every few years and floods the whole friggin' county."

"The file was destroyed?"

"The basement took hits in '99 and '04."

"Did you ask Trout about Menard and Catts?"

"Let's see. How'd he put it? Given that both are dead, have been for years, and will remain so in the future, he couldn't waste time researching their bios."

For a very long moment, empty air filled the line. Through the windshield, I could see Ryan talking on his mobile. Then Slidell shared the only good news I'd heard in a while.

"We may get lucky with Leal's computer. The IT guy's using some sort of mojo recovery software, getting fragments, whatever the hell that means."

181

"Pieces of the browser history."

"Yeah. He says the deletions were amateur-hour. Thinks he might be able to nail some sites the kid visited."

"That's fantastic."

"Or a big waste of time."

"I have a feeling something is there. Otherwise why would somebody want the child's Internet history destroyed?"

"Eeyuh."

I told Slidell what Ryan and I were doing.

"The media's screaming for blood down here. So far it's staying local."

"How's it going with Tinker?"

"You gotta go ask that and wreck my day?"

"Keep me in the loop," I said.

I joined Ryan on the sidewalk. He'd finished his call and was surveying our surroundings. The block was a quiet one shaded by large trees, now bare, and lined with what appeared to be single-family homes. Each home was fronted by a well-kept lawn, now brown, and burlap-wrapped bushes and shrubs. Several had the portable plastic garages that *les Montréalais* call *abris tempos*.

I looked at the conjoined structure at our backs, then at Ryan.

"The place was converted into a nursing home back in the eighties," he said.

"The PC term is 'assisted living.'"

"More like assisted dying."

Nothing like witty repartee to buoy one's soul.

Steps rose from a short walk to a wooden door at the left end of a porch spanning the width of the building. On the porch were six Adirondack chairs, each painted a different color, probably at the time of the home's conversion. A second-floor balcony provided overhead shelter from rain or snow. The upper balcony held four more weathered chairs. In one, bundled like an Inuit hunter, was an elderly man with his face tipped to the sun.

Ryan and I climbed up and let ourselves in.

The house's interior was cloyingly warm and smelled of disinfectant and urine and years of institutional food. To the right was a small waiting room, once a parlor, to the left a staircase. Ahead were a dining room and a hall leading straight back to what looked like a sunroom. Doors opened off both sides of the hall, all closed.

A signal must have sounded when Ryan opened the door. As he closed it, a woman was already coming toward us. Her skin was chocolate, her hair thick and silver and braided on top of her head. She wore a generic white uniform, size large. A small brass rectangle above her right breast said *M. Simone, LPN.*

"Puis-je t'aider?" May I help you? A broad smile revealed teeth way too white to be real.

"We're here to see Sabine Pomerleau," Ryan responded in French.

"Are you family?" Undoubtedly knowing we weren't.

Ryan held up his badge. Simone eyed it. Then, "I'm afraid Madame Pomerleau is asleep at the moment."

"I'm afraid we'll have to wake her." No attempt at the old Ryan charm.

"Disruptions are unhealthy."

"She set the alarm for an early shift at the plant?"

I detected a flash of annoyance beneath Simone's sunny demeanor. A flash of something. But the smile held. "Does this have to do with her daughter?"

Ryan just looked at her.

"I will warn you. Conversations with Madame Pomerleau can be problematic. She has Alzheimer's, and a recent stroke has compromised her speech."

"Noted."

"Wait here, please."

Simone returned in less than five minutes and led us to a tiny second-floor room holding two beds, two dressers, and two straight-back chairs. Faded green floral wallpaper made the cramped space feel as claustrophobic as possible.

The room's sole occupant sat propped in bed, a ratty stuffed cat cradled in one arm. As she stroked the doll, the bones visible below the sleeves and at the collar of her pink flannel gown looked as fragile and weightless as those of a bird.

"You have visitors." Simone had the volume on high.

Sabine's face was wrinkled, her cheeks flecked with

tiny red and blue capillaries. The watery green eyes registered nothing.

"I'll be back in ten minutes." Simone spoke to Ryan.

"We'll be careful not to upset her," I said.

"You won't." With that odd comment, Simone hurried off.

Ryan and I maneuvered both chairs to the bed and sat.

"*J'espère que vous allez bien.*"

Getting no response, Ryan asked in English if she was well.

Still no indication that she'd heard.

"We'd like to discuss Anique."

Not so much as a blink.

Ryan amped up the decibels and switched back to French. "Perhaps you've heard from Anique."

One hand continued stroking the cat, blue veins snaking like night crawlers beneath the liver-spotted skin.

A full minute passed. Ryan tried again, with the same result.

I signaled that I'd give it a go.

"Madame Pomerleau, we are hoping you can help us locate your daughter." I spoke loudly but soothingly. "Perhaps you've heard from Anique?"

Silence. I noticed that the cat had no whiskers on the left side of its snout.

"Perhaps you have ideas where Anique might have gone following the troubles?"

I may as well have been speaking to the gargoyle in my garden.

I posed several more questions, slowly and forcefully.

No go.

I looked at Ryan. He shook his head.

As I checked my watch, footsteps sounded on the stairs. I tried one last time. "We fear Anique may come to harm if we don't find her soon."

It was as though we weren't there.

Simone appeared in the doorway, a "Told you so" expression dulling the snowy smile. Ryan and I replaced our chairs, then crossed to her.

The voice was raspy and deep. Over a phone, I'd have pegged it as male.

"*Avec les saints. Saint-Jean.*" Then, in heavily accented English, "Buried."

Ryan and I turned. The ancient hand had stilled on the ragtag toy.

"Anique is with the saints?" I repeated. "She's buried with Saint John?"

But the moment had passed. The ancient hand resumed its relentless caressing of the matted fur. The watery eyes remained pointed at a memory no one else could see.

Outside, the sun was filtered by long white fingers of cloud. The air seemed even more frigid than earlier. I glanced up. The old man was gone from the balcony.

"What's your take?" I asked Ryan as I pulled on my gloves.

"Nurse Smiley tipped her patient that cops were in the house."

"Does she really think Anique is dead?" Sudden thought. "Marie-Joëlle Bastien is buried in the cimetière Saint-Jean-Baptiste in Bouctouche. Could Sabine be confusing Anique with Marie-Joëlle?"

Ryan raised both shoulders and brows.

"Or was she stonewalling?"

"If that was acting, the performance was Oscar-quality."

"Do you know who pays for her care?"

"A nephew in Mascouche. The money comes from the estate, so he's not exactly splurging."

We got into the Jeep. Ryan was turning the key when his mobile buzzed. He picked it up and clicked on. I listened to a lot of *oui*s, a few one-word questions, then, "Text me the address."

"The address for who?" I asked as he disconnected.

"Whom."

"Seriously?" Though I welcomed a glimpse of the old Ryan wit, the two visits we'd paid that day had left me in no mood for humor.

"Tawny McGee."

18

As we drove, Ryan briefed me on what he and his colleague had learned. I was aware of Tawny McGee's backstory, but not of her movements since 2004.

What I knew: Bernadette Higham lived for five years with a man named Harlan McGee. She worked as a receptionist for a small Maniwaki dental practice. He was a long-haul trucker.

Though unmarried, the couple had two daughters. Sandra was born in 1985, when Bernadette was nineteen and Harlan was twenty-nine. Tawny followed in 1987.

A week after Tawny's second birthday, Harlan left on a run to Vancouver and never returned. Four months later, Bernadette received a letter stating that he wouldn't be back. The envelope also contained four hundred dollars.

In 1999 Bernadette's younger daughter vanished while playing in a park. Tawny McGee was twelve years old. Years passed with no progress in the investigation of her disappearance. In 2004 Tawny was released from captivity in Anique Pomerleau's dungeon of torture.

What I learned from Ryan: four months after Tawny returned home, the Maniwaki dentist retired and closed his office. Appreciative of his employee's years of loyal service, he secured Bernadette a position as receptionist and bookkeeper at his brother's pest-control company, if she was willing to move to Montreal. Dissatisfied with the psychological counseling Tawny was receiving, and hoping for better, Bernadette packed up and headed east.

Within a year Bernadette married Jacob Kezerian, the exterminator's son. The Kezerians now lived in the Montreal suburb of Dollard-des-Ormeaux.

Bernadette had agreed to talk with us. So at three P.M. we were heading her way.

The city of Montreal sprawls across a small hunk of land in the middle of the St. Lawrence River. The West Island—in French, l'Ouest- de-l'île—is a handle for the burbs on the western end.

The West Island is composed of green spaces, bike paths, cross-country ski trails, golf courses, and eco-farms sandwiched among affluent bedroom communities. The area is lousy with stockbrokers, lawyers, bankers, and business owners.

Historically, Montrealers divided themselves linguistically, with the French staying east and the English staying west. That separation has softened in recent years. Still, the West Island remains strongly anglophone. Ironic. As late as the '60s, the region was largely farmland populated by les Français.

Thirty minutes after we left Sabine Pomerleau, Ryan turned the Jeep onto a street that could have been a backdrop for Wally and the Beav, Quebecois-style. The front lawns were uniform in size and shape. Each was bisected by a center walk bordered with winter-empty swatches of dirt or with burlap-wrapped shrubs.

The homes were equally homogeneous, each a variation on *la belle province*'s basic bungalow design— stone or stucco facing, blue or brown wood trim, dormer windows up, small porch below.

"Tawny lives with her mother and stepfather?"

"I thought we'd ease into this. First get the lay of the land."

"Your guy didn't ask?"

"I didn't say that."

"Did he?"

"No."

I cocked a questioning brow.

"The kid might still have problems."

"Tawny isn't a kid. She's twenty-seven."

"I didn't want Bernadette going all mother bear."

"She knows you were instrumental in finding her daughter."

"She does."

"How did she react to your call?"

Ryan gave that some thought. "She seemed wary."

"So you implied we were coming just to talk to her?"

"I didn't imply. Though she might have inferred."

Eyes rolling, I followed Ryan between the rows of bundled flora leading to the house. The door and flanking windows were trimmed with strings of multi-colored lights. A plastic Santa hung from a fleur-de-lis iron knocker. Ryan tapped twice, then stepped back.

The woman who answered was a trim brunette trying hard to look younger than her age. Her eyes were a startling turquoise made possible only with tinted contacts. Her makeup was overdone, the streaks in her hair far too blond to look natural. She wore a red-and-green floral shirt unbuttoned over a red tank top. Skinny jeans. Faux equestrian boots.

I'd never met Tawny's mother. But I knew from the file that she was now forty-eight. The man behind her looked at least ten years her junior. His hair and eyes were dark, his five o'clock shadow darker. His heavy brows met in an unhappy V above the bridge of his nose.

"I'm Bernadette Higham. At least that's the name the officer used on the phone." Bernadette started to offer a hand, stopped. "But of course you know that. It's Kezerian now. But you know that, too."

"It's nice to see you, Mrs. Kezerian."

"I expected the other detective. The fancy dresser."

"Luc Claudel."

"Yes. Where is he?"

"In France."

"I see." Bernadette's half-proffered hand curled back to her chest, as though embarrassed at hanging alone in midair. The nails were acrylic, painted the color of uncooked beef.

"This is my colleague, Dr. Temperance Brennan." Ryan left it at that.

"A doctor?" She glanced at me.

"Dr. Brennan works at the medico-legal lab."

The turquoise eyes went wide. The fingers curled tighter. Why such fear? I felt a sense of unease.

"My wife has health issues. You got something to tell us?"

Bernadette turned at the sound of her husband's voice. "I'm okay, Jake."

Jake placed a hand on his wife's shoulder. He was muscled and toned beyond what I'd expect of a guy just spraying for bugs. His forearm was inked with an intricate Asian design. I wondered if his gesture was meant as support or warning.

"May we talk inside?" Ryan asked.

"Of course. Please," Bernadette said.

Jake stepped back, his expression unchanged. As we passed, he lingered to close the door.

Bernadette led us down a wide hall and turned right through an archway into a small living room with a bay window in front and a fireplace at the far end. The decor was not what I'd visualized.

Every wall was white, and off-white plush carpeting

covered the floor. The sofa and armchairs were upholstered in ivory cotton trimmed with pale piping. The room's only color came from throw pillows and paintings. Both featured bright geometric designs.

Bronze sculptures of indeterminate form covered the mantel. A reindeer skin lay in front of the hearth.

The end and coffee tables were made of glass and antique brass. A sole photo sat on one. Its frame was mother-of-pearl edged with silver, the quality much higher than that of the image it housed. The picture was grainy, maybe taken with a cellphone or inexpensive camera, then blown up beyond what the pixels could handle.

The subject was a tall young woman, maybe nineteen or twenty, on a boat with a harbor or bay behind her. She was wearing a turtleneck and jacket, a bead necklace with some sort of pendant. The wind was lifting the jacket's collar and blowing her long dark hair across her face. She didn't look happy. She didn't look sad. She was pretty in a disturbingly detached sort of way.

Her face was more fleshy, her breasts fuller, than when I'd last seen her. But I knew I was looking at Tawny McGee.

Ryan and I did our usual and sat on opposite ends of the couch. Bernadette took an armchair, fingers clasped like red-tipped claws in her lap. Jake remained standing, arms folded across his chest.

"May I get you something? Coffee? Tea?"

Bernadette's offer sounded rote, insincere.

"No, thank you," Ryan and I answered in unison.

A cat appeared in the doorway, gray with black stripes and yellow-green eyes. A notch in one ear. A scar on one shoulder. A scrapper.

Bernadette noticed. "Oh, no, no, Murray. Shoo."

The cat held.

Bernadette started to push to her feet.

"Please let him stay," I said.

"Get him out of here," Jake said.

"I own a cat." I smiled. "His name is Birdie."

Bernadette looked at Jake. He shrugged but said nothing.

Murray regarded us a moment, then sat, shot a leg, and began cleaning his toes. Something was off with his upper left canine. I liked this cat.

Bernadette settled back, spine stiff, neck muscles standing out sinewy-hard. She glanced from Ryan to me, back to Ryan. Hopeful we had news. Frightened we had news.

I understood that yesterday's call was undoubtedly a shock after so many years. But the woman's anxiety seemed out of proportion. The shaking hands. The terrified eyes. I didn't like what I was sensing.

"Your home is beautiful," I said, wanting to reassure.

"Tawny likes things bright."

"Is this Tawny?" Gesturing at the woman framed in mother-of-pearl.

The parakeet eyes looked at me oddly. Then, "Yes."

"She's grown into a beautiful young woman."

"You're sure about the cat?"

"I'm sure. Do you have other pictures?"

"Tawny hated being photographed."

As with the Violettes, Ryan allowed silence, hoping one or the other Kezerian might feel compelled to fill it. Neither did.

Murray switched legs. Behind him, through a matching archway across the hall, I noted a dining room of identical footage with an identical bay window. The table was glass. The chairs were molded white acrylic and made me think of the Jetsons.

When Bernadette spoke, her words were not what I expected. So far, nothing was. "Is she dead?"

"We have no reason to think that." Ryan indicated no surprise at the question.

Bernadette's shoulders rounded slightly as her expression melted. Into what? Relief? Disappointment? I really couldn't read her.

Jake spread his feet. Frowned his frown.

"But we have new information," Ryan said.

"You've found her?"

"We haven't determined her exact location. Yet."

Bernadette's knuckles blanched as her fingers tightened again.

Ryan leaned toward her. "I promise you, Mrs. Kezerian. We are closing in."

"Closing in?" Jake snorted. "You make it sound like the play-offs."

"I apologize for my poor choice of words."

It struck me. Unlike the Violettes, the Kezerians were asking no questions about the nature of the "new information." Or about Pomerleau's movements over the last decade.

Jake pinched the bridge of his nose. Again crossed his arms. "If you have nothing to tell us, why are you here?"

"We were hoping Tawny might agree to an interview."

I heard a sharp intake of breath. Looked at Bernadette. Her face had gone as white as the walls around us.

In my peripheral vision, Jake's arms dropped to his sides. I ignored him and focused on his wife. Bernadette was trying to speak but managing only to swallow and clear her throat.

I reached out and took her hands in mine. "What is it? What's wrong?"

"I thought you'd come to tell me you'd located Tawny." More swallowing. "One way or the other."

"I'm sorry. I don't understand." I didn't.

"Who we talking about here?" Jake demanded. "Who is it you're tracking?"

"Anique Pomerleau," Ryan said.

"Sonofabitch."

"Tawny's not here with you?" I asked Bernadette.

"I haven't seen my daughter in almost eight years."

19

"Oh, God." A tiny sob bubbled from Bernadette's throat.

"I am so sorry," I said. "Obviously, Detective Ryan and I were unclear."

"You're here about the woman who kidnapped my child?"

"Yes," I said. "Anique Pomerleau."

Bernadette slipped her hands free of mine and extended one back toward Jake. He made no move to take it. "You came to question Tawny?" she asked.

"To talk to her."

Bernadette brought the unclaimed hand forward onto the armrest. It trembled.

"We were hoping—" I began.

"She's not here." Bernadette's voice was flat, as though a door had slammed shut somewhere inside her. She began picking at a thread poking from the piping.

"Where is she?"

"Tawny left home in 2006."

"Do you know where she's living?"

"No."

I glanced at Ryan. Tight nod that I should continue.

"You haven't heard from your daughter in all that time?"

"She called once. Several months after she moved out. To say she was well."

"She didn't tell you where she was?"

"No."

"Did you ask?"

Bernadette kept working the errant strand. Which had doubled in length.

"Did you file a missing persons report?"

"Tawny was almost twenty. The police said she was an adult. Free to do what she wanted."

Thus nothing in the file. I waited for Bernadette to continue.

"It's crazy, I know. But I figured that was the reason you'd come. To tell me you'd found her."

"Why did she leave?"

"Because she's nuts."

Ryan and I looked past Bernadette toward her husband. He opened his mouth to continue, but something on our faces made him shut it again.

Bernadette spoke without taking her eyes from the thread she was twisting and retwisting around one finger. "Tawny endured a five-year nightmare. Anyone would have issues."

My gaze slid to Ryan. He did a subtle "Take it away" lift of one palm.

"Can you talk about that?" I urged gently.

"About what?"

"Tawny's issues."

Bernadette hesitated, either reluctant to share or unsure how to put it. "She came back to me changed."

Sweet Jesus! Of course she did. The child was raped and tortured her entire adolescence.

"Changed how?"

"She was overly fearful."

"Of?"

"Life."

"For Christ's sake, Bee." Jake threw up his hands.

Bernadette rounded on her husband. "Well, aren't you Mr. Compassionate." Then to me, "Tawny had what they called body-image issues."

"What do you mean?"

"My baby lived in conditions you wouldn't wish on a dog. No sunlight. No decent food. It all took a toll."

I pictured Tawny in my office, overwhelmed by a trench coat cinched at the waist.

"She didn't grow properly. Never went through puberty."

"That's understandable," I said.

"But then her body, I don't know, started playing some kind of high-speed catch-up. She grew very fast.

Developed large breasts." Bernadette shrugged one shoulder. "She was uncomfortable with herself."

"She was irrational." Jake.

"Really?" Bernadette snapped. "Because she didn't like to be seen naked? News flash. Most kids don't."

"Most kids don't go batshit if their mother accidentally peeps them in the crapper."

"She was making progress." Cold.

"You see what I'm dealing with?" Jake directed this comment to Ryan.

"You knew about Tawny from the day we met." Bernadette's tone toward her husband was acid.

"Oh, you've got that right. And we haven't stopped talking about the kid since."

"She was seeing a therapist."

"That asshole was part of the problem."

Bernadette snorted. "My husband, expert on psychology."

"The quack took her to the cellar where they caged her. In my book, that's over-the-top fucked up."

That surprised me. "Tawny and her therapist visited the house on de Sébastopol?"

"Perhaps the treatment was a bit harsh." Softer, almost pleading. "But Tawny was doing well. She was attending community college. She wanted to help people. To heal the whole world. When she called that one time, she said she was back in school."

"But she didn't say where."

"No."

I glanced at Ryan. He was studying Jake.

"How did you two get along?" he asked.

"What? Me and Tawny?"

Ryan nodded.

Jake's voice remained even, but the set of his jaw suggested his annoyance was no longer just with his wife. "We had our spats. The kid wasn't easy."

"Spats?" Bernadette snarled. "You two hated each other."

Jake sighed, impatient with accusations clearly aired more than once. "I did not hate Tawny. I tried to help her. To make her understand that life involves boundaries."

"Be honest, Jake. She left because of you."

"She never embraced me as a father, if that's what you mean."

"You drove her away."

The Kezerians exchanged a glance boiling with anger. Then Bernadette turned back to me. "Tawny moved out after a blowup with my husband. Stormed upstairs, packed her things, and left."

"When was that?"

"August 2006."

"What did you argue about?"

"Does it matter?" Jake's voice remained level, but something unreadable flickered in his eyes.

"Where do you think she went?" I asked Bernadette.

"She often spoke of California. And Australia. And Florida, especially the Keys."

"She could have gone anywhere she wanted, right, Bee?" Jake's mouth pursed up in a humorless smile.

A flush climbed Bernadette's throat, splotchy red against the colorless skin. She said nothing.

"As a final adios, Tawny helped herself to the stash my wife kept in her closet."

"How much did she take?" Not sure why I asked.

"Almost three thousand dollars." Jake flicked two fingers off his forehead in a goodbye salute. "Adios and fuck you."

Ryan asked a series of questions. Did Tawny ever mention Anique Pomerleau? Did she make friends during the two years she lived in Montreal? Was there a person at the college in whom she might have confided? Did they have any names or numbers of anyone with whom she worked, attended class, or interacted in any way? Might it be helpful to speak with her sister, Sandra? Was Tawny's room intact enough to warrant a visit? The answer to each was a definite no.

Ryan concluded by asking them to phone him if Tawny contacted them. If they remembered anything she'd said about her captor or captivity. The usual.

Then, placing our cards on the coffee table, we rose to leave.

Mrs. Kezerian escorted us. Mr. Kezerian did not.

At the door, we assured Bernadette that we were doing everything possible to find her daughter's abductor.

And Tawny? she asked.

Ryan promised to send out queries.

Not a single question about Pomerleau. About where she was. About how or why she'd surfaced.

And that was it.

I'd never felt more discouraged in my life.

It was four-thirty by the time we wound our way out of Dollard-des-Ormeaux. Lights were on in most of the homes we passed, yellow rectangles warm against the thickening darkness. Here and there, electric icicles or colored bulbs heralded the coming of a season that would bring joy for some, a reminder of loneliness for others.

Traffic on the Metropolitan was heavy and slow. We crept east, taillights ahead, double beams behind, through cones of illumination thrown by halogens arching over the highway.

Like frames on an old movie reel, Ryan's silhouette flashed into focus, receded into shadow. He offered nothing. The silence in the Jeep grew deeper and deeper.

"Not exactly *Happy Days*." When I could take it no longer.

"If I was the kid, I'd have left, too."

"Do you think Jake could be physically abusive?"

"The guy's an arrogant bastard."

"That wasn't my question."

"I think it's conceivable."

So did I. And another unpleasant possibility had

crossed my mind. "Do you suppose he came on to Tawny?"

"Speculation is pointless."

"Will you try to find her?"

"Yes. But she's not my priority."

"You don't feel she can help us?"

Ryan glanced my way, then back to the road. "At what cost?" The bitterness in his voice was so tangible, I could feel it on my skin.

Several long moments passed.

"Did you find it odd that the Kezerians showed no interest in Pomerleau?" I asked.

"No."

"No?"

"They're too focused on their own soap opera."

"Yes, but—"

"We weren't what they expected."

I leaned into the seat back. Beyond the windshield, the day's clear sky had lost out to dense cloud cover. Overhead, nothing twinkled. Ahead, brake lights smeared crimson across the top of our hood.

Beside us, a yellow Mini lurched and braked in tandem with our Jeep. The driver steered with one elbow while thumb-tapping a mobile phone. Texting. Emailing. Tweeting about the burger he'd have for dinner. Impressive. A multitasker.

I closed my eyes. Pictured a girl with bitter white skin, haggard eyes, and a braid snaking down vertebrae sharpened by years of deprivation. That image yielded to one of a small dark-haired girl in a trench coat and beret. To a young woman on a boat in a windswept harbor.

Tawny McGee was seventeen when she was finally set free. I imagined her somewhere in the sun, laughing over lunch with women her age. Pushing a stroller. Walking a golden retriever or a Saint Bernard. Free of the rancor we'd just witnessed. The constant bickering.

Was Bernadette correct in her optimism? That her daughter was doing well? Or did Jake have it right in viewing Tawny as permanently broken?

I understood Ryan's desire to focus on the hunt for which I'd dragged him from Costa Rica. Pomerleau had scripted the nightmare that had robbed Tawny of her childhood. Perhaps her sanity.

Still. I wondered where Tawny was and what she was doing.

Ryan dropped me at my condo. No goodbye. Just a promise to call in the morning.

I phoned Angela's and ordered a small pizza with everything but onions. Then I walked to the corner *dépanneur* for coffee and a few breakfast items. No point in provisioning when I'd be returning south soon. Groceries in hand, I picked up the pizza and headed home.

I ate with Wolf in the Situation Room. The pizza was good. The conversation did nothing to brighten my mood.

Then, all of a sudden, I was exhausted. The grueling trip to Costa Rica, followed by draining days in Charlotte. The long hours yesterday, then the late-night flight. Today the disturbing file review, then ping-ponging across the island to visit people not happy to see us.

Had we learned a single useful fact? Or simply wasted our time?

I stretched out on the couch and replayed each interview in my mind.

The Violettes had been a bust. Fair enough. We'd anticipated little from them.

Ditto for Pomerleau. Barely lucid. What was the one thing she'd said? That her daughter was in the cimetière Saint-Jean-Baptiste. Marie-Joëlle Bastien was buried there, not Anique. Anique was alive.

Tawny McGee was the only person I'd thought might prove helpful, but we hadn't laid eyes on her. Bernadette and Jake were clueless concerning her whereabouts. They themselves were pathetic.

Maybe the therapist? Had we gotten her name? Easy enough. But Tawny wasn't dead. The woman would invoke doctor-patient privilege. If they were still in contact, might she deliver a message to Tawny?

Wolf reported that the fires in Australia were worsening.

Ryan said that Pomerleau was in Vermont. Jake Kezerian strode toward him, angry. Thrust a paper in his face. Ryan took the paper and placed it in a bright yellow folder.

Wolf said something about economic indicators.

Kezerian crossed his arms on his chest. Spread his feet. "Grand-mère and Grand-père."

The sky behind Ryan transformed into a green floral web. Ivy, twining nothing, meandering free-form in space.

Ryan opened the file.

The ivy snaked and twisted.

Ryan looked up. Slowly, his face morphed to that of Nurse Smiley. Simone.

"Qu'est-ce que vous voulez?" Kezerian asked. What do you want?

"Saint John," Simone said.

This was backward. The nurse was speaking English, Kezerian French.

"Maladie d'Alzheimer." Kezerian.

"She's not buried." Simone.

"Qui est avec les saints?" Who is with the saints?

Simone wagged her head slowly from side to side.

My eyes flew open.

Wolf had been replaced by Anthony Bourdain.

I rewound the dream.

Juggled the pieces my id had gathered and stored.

They fit.

Jesus. Could that be it?

I lunged for the phone.

20

I checked the time as I punched in the number. 11:15. A twinge of guilt. I ignored it.

"Umpie Rodas."

"It's Dr. Brennan. Tempe."

A sliver of a pause as the name registered.

"Yes."

"I'm in Montreal. With Ryan."

He waited.

"This may be nothing."

"You wouldn't phone this late about nothing." A mild reprimand?

"In the course of your investigation, did you ever come across the name Corneau?"

"No. Why?"

"When we shut Pomerleau down back in '04, she was working with a guy calling himself Stephen Menard. The story's complicated, so I'm simplifying. The house they occupied on de Sébastopol originally belonged to a couple named Corneau, Menard's grandparents. The Corneaus died in a car wreck in Quebec in 1988. You with me?"

"I'm listening."

"Menard's mother was Genevieve Rose Corneau, an American. She and her husband, Simon Menard, owned a home near St. Johnsbury, Vermont. The deed was in Simon's name. Stephen Menard lived there for a time before relocating to Montreal."

"To set up his twisted little fantasyland."

I figured Rodas had learned about Menard recently, either from Ryan or Honor Barrow, or perhaps on his own, when the DNA recovered from Nellie Gower's body led to Anique Pomerleau.

"Right. This afternoon Ryan and I visited Sabine Pomerleau, Anique's mother. She's eighty-two and suffers from dementia. But she said one thing. Could be I'm reading too much into the ramblings of a senile old woman—"

"What did she say?"

"That Anique is *avec les saints. Saint Jean.* Then in English she said buried."

Silence hummed as Rodas considered that.

"Ryan and I took it to mean she believes Anique is in the cimetière Saint-Jean-Baptiste, where Marie-Joëlle Bastien is buried."

"Another of Pomerleau's victims."

"Yes. But thinking back, it's possible she also said *Jean*, in English. That we misunderstood her completely."

Rodas got it immediately. "Saint John. Buried. St. Johnsbury. The home in St. Johnsbury, Vermont."

"It's a long shot, I know. But if there's other family property there registered in the name Corneau—"

"I never would have made that connection."

"Anique might have learned of the property from Menard. Perhaps they discussed it as a safe house. Or a meeting-up point."

"Vermont is a bump down the road from Quebec."

A ping dragged me up from a miles-deep sleep. Another followed. Groggy, I thought my house alarm was announcing a burglar or fire.

Then recognition. I reached for my iPhone.

The text was maddeningly short: *You were right. En route now. Will call with updates. UR*

I sat up, fully awake. What the hell? Had Rodas found a place deeded to the proper Corneaus? Was he on his way there? Where?

The room was dim. The bedside clock said 8:42. Christ. Had I really slept that late?

Jamming a pillow behind my back, I punched a speed-dial entry.

My call was answered quickly. "Ryan."

I started to tell him about my theory. About Rodas.

"I know."

"You know?"

"He phoned."

"When?"

"An hour ago. Not bad, Brennan."

I felt a rush of irritation. Said nothing.

"Where is he?"

"Driving to the location."

"What location?"

"You nailed it. The Corneaus own ten acres with a house and outbuildings a bit south of St. Johnsbury. It's about twenty miles from the farm where Menard holed up before moving to Montreal."

"Rodas couldn't have waited?"

"He thought it wise to have a look."

"He has backup?"

"He's been a cop for a very long time." A note of condescension?

"Did he take a CSS team?" I knew that was stupid. Asked anyway.

"It's a bit premature for that."

"What's his plan?"

"Observe. See if anyone's living there."

"He couldn't determine that before heading out?" Sharp.

"Rodas has someone running a search. Tax records. Phone and utility bills. You know the drill."

I did. "How long is the drive to St. Johnsbury for him?"

"He estimated forty minutes."

I looked at the clock. It was now 8:57. "If it's been an hour since you spoke, why hasn't he called?"

"Probably nothing to report."

"So what are we supposed to do?"

"Wait."

"Fine. I'll wait. While you and Rodas bust your asses protecting and serving."

With that clever retort, I clicked off and tossed the phone.

I knew my peevishness was juvenile. I needed to vent, and Ryan had taken the hit. But Rodas had left me out of the loop. So had Ryan. Not even a text from him. I was furious.

Throwing back the covers, I shoved to my feet. Yanked on sweats. Stomped to the bathroom and brushed my teeth.

9:08.

Into the kitchen for a bagel and coffee. Dining room table. Back to the bed for my mobile. Back to the table.

Out the French doors, the sky was the color of old nickels. The shrubs in the courtyard looked dark and droopy, as though dispirited by the prospect of sleet or snow.

At 9:29 the phone rang. I knocked over my coffee snatching it up. Grabbed a towel from the kitchen as I answered.

Slidell was talking before I could say my name. "Pastori's getting some of Leal's browser history." He took my nonresponse as puzzlement over the name. "Pastori's the computer geek."

"I know who he is."

"Whoa. We got a bug up our ass today?"

"What is Pastori finding?" Diverting a brown tentacle coursing toward the edge of the table.

"I'll spare you the bullshit about URLs and partial URLs and embedded sites, blah, blah, blah. Bottom line, it don't seem like much."

I heard a wet sound as Slidell thumbed his tongue, flipped a page, went on. "No shopping trips to eBay, Amazon, that kind of thing."

"Not surprising. Shelly Leal was thirteen years old."

"She visited some game sites let kids play dress-up with cartoon characters. You know. Put Barbie in a tube top and braid her hair."

I held the phone with my shoulder as I lifted and blotted.

"There was a site lets kids create aviators for moving around virtual worlds."

Knowing Slidell hadn't a clue about avatars, I didn't bother to correct him.

"What the hell's a virtual world? That some kinda make-believe where everyone's good?"

"That would be virtuous. What about chat rooms?"

"The kid didn't hit porn sites, if that's what you're asking."

"You know it isn't." Wiping off the chair seat.

"She linked to a site called AsktheDoc.com. You put in questions about your prostate, someone claiming to be a doctor answers."

"Is that what she did?"

"What?"

"Ask about her prostate?" What little patience I had was fast disappearing.

"You could try tweezers."

"What?"

"To pluck that bug crawled—"

"What questions did Shelly ask?"

"Pastori couldn't get that." Paper rustled. "The only other site he managed to pull out was a forum on a disease called dysmenorrhea." He pronounced it "dies-men-o-ree-ah."

"It's not a disease. The term refers to severe pain associated with menstruation."

"Yeah. I don't need no details."

"What did she do there?"

"He couldn't get that, either."

"Why not?" Sharper than I intended.

Slidell let a few beats pass, his way of telling me to lose the attitude. "First of all, you've got to have an ID, and the forum's got a shitload of members. Pastori says he skimmed through a couple hundred posts. But he had no idea what to look for. And even if he did figure out who Leal was, she could have been a lurker. That's someone—"

"I know what a lurker is. Did he attempt to figure out her ID?" I almost said "aviator."

"With what little I could give him, yeah. Family names, pets, initials, birthdates, phone numbers. Got nowhere."

I thought about that. "Was he able to determine

what cartoon characters she chose on the game sites?"

"Hmm," Slidell said.

I bunched the towel, walked to the door, and tossed it into the sink. Coffee dribbled on the floor as it arced across the kitchen.

"This whole Internet angle may be a dead end," Slidell said.

"Or she may have met someone in that chat room."

"It's a site for people whining about cramps."

Seriously? "Gee. You think some of those whiners could be adolescent girls?"

"You're saying our target visits this chat room hoping to hook up with kids? Maybe pretends to be a doctor or something?"

"A doctor, a teacher, another kid having difficult periods. People lie on the Internet."

"No shit."

"No shit. Have Pastori stay on it. If someone walked Leal through the process of wiping her browser history, it was for a reason."

Slidell gave a long dramatic sigh. But he didn't disagree.

"And talk to the mother. See if she has suggestions about passwords or IDs Leal might have used. Find out how much freedom she allowed Shelly online. And ask why her daughter was interested in dysmenorrhea."

"Eeyuh."

"Maybe revisit Leal's bedroom? See what she was

reading. What dolls or animals she had. Anyway, get what you can for Pastori."

"You know the guy is an Olympic-class gasbag. Runs on and on, I'm guessing to fluff his geeky little ego. Every time I call him, it's half my day."

I imagined the exchanges between Slidell and Pastori. My sympathies were definitely with the latter. "Is the media still clamoring?"

"Some asshole videoed us working Leal's body at the underpass, can you believe that? Wanted their fifteen fucking minutes of fame."

I changed the subject. "What about the age progression on Anique Pomerleau?"

"Yeah. I got that."

"Did you plan to tell me?"

"I am telling you."

"How does it look?"

"Like she got older."

"Send it to my iPhone. Please."

I briefed Slidell about events on my end. The unsatisfying interviews. My subliminal breakthrough after studying the dossiers from 2004 and talking with Sabine Pomerleau. The property in Vermont.

"Not bad, Doc."

"If she did use the Corneau home as a hidey-hole, she's long gone now."

"When will you toss the place?"

"When Rodas gives the word."

"He ask for a warrant?"

I hadn't thought of that. "Gotta go." I disconnected.

9:46.

I cleaned the coffee off the kitchen tile, then unpacked the carry-on I'd brought from Charlotte. Took a shower and dried my hair. Dressed in jeans, wool socks, and a sweater.

10:38.

I checked my phone, hoping a text had landed while I was engaged in toilette. Nope.

I paced, too wired to sit still. Why such angst? I felt what? Stunned that I'd been right? Maybe right. Thrilled that we might have found the spot Pomerleau first went to ground? Might have. Outraged that Rodas and Ryan had sidelined me? Definitely.

The phone finally rang at ten past eleven. Area code 802.

"Brennan." Cool as snow in Vermont.

"Ryan's on his way to pick you up."

"Is he."

"You need to get down here. Fast."

21

The snow started as we crossed the Champlain Bridge. Turned to sleet as we hit Stanstead, just north of the border.

I watched the wipers chase fat flabby flakes, later slush, from the windshield. Now and then a wind-tossed leaf hit the glass and was whipped free, brittle and shiny with moisture.

The car's interior smelled of wet leather and wool. Stale cigarette smoke.

"Look for the Passumpsic Cemetery."

The first words Ryan had spoken in almost two hours. I was good with it. After he'd relayed what he knew, which was virtually nothing, we'd both burrowed deep into our own thoughts.

Occasionally, I'd check my iPhone. An email with an attachment arrived from Slidell just past noon. I downloaded and enlarged the image.

You've seen pictures of Charles Manson. No matter

what his age is, his eyes send a frigid wind knifing straight through your soul. His hair may be shaggy or shaved, his cheeks full or gaunt. You feel like you're gazing straight into the heart of evil.

That's how it was with Pomerleau. She was in her teens when the sole existing photo was taken. Now she would be thirty-nine.

The computer had softened the jawline, drooped the lids, and broadened the lips and facial contours, transforming the child face into that of a woman. Still the eyes looked stony cold, reptilian, and unfeeling.

As they had on our last encounter. When she'd doused me with accelerant, then coolly lit a match.

I did as Ryan asked. We'd just passed through St. Johnsbury, were now seeing mostly farm fields, trees, a few clusters of homes.

"There." I pointed to the cemetery. It was old, with headstones and pillars, rather than ground-level plaques for the convenience of mowers. A perfect Poe tableau in the wintry gloom.

Maybe a quarter mile more, then Ryan slowed, signaled, and made a left from Highway 5 onto Bridge Street. We passed a church, a general store and post office combo, a gray building with an old red auto seat on the porch and a red plastic kayak affixed to the top of the front overhang. *Passumpsic* was written in white on the kayak's side. A wooden sign above the door identified the *Passumpsic River Outfitter, LLC.*

Just beyond the outfitter was a bridge, a narrow

latticework of metal girders and wooden beams painted green. Not the covered New Englander I'd envisioned. The Passumpsic River looked dark and menacing as we crossed over. On one bank, an ancient brick power station.

Soon the road's name changed to Hale. Forest took over on both sides. Lofty pine, less lofty spruce. Hardwoods, their branches nude, their bark black and sparkly wet.

Then there were no homes, no barns. Just the Hundred Acre Wood.

Seven minutes of silence, I kept checking my watch. Then Ryan made a right beside a battered post that at one time may have held a mailbox. A sign nailed to a tree said *ORNE* in letters sun-bleached to the color of old denim. Below the truncated name, an equally faded fleur-de-lis.

The track was little more than an absence of trees and two ruts undecided between mud and ice. As the Jeep bounced and swayed, I braced myself with palms to the dash. My fillings were loosening when Ryan finally braked to a stop.

Across a clearing, maybe ten yards distant, sat a small frame house that had seen better days. Single-story, once probably yellow with white trim. But, as with the mailbox, the paint was long gone.

The front door, accessed by one concrete step, was propped open with a rock. The windows visible on the front and right were boarded on the inside with plywood. To the left, up a slight rise and nestled under a stand of tall pines, stood three sheds, one large, two small. Dirt paths connected the trio to one another and to the house.

Parked in front of the house was a Hardwick PD cruiser. I assumed it belonged to Umpie Rodas. Beside the cruiser was a crime scene truck. Beside the truck was a black van with double doors in back. My gut told me the vehicle had ties to a morgue.

"Tabernac!"

I swiveled toward Ryan, ready to be livid for what he'd held back. He looked as surprised as I felt.

"What's the deal?" I asked.

"Damned if I know."

"Rodas didn't tell you?"

"He just said they'd found something we needed to see. Sounded distracted."

"No doubt. He was busy making a whole lot of calls."

I raised the hood of my parka to cover my head. Pulled on gloves. Got out and started toward the house. The wind was gusting hard, blasting sleet at my face like fiery little pellets. My mind was racing, running possibilities. Senseless. I'd know in seconds. Behind me, Ryan's boots made swishing sounds in the slippery leaves and grass. Mimicking my own.

A uniformed cop stood inside the front door, thumbs hooked in a belt half hidden by a substantial roll of fat. His hat and jacket bore insignia patches saying *Hardwick PD*.

The cop straightened upon seeing us.

"Dr. Temperance Brennan." I flashed my LSJML security card as Ryan badged him. "Rodas requested our presence."

The guy barely glanced at our IDs. From another room, I heard the sound of drawers opening and closing. "He's in the big shed out back."

"Thanks."

"Tight security," Ryan said when we'd rounded the corner of the house.

"It's rural Vermont."

We followed the path up the hill. Added ours to dozens of boot prints in the half-frozen muck.

The shack was made of unpainted boards barely maintaining contact. The roof was rusted tin, louvered at the top, curling free of the nails securing it at the bottom.

The shed's two barnlike doors were thrown wide, and its interior was visible in bright detail. The scene looked surreal, like a movie set lit by an overzealous gaffer. I assumed portable lights had been brought in and set up.

Set up for what?

In a far corner, partly in shadow, two figures stood talking beside a blue plastic barrel. One was Umpie Rodas. The other was a tall woman with a red knit hat pulled low to her brows. A full-length black coat obscured her shape. Both turned at the sound of our footsteps. Rodas was hatless, and his jacket was unzipped. He may have had on the same red shirt he'd worn in Charlotte. Or maybe he had a collection.

"Glad you made it. Sorry about the weather."

Ryan and I entered. The shack smelled of smoke, moist earth, and something sweet, like a pancake house on a Sunday morning.

I was right about the lights. There were three, the standard tripod variety often used at crime scenes. The generator was gas-powered, the kind you can buy at any Home Depot.

Rodas made introductions. The woman, Cheri Karras, was with the chief ME's office in Burlington. Instead of mittens, she wore surgical gloves. So did Rodas.

I felt a knot begin to form in my gut.

Behind Karras, a man in a thick padded jacket was snapping photographs. His breath glowed white each time his flash went off.

I took a quick look around. The floor was hard-packed dirt, filled with a hodgepodge of items. Enormous cauldrons, blackened by fire. An open box containing blue plastic bags. Beside it, dozens of identical boxes, unopened. Circling the walls, rusty buckets, saucepans of differing sizes, screens, juice and milk cartons, five-gallon white plastic tubs stacked to form wobbly five-foot towers.

Crude shelving held wooden boxes filled with small

metal implements that had a spike at one end and a downspout opposite. Others held metal hooks. Two drills. An assortment of hammers. A half-dozen coils of blue tubing. Jugs of household bleach.

At the shack's center, directly below the vented part of the roof, was a three-by-five brick-lined pit with iron bars running between the long sides. On the bars sat a rectangular flat-bottomed metal pan, empty, its interior yellowed by some sort of residue. The bricks and bars were fire-blackened and covered with soot. Ditto the outside of the pan.

I was stumped. But one thing was clear. Whatever the shed's purpose, cobwebs and grime suggested years of disuse.

"—got word no one was occupying the property, I decided to take a look around, be sure vandals weren't up to mischief. We get squatters sometimes, folks find an empty summer home, decide to move in for the winter."

My attention refocused. On Rodas. On Karras. On the ominous blue barrel between them.

"House had been breached, all right. Lock was jimmied. That was my green light. No damage inside, nothing worth stealing, so I took a peek out here."

"Cabane à sucre." For some reason, Ryan said it in French.

Of course. The shed was a sugar shack, a place to convert maple sap into syrup.

I eyed the barrel. The knot tightened.

Rodas nodded. "A Quebecer would know, eh?"

Karras's phone buzzed. Wordlessly, she stepped outside. I watched her as Rodas continued talking. She seemed untroubled. A raccoon in the barrel? Or just another day with death?

"The property's deeded to Margaux and Martin Corneau. Ten acres, eight of 'em mixed red and sugar maple. Until the late '80s, the Corneaus ran a small operation, provided ten, twenty gallons a year to an outfit that bottled and sold locally." Rodas arced an arm at the paraphernalia around us. "The old stuff's theirs, cauldrons, aluminum buckets and lids. The plastic collection bags and polyethylene tubing, now, that's something else."

"Meaning?" Ryan asked.

"Meaning they're new."

"Suggesting a more recent operation."

Rodas nodded, his expression grim. But something else. Excited? Eager?

"By whom?" Ryan asked.

"I'm working on that."

"What's in the barrel?" Not trying very hard to hide my impatience.

"We'd best wait for Doc Karras."

"Where do you buy sugaring equipment?" Ryan asked.

"Anywhere. The barrels are widely used for food storage. The tubing's multipurpose."

"The taps and bags?"

"Sugaring supply companies. The capture bags aren't expensive, maybe forty cents each. Most small producers now prefer them to buckets. Slip the bag over a collar, run the tubing straight in from the tap, empty the sap into a collecting point, toss the bag, repeat until the tree runs dry. Bags are also better at keeping out bugs and debris."

"Can't be that many sold."

"More than you'd think."

"Can you purchase them online?"

Rodas nodded. "Got someone making calls."

Karras was still on her phone.

I wrapped my arms around my torso, hands tucked under my armpits for warmth. Cold was rising through the soles of my boots and spreading through my bones. The chill coming from more than the weather.

"That an evaporator?" Ryan chin-cocked the fire pit.

"Yeah. Better than the cauldrons, but still takes a lot of fuel."

"Seriously?" I snapped. "We're discussing advances in the art of syrup production?"

"The woodshed's beside this one." Rodas ignored my outburst. "Not much left. I suspect the neighbors helped themselves over the years." Turning to me. "You know much about maple syrup?"

"We're wasting time here." Rude, but I was freezing. And anxious. And fed up with the male-bonding routine.

"Then let's use it to learn something." Rodas took my nonresponse as invitation to continue. "During the growing season, starch accumulates in the roots and trunks of maples. Enzymes transform the starch into sugar, then water absorbed through the roots turns it into sap.

"In the spring, alternating freezes and thaws force the sap up. Most folks tap once daytime highs hit the forties. Around here, that's usually late April.

"The sap then has to be processed to evaporate out the water and leave just the concentrated syrup. That means boiling between five and thirteen gallons of sap down to a quarter of a gallon of syrup. You can do that entirely over one heat source." Rodas gestured at the fire pit. "Or you can draw off smaller batches as you go, and boil them in pots." Pointing at the pots.

"Is this really relevant?"

Rodas grinned at me. "You need some coffee? I have a thermos."

"I'm good." Curt.

"The bottom line is, maple syrup is roughly sixty-six percent sugar. Just sucrose and water, with small amounts of glucose and fructose created during the boiling process. Some organic acids, malic, for example. A relatively low mineral content, mostly potassium and calcium, some zinc and manganese. A variety of volatile organic compounds, vanillin, hydroxybutanone, propionaldehyde."

"Hallelujah. A chemistry lesson." I wasn't believing this.

"Sucrose, glucose, and fructose. Gooey and sweet. That bring anything to mind?"

Holy shit. I got it.

Before I could respond, Rodas's eyes went past me toward the open doors. As I turned, Karras stepped into the light. Droplets glistened on her shoulders and hat.

"Good to go, Doc?" Rodas asked.

"Bring on the show."

Rodas inserted gloved fingers under the metal lever securing the lid. Flipped it outward.

The lid lifted easily. But nicks and gouges on its periphery and on the barrel's rim suggested much more effort had been needed the first time around.

Rodas stepped back, lid held up and away from his body.

Ryan and I moved in.

22

Sleet hissed on the tin overhead.

The generator hummed.

The CSS camera clicked softly.

The corpse was floating just below the surface, head up and tilted sideways, crown pressed to one side of the barrel. Long blond hair wrapped its face, molding the features like a wet suit on a surfer.

No. Not floating. Submerged in thick brown goop.

An image flashed. An exhibit at the Centre des sciences de Montréal. Bodies preserved by replacing the water and fat in the tissues with polymers. Plastination. Not the same process here, but the effect was eerily similar.

Karras spoke first. Brisk and cool. Here to do her job, not make friends. "I've made arrangements to take the whole barrel."

"How long has she been in there?" Rodas asked.

"I'll know more after I examine the body. And *if* the victim is male or female."

"Point taken."

"I'm happy to help," I said.

"Our facility is closed to the public." As though addressing an amateur.

I explained my qualifications.

"Given the state of preservation, an anthropologist shouldn't be necessary."

"First looks can be deceiving."

"Really."

"I know I'm out of jurisdiction." Trying to appease for my indelicate comment. And my churlishness earlier. "And I understand—"

"Probably not."

Easy. "May I at least observe?"

"Dr. Brennan and Detective Ryan are working homicides potentially linked to Nellie Gower." Rodas intervened on my behalf.

"That what this is about?" Karras tapped the rim of the barrel with one gloved hand.

"Possibly."

Karras eyed me flatly. "You know your way around an autopsy?"

"I do."

"Once the body's out of the syrup, it'll head south fast."

"It will."

"I'll be working through the night."

"As would I." Holding her gaze.

"In Burlington."

"Take the Jeep," Ryan said to me. "I'll stay and help with things on this end."

And that's what we did.

Vermont's chief medical examiner is headquartered in the Fletcher Allen medical complex on the western edge of Burlington. Burlington is on the western edge of Vermont, all the way across the state from St. Johnsbury. Fortunately, it's a small state.

Nonetheless, the drive was brutal. I was unfamiliar with Ryan's Jeep. And with dusk, the temperature dropped and the sleet turned to ice, clogging the wipers, reducing visibility, and turning the roads treacherous.

I arrived at 6:40. Karras and the barrel were already there.

The facility was not unlike many others in which I'd worked, including those at the MCME and the LSJML. There were multiple autopsy rooms, each with a tile floor, erasable board, metal and glass cabinets, stainless steel counters and centerpiece table.

Without the outerwear, I could see that Karras was a large woman with thick limbs and pendulous breasts. I doubted she cared. Her demeanor suggested cotton briefs and sensible shoes.

After the normal routine of logging in, the barrel was X-rayed with a Lodox scanner that allowed real-time viewing on video displays. Karras and I observed the body section by section: bones, skull, and teeth white; soft tissues gray; air in the gut and passageways black.

The barrel held a single human corpse, legs flexed at the knees, arms tucked to the belly. Nothing radio-opaque. No belt buckles, zippers, watches, or jewelry. No dental restorations. No bullets. I spotted no obvious skeletal trauma.

X-rays completed, a technician wheeled the barrel by dolly to an autopsy room. He took samples of the syrup while Karras recorded observations concerning the barrel's particulars and condition.

After shooting a zillion photographs, the tech placed a screen over a floor drain, and together we all laid the barrel on its side. With much effort and considerable swearing, we freed the body and transferred it to the table.

When finished, we were all coated with syrupy sweat. Here and there, we wore leaves that had transferred and pasted to our skin.

As Karras dictated and took more photos, the tech placed additional screens over large stainless steel pots into which the remaining syrup would be transferred for inspection. Perhaps the vegetation, maybe pollen or an insect, might pinpoint the season the individual had died.

Prelims completed, Karras sent the tech home. Hazardous road conditions. Perhaps a vote of confidence in me. She'd noted my comments in radiology.

Observed as I'd helped dislodge and maneuver the corpse.

Then Karras and I went to shower and change into fresh scrubs.

By 8:40 we were regoggled, regloved, and re-aproned. Though I'd done a quickie shampoo, my hair felt itchy under the surgical cap holding it back from my face.

The barrel victim was female. She lay on the table, hair glued over her face, syrup dripping from her body with soft little *tick*s. She was nude and her skin looked oddly bronzed, an effect of the amber liquid in which she'd been stored.

I waited as Karras dictated height, weight, and gender, holding off on age until we could get to the teeth. I watched her search the scalp, displacing what hair she could disengage, clump by clump.

After several minutes. "Look at this."

I stepped to her side. Sticky with syrup, the blue plastic sheeting protecting the floor pulled at the footies covering my shoes.

The victim's hair was blond, with a half inch of dark growth at the roots. A bleach job, amateur, probably done at home from a box.

Karras lifted a handful of strands, revealing an oval lesion roughly two inches long by one inch wide. The scalp was gone, and yellowed bone gleamed naked in the egg-shaped defect.

"What is it?"

Kathy Reichs

No response. The woman was definitely not a talker.

"An abrasion due to contact with the barrel?" I suggested.

"Her head was resting on the other side."

"Rodents?" I didn't believe it.

"No tooth striations in the bone or tissue. And she was too far below the surface. Besides, how would mice exit the barrel after gnawing on her scalp?"

"Are there other lesions?"

"Two. Hand me the magnifier."

I did.

"The edges appear mushy, not clean. But that could be an artifact caused by the syrup."

I ran through possibilities in my mind. "Something external? A burn? Exposure to a caustic chemical?"

"None of the surrounding hair or tissue is affected."

"Mites? Ticks? Bedbugs? Lice? Brown recluse spiders?"

"I didn't spot any eggs or excrement. But I suppose areas of infestation could have become infected, eventually necrotic."

"An autoimmune response? Something like Pemphigus?" I was referring to a group of skin disorders that caused blistering of the skin and mucous membranes.

"Mmm."

"An infectious process? Leishmaniasis? MRSA?" Methicillin-resistant *Staphylococcus aureus*.

That drew another noncommittal response.

"Eczema? Pustular psoriasis? Either could lead to skin abscess."

"We'll have a better look when I retract the scalp."

Discussion over.

Karras took measurements, dictated, made notes on a diagram. Then, using her index finger, she tried teasing hair from the face. It held firm.

I withdrew as Karras ran the lens over the neck, shoulders, breasts, belly, and tops of each leg, checking for moles, tattoos, birthmarks, scars, fresh wounds.

"Hello." Holding the right arm. She switched to the left. Gestured me over.

Under magnification, I could see a cluster of pinpoint discolorations on the inside of the right elbow. "Same on the left?"

"Three."

"Injection sites?" It didn't look right.

"If so, the pattern is atypical."

Karras continued examining the body. The skin on the palms looked rough and chapped, the nails unkept. *Working hands,* I thought.

"Both wrists show bands of reddening."

"Ligatures?"

"Maybe."

Several beats passed.

"Ever work one of these?" Karras asked.

"I once got a corpse in a barrel of asphalt. Maple syrup, no."

"Any sense how long she's been in the stuff?" Checking the right armpit.

"She's in good shape," I said. "Some skin sloughing on the tip of the nose, the shins, a few toes. That's about it."

"Probably contact points."

Several more beats. Then Karras made her first sortie into non-autopsy-related conversation. "I live near an old cemetery. Small, just a few graves. There's a kid buried under a headstone that says he died in England in 1747. Says they shipped him home in a barrel of honey."

"Embalming didn't exist back then."

"Alexander the Great." Left armpit. "Died in 323 B.C. They preserved him in a coffin filled with honey."

"Yes." Hiding my surprise that she knew.

"Can't recall why they did that."

"Alex kicked in Babylon but needed to get to Macedonia."

No chuckle. Rule of thumb. If a joke needs explanation, there is no point. I let it go.

"The Assyrians used honey as a means of embalming," I said. "So did the Egyptians."

"How's it work?" Karras moved down the table to the feet. Started spreading and checking inter-toe spaces.

"Honey is composed mainly of monosaccharides and H_2O. Since most of the water molecules are associated with the sugars, few remain available for microorganisms, making it a poor environment for bacterial growth."

"No access to the body's exterior, and no anaerobic action in the gut. End result, no decomp. Syrup has the same effect?"

"Apparently." The point Rodas had been making with his lecture on maples and sugaring.

My cellphone buzzed. I walked to the counter and, without touching it, checked caller ID. Slidell.

"I'd better take this."

No reply.

I pulled off a glove and clicked on.

"The mother says Leal had problems with her monthly time."

My eyes sought the ceiling at Slidell's outdated euphemism.

"Didn't ask details, but sounds like the kid got some real bad bellyaches. Mother once took her to the ER. She thinks that's the reason for the Internet sites."

"Did she have any thoughts on possible passwords?"

Across the room, Karras was collecting scrapings from under each nail.

"A few. I bounced them to Pastori."

"Did she regulate Shelly's use of the Internet?"

"She says yeah, but I get a different vibe."

Karras crossed to the counter and opened the fingerprint kit. Not wishing to disclose confidential information, I turned my back and lowered my voice. "Did you circulate the Pomerleau sketch?"

"Issued an updated BOLO right after I emailed it to you."

"Any action?" I asked.

Karras returned to the table.

"Geraldo called pronto. Pomerleau wants on the show."

I let that go without comment.

"What's happening up there?" Slidell asked.

I heard movement behind me. Knew Karras was inking and then pressing each fingertip to a print sheet.

"I'll tell you later."

"Where's Ryan?"

"Tossing a sugar shack."

"What's that supposed to mean?"

"Later."

I heard a metallic rattle, then water hitting stainless steel. I turned. Karras was using a spray nozzle on the hair covering the face. Slowly, the strands yielded and drifted back toward the temples.

The features came into view.

My jaw dropped.

23

"God Almighty!"

Karras was eyeing me, stony with disapproval.

I found an image on my phone, crossed to her, and held the screen so she could see. Her gaze moved between my iPhone and the glistening bronzed face on the table. A very long moment passed.

"Who is she?"

"Anique Pomerleau."

Blank stare.

"Pomerleau may have murdered Nellie Gower and several other children."

"Go on."

I did. But kept it short.

"You're sure it's her?" Studying the corpse.

"It's her."

"We'll run the prints and take samples for DNA testing."

"Of course."

"How did your suspect end up in a barrel of syrup?"

"I'm hoping you'll help clarify that."

At 2:45 A.M. Karras snipped the thread closing the Y on Pomerleau's chest.

By then bacteria, long denied, had begun to have their way with her flesh. The air was thick with the foul smell of putrefaction mingling with the sweet smell of syrup.

Sadly, the autopsy had left us with many more questions than answers.

Rigor, a transient condition causing the muscles to stiffen, had long since come and gone. No surprise. We'd noted that when handling the body.

Livor, discoloration due to the settling of blood on a corpse's downside, was evident in the buttocks, lower legs, and feet. Either Pomerleau had died in the barrel or she'd been placed there immediately after death.

No syrup was present in the paranasal sinuses, air passages, lungs, or stomach, meaning Pomerleau hadn't inhaled or ingested it. She hadn't drowned in the barrel; ergo, she'd gone into it dead.

Pomerleau's gut held only a few fragments of tomato skin. She hadn't eaten for roughly six to eight hours before she died.

Karras found no bullets, bullet fragments, or bullet tracks. No blunt instrument trauma. No hyoid fractures pointing to strangulation. No significant petechiae suggesting asphyxiation.

Under magnification, she spotted three parallel grooves on the ectocranial surface near the border of one oval defect, V-shaped and extremely narrow in cross section. Neither Karras nor I had a satisfactory explanation.

Other than the tiny marks on each inner elbow, the body lacked the constellation of features typically seen in habitual drug users.

Karras did a rape kit. Drew what blood she could for toxicology testing. Wasn't optimistic on either front.

Bottom line, Pomerleau was a healthy thirty-nine-year-old white female showing no evidence of trauma, infection, systemic disease, or congenital malformation. We didn't know how or when she died. We didn't know how or why she'd ended up in the barrel.

Icy sleet was still coming down when Karras drove me to a Comfort Inn about a mile from the medical complex. En route, we shared theories. I thought it likely Pomerleau had been murdered. Karras, more cautious, planned to write cause of death as "undetermined," manner as "suspicious."

She was right. Though unlikely, other possibilities existed. A drug overdose, then a cover-up. Accidental suffocation. I didn't believe it.

We agreed on one point: Pomerleau hadn't sealed herself in that barrel.

After checking in to my room, I considered phoning Ryan. Slidell. Instead, I took a second shower and dropped into bed.

Kathy Reichs

As sleep descended, the truth hammered home.

Pomerleau was finally dead. The monster. The one who got away. I tried to pinpoint the emotions twisting my gut. Failed.

Facts and images ricocheted in my brain.

A lip print on a jacket.

Male DNA.

Stephen Menard.

A soundproof prison cell in a basement.

Questions. Lots of questions.

Had Pomerleau found a new accomplice? Was that man involved in her death?

Had he murdered her? Why?

Who was he? Where was he now?

Had he taken his malignant freak show south?

This time it was banging that breached the thick wall of sleep.

I awoke disoriented.

From a dream? I couldn't remember.

The room was dark.

Fragments began to congeal. The sugar shack. The barrel. The autopsy.

Pomerleau.

Had I imagined the pounding?

I listened.

The thrum of traffic. Heavy now, uninterrupted.

No sleet or wind thrashing the window.

"Brennan." *Bang. Bang. Bang.*

8:05.

Shit.

"Ass out of bed."

"Coming." I pulled on the clothes I'd worn the day before. All I had.

The sun blinded me when I opened the door. The storm had ended, leaving an unnatural stillness in its wake.

Aviator shades distorted my face into a fun-house version of itself. Above them, a black wool tuque. Below them, windburned nose and cheeks.

"You're here." Lame. I was still wooly.

"You should be a detective."

One of Ryan's old lines. Neither of us laughed.

"Rolling in ten."

"Twenty," I said, shielding my eyes with one hand.

"I'll be in the Jeep."

Twelve minutes later, I was buckled in, fingers curling around a wax-coated polyethylene cup for warmth. The Jeep smelled of coffee and overcooked pork.

"Anyone could have boosted this ride."

"No one did."

"I need this Jeep."

"I'm sure it needs you."

"You're not vigilant."

"Ease up, Ryan. You had keys."

"Leaving it at the medical complex was just plain lazy. Good thing Karras let me know."

243

An Egg McMuffin lay in my lap, grease turning the wrapper translucent in spots.

"How did you get here from St. Johnsbury?" I asked.

"Umpie hooked me up with a lift."

It was Umpie now.

"Where are we going?"

Ryan merged into traffic. Didn't answer.

I unwrapped the sandwich, took a few bites. Minutes later, we fired up the entrance ramp onto I-89. Heading north.

"There it is." I pointed at Ryan. "There's that smile."

He was clearly not in the mood for teasing.

Fine.

I watched Vermont slide by.

The morning sun was melting a world made of ice. Still, the countryside looked glistening brown, caramelized. Perhaps coated with maple syrup.

"Okay, sunshine. I'll start." Jamming my McMuffin wrapper into the bag between us. "It was Anique Pomerleau in that barrel."

The aviators whipped my way. "Are you shitting me?"

"No."

"How'd she die?"

"I can tell you how she didn't."

I outlined the autopsy findings. Ryan listened without interrupting, face tight and wary. When I'd finished, he said, "Rodas's team tossed the property top to bottom. Found no drugs or drug paraphernalia."

"What was in the house?"

"Crap furnishings and appliances. Canned food in the pantry, cereal and pasta that delighted generations of rodents."

"With readable expiration dates?"

"A few. The most recent was sometime in 2010."

"What about the refrigerator?"

"Variations on rot. Bugs, mouse droppings, mold. Looks like the place was occupied for a while, then abandoned."

"Abandoned when?"

"Old newspapers got tossed into a basket. *Burlington Free Press*. The most current was from Sunday, March 15, 2009. That and the food dates suggest no one's been living there for over five years."

"Did you check light switches? Lamps?"

Ryan slid me a look. "All were turned off except a ceiling fixture in the kitchen and a lamp in one bedroom. Those bulbs were burned out."

"Were the beds made?"

"One yes, the other one no."

"Whoever was there last made no effort to close up. You know, clean out the refrigerator, strip the beds, turn off the lights. They just left. Probably at night."

"Very good."

"How'd the papers arrive?"

"Not by mail. The post office stopped service because the resident at the address provided no mailbox."

"When was that?"

"1997. According to Umpie, there's no home delivery."

I thought a moment. "Pomerleau did her shopping in or near Burlington."

"Or at a local store that sold Burlington papers."

"Any vehicle?"

"An '86 Ford F-150 was parked in one of the sheds."

"That's a truck, right?"

"Yes, Brennan. A half-ton pickup." Ryan jumped my next question. "Quarter tank of gas in the truck. No plates. Obviously no GPS to check."

"Obviously. Anything else in that shed?"

"An old tractor and cart."

"I assume the house had no alarm system."

"Unless they had a dog."

"Was there evidence of that?"

Ryan only shook his head. Meaning no? Meaning the question annoyed him?

"There were no close neighbors," I said to the windshield, the armrest, maybe the air vent. "No one to notice if lights failed to go on and off."

Ryan cut left to overtake a Budweiser truck. Fast. Too fast.

"Did the house have a phone?" I couldn't recall seeing wires.

"No."

"I'm guessing no cable or Wi-Fi."

No response.

"What about utilities? Gas? Water? Electric?"

"They're on it."

"The Corneaus died in 1988. Who paid the taxes after that?"

"They're on that, too."

"Do you really think Pomerleau was living there, tapping trees, and keeping a low profile?"

"One bedroom had a collection of books on maple sugar production. All the equipment needed was already on-site."

"What do the neighbors say?"

"They're—"

"On it. Why are you being such an ass?"

Ryan's hands tightened on the wheel. He inhaled deeply. Exhaled through his nose. "We found something else in there."

"Must have been flesh-eating zombies, the way you're acting."

It was worse.

24

"Me?"

"Yes, Brennan. You."

"What magazine?" My gut felt like I'd just drunk acid. It wasn't the McMuffin.

"Health Science."

"I don't remember being interviewed—"

"Well, you were."

"When did the story appear?"

"2008."

"What was the subj—"

"Only one page was saved. A picture of you measuring a skull in your lab at UNCC."

A vague recollection. A phone call. A piece profiling changes in physical anthropology over the past five decades. Would I comment on my subspecialty of forensics? Could I share a graphic?

I'd thought the article might dispel Hollywood myths about crime scene glamour and hundred-percent solve rates. Had it been six years?

The heartburn was spreading from my stomach to my chest. I swallowed.

Pomerleau had clipped a photo of me. Had known I lived in Charlotte. Had known since 2008.

Lizzie Nance had died in 2009. Others had followed. Estrada. Leal. Maybe Koseluk and Donovan. ME107-10.

Before I could comment, Ryan's phone buzzed in his pocket. He checked the screen, clicked on, listened. "Pomerleau."

The expletive was muted by Ryan's ear. Questions followed. Ryan responded with mostly one-word answers. "Yes." "No." "Undetermined." "Suspicious."

"I'll put you on speaker." He did, then placed the phone on the dash.

"How's it going, Doc?" Rodas.

"Hunky-dory."

"Here's what we've got so far. A canvass of the neighbors took about five seconds, practically no one out there. The couple to the south are both in their eighties. Can't hear, can't see. They knew the Corneaus, said they used the place in spring for sugaring, sporadically in summer. Lamented their passing. The husband thought a granddaughter lived there for a while."

"When did he last see her?"

"He didn't know."

"Was she blond?"

"I'll ask."

"I'm sending two images. An age progression done on Pomerleau's mug shot." As I texted the files. "And a close-up I took at autopsy. Show those to him."

"Will do. The neighbor to the north is a widower, stays out there only part of the year. He knew zilch. Ditto for those living along Hale."

"No one noticed that the house had gone permanently dark?"

"It's set too far back. I checked last night. You can't see spit through the trees."

"No one recalls vehicles entering or leaving?"

"Nope."

"No one ever visited? Went looking for a lost puppy? Took cookies to say welcome to the 'hood?"

"Vermonters tend to keep to themselves."

"Did you ask in town?"

"Apparently, Pomerleau took her trade elsewhere. So far we've found no one who remembers a woman fitting her description. If she did hit a store now and then, folks probably figured she was a tourist up for fishing or kayaking. Paid no attention."

That fit my theory that Pomerleau had shopped near Burlington. A bigger city where she could remain anonymous.

I heard a muted ping. Another. Knew my texts had landed on Rodas's phone.

"Where'd she get wood?" I asked.

"We found a guy who says he took a truckload

each March for a few years. He says a woman paid in cash."

"When was the last delivery?"

"His record-keeping's a bit glitchy. He thinks maybe 2009."

"Show him the photos."

"Will do. Andy?"

"I'm here."

"Did you tell her about the newspapers and food expiration dates?"

"Yes."

"Here's what I'm thinking. Pomerleau makes her way from Montreal to Vermont in '04. She moves in and lays low. The house is abandoned in 2009. You and Doc Karras think she could have been dead that long?"

I pictured the barrel. The body. The leaves preserved in pristine condition. "Five years is possible," I said. Then, "Who owns the property?"

"There it gets interesting. The deed is still in the name Margaux Daudet Corneau."

"Stephen Menard's maternal grandmother."

"I'm guessing since Corneau died in Canada, no one caught that the title never transferred after she passed away. The taxes, a staggering nine hundred dollars per year, were handled by auto payment from an account in Corneau's name at Citizens Bank in Burlington."

"When was the account opened?"

"I'll know more once I get a warrant."

"What about utilities?"

"The place has its own well, there's no gas. Green Mountain Power was paid from the same account as the taxes. But the money finally ran out. Notices were sent—"

"But not received, since there was no mail delivery or phone."

"The electricity was cut off in 2010."

"The state took no action due to default on the taxes?"

"Notices were sent. No follow-through yet."

I heard a click.

"Hold on. I've got another call coming in."

The line went hollow. Then Rodas returned, tension in his voice up a notch. "Let me call you back."

"You're right," Ryan said when we'd gone a few miles. "I've been acting like an ass."

"You have," I agreed.

"I hate that Pomerleau knew your whereabouts." The lane markings sent double-yellow lines tracking up Ryan's lenses. "That she wanted to know."

"I don't like it, either."

"I'm glad the bitch is dead. Hope she rots in hell."

"Someone killed her."

"We'll get him."

"And in the meantime?"

"We'll get him." Ryan continued not looking at me.

"If I hadn't granted that interview, Pomerleau never would have gone to Charlotte."

"We don't know that she did."

"Her DNA was on Lizzie Nance's body."

"She'd have continued the carnage here in Vermont. Or someplace else."

"Why Charlotte? Why my home turf?"

We both knew the answer to that.

We'd crossed into Quebec when Ryan's phone buzzed again. As before, he put Rodas on speaker.

"One of my detectives found a mechanic who says he serviced a furnace at the Corneau place, once in '04, again in '07."

"Did he recognize the images I sent?"

"Yes, ma'am. He says Pomerleau was alone the first time. The second visit, someone else was there."

I shot Ryan a look; his jaw was set, but he didn't return it.

"Can someone work with him to create a sketch?" I asked.

"Negative. He says the person was too far off, way back at one of the sheds and all bundled up for winter. All he's sure of is that the guy was tall."

"It's something," I said.

"It's something," Rodas agreed, then disconnected.

Ryan and I took some time digesting this latest piece of information. He spoke first. "By 2007 Pomerleau has hooked up with someone willing to share her psychosis. They kill Nellie Gower. A year and a half later, they travel to North Carolina, kill Lizzie Nance, then return to Vermont to tap their maples. The relationship tanks—"

"Or there's an accident." Caution, à la Karras.

"—he kills her, seals her body in a barrel, and splits for North Carolina."

"It plays," I said.

"Like a Sousa march."

"What now?"

"We shut the fucker down."

Ryan and I decided on a two-pronged approach. Neither clear on what those prongs would be.

He would stay in Montreal. This didn't thrill him, given that Pomerleau or her housemate had posted my face on a wall. But after much discussion, he agreed that it made the most sense.

I took the early-morning flight to Charlotte. As we parted, I wondered when I'd see Ryan again. Given our past, and the fact that my presence now seemed painful to him, I suspected that, going forward, he might request cases that didn't involve me.

Just past eleven, a taxi dropped me at the annex. I paid and dug out my keys. Found I didn't need them. The back door was unlocked.

Momentary panic. Check it out? Call the cops?

Then, through the glass, I saw Mary Louise enter the kitchen, Birdie pressed to her chest.

Relief flooded through me. Followed by annoyance. "You should always lock the door." Upon entering.

Mary Louise was wearing the same flapper hat. Below the scoopy bell brim, her face fell.

Cool move, Brennan. Your first words to the kid are a rebuke.

"I just mean it's safer."

"Yes, ma'am."

Birdie looked at me with round yellow eyes. Reproachful?

"Looks like you two have really hit it off."

"He's a great cat."

Birdie made no attempt to push free and come to me, his normal response after I've been away.

"I was going to give him a treat." Hesitant.

Birdie gave me a long judgmental stare. Daring me to interfere?

"He'll like that," I said, smiling broadly.

Mary Louise went to the pantry. I set my carry-on aside and placed my purse on the counter.

"Your mother called." As Birdie ate Greenies from her palm. "I didn't pick up. But I heard her leave a message. My grandma has an answering machine like that."

Great. I was a fossil. I wondered how old she was. Twelve, maybe thirteen. "Any other calls?"

"The red light's been flashing since Wednesday. So, yeah, I guess."

"What do I owe you?"

She stroked Bird's head. The drama queen arched his back and purred. "No charge. I really like this little guy."

"That wasn't our deal." I dug out four tens and handed them to her.

"Wow." Pocketing the bills. "My mom has allergies. I can't have pets."

"That's too bad."

Awkward pause.

"Can I come visit him? I mean, like, even if you're home?"

"Birdie and I would both enjoy that." I thanked her, then, through the window, watched her skip down the walk. Smiling, I hit play on my relic machine.

Mama, complaining about Dr. Finch.

Harry, recommending books about cancer.

Outside, Mary Louise did two cartwheels in the middle of the lawn.

The last message was Larabee, saying he had DNA results on the hair found in Shelly Leal's throat. Odd. I checked my iPhone. He'd called there, too. I'd forgotten to turn it on after landing.

I phoned the MCME. Mrs. Flowers put me through after a few comments on container-grown lettuce.

"Larabee."

"It's Tempe."

"How was Canada?"

"Cold. Ditto Vermont." I briefed him on the inter-views with Sabine Pomerleau, the Violettes, and the Kezerians. Then I dropped the bombshell about Anique Pomerleau.

"I'll be damned."

"Yeah." I recalled Ryan's comment. Felt almost no guilt at sharing his sentiment about Pomerleau's death. Almost.

"The hairs we found in Leal's throat were forcibly removed from the scalp, so the lab was able to sequence nuclear DNA." Larabee's voice sounded odd. "It's a match for Pomerleau."

I was too shocked to respond.

"The hair was bleached, so that fits with your corpse. Pomerleau was probably trying to disguise her appearance."

"But Pomerleau was dead long before Leal was killed."

"Hair can transfer in so many ways. On clothing. On blankets. Looks like her accomplice got sloppy."

My mind was racing with images, one worse than the next.

"What now?" Larabee asked after a pause.

"Now we shut the fucker down." Quoting Ryan.

I was in my bedroom unpacking when pounding rattled the front door.

25

I jetted to the hall window to look down at the porch. A plaid shoulder was half visible under the overhang. A man's rubber-soled Rockport, scuffed and worn.

I hurried downstairs. Verified the identity of my visitor by squinting through the peephole. Slidell was working a molar with one thumbnail.

His hand dropped when I opened the door. "Barrow wants Lonergan's spit on a stick."

It took me a minute to process that. "Lonergan is Colleen Donovan's aunt," I said.

"Yeah."

A prickle of fear. "Have remains been found?"

"Nah."

"Why collect Lonergan's DNA now?"

"The lady don't have what you'd call a stable lifestyle. Barrow wants her on file. You know. In case she hops it and fails to leave a forwarding."

In case Colleen turns up.

Slidell's gaze drifted to the parlor behind me. "Hey, cat."

I turned. Birdie was watching from the middle of the room. He liked Slidell. No accounting for feline taste.

"I was thinking you might ride along."

I knew the reason for that. Slidell is revolted by the bodily fluids of others. Loathes the contact needed to obtain them.

"Have you talked to Larabee?" I asked.

"He briefed me on Pomerleau when I picked up the Q-tip. Guess we won't be lighting no candles for her."

I didn't disagree.

"Rodas got any theories who her sidekick might be?"

"No," I said.

"Let's roll. It'll give you a chance to recap the highlights."

Laura Lonergan lived on Park Road, not far from uptown. Geographically speaking. Economically, the address was light-years away.

En route, Slidell handed me a printout:

AVAILABLE 24/7. Massage. Companionship. For mature men who want a sexy, sensitive female. Real curly hair, spicy tits, juicy butt!!! Call me now! No black men. No texts or blocked numbers. Princess.

Poster's age: 39.
Location: Uptown Charlotte.

A photo showed a woman in a thong and push-up bra contorted on a bed like a boa on a vine. In another, she was smiling from a not-quite-chin-deep bubble bath.

"Where's this from?" I asked.

"Backpage.com. Under *Escorts, Charlotte.*"

"She's very broad-minded."

"We all got our limits."

"She goes by Princess?"

"Pure gentry."

"I guess marketing on the Internet is easier than walking the streets." Placing the ad on the center console.

"She does her share of that."

Slidell slowed. Checked his spiral.

The block was lined with two- and three-story buildings, many with apartments converted to accommodate small businesses. Lonergan's was a six-unit affair with large-leafed vegetation crawling the brick. Maybe kudzu.

"Is she expecting us?" I asked.

"No." Slidell shifted into park. "But she's here."

We got out and entered a postage-stamp lobby. The air smelled of mold and rugs not cleaned in a decade. Of chemicals used to perm and dye hair.

To the right, past an inside door, was a tax

accountant's office with not a single employee or customer present. A narrow stairway lay straight ahead. To the stairway's left, a hall led to another hall cutting sideways across the back of the building.

Lonergan's unit was on the second floor, beside a beauty salon and across from an aesthetician who also did nails. Both doors were shut. Beyond them, no indications of human life.

A sign on Lonergan's door offered massage therapy and instructed patrons to knock. Slidell did.

We waited. My gaze wandered. Landed on a spiderweb that could have made *Architectural Digest*.

Slidell knocked again.

A voice floated out, female, the words unclear.

Slidell gestured me to one side, out of view. Then he banged again, this time with gusto. After some rattling, the door opened.

Laura Lonergan was a portrait titled *The Face of Meth*. Fried orange hair. Rawhide skin peppered with scabs. Cheeks sculpted with deep hollows created by the loss of dentition.

Lonergan smiled, lips closed, undoubtedly to cover what unsightly teeth she'd managed to retain. One hand brushed breasts barely altering the topography of a pink polyester tank. Her chin rose, and one shoulder twisted in under it. The coy seductress.

"Save it, Princess." Slidell held out his badge.

Lonergan studied it for about a week. Then she straightened. "You're a cop."

"You're a genius."

"I'm closed." Lonergan stepped back and started to shut the door.

Slidell stopped it with one meaty palm. "Not anymore," he said.

"I don't have to talk to you."

"Yes. You do."

"What have I done?"

"Let's skip the part where you play innocent."

"I'm a masseuse."

"You're a tweaker and a whore."

Lonergan's eyes skittered up and down the hall. Then, softer, "You can't talk to me like that."

"Yes. I can."

Lines crimped Lonergan's forehead as she thought about that. "How about you cut me some slack?"

"Maybe."

A beat as she considered what that might mean. "Yeah?"

"Yeah."

"You won't bust me?"

"That depends on you."

The skittery eyes narrowed. Bounced to me. Back to Slidell. "A three-sixty-nine is cool. But it'll cost."

I felt the urge to scrub down with antibacterial soap.

"Let's move this inside," Slidell snapped.

Lonergan didn't budge.

"You feeling me, Princess?"

"Whatever." Trying for indifference, not even coming close.

The front entrance gave directly onto a small living room. Lonergan crossed it and dropped onto a couch draped with leopard-skin fabric, one skinny-jeaned leg outstretched, the other hooked over an armrest.

The sofa faced two ratty wicker chairs and a coffee table scarred by dozens of cigarette burns. Beyond them, against the far wall, which was red, a desk held a TV and a plastic banker's lamp repaired with duct tape. Black plastic trash bags lined the walls, bulging with treasures I couldn't imagine. An unshaded halogen bulb threw sickly light from a pole lamp twenty degrees off-kilter.

Through a door to the right, I could see a shotgun kitchen, the counter and table stacked with dirty dishes and empty food containers. I assumed the bedroom and bath were in back. Had no desire to view them. I eyed the chairs. Chose to remain standing.

Slidell balanced one ample cheek on the edge of the desk. Folded his arms. Stared.

"This gonna take all day?" Picking at a scab on her chin. "I got things to do."

"Talk about Colleen."

"Colleen?"

"Your niece."

"I know she's my niece. You here to tell me something bad about her?"

Slidell just stared.

"Where is Colleen?"

"You tell me."

"I don't know."

"You heard from her lately?"

"Not since she split."

"When was that?"

The ravaged face went slack as she searched through the rubble of her mind. "I don't know. Maybe Christmas." Back to the scab, the perimeter now smeared with blood. "Yeah. She was here for Christmas. I got her a six-pack. She got me the same. We had a laugh over that."

"Where'd she go?"

"To crash with friends. To shack up with a guy. Who the hell knows?"

"Hard to imagine her leaving, you providing such a nurturing environment and all."

"The kid got tired of sleeping on the couch."

"Tired of watching you tweak and bang johns."

"That's not how it was."

"I'm sure you prayed the rosary together."

"Colleen was no angel." Defensive. "She'd spread her legs if a dude made it worthwhile."

"She was sixteen." Sharp. I couldn't help myself. The woman was repulsive.

"Colleen's a survivor. She's probably dancing in Vegas." Flip. But I could hear question marks in her voice.

Slidell withdrew a clear plastic vial from his jacket

pocket. Handed it to me. "We need your spit," he said to Lonergan.

"No way."

"The procedure is painless." I pulled the swab from the vial and showed it to her. "I'll just run this over the inside of your cheek. That's it."

Lonergan swung the armrest leg down to meet the floor leg, drew both in, and sat forward, arms wrapping her knees, head wagging from side to side.

Slidell drilled her with one of his tough-cop looks. Wasted effort, since she was staring at the floor.

"This is a trick to prove I'm using." Gaze still on her boots. Which had heels higher than the wheels on my car.

"Don't need no swab to see that." Slidell's tone said he was out of patience.

"I'll puke."

Slidell spoke to me. "The witness says she don't feel good. I should take a spin around the premises, see if there's something might be making her sick." He pushed to his feet.

When Lonergan's head snapped up, the cartilage in her throat stood out like rings on a Slinky. "No."

We waited.

"Why are you doing this?" The skittish eyes bounced around the room and settled on me, a less threatening foe.

"We need your DNA on file," I said gently.

"In case Colleen—"

"It takes only a second." I pulled on surgical gloves and stepped closer. I expected Lonergan to turn away. To clamp her jaw. Perhaps to spit at me. Instead, she opened her mouth, revealing teeth so rotten that I wondered how she could chew.

I scraped her cheek, sealed the swab in the tube, and marked it with a Sharpie. Slidell took the specimen without comment. Then he turned on his heel and headed for the door.

Looking at Lonergan, I felt a bubble of pity rise in my chest. The woman had nothing. Her sister was dead. Her niece was missing, probably dead. She had no present. No future. Only enslavement to a habit that would inevitably take her life.

"I know you care about Colleen," I said softly.

Lonergan's snort was meant to show apathy. What I heard was guilt and self-loathing.

"You did the best you could, Laura."

"I didn't do shit."

"You haven't given up."

"Yay, me. I leave the porch light on."

"You didn't let it drop." Desperate to find something comforting to say. "You reached out to check on your niece's case."

"No, I didn't."

"According to Colleen's file, you phoned last August to ask for an update."

Lonergan looked at me in genuine confusion. "Phoned who?"

"Pat Tasat."

"Never heard of him."

"Do you know a woman named Sarah Merikoski?"

One bony shoulder rose, dropped. "Maybe."

"She reported your niece missing. Tasat was the detective looking into it."

"Lady, I'm not sure of much. But one thing you can take to the bank: I've never dimed a cop in my life."

Was the meth speaking? Had Tasat gotten it wrong? Or had he missed something?

"Does Colleen have more than one aunt?" I asked.

"If the kid had options would she have stayed in this dump?" Sweeping a skeletal arm to take in the room.

A buzz rippled my nerves.

My eyes shifted to Slidell.

He was listening.

26

I was so pumped, I overlooked the mélange of odors polluting Slidell's Taurus.

"If Lonergan didn't call Tasat, who did?" I said.

"You can count on one hand the cells still firing in that chick's head."

"She sounded so certain."

Slidell offered a sniff.

"I can't recall if the notation included a callback number."

"Knock yourself out. I'm gonna run the swab by the lab."

We were at the LEC in minutes. Rose through the building in silence.

My pulse was high-stepping. Was the discrepancy due to Lonergan's impaired wiring? Had Tasat gotten it wrong in his notes? Or had we stumbled on to one of Ryan's big bang breaks?

I got off on two and headed past the CCU to the

conference room. Slidell continued up to four.

The Donovan file was on the table with the others. It took little time to locate the entry.

Investigative Notes (Tasat) (8/07/14)

Laura Lonergan, family member, phoned to ask about progress on MP Colleen Donovan. Lonergan is Donovan's maternal aunt. When asked if she had thoughts where Colleen might be, Lonergan stated that she did not. When asked where she could be reached, she provided a cellphone contact and stated she had no work or home lines.

Lonergan's mobile was listed at the end of the entry.

After blocking my own caller ID, I tried the number. A voice told me it wasn't in service.

I was sitting there, frustration oozing from every pore, when Slidell lumbered through the door. "What?" Seeing my face.

"There's nothing in the file to indicate where the call was made. The mobile number given by Lonergan"—hooking the name with air quotes—"is bogus. And Tasat's not around to take questions."

"I'm telling you. The woman's brain is hamburger."

"I think we should check it out."

Slidell sighed, über-patient. Yanked out his spiral. "You got the date the call came in?"

"August seventh."

Kathy Reichs

"The time?"

"No."

"I'll have to get Tasat's number."

"That's easy enough."

"Then I'll have to subpoena Ma Bell."

"How long will that take?"

"A couple weeks, a couple days. Some companies are friendlier than others."

"Shall we tell Barrow?"

"Tell him what? A tweaker's having memory issues?"

Easy, Brennan. "Where is Barrow?"

"Heading here now."

Slidell's words were barely out when the head of CCU stepped into the room.

I explained the call. And my suspicion that someone other than Lonergan had placed it.

"Nice catch."

"Maybe." I knew in my gut that it was. "The mobile number Lonergan gave Tasat isn't in service. And it's not the one she's currently posting on Backpage.com."

"So she got dropped or switched carriers." Slidell's skepticism was a real buzzkill.

"You on the trace?" Barrow asked him before I could respond.

"Wanna bet it's a waste of time?"

"I could pass it to Tinker."

Slidell took his leave, muttering about paperwork. And horseshit.

Barrow took the chair opposite mine. "How was the far north?"

"Cold."

"Bring me up to speed."

I did.

Barrow listened, now and then clearing his throat.

When I finished, he sat thinking about it. Then, "The brass wanted stronger links between Leal and the other cases. Said they'd reassess when the situation changed."

"They did."

"We need to share this with the deputy chief."

"When?" I looked at my watch. It was ten past five. I'd risen before dawn to fly back to Charlotte.

"Now."

"Since 2007, three adolescent females have been abducted in broad daylight and later found dead. Nellie Gower, Hardwick, Vermont, 2007. Lizzie Nance, Charlotte, 2009. Tia Estrada, Salisbury, 2012. The victims are of a type. The VICAP crime profiles show striking similarity. In each case, the body was left in the open, fully clothed, and posed. In no case was there evidence of sexual assault. In no case could cause of death be determined." At Barrow's urging, I was taking the lead.

Deputy Chief Denise Salter kept her eyes level on mine. They were brown, darker than her caramel skin, lighter than the black hair pulled back and knotted at the nape of her neck. Her shirt was eye-scorching white, the creases on its long sleeves sharp enough to perform microsurgery. Black tie, black pants, black patent-leather shoes gleaming like marble.

Salter had rescheduled another meeting to make time for us. She was listening, her expression neither kind nor unkind.

"Over the same seven-year period, at least two others girls have disappeared in North Carolina. Avery Koseluk from Kannapolis in 2011. Colleen Donovan from Charlotte in late 2013 or early 2014."

Barrow placed five photos on the desk facing Salter. She slipped reading glasses onto her nose and scanned the lineup. Then looked pointedly at me.

I went on, "Koseluk was thought to be a noncustodial-parent abduction, Donovan a runaway. Both remain open MP files."

"Cut to the chase." Behind the lenses, Salter's eyes looked E.T. huge.

"Identical DNA was found on Gower and Nance."

Barrow added the age-progressed pic of Pomerleau to the blotter. Salter picked it up and studied the face. "Hers?" she asked.

"Yes."

"Where'd you get the hit?"

"The NDDB, the Canadian equivalent of CODIS."

If that surprised Salter, she hid it well.

"Who is she?"

"A Canadian national named Anique Pomerleau. She and an accomplice, Neal Wesley Catts, aka

Stephen Menard, are wanted for the deaths of at least three individuals. Their MO was to imprison, torture, and rape young women. Angela Robinson, Menard's first victim, was kidnapped in Corning, California, in 1985. Marie-Joëlle Bastien and Manon Violette were taken in Montreal in 1994. All three died in captivity."

"You know this because?"

"I identified their remains."

"Go on."

"In 2004, Pomerleau slipped the net just as the Montreal cops closed in. She's been in the wind ever since. Until now."

"And Menard?"

"She either killed him or he killed himself just before she disappeared."

"You think Pomerleau is now murdering kids on my turf?"

"No."

Salter's brows floated up in question.

"Two days ago I assisted at Pomerleau's autopsy."

I summarized my trip to Montreal and St. Johnsbury. Ryan. The interviews with the Kezerians, Sabine Pomerleau, the Violettes.

I described the Corneau property, the barrel, the autopsy. The furnace mechanic who'd seen a second person present at the farm.

"You think Pomerleau and an accomplice killed Nellie Gower. Then, a year and a half later, the pair came here and killed Lizzie Nance."

"We do."

Barrow and I exchanged glances. He nodded. "And we believe there were others," I added.

A flick of Salter's wrist told me to continue.

"A skeleton was discovered in Belmont in 2010. I determined that the bones were those of a twelve- to fourteen-year-old female, probably fully clothed when her body was dumped."

"Probably?"

"The remains had been scavenged by animals."

Salter tossed her glasses to the blotter and leaned back into her chair.

"During Shelly Leal's autopsy, Larabee pulled hair from her throat," I said.

"The child just discovered under the I-485 overpass."

I nodded. "DNA sequencing says at least one of those hairs came from Anique Pomerleau."

"That's big."

"But puzzling. Circumstantial evidence suggests Pomerleau died in 2009."

"Explanation?"

"The hairs could have transferred from Pomerleau to her accomplice," Barrow said. "Maybe via a shared article of clothing. Or his ritual could include wearing something Pomerleau wore."

"Larabee also found a lip print on Leal's jacket," I said. "It contained DNA. Amelogenin testing indicated the DNA came from a male."

"I'm guessing lip boy is not in the system."

"No."

Silence filled the room for a very long moment. Salter broke it. "Let me get this straight. Pomerleau and a male accomplice operated out of a farm in Vermont until 2009."

"Yes."

"Was anything found to suggest kids were held there? A soundproof room? Handcuffs bolted to a wall?"

"No."

"Uh-huh." Neutral. "This mysterious accomplice eventually kills Pomerleau and stashes her body in a barrel of syrup."

"Yes."

"Motive?"

"We have none."

"He then moves south. Does Nance, Estrada, maybe Koseluk, Donovan, and the kid found near Belmont. Now Leal."

"Yes."

"Why shift his blood sport here?"

I described the *Health Science* article. The picture of me clipped and saved at the Corneau farm.

"You're saying the perp's in my town because of you."

"I'm saying it's a possibility."

"Why?"

"Revenge? Taunting? Who knows?"

Salter's phone rang. She ignored it.

"Explain the dates again," Barrow said to me.

I did, leaving out Mama's role in spotting the pattern.

"So victims are taken on the anniversaries of abductions in Montreal." Statement, not question, Salter wanting affirmation.

"That's the idea," I said. "Possibly on the dates they died."

"And Pomerleau's accomplice continues the game even though he's taken her out."

"So it appears."

"And the intervals are decreasing."

"Yes," Barrow said. "And another anniversary comes up in two months."

I could hear my own breathing in the silence that followed. Salter's folded glasses tapping the desktop. Finally, when I thought she was about to blow us off, "Slidell's working Leal, right?"

"Yes," Barrow confirmed.

"Anyone else assigned to this?" She swept a hand over the photos.

"Ex-officio, a detective from Montreal, another from Hardwick, Vermont."

"I've seen Beau Tinker in the halls. The SBI here at your invitation?"

"Not exactly."

Another beat. Then Salter pocketed the glasses. "Write it up. Everything you've got."

27

The weather had turned colder while I was in the LEC. Not enough to make me hate it. But enough to make me think about getting out gloves I'd stashed in a closet last March.

Birdie showed more interest in the contents of my Roasting Company bag than in my return. I filled his bowl, clicked on CNN, and settled at the kitchen table.

The Situation Room had closed for the night. A Democrat was bickering with a Republican about health care and immigration reform. Irritating. I want news at the end of the day, not a bout of extreme verbal sparring.

I turned off the set. Tossed down the remote.

Birdie jumped onto the chair beside me, preferring warm chicken to the hard brown pellets I'd served up. Couldn't blame him.

As I ate, Tasat's note filled my thoughts.

"Lonergan didn't make that call," I said through a mouthful of succotash.

Birdie cocked his head. Listening, or hopeful for poultry.

"So who did?"

The cat rendered no opinion.

"A relative? A friend? Supposedly, Donovan had none."

I placed a sliver of drumstick on the table. Bird tested it with one in-curled paw, then seized it delicately with his front teeth.

"Donovan's killer, that's who. It's classic felon behavior. Like returning to a crime scene."

Bird and I looked at each other, thoughts definitely not on the same page.

My mobile rang.

"Your flight went well?" Ryan sounded as exhausted as I felt.

"I can't remember that far back."

"I'm beat, too."

"Any progress?" I offered Bird another scrap of fowl. He repeated his pat-and-snatch maneuver.

"None. Where are you?"

"Home. I spent the day with Slidell."

"And?"

"He often addressed me in an ill-mannered fashion."

"Any breaks?"

"Maybe."

I described the visit with Lonergan and the meeting

with Salter. Explained Tasat's notation and Lonergan's denial about making the call. "Slidell's convinced there's nothing to it."

"Has he agreed to subpoena the phone records?"

"Grudgingly. Says it could take weeks. Meanwhile, we—" A bottle rocket exploded in my head. "Shit!"

"What?"

"How did I miss it? I must be totally brain-dead."

"Earth to Brennan."

"Tia Estrada."

"The kid from Salisbury."

"I was distracted by Slidell and Tinker sniping at each other."

"Stay on point."

"According to the case log, a journalist called six months after Estrada went missing."

"And?"

"I'm almost certain that was the last entry in the chronology. And the file contained no news clipping dating to 2013."

"You're thinking that call might also be bogus?"

"It's identical to Donovan. Someone calls six months after the child vanishes. Maybe it was the same person who phoned for info on Donovan. If so, there's a pattern. Something linking the cases."

"Worth some following through."

Suddenly, I was on fire to hang up. "I've got to go."

"Slow down."

"Slow down?"

"Don't get ahead of yourself."

"Jesus, Ryan. You sound like Slidell."

There was a long empty pause on the line. Then he asked, "Anson County, wasn't it?"

"Yes. Do you remember who caught the case?"

"Cock."

"Very helpful." Actually, it was. "Henrietta something, right?"

"I think so."

"And I thought of something else. We need to compare pics of the Gower, Nance, and Leal scenes. See if any gawker makes a repeat appearance."

"No one's done that?"

"Not that I know of."

I disconnected, my weariness dispelled by the prospect of a big bang.

After clearing the table, I grabbed my purse and jacket, and bolted.

The second floor of the LEC was quiet. I went straight to the conference room and spread the Estrada file on the table.

The last article ran in the *Salisbury Post* on December 27, 2012, roughly three weeks after Tia was found. At least that was the last one saved.

The story was little more than a summary of facts. The child's disappearance. The discovery of the body four days later, near the Pee Dee National Wildlife Refuge. The mother's deportation to Mexico. It ended with an appeal to the public for further information. There was no byline credit.

I got online and Googled the *Salisbury Post*. A woman named Latoya Ring seemed to be covering a lot of the crime beat. A link provided her email address. I composed a brief message, explaining my interest in the Estrada case and asking that she call me.

Setting aside the *Post* clipping, I reread the entire file. Every few minutes checking my iPhone. When finished, I'd learned nothing.

But I had the name I needed. Henrietta Hull, Anson County Sheriff's Office.

My head was pounding from struggling over lousy handwriting and blurry text. And the fatigue was back double-time.

I closed my eyes and rubbed circles on my temples. Call Hull? Or wait to hear from Ring?

It was after nine on a Friday. Unless Hull was working the night shift, she was probably home enjoying a beer. Maybe at church or bowling with her kids. Better to talk to Ring first. If she or a colleague had phoned about Estrada, end of story.

Screw it.

I dialed.

"Anson County Sheriff's Office. Is this an emergency?"

"No. I—"

"Hold, please."

I held.

"All right, ma'am, what's your name?"

"Dr. Temperance Brennan."

"The purpose of your call?"

"I'd like to speak to Deputy Hull."

"All right, can I tell her what it's about?"

"The Tia Estrada homicide."

"Okay. May I ask for specifics?"

"No."

A slight hesitation. Then, "Hold, please."

I held. Longer than before.

Things clicked.

"Deputy Hull." The voice was guarded. Husky but softer than I'd expected. Perhaps a bias on my part due to the nickname.

I explained who I was and my reason for contacting her.

"Suddenly, everyone's interested."

"I'm sorry?"

"Two years go by, nothing. Then three queries in a week." I could hear dialogue in the background, the cadence of a sitcom laugh track.

"You've spoken to Detectives Ryan and Slidell."

"Slidell. He's a pip."

"Did he mention Colleen Donovan?"

"No."

"Donovan was reported missing in Charlotte last February. We suspect her case may be linked to that of Tia Estrada."

"Who did you say you're with?"

"The medical examiner. And the CMPD cold case unit."

"Okay."

"Six months after Colleen Donovan vanished, an aunt phoned asking for an update. Donovan's only aunt denies making that call. Six months after Estrada was abducted, a journalist contacted your office. We're wondering if that call was also a sham."

"Who's the journalist?"

"The notation is handwritten, one line that provides no name or number. And there's no clipping in the file."

"I'm not surprised. Estrada was killed on Bellamy's watch, and he already had one flip-flop out the door. I inherited the case when he retired to Boca."

"I've left a message for Latoya Ring. Do you know her?"

"Ring is solid."

"This might turn out to be nothing. Donovan's aunt is a tweaker and pretty wasted. But if no one at the *Post* made the call, do you think you can find and trace the number?"

Twice, canned laughter cued me that something was funny. Finally, "Done. Now tell me what you know."

I did. Along the way remembered another loose end. "According to the autopsy report, the local ME found hair in Estrada's throat. Do you know if that hair was tested for DNA?"

"I'll check."

"If not, find out what happened to it."

"Will do."

A long silence came down from Wadesboro.

"Thanks, Dr. Brennan. This kid deserves better."

"Tempe," I said. "I'll call if I hear back from Ring."

"You'll hear back."

I spent another hour going over photos from the Gower, Nance, Estrada, and Leal scenes. Scrutinizing faces with a handheld magnifier. Comparing features, body shapes, clothing, silhouettes. It was no good. The vessels in my head were trying to blast through my skull. Someone with superior skills and equipment would have to do it.

At ten I packed up and headed home. I'd just pulled in at the annex when my mobile launched into "Joy to the World." I'd switched the ringtone to try to be festive.

The number was blocked. I hesitated a moment, then clicked on. "Brennan." Shifting into park.

"It's Latoya Ring. I've just spoken with Hen Hull."

"Thanks for returning my call."

"No one here at the *Post* phoned the sheriff."

I felt an electric shock fire through my body. "You're certain?"

"We're not *The New York Times*. Only two of us cover the crime beat. He didn't call, I didn't call."

Across the yard, something rippled the tangle of shadows thrown by an enormous magnolia. A dog? A late-night walker? Or did I imagine it?

"And I phoned my editor just to make sure," Ring continued. "A move that will not contribute to my being named employee of the month. He green-lighted no follow-up on Estrada."

"You're certain of that?" Straining to see through the dark.

"The assignment would have fallen to me. I'd asked several times. Was repeatedly told no."

"Why?"

"There was no point. The cops had zip—no suspects, no leads. The mother wasn't even in the country by then."

Tia Estrada wasn't a blue-eyed darling with Shirley Temple curls.

"Thanks for jumping on this," I said.

There. Was that movement just past the coach house? A deer?

"The whole thing stinks."

I waited for Ring to elaborate.

"Some bastard murdered this kid. Then the system let her fall through the cracks."

"We'll get him," I said, squinting into the thick vegetation surrounding my car.

"Take care."

I sat a moment, mildly uneasy. Then got out and scurried to the annex.

I was in bed in seconds.

Unconscious in minutes.

Unaware of what I'd set in motion.

28

That weekend it rained in Charlotte, not hard but constantly. At times a mist, at times ramping up to a halfhearted drizzle. A cold dampness saturated the air, and water dripped from the eaves and off the broad green leaves of the magnolias outside.

On Saturday, Mary Louise dropped by to see Birdie. That day's hat was a striped bucket affair with a tassel on top.

Maybe I was lonely for Ryan. Maybe just lonely. Or maybe I was avoiding a stack of reports that needed my attention. Hell, maybe it was the weather. I surprised myself by asking Mary Louise to stay for lunch.

After gaining parental clearance, we made and ate ham and cheese sandwiches. Then we baked cookies and decorated them with M&M's. Mary Louise talked about her desire for a dog. Her problems with math. Her love of Katniss. Her goal of becoming a fashion designer. The kid was good company.

On Sunday I drove up to see Mama. At higher elevations, the precipitation hovered on the brink of snow. We sat by the fireplace, watching soggy flakes dissolve into puddles on the deck.

Mama seemed tired, distracted. She asked only once about the "poor lost angels," drifted through other topics, as though she'd forgotten or lost interest in what had energized her less than two weeks earlier.

Mama's stance on chemotherapy hadn't softened. When I broached the subject, she shut me down. The only spark she showed all day.

On my way out, I conferred with Dr. Finch. She urged acceptance. I asked how long. She refused to speculate. Inquired what hospital I preferred should the time come when Heatherhill was no longer adequate. As before, her eyes said more than her words.

Once in the car, I phoned Harry. She refused to acknowledge the inevitable. Talked only of new therapies, miracle cures, a woman in Ecuador who had lived a decade following diagnosis. Classic baby sister.

After disconnecting, I let the tears flow. Riding the salty gush, I focused on my headlights arrowing through the dark.

The trip down the mountain seemed endless. The slushy snow triggered thoughts of my trip from St. Johnsbury to Burlington. I almost welcomed them. But not the horrendous collage that followed in their wake.

A pale body floating in amber liquid. A small

bloated corpse on a stainless steel table. Adolescent bones stored in a box on a shelf.

That night the same images kept me awake. When sleep finally came, they invaded my dreams.

Nellie Gower on the edge of a quarry. Lizzie Nance in a field at Latta Plantation. Tia Estrada beside a gazebo at a campground. Shelly Leal under a highway overpass.

Facts. Leading to questions. Which looped into more questions. Never to answers.

Anique Pomerleau hadn't acted alone in Montreal. Her MO had involved an accomplice.

Pomerleau's second killing season had begun at a farm in Vermont. Her DNA was found on a victim there, on another in Charlotte.

DNA from a lip print said the current doer in Charlotte was male. That fit the theory that Pomerleau had a killing partner.

But Pomerleau was dead. Had her accomplice taken her off the board? Why? When?

Had he brought his perverse delusions south? Why North Carolina? Was I the draw? Why?

Was he following Pomerleau's pattern of kidnapping on the anniversaries of previous abductions? Why continue the legacy without her?

Would he strike again soon?

I awoke to bright sunlight. Made coffee and went to bring in the paper.

Blown leaves dotted the patio bricks. The sky was

blue. The trees were alive with the businesslike twitter of mockingbirds and cardinals.

I'd just filled my mug when my mobile sounded. At first I didn't recognize the caller ID. Then I did.

"Hope I didn't rouse you." Something in Hen Hull's voice kicked my pulse up a notch.

"Awake for hours," I lied.

"Took some doing, but I got it," Hull said. "Ready?"

I grabbed pen and paper from the counter. "Shoot." She read off a number, and I wrote it down. "Can you trace—?"

"Ready?"

"Shoot."

"The call to Bellamy inquiring about the Estrada case came from a pay phone near the intersection of Fifth and North Caswell in your fair city. I thought mobiles had put pay phones up there with the horse and buggy. That and vandalism."

"The line might be long gone."

"Or the booth could be a toilet stall."

I thought a moment. "Even if the phone exists, and there's video surveillance on that corner, there's no chance footage would still be around."

"Not after two years."

The number was another dead end. I wanted to scream in frustration. "You think the caller was Estrada's abductor?"

"It wasn't a journalist at the *Post*."

"Any word on the hair?" I asked.

"The autopsy was done by a guy named Bullsbridge. I'm waiting for a callback."

"Is he competent?"

"I'm waiting for a callback."

"I'll brief Slidell," I said.

"Keep in touch."

I disconnected. Redialed. The line was busy.

I left a message. The device was still in my hand when Slidell phoned back.

"I got—"

"Hull got—"

We both stopped.

"Go ahead," I said.

"I got the number of the call on Colleen Donovan. From Tasat's phone."

I read off the digits I'd written down.

"Where the hell'd you get that?"

I told him about the caller claiming to be a journalist at the *Salisbury Post*.

"Same phone. I'll be goddamned."

"Undoubtedly the same person. A solid link between Estrada and Donovan."

"Still don't tie 'em to Gower and Nance. Or those two to the others."

"Jesus, Slidell. What do you need?"

"I'm advocating the devil."

I was too amped to point out that he was garbling the metaphor.

"Now what?" I asked.

"Now I get my nuts handed to me by the DC."

"You've asked for another meeting with Salter?"

"No. Special Asshole Tinker has."

"Why?"

"He's got issues with my attitude."

"Tell Salter about the calls."

"Eeyuh."

I tried Ryan. Got voicemail. Rodas. Barrow. Voicemail. Voicemail.

My pulse was humming. I couldn't sit still.

I changed my ringtone. Did a load of laundry. Ran the vacuum. Put eggs on to boil. Forgot them until the smell of burning shells made me race to the kitchen.

At noon I pulled on gym shorts, a sweatshirt, and Nikes and pounded out two miles on the booty loop. Breathing hard, I inhaled a mixture of wet cement and rain-soaked grass and leaves. Of sun-warmed metal from the cars lining the curbs.

When I finished, students were streaming between the buildings at Queens University. As I walked the last block back to Sharon Hall, the air felt cool on my sweat-slicked skin.

At home, I checked my mobile and landline. No one had called. I wondered if Slidell was still in his meeting with Salter. Or if he'd left it too peeved to bother with me.

I showered and changed into jeans and a sweater. Continuing to feel agitated, I pulled out the copy I'd made of the Nance file.

What was the definition of insanity? Repeating the same action and expecting different results?

Knowing it was futile but needing to do something, I began going through every entry again. Photos. CSS and ME reports. Interview summaries. As with the files in Montreal, the exercise felt like a faded letter from another time.

But today there was an added element. Something nagging at the periphery of my thoughts. Something that refused to come into focus.

Was my subconscious noting a detail that I was missing?

At three I tried Slidell again. With the same result. I thought about calling Tinker. Didn't, knowing Skinny would rip the skin off my face.

Harry called at four. Should she send Mama flowers? Should she come for a visit? For now, I endorsed FTD.

A cup of Earl Grey, then back to the file.

Still my subconscious tickled. What? A photo? Something I'd read? Something Ring had said? Hull?

At five I gave up.

Out of ideas but unable to rest, I got online and called up a map of Charlotte. After locating the intersection of North Caswell and Fifth Street, I switched to satellite view and zoomed in.

I spotted the pay phone. Beside it was a parking lot filled with vehicles. Below that a sprawling brick structure.

I activated the label function. A purple bubble

appeared. I clicked on it. Saw the words "CMC—
Mercy."

Carolinas Medical Center—Mercy Hospital.

Something flickered in my lower centers. Was gone.

I stared at the screen, willing the pesky spark to
burst through.

It did. With a high-voltage jolt.

Lizzie Nance had been researching ER nursing for a
school project. They'd found the report on her laptop
after she died.

Shelly Leal had gone to an ER for dysmenorrhea.

Colleen Donovan had been transported to an ER
after falling and hitting her head.

A caller using fake identities had dialed from a pay
phone across from a hospital. To check on Estrada. To
check on Donovan.

As I thought about it, I could feel my blood pumping
faster.

I grabbed the phone. Had to key the digits twice.
"Come on. Come on."

"Yo." Slidell was chewing on something.

My words came out at breakneck speed. In
finishing, "You need to call Shelly Leal's mother. Ask
what hospital they took her to. Then find out where
Donovan was treated."

"I'll get back to you." Gruff.

The wait seemed endless. In fact, it was under an
hour.

"CMC—Mercy," Slidell said.

"Sonofabitch," I said. "That's where the victims were chosen."

"I'll get a list of employees."

"Without a warrant?"

"I'll persuade them."

"How?"

"Personal charm. If that don't work, I'll threaten to dime the *Observer*."

Slidell had the roster by ten. "You got any idea how many people work at a hospital?"

"Now what?" I asked.

"I'm running the names against those I got from the DMV on the license plate ID. Special Asshole's gonna start sending 'em through the system."

"Doesn't every hospital employee undergo a background check?"

"Yeah. That stops the bad guys."

"Focus on those with an ER connection."

We hung up.

While waiting to hear back from Slidell, I tried Ryan again. This time he answered.

He was as pumped as I was. Congratulated me. "Not much dropping here," he said.

"Have you found Tawny McGee's psychologist?"

"Yeah. Pamela Lindahl. She's actually a social services psychiatrist."

"Is she still affiliated with the General?"

"Yes. But she sucks at returning calls. I'll keep on it. But I doubt finding McGee will lead anywhere."

I couldn't disagree. And wondered if opening the wound was worth the cost. "What about Rodas?" I asked.

"He called in some chits with the press. Had Pomerleau's face published statewide, along with a description and a plea to the public for pics or video taken between 2004 and 2009 in which she might be seen in the background. You know, photo bombing at a store, a gas station, a parking lot."

"If she's with a guy, it could put a face to her playmate."

"Exactly. It's unlikely, but you never know. He's also got people canvassing door-to-door in Hardwick and St. Johnsbury."

I asked Ryan if he was planning to return to Charlotte. He said soon.

There was an awkward pause. Or I imagined one. Then we disconnected.

Knowing I wouldn't sleep, I made tea and returned to the Nance file.

Gran's clock ticked softly from its place on the mantel.

As expected, I found nothing further.

At midnight I switched to the reports awaiting my attention. My mind kept drifting. I speculated. Pomerleau's accomplice was an EMT. A nurse. A security guard.

The hours dragged by at glacial speed.

Slidell finally called at two A.M.

He had learned three things.

29

"Leal went to Mercy."

"When?"

"Sometime last summer. The mother thinks late July."

"Does she know who treated her daughter?"

"No."

"The ER will have a record of the visit."

"Really?"

"They'll probably insist on a subpoena."

"You want to hear this?"

Easy. You're both tired.

"The good news is the place has security cameras up the wazoo. The bad news, they got storage issues. Only keep tapes ninety days."

"You need to requisition the most recent set."

"Hadn't thought of that."

There was a censorious pause. Then I heard pages flip, knew the spiral was being thumbed.

"Got a possible hit from my DMV list."

Slidell delivered it so flatly I thought I'd mis-understood. I waited for him to clarify.

"Hamet Ajax. Drives a 2009 Hyundai Sonata. Dark blue. First two digits match the tag spotted by the genius on Morningside."

"The witness who saw Leal outside the convenience store?"

"Maybe saw her."

"How did you narrow in on Ajax?"

"Jesus, I already told you. I cross-checked the names from the DMV against the hospital employee list."

Easy, Brennan.

"So Ajax works at Mercy?"

"Since 2009."

"Doing what?"

"Part-time ER doc."

"Why didn't you just say that?"

"I did."

"And now?"

"I do some digging."

"On Ajax."

"No. On the guy served my steak too rare last night."

Deep breath. "Let me know what you learn."

It took me a long time to drift off after that, and I slept fitfully, floating in and out of dreams starring Mama. On waking, I retained nothing but a sense of her presence and a potpourri of disjointed images.

Hands braiding long blond hair. A delicate brass bell on a bedside table. A glossy white vase with shamrocks curling its rim. Tears. The word "Belleek" coming from trembling lips.

I got out of bed feeling anxious. Useless.

I was pouring my second coffee when the phone rang.

Reflex. Time check: 7:40.

Slidell sounded drained, I guessed from working all night. He wasted no time on sarcasm or his version of wit. "Ajax is a pedophile."

The word drove an icicle straight into my heart.

"Did a nickel in Oklahoma for molesting a kid."

"Now what?"

"Now I invite the slimeball in for a chat."

"I want to observe."

"'Course you do."

The interview was supposed to take place at three that afternoon. Turned out Slidell hadn't been able to wait. When I got to the LEC, he and Ajax were already in an interview room. I walked past it to the adjacent one.

Barrow and a handful of CMPD detectives stood watching a monitor to which Ajax's image was being transmitted. They looked up when I entered, expressions empty, expecting little, or unimpressed with what they were seeing. Barrow nodded and stepped to his left. The others shifted right. I moved into the space created for me.

Ajax took up most of the screen. He was a tall bony man in a suit made for a tall muscular man. His hair was black, his skin surprisingly pale. Tortoiseshell glasses magnified eyes already too large in a face overcommitted to nose. I thought he might be Middle Eastern, perhaps Indian or Pakistani.

He sat at a metal table, hands motionless on the simulated wood top. Behind him, the wall was mauve above waist level, white cinder block below. The floor-bolted cuffs had not been clamped on his ankles.

Slidell was opposite, one shoulder and a bit of greasy scalp visible on-screen. An unopened folder lay on his side of the table.

"Anything so far?" I asked.

Barrow shook his head.

"I worked last night as well as today." Ajax's tone was serene, his English subtly accented. "I'm quite weary now."

"That what you used to tell the missus so you could bang that kid?"

No reaction from Ajax.

"Good scam. Claim to be at the hospital, go cruising instead."

"I've told you. It wasn't like that."

"Right. The kid was your family's babysitter. That made it okay."

"I'm not saying my conduct was appropriate. I'm saying I never sought children out."

"Easier to hit on the ones who already trusted you." Slidell's tone dripped with disgust.

"There were no others."

"Bullshit."

"I made a mistake. The circumstances were ... unusual."

"How's that?"

"The girl in question was mature for her age. Her behavior was provocative."

I felt my whole body cringe with repugnance.

"You perverted piece of scum." On-screen.

"Gives scum a bad name." The detective behind me.

"I served my time," Ajax said, unruffled. "I underwent therapy."

"Last I checked, the sex registry ain't optional for mutants like you."

"I submitted my name in Oklahoma."

"This ain't Oklahoma."

"My offense was fifteen years ago. I was required to register for ten."

"You do that back when you landed here?"

Ajax pulled a wry grin. "I am a changed man."

"A real humanitarian."

"I cure the sick."

"Let's go back over that. You stitched up a sixteen-year-old name of Colleen Donovan. Street kid brought in by the cops. Head wound."

"I repeat. I treat hundreds of patients each year."

"How about Shelly Leal. Came in last summer complaining of cramps."

"Without access to charts, I can't possibly know."

"Yeah? Well, we know." Slidell's hand came into view. Flipped open the folder and removed a printout.

I looked at Barrow. He shook his head, indicating it was a ruse.

"Perhaps I treated this patient." Unruffled. "What of it?"

Slidell's hand took a second paper from the folder and winged it across the table. "That your car?"

Ajax rotated the page and glanced down. "I drive a Hyundai."

"Check the plate."

He did. "The vehicle is mine. And legally registered."

"We got a witness saw you shove Shelly Leal into that car."

"That person is lying."

"Some cold-blooded bastard killed both these kids." In Donovan's case, another lie.

Behind the lenses, the dark eyes narrowed a hair. "Surely you don't suspect me."

"Now, why would we do that?"

"I've told you. I never hurt anyone."

"How's that babysitter doing these days?"

"I have never shown physical violence toward any human being."

"Where were you on April 17, 2009?"

Ajax's chin hiked up, sending a slash of white across each lens, a double reflection of the overhead fixture. The slashes reversed course as his chin leveled. "I must check my agenda."

"How 'bout November 21, 2014?"

"Should I engage an attorney?"

"Should you?"

Ajax sighed. "If you had proof of my involvement in these homicides, you'd be charging me with a crime. Since you are not, I assume I am free to go."

"We're trying to clear you here, Doc."

The voice surprised me. Beau Tinker was also in the room.

"Your partner's tone has suggested otherwise all afternoon."

"Look, you're a smart man. Given your past, you know we have to check you out. You get that, right? In order to exclude you."

"You took me away from my work. I've answered your questions to the best of my ability."

"Still, there are gaps."

"I can provide more precise answers once I have access to charts and personal records."

"You don't remember treating Colleen Donovan?"

"No."

"Or Shelly Leal."

"No."

"You recall no contact with either?"

"None. I've made that clear."

"We want to get it straight."

"I've agreed to be recorded." Ajax looked straight into the camera, obviously familiar with police interview rooms. "You can refer back to your tape."

A pause.

"You know a kid named Tia Estrada?" Slidell jumped back in.

"No."

"Avery Koseluk?"

"No."

"Lizzie Nance."

Ajax sat silent and unmoving.

"That one ring a bell?"

"No."

"How about Nellie Gower?"

"I know none of these persons."

"Ever been to Vermont?"

"I have answered that in the negative."

"Talk about Anique Pomerleau."

"Who?"

Slidell lurched forward across the table, close to Ajax's face. "Cut the crap, you worthless piece of shit."

"I don't know what you are talking about." Looking Slidell straight in the eye.

"Can you think of anyone at Mercy we should question?" Tinker again.

"I promise to give serious thought to that question."

"Please do."

Kathy Reichs

"Yeah. Please do." A chair scraped. The visible parts of Slidell jerked from view. "In the meantime, I need air what ain't fouled."

A door opened. Closed. Ajax sat still as a carving on Rushmore, eyes on the corner, where, I assumed, Tinker was standing.

"I have never physically hurt anyone. Not then. Not now."

"I believe that's true, Doc." Tinker, good cop extraordinaire. "Listen. You need a soda?"

The twitch of a lip. A smile? "I will accept nothing to eat or drink."

"Suit yourself."

Our little gaggle divided. The detectives turned left, toward the violent crimes division. Barrow and I turned right, toward the conference room. Slidell was already there, standing by the table. His face looked drawn, his eyes puffy and red from lack of sleep.

"You get anything?" Barrow asked.

Slidell shook his head. "The guy's a fox. Knows how to play his hand."

"When did you start in on him?"

"Just past one."

I may have made a sound. Or moved. Slidell's eyes flicked to me. Before I could say anything, voices sounded in the hall, then Tinker joined us, followed by Salter.

"I wanted to go at him alone." Directed to me but loud, for Tinker's benefit. Maybe Salter's.

"The whole interview, Ajax never changed his story?" Barrow had also missed the start of the show.

"Can't remember treating Donovan or Leal. Didn't know they were dead. Had nothing to do with killing 'em."

"Leal's been all over the news," I said. "Ajax doesn't read papers or watch TV?"

"Claims he's too busy saving lives."

"And no one at the hospital once mentioned Leal? Does that sound right?"

"The slimy—"

Salter truncated Slidell's response. "Just what have you got on this guy?"

"He's a pedo. And his vehicle and tag square with a witness account from the spot Leal was grabbed."

"Full match?"

"Two digits."

"That's it?"

"Four girls are dead. Maybe six. This creep likes girls."

"It's weak."

"Two of our vics walked through his ER."

"Did he treat them?"

"We're getting the records."

"Anything else?"

"Tell her about the pay phone," Slidell ordered me. I did.

"Outside Mercy."

"Yes."

Salter nodded, turned back to Slidell. "Any shot at DNA?"

"He's not falling for it."

"How do you want to proceed?"

"Let me go back at him."

"Has he requested a lawyer?"

"Not yet."

"He's supposed to register as a sex offender," Tinker said. "Hasn't in years, never did in North Carolina."

"That buys us some leeway." A few beats, then, "You seriously think Ajax could be our guy?"

"He's our only real suspect."

"You getting his history?"

"Every dump he ever took."

"Okay. Let him cook awhile, then go back in." Looking from Slidell to Tinker. "If nothing breaks by six, we cut him loose." Slidell started to protest. "And this goes by the book. I want to see fast footwork, I'll watch *Chinatown*." Pointedly to Slidell. "Ajax asks to lawyer up, we shut it down. Are we straight?"

Slidell inhaled deeply, exhaled through his nose.

"Are we straight, Detective?"

"We gotta kick him, we stay up his ass?"

"Right between the cheeks."

30

At five, Ajax requested counsel.

Thirty minutes later, a cruiser dropped him at his home. An unmarked car was already parked up the block.

At six, Slidell got a call from an attorney named Jonathan Rao. Henceforth, Rao's client would answer questions only through him or in his presence.

At seven, Slidell, Barrow, and I were in the conference room eating King's Kitchen takeout. Between mouthfuls of fried flounder, Slidell was sharing what he'd learned about Ajax's past.

"Back in Oklahoma, he was Hamir Ajey. His story squares with what I dug out of court records. Ajey, aka Ajax, began nailing a babysitter when she was fourteen and he was thirty-three. The abuse stopped two years later, when the kid confided in a teacher. He was charged with rape and lewd acts on a minor, copped a plea."

"To spare the child having to endure a trial," Barrow said. "That's often how it goes."

"The sick fuck did forty-six months and walked."

"Wasn't he required to register as a sex offender?" I asked.

"He did." Bite of flounder. "When he got out of the box in 2004. In Oklahoma."

"Didn't the state yank his medical license?"

"That state." Slidell licked his fingers. "So Ajey/Ajax goes underground a couple years, surfaces in New Hampshire at an urgent care clinic ain't so picky about background checks."

"You're kidding."

"A couple pen strokes on the ole license, his name changes from Hamir Ajey to Hamet Ajax. He figures no one will bother phoning Mumbai."

"And no one did. Jesus."

"A few more years, he uses the New Hampshire job to springboard to an ER in West Virginia."

"From there to Charlotte," Barrow said.

"Along the way, he stops mentioning he's a perv."

"And no one asks." I was disgusted.

"Why Charlotte?" Barrow asked.

"Who knows?"

"How long was Ajax required to register?" I asked.

"I'm getting to that," Slidell said. "He claims ten years."

"Is he married?"

"Back in Oklahoma. The wife left him."

"How many kids?"

"Two girls."

I felt clashing emotions. Revulsion for Ajax. Sympathy for his daughters. Fear for future victims. I wanted to scream, to cry, to throw something at a wall.

"Any other incidents? Patient complaints, that sort of thing?" Barrow asked.

"Nothing popped in the four states I ran the two names. Apparently, Ajax kept his nose clean."

"Or improved his technique." Barrow.

"Where's he living now?" I asked.

"One of those cuter-than-shit neighborhoods off Sharon View Road."

"Does Oklahoma have his DNA?"

Slidell shook his head.

"Was Ajax working on the dates Donovan and Leal presented at Mercy?"

"I got a warrant in the works. Should know in an hour or two."

"What's your thinking?" Barrow asked.

"I want inside Ajax's house."

"Without cause that's a nonstarter."

"Yeah. Yeah. So we keep a team up his butt twenty-four/seven. The asshole so much as glances at a playground, we yank him back in."

Impressive. Slidell had worked two buttocks references into one comment.

"If he's no longer required to register, that won't fly."

"Confusing, ain't it? But we're awaiting confirmation from Oklahoma."

"And if Ajax does nothing?" I asked.

"These dickheads always do something. Meanwhile, I find out when Leal and Donovan went to Mercy. I check the ER records for MD signatures or printed names or ID numbers or whatever it is they use. And I get a list of any ER employee present both times. Talk to them. That goes nowhere, I branch out to the rest of the hospital."

"Where's Tinker?" I asked.

"Following up with Ajax," Barrow said. "Getting alibis for the dates Leal, Estrada, Nance, and Gower were abducted. Then he'll run checks."

"You two kiss and make up?" My lame attempt to lighten the mood. Also, I was curious. Slidell glowered at me, clearly not open to a discussion of his rapport with Tinker. I changed the subject. "New Hampshire shares a border with Vermont."

"I'll shoot Ajax's face to Rodas," Barrow said. "See if that shakes anything loose up there. In the meantime, I got hours of video from places Leal might have gone the week before she died. I'll keep plowing through that, see if the kid appears. See if anyone suspicious is near her. And I got people going through footage taken in the time window our guy must have off-loaded Leal. Roads he might have driven to get to the overpass."

"How many hours you talking about?"

"You don't want to know."

"Ajax thinks he's smart." Slidell pushed to his feet. "The arrogant prick is going down."

"What can I do?" I asked.

"Take me off speed dial."

I glared at Slidell's retreating back.

I was at the MCME when Slidell finally phoned. I could have written the reports at home, but somehow, being at the morgue made me feel less marginalized.

"Donovan arrived at Mercy at 11:40 P.M. on August 22, 2012. Got three stitches in her forehead. She was discharged at 1:10 A.M. The uniforms who brought her drove her to a shelter. Ajax is on record as the treating physician."

I felt my pulse rush. Made a very special point of not interrupting.

"Leal arrived at 2:20 P.M. on August 27, 2014. A Dr. Berger treated her for abdominal cramping, advised over-the-counter meds. The parents took her home at 4:40 P.M."

"Was Ajax working that day?"

"Yes."

"Any other ER staff coincide on those two occasions?"

"Five."

"I thought the list would be longer."

"Two years go by, people move around. Plus, we got lucky. One kid landed at night, the other during the day."

"Different shifts."

"Eeyuh."

"Do any of the five still work at Mercy?"

"Three." I heard the flutter of the ubiquitous spiral. "A CNA name of Ellis Yoder. That's a certified nurse's assistant."

I knew that. Said nothing.

"Alice Hamilton, also a CNA. Jewell Neighbors, a guest relations specialist. Makes the place sound like the friggin' Ritz."

GRS. That one I didn't know.

"One nurse, Blanche Oxendine, retired. Another, Ella Mae Nesbitt, moved out of state."

"Have you talked to any of them?"

"Been too busy touching up my spray tan."

I waited out a brief pause.

"Oxendine's sixty-six, widowed. Worked ten years at Mercy, thirty-two at Presbyterian before that. Lives with her daughter and two grandkids. Has arthritis, weak bones, and a bad bladder."

I could only imagine that conversation. "Did Oxendine remember either of the girls?"

"Leal, vaguely. Donovan not at all."

"What did she think of Ajax?"

"Liked that his breath always smelled nice."

"That's it?"

"Feels too many jobs these days are going to foreigners."

"Is she Internet-savvy?" Not sure why I asked that.

"Thinks computers are the ruin of today's youth."

"What about Nesbitt?"

"Thirty-two, single, worked at Mercy four years after getting her degree. Moved to Florence in September to take care of her eighty-nine-year-old mother. The old lady fell and broke a hip."

"So Nesbitt wasn't living in Charlotte on the dates Nance and Leal were killed."

"Nope."

"Does she use a computer?"

"For email and online shopping."

"Her thoughts on Ajax?"

"Said he was a little too stiff for her taste. Chalked it up to cultural differences. Whatever that means. Felt he was a decent enough doctor."

"Did she—"

"Remembered Donovan because she assisted Ajax with the suturing. Said the kid was belligerent, probably on something. Drew a blank on Leal."

"So neither one raised an alarm?"

"Hell-o. Our doer plays for my team."

Slidell was right. The DNA on Leal's jacket said her killer was male.

"What about the others?" I asked.

"Thought I'd swing by the hospital now."

"See you there," I said, and disconnected before Slidell could object.

I arrived first. At nine P.M. on a Monday, the place was quiet.

Knowing Slidell would go batshit if I did anything but breathe, I settled in the waiting area, hoping no one there had anthrax or TB.

Across from me, against one wall, a man in full-body camouflage clutched a shirt-wrapped hand to his chest. To his left, a kid in a tracksuit observed me with crusty red eyes.

Down the row to my right, a girl held a swaddled baby who wasn't moving or making a sound. I guessed the girl's age at sixteen or seventeen. Now and then she patted or bounced the still little bundle.

Beyond the girl, a woman coughed wetly into a wadded hankie. Her hair was thin and gray over a shiny pink scalp, her skin the color of uncooked pasta. The fingers on one hand were nicotine yellow.

I focused on the staff, reading names when anyone came into view. Soon spotted one of our targets.

A tall, doughy guy with a stringy blond pony wore a tag identifying him as *E. Yoder, CNA*. When Yoder passed me to collect Crusty Eyes, I noticed that his arms were flabby and covered with freckles.

Ten minutes passed. Fifteen.

The old woman continued her phlegmy hacking. I was considering relocation when Slidell finally came through the door. I got up and crossed to him. "Yoder's here. I haven't spotted Neighbors."

"I talked to her."

"What?"

"She's a cretin."

"Where did you see Neighbors?"

"Does it matter?"

I drilled Slidell with an inquisitional stare.

"In the lobby."

"And?"

"She handles a lot of patients with bellyaches and scrapes."

"That's what she said?"

"I'm paraphrasing."

"Why is she a 'cretin'?" Hooking air quotes.

"She's twenty-four, has a husband and three kids, wasn't working at Mercy when Nance or Estrada were killed."

"That makes her a cretin?"

"She's been outside the Carolinas once in her life, on a school trip to D.C. Thinks the Lincoln Memorial is one of the seven wonders of the world. Never been on a plane. Doesn't own a computer. You getting the picture?"

I was. Jewell Neighbors didn't fit the profile of a child killer. Or a child killer's apprentice.

"And note the pronoun. As in female."

"You're assuming no one else is involved."

Now I was the recipient of a questioning stare.

"A woman would be less threatening."

"So a woman recruits victims."

"Maybe here, in person. Maybe online."

"And why would she do that?"

"It's not impossible." Defensive. "Pomerleau did it for Menard."

"If our perp's getting help, it ain't Neighbors. Or Oxendine. And Nesbitt wasn't around for Nance or Estrada."

"If Estrada is even linked." I thought a moment. "Nesbitt was nineteen in 2009. Where was she?"

"I'll ask."

"What did she say about Ajax?"

"Kept to himself, didn't schmooze in the lunchroom, didn't attend social events. She never saw him outside the workplace. Didn't know him at all. Same picture I got from Neighbors."

"Ajax is a loner."

"Yes. Now you mind if I talk to a guy has history?"

"What does that mean?"

"I ran Yoder. He's got a jacket."

"For what?"

"Two 10-90s."

"Who did he assault?"

"A guy in a bar."

I started to ask a question. Slidell cut me off.

"And a seventeen-year-old kid named Bella Viceroy."

31

Ellis Yoder wasn't openly hostile. Nor was he terribly forthcoming.

After badging him and vaguely explaining me, Slidell asked to speak in private. Yoder led us to an unoccupied office.

Slidell opened with the arrest record. "Remember Chester Hovey? The guy whose face you retooled with a bottle?"

"The guy who smashed my girlfriend onto a windshield to feel up her tits. You know where Hovey is now?"

"I don't."

"Doing time for slapping a hooker around."

"And Viceroy?"

"Bella." Yoder wagged his head slowly. "That what this is about?"

Slidell gave him the long stare.

"We fought. The bitch bit me. I smacked her. She

317

brought charges. She was seventeen. I was nineteen, so I took the heat."

"Sounds like you got anger management issues, Ellis."

"Oh, right. I'm the one with issues." Yoder gave a mirthless snort. "Look. Bella and I were both jerks. I've been clean since. Check it out."

"You can take that to the bank."

"You guys never let up."

"Do you remember a patient named Shelly Leal, came in last summer complaining of cramps?"

"Hell, yeah. She's the one got murdered."

"Tell me about her."

"I don't actually remember *her*."

"You just said you did."

"I mean when I heard her name later, you know, in the news, I remembered she was here."

"You know the name of every patient comes in?"

"No." Yoder crossed his arms and scratched the outer side of each with long, nervous strokes. His nails left white trails across the freckled landscape.

"But you remember her."

"Holy shit. Are you thinking I had something to do with that?"

"Did you?"

"No." A flush colored Yoder's face.

"How about a patient named Colleen Donovan? Street kid brought in with a gash in her head."

"When?"

"August 2012."

"Maybe. I don't know." More scratching. "Wait. I think Doc Ajax sewed that one up. I didn't assist."

"You see either of these kids outside the ER?"

"ED."

"What?"

"It's called the ED. Emergency Department."

"You trying to piss me off?"

"No!" The vehemence caused his nostrils to blanch at the edges.

"Answer the question."

"The answer is no."

"Talk about Hamet Ajax."

"Doc Ajax?" Yoder's nearly invisible brows rose in surprise. "What about him?"

"You tell me."

"He's Indian."

Slidell offered an upturned palm.

"Not a talker, it's hard to know."

"He a good doctor?"

"Good enough."

"Go on."

"What do you want me to say? Patients seem to like him. He treats the staff okay. I don't know anything about his personal life. The docs don't hang with the drudges."

"Ever hear any complaints? Rumors?"

"What are you getting at?" Yoder's eyes hopped

to me, back to Slidell. They were a peculiar avocado green.

"Just asking."

"No."

"Ever get any bad vibes?"

"From Doc Ajax? No."

"What else?"

"Nothing else."

"That's it?"

"That's it."

"Is Alice Hamilton working today?"

Yoder's fingers stopped. "Now I get it."

"Yeah?"

"Her and the doc."

"Go on."

"I wouldn't mind a piece of that myself." His lips squashed up in a smarmy grin. "If you catch my meaning."

Slidell looked at him coldly.

"Hey, I'm not casting stones." Raising and splaying both hands. Which were peppered with tiny flakes of dry skin.

"You saying Ajax and Hamilton are doing the two-headed roll?"

Yoder hiked both shoulders and brows.

"Where is she?"

"Hell if I know."

"When did you see her last?"

"Not for a while."

"Is that unusual?"

Yoder considered the question. "Nah. She's a part-timer."

Slidell gave Yoder the usual mantra about calling if he thought of anything further. We left him scratching and staring at Slidell's card.

Before leaving the hospital, Slidell asked a supervisor about Hamilton's next scheduled shift. Learned she was off until Wednesday. Obtained contact information, a mobile.

Slidell dialed as we crossed the parking lot. Got a recorded voice. Next he phoned the surveillance team. Learned Ajax hadn't left home since being deposited at six.

I glanced at my watch. Half past ten and we'd accomplished zip. The adrenaline fizz had long since faded.

Still smarting from Slidell's speed-dial remark, I didn't ask his plans.

I got into my car and headed home.

Inspired by Yoder's skin storm, I took a quick shower.

Ryan called as I was dropping into bed. I stacked pillows behind me and put him on speaker. In the background, I could hear frenetic male voices.

"How goes it?"

"Good. You?"

"Watching the Habs pummel the Rangers."

"At eleven P.M.?"

"DVR, baby."

I told Ryan about the phone calls made outside Mercy. About Ajax.

"Sonofabitch. How'd he act?"

"Cool as a snake. Ajax was on duty in the ER when Donovan and Leal presented. Slidell and I are talking to everyone else who worked both shifts."

"What do his co-workers say about him?"

"One CNA hinted he had something going with another CNA. Otherwise the interviews were a bust. No one knows diddly about Ajax. No one remembers much about Donovan or Leal. How about you? Any luck with McGee?"

"The mother was on the level. Tawny did take some CEGEP courses." Ryan used the acronym for Collège d'enseignement général et professionnel, a type of post-secondary school unique to Quebec.

"Where?"

"Vanier. I talked to some profs. No one remembers her. Not surprising. She attended for a little while, dropped out in 2006. Then it's as if she fell off the planet."

"Did you ever hear back from the psychiatrist?"

"Yeah. Pamela Lindahl. You met her in '04, right?"

"Only briefly."

"Your impression?"

"She seemed genuinely interested in Tawny's welfare. Why?"

"I don't know. She's odd."

"Psychiatrists are all odd."

"I can't put my finger on it. She seemed to be hinting at something she wouldn't come out and say."

"Did you ask why she took Tawny to de Sébastopol?" Not relevant. But the outing still troubled me. I couldn't see the upside.

"She claims she was opposed to the idea, but Tawny insisted, like it was some rite of passage. When the kid wouldn't let up, Lindahl consulted colleagues, they said go for it, so she finally agreed."

"The house was sealed after the fire. How'd they get in?"

"Lindahl called the city, and someone did a safety inspection. Though damaged, the building was structurally sound. Given the special circumstances, they were allowed to visit. I'm not sure of the whole story."

"What did they do there?"

"Mostly sat in the parlor."

"Did Tawny venture into the basement?"

"Yeah. Lindahl passed on that. Figured the kid needed to be alone."

"Jesus."

"Lindahl stayed in contact even after funds for treatment ran out."

"How long?"

"Until the kid cut herself off in 2006."

"Does she have thoughts on where Tawny might be?"

"If so, she's not sharing them."

"Did you ask about Jake Kezerian?"

"Lindahl's comments weren't flattering."

"Does she think he's the reason Tawny took off?"

"She refused to speculate."

"Did Anique Pomerleau come up in their sessions?"

"She's not at liberty to say."

"Seriously?"

"Tawny is a patient. And an adult. Anything they discussed is privileged."

"Did you ask about the potential impact of our contacting Tawny?"

"Lindahl felt revisiting the past would be painful."

"No kidding."

A pause.

"You really think Ajax could be our guy?" Ryan asked.

"Slidell does."

"How'd he hook up with Pomerleau?"

"Unless Ajax cracks, we may never know. But after Oklahoma, he worked in New Hampshire."

"Somehow they meet. Paired with Pomerleau, things escalate to murder."

Nothing but hockey as we thought about that.

"Here's what bothers me," I said. "Ajax is a pedophile. But these homicides show no sexual component."

"Who knows what's sexual to these freaks. Our doer takes souvenirs. Maybe the rush comes after the kill."

"Maybe it comes from controlling the victim." Continuing Ryan's train of thought. "From dictating minute personal choices—hair, clothing, body position."

"Moment of death."

I heard a match strike. An expulsion of breath.

"Why kill Pomerleau?" Ryan asked. "And why shift to Charlotte?"

"Better climate?" I didn't believe it.

"Then why the delay? Why go to New Hampshire, then West Virginia?"

"Ajax needed time to rebrand himself."

"Maybe."

"Pomerleau probably told him about Montreal. About my role in bringing her down. Maybe that excited him. It's not uncommon for serial killers to try to up the ante."

"Increase the danger, increase the thrill."

"The danger being me."

We both considered whether that had legs.

"How about this," Ryan said. "Ajax wants to be arrested. He loathes what he's doing but can't stop himself."

"Subconsciously, he wants me to catch him?"

"While consciously, he tries to avoid it."

"Hmm."

The voices exploded into a frenzy.

"Who scored?"

"Desharnais."

Kathy Reichs

"Why would Ajax, or anyone, continue to strike on dates significant to Pomerleau?"

"He's taken over her compulsion? Or maybe, unknowingly, he's sending out a clue."

"A clue I would understand."

"That plays."

"And the next date comes in less than six weeks."

32

Little happened over the next forty-eight hours.

Turned out Ajax couldn't reconstruct his movements on the day in 2007 when Nellie Gower disappeared. He was in New Hampshire by then, but the clinic's pay records didn't reflect exact dates worked, and it didn't keep schedules going that far back. Neither did the doctor.

As in Charlotte, Ajax had lived alone, in a rental home on the edge of Manchester. He ventured out only to work, shop, and run errands, never socially. He did not attend church. He had no colleague with whom he was close, no friend or neighbor with whom he discussed gardening or sports. No one to contact to help jog his memory.

Ajax claimed to be at the hospital or at home on the dates Koseluk and Estrada went missing. Tinker worked on verifying his hours with Mercy. Talked to people there.

Ajax's lawyer refused access to phone, credit card, and bank records. Tinker started the process to obtain warrants.

Leal was a different story. Ajax knew exactly where he was the Friday she was abducted.

November 21 was a rare day off. That afternoon he shopped at the Morrocroft Village Harris Teeter, then at a Walmart on Pineville-Matthews Road. Filled and washed his car at a service station one block up.

That evening he ate dinner at home, then went solo to see a film at the Manor Theatre. Unfortunately for him, he'd used no credit card, kept no receipt, no ticket stub.

Slidell showed Ajax's photo to employees at the stores, gas station, and theater and requested surveillance video for the day in question. Began viewing it.

Barrow continued with video taken from locations Leal had frequented in the months before her death. Phoned out to Oklahoma. Learned Ajax's wife and daughters had moved back to India.

Rodas floated Ajax's picture in Hardwick and St. Johnsbury. No one recognized him. The man who serviced the furnace at the Corneau farm said he'd been too far away to see the guy's face.

Tuesday morning the IT tech phoned Slidell. He'd found a visitor to the dysmenorrhea chat room he thought might be of interest. HamLover. Ham. Hamet. Slidell told him to do what it took to identify the user.

Tuesday afternoon, under increasing pressure from the media, the CMPD press office agreed to a news conference. It took place in the courtyard outside the LEC. Under a sunny sky, Salter and Tinker fielded queries on the Leal homicide. Gave no real answers. Didn't mention Lizzie Nance or the other girls. Didn't mention Hamet Ajax.

Leighton Siler asked question after question, face knotty, clearly frustrated. Got nothing. Didn't matter. Eventually, Siler or some hungrier or craftier rival would reveal details of the investigation in braying headlines.

I phoned Heatherhill several times, never reached Mama. Left messages knowing she wouldn't call back. When the demons stir, my mother distrusts all forms of communication. Calls, texts, and emails stop.

Luna Finch said Mama was listless, sleeping more than usual. And that she'd contacted Cécile Gosselin.

I hung up, breath coming in wobbly heaves. Mama had summoned Goose to her side.

Wednesday morning Ajax made a mistake.

To my amazement, Slidell came by the annex to share the news. It was just past nine. He looked haggard and smelled of coffee and too much drugstore cologne.

"The dumb shit drove right up to a school."

"When?"

"Seven-twenty this morning."

"Where is he now?"

"In a cage at HQ."

"What's his story?"

"He was dropping off food for a Christmas campaign for the poor. Says he drives by the school every day, noticed their thermometer thingy wasn't indicating a whole lot of donations. Wanted to give them canned peas and pasta."

"Is that true?"

"Don't matter. A pedo can't go within a thousand feet of a school."

"A thousand feet?"

"Whatever."

"The restriction doesn't apply if Ajax is no longer required to register."

"We're checking that out."

"Why is it taking so long?"

"Must be a glitch out in cyberspace."

"When did you—"

"Jesus Christ and the freakin' Mousketeers. The guy raped a kid. He pulled into a school yard."

"Would you like coffee?" *A kick in the nuts?*

"I got a warrant coming."

"Allowing you to do what?"

"Toss Ajax's house."

"You're going there now?"

Slidell nodded. "I want to be done and gone before Ajax's lawyer finds out. Same goes for Siler and his bloodsucking cronies."

"How long does that give you?"

"We got full radio silence on this. Still, not long."

"Where does he live?"

Slidell held up a small page with ripped and twisted tabs running along one edge. An address was scrawled sideways across the blue lines.

"You got us to this turd," he said. "Figure I owe you."

Larabee called as I was brushing my teeth. A kid had found a trash bag full of bones in the northern part of the county. Nothing urgent, but he wanted me to examine them.

Then it was Harry. That was a long one.

I was pulling on jeans when Rodas took a turn. The toxicology report had come back on Pomerleau. She had neither drugs nor alcohol in her system at the time of death. I told Rodas about Ajax's trip to the school. About the search warrant.

Ninety minutes after Slidell's departure, I finally broke free.

Ajax lived in the southeastern slice of the Queen City pie, close to Charlotte Country Day School, Carmel Country Club, Olde Providence Racquet Club. Big homes, big yards. Golf and pinot on the links. Lacrosse and Milton at school. Land of the nouveaux and not so nouveaux riches.

Slidell's scrawled note led me to Sharon View Road, a narrow two-laner with old-growth trees lining both shoulders. Sunrise Court was a small spur shooting from the south side.

The block held ten residences, all the creation of a single developer enthralled with timber and stone. Entrance was through a faux wrought-iron gate decorated with a plastic wreath. I keyed in the code Slidell had provided, and drove through. No big pines or live oaks here. The scraggly saplings suggested fairly recent planting. Or a paltry landscaping budget at the time of construction.

Ajax's house was at the far end, above the others on a slight rise. Like its neighbors, upmarket but not over-the-top. Unlike its neighbors, devoid of Santas, reindeer, icicles, or elves.

Ajax's lawn was neat, the shrubbery basic. Hollies. Boxwoods. Nothing requiring attention.

Slidell's Taurus headed a line of vehicles circling the cul-de-sac curb. Two cruisers. A CSS truck. An unmarked SUV. Skinny wasn't messing around.

I added my Mazda to the assemblage and got out. Walking up the drive, I noticed movement in the front window of the house to my left. A silhouette stood with arms crossed, eyes pointed in my direction. Though a reflection off the glass obscured the face, body form suggested the curious neighbor was male.

I hurried up stone steps to a darkly stained door. Tried the handle and found it unlocked.

The foyer had a slate floor, oil-rubbed bronze sconces, and a matching bronze fixture overhead. To the left, a powder room. Straight ahead were living and dining rooms. In each was a CSS tech in white Tyvek coveralls. One was taking pictures. The other was dusting dark powder onto a door frame.

Voices came from somewhere in back and to the left. Loud. Unhappy.

A mound of disposable Tyvek shoe covers lay on the slate. I slipped on a pair and moved forward.

The house's interior looked like an attempt to re-create an old black-and-white photo. The upholstery, rugs, and walls were all variations on gray. Fog. Ash. Sweatshirt. Steel. Chartreuse accessories added splashes of color. Throw pillows. A mirror frame. A chair. DVDs crammed built-ins beside a fieldstone fireplace. A small flat-screen TV hung above.

In the dining room, a dove-gray drum chandelier dangled over a table set with chartreuse place mats. In the middle, candles that had never been burned. A chartreuse ceramic bowl sat perfectly centered on a sideboard. A painting of bright green poppies decorated a wall.

I wondered if Ajax or the builder had chosen the decor. Suspected the latter. The place had a cold, impersonal feel. As though the furnishings had been purchased at Rooms To Go and Pottery Barn, then placed exactly as displayed in a magazine spread.

I nodded to the techs as I wound my way toward the kitchen. They nodded back.

Slidell was on one side of a brown-granite-topped

island. Tinker was on the other. Both wore shoe covers and latex gloves.

"—couldn't like him or not like him. They don't know him. The woman next door thought he worked at an Apple store." Tinker looked red-faced and cross.

"Track down the ones you missed." Slidell looked crosser.

"I'll get the same story."

"You're the one pushed for this."

"You don't think Ajax is dirty?"

"I'm not saying that," Slidell snapped.

"What are you saying?"

"I'm saying if Salter learns about the stall on Oklahoma, it's my balls on a rusty hook, not yours. Not to mention blocking Ajax from his lawyer right now."

"Or is it that those balls are already gone? Once burned, twi—"

"Get the fuck out there and bring me something!"

Tinker started to reply, heard my plastic-bottomed footies slapping the tile. Mouth tightening into an inverted U, he spun and stomped off.

"What's happening?" I asked.

"We've been through the whole friggin' place. So far, nothing. No porn. No girls' clothing. No key, no ring, no ballet slippers. No boarded windows, no padlocked doors. Nothing to suggest a kid was ever in here."

"Prints?"

"One set, which, you can bet your ass, will come back to Ajax. Same for hairs, fibers. Either he's the tidiest fucker on the planet or the most careful."

"Have the techs checked the vacuum cleaner?"

"Bagged the contents."

"The trash?"

Slidell just looked at me.

"Did they get anything that might yield DNA?"

"Toothbrush. But Ajax ain't on file."

"We can compare it to DNA from the lip print on Leal's jacket."

"Right."

"Did you find a computer?"

A moment of hesitation. Then, "No."

"A charger for a laptop?"

"No."

"A modem? A router?"

Tight shake of the head.

"He could have gone online elsewhere. Maybe at the hospital."

"Yeah."

"Is there a basement?" I was almost afraid to ask.

"Just a crawl space. Empty except for crap the builder shoved under there. And a whole generation of spiders."

"Garage?"

"Clean."

"Where's his car?"

"Uptown."

"Is it included in the warrant?"

"No." Slidell's jaw muscles bulged, relaxed. We both knew. If this search came up empty, there would not be another.

"May I look around?"

"Don't touch nothing."

Slidell looked so glum, I let the grating command pass without comment.

After retracing my steps, I turned left at the foyer. The hall led to a pair of bedrooms, each with an en suite bath.

I entered the one at the front of the house. Here the theme was green. The furnishings included a bed, a side table with lamp, a desk. Their boho styling screamed Restoration Hardware. Two bookshelves by the desk looked more Staples or Costco.

I believe bathrooms reveal a lot about a person. I started there.

The medicine cabinet was open, its mirror coated with fingerprint powder. Ditto the glass shower stall. Both were empty. No soap, no shampoo, no washcloth or loofah. The sink was pedestal, zero place to stash anything. The room was sterile. Not a hint of personality.

I returned to the bedroom.

The shelves held sets of professional journals. I crossed to observe them up close. *Emergency Medicine Journal. The Journal of the American Medical Association.*

The New England Journal of Medicine. Annals of Emergency Medicine.

I shifted to the desk. Centered on it was the most recent issue of *JAMA*, closed, with a small plastic ruler marking a page. I wondered what Ajax had been reading. Remembered Slidell's warning and didn't look.

Stapler. Tape holder. Letter opener. Leather cup with pens and pencils. A small stack of envelopes that looked like bills.

Nothing in the wastebasket. Probably the work of the CSS techs.

The room was clearly Ajax's office. Yet he went elsewhere to use the bathroom. At least for more than toilet needs. Habit? Eliminating the need to clean more than one?

I crossed the hall to the bedroom opposite. It was marginally larger and done in shades of blue. Same RH vibe but different finish and detail work on the wood. A more urban-chic style. As before, I started in the bathroom.

Unlike its counterpart, this one was used. Black flannel pajamas hung from a hook on the door. The shower stall held one bottle each of shampoo and conditioner, a bar of Ivory soap, and a long-handled brush.

The medicine cabinet contained Advil, Afrin, ChapStick, CVS-brand plastic bandages, Degree anti-perspirant, a Gillette disposable razor, a can of Edge shaving gel, Oral B dental floss, and a tube of Crest.

The sink was set into a black wooden vanity. Open drawers revealed a brush and comb set, tweezers, scissors, a home barber kit, and a battery-operated nose- and ear-hair trimmer. Linens, toilet paper, and backups for all toiletries were stored in a tall slatted cupboard that matched the sink. When Ajax shopped, he bought to last months.

I thought of the array of products in my bathroom. Of the state of hygiene in my cabinets and drawers. Slidell was right. The place was extraordinarily clean. An obsession? A covering of tracks?

Back to the bedroom.

A book of crossword puzzles was propped against the lamp on the bedside table, a pen clipped to its cover. A reprint from the *European Journal of Emergency Medicine*. I twisted sideways to read the title. "Reducing the Potential for Tourniquet-Associated Reperfusion Injury." *Yep. That'll get you to sleep.*

Three framed photos sat equidistant from one another on the dresser. I crossed to study them.

And felt my skin goose up into tiny bumps.

33

None of the photos looked recent. One was posed. A woman, seated, a baby on her lap and a toddler at her side. A red velvet band held long black hair back from her face. The woman looked straight at the camera with large brown eyes. Sad eyes.

The other two pictures were snapshots. One captured the woman walking hand in hand with two little girls. They looked about three and five. In the other, the trio was seated on a wall. Same kids but older, maybe six and eight.

Both girls had the woman's dark eyes and hair. On both occasions, their hair was center-parted, braided, and tied off with bows.

My mind popped a series of flashbulb images. Leal. Donovan. Estrada. Koseluk. Nance. Gower.

I hurried back to the kitchen. Slidell was peering into the fridge. "Did you check out the photos in the bedroom?"

"Probably the wife and kids." Slamming the door.

"Did you see the resemblance—"

"You telling me how to do my job?"

Cutting, even for Slidell. Knowing pressure from Salter and friction with Tinker were combining to make him overly defensive, I let it go. "Are you getting any feel for who Ajax is?"

"Bollywood freak." Far from apologetic but more tempered.

"The DVDs?"

Slidell nodded. "Lousy dresser. Eats healthy. Likes baseball." I cocked a questioning brow. Wasted, since Slidell wasn't looking at me. "He gets the major league package on cable."

I scanned the countertop beyond the island. Not a crumb or smudge. No canisters or cookie jar. Only a portable phone in a charger.

Slidell turned and saw where I was looking. "Yes. I hit redial. The last call went to Mercy."

"Any stored numbers?"

"No."

"Any messages?"

"No."

"You're right about the place being spotless."

"The worm's got every spray and polish ever put in a bottle." Jerking a thumb at a pantry I hadn't noticed before.

"Does he use a cleaning service?"

"None of the neighbors ever saw anyone but him

come and go. Hell, they hardly ever saw him."

"Yard service?"

"No."

"What about mail?" I noticed a small white box on the wall beside the back door.

"Utility bills. Circulars. Catalogues. Nothing personal."

"No indication he maintained contact with his family?"

"They're in India."

"They have phones and mailboxes there."

"No shit."

"Catalogues might mean he shopped online." The box had a sticker.

"I don't shop online, and I get the same crap."

"Was the security system activated when you came in?" The sticker had a logo. ADT.

"Yeah."

"Ajax gave you the code?"

"I persuaded him that sharing was in his best interest."

"So he sets the alarm when he's away."

"Where you going with this?"

"If ADT keeps records, they could tell you when Ajax entered and left the house."

"They could tell me when someone entered and left the house."

"So this was a bust," I said.

"You kiddin'? Double score." Slidell stripped off

his gloves. "First, this house ain't a crime scene."

Slidell's phone buzzed. He yanked it from his belt. Checked the screen. Sighed and raised it to his ear. "Slidell."

A tinny voice. Female. Strident.

"Yeah?"

The voice boiled again.

"Musta been a misunderstanding."

More boiling.

"On my way." Hooking the device back into place. "Salter's putting me up for cop of the year." Slidell looked at me, eyes bloodshot from worry and unrest. Then strode toward the door.

"And the second?" I asked.

"What?" Turning.

"What's the second thing you learned?"

"The prick keeps another crib for his dirty work."

While Slidell reported to Salter, I went to the MCME.

Larabee's bones weren't as straightforward as he'd hoped. Though far from complete, the skeleton was obviously human. A male, middle-aged, edentulous, probably white. Cortical flaking, discoloration, and adherent fibers suggested the man had occupied a coffin for many years.

Larabee was off somewhere. I wrote a preliminary report and left it on his desk. It would be up to him to investigate or not.

Slidell phoned late in the afternoon. His mood

made the morning's seem happy-go-lucky.

Salter had gotten two calls before noon. One was from Ajax's lawyer, Jonathan Rao, accusing the CMPD of denying his client the constitutional right to counsel. The other was from the judge who'd issued the search warrant—Rao had also reamed out Her Honor.

Since neither caller was happy, Salter wasn't happy. After laying into Slidell, she'd relented and said he could re-interview Ajax. Wearing gloves made of very young goat. The session yielded nothing. The few answers Ajax gave were filtered through Rao. At three, both walked out the door. It was the last time anyone would talk to Hamet Ajax.

Slidell had received video from Walmart and Harris Teeter that covered the day Leal went missing. So far, he hadn't spotted Ajax or his car. He planned to continue working through the footage.

I got through two reports, knocked off at five. Back home, I ate Bojangles' chicken with Bird and watched a rerun of *Bones.* For some reason, the cat is nuts about Hodgins.

Slidell called again at nine. "He's on tape."

"Which one?"

"Walmart and the Manor." Gloomy. Obviously not wanting Ajax to be there.

"LSA for Leal was 4:15 at the convenience store on Morningside."

"Ajax was in the Walmart on Pineville-Matthews Road. Entered at 3:52. Left at 5:06."

"Rush hour, and those locations are at least ten miles apart."

We both gnawed on that.

"Maybe you were right." Slidell sighed. "Maybe this douchebag don't work alone."

Or maybe. Just maybe.

I didn't say it.

That night, sleep was elusive.

The rain was back. I lay in the dark, listening to drops hit the screen and patter on the sill. To the subtle hum of my bedside clock.

And thought the thought again.

Impossible.

I reviewed what I knew about serial killers. Their victims usually conform to a type. A tall blond woman. A teenage boy with short brown hair. Cher. A hooker. A homeless codger with a cart full of trash.

The individual means nothing to the killer. He or she is irrelevant, a bit player in a carefully constructed ballet. The dance alone matters. Each battement and pirouette must be carried out with precision.

The killer is both dancer and choreographer, in control at all times. Victims enter and leave the stage, interchangeable, bit players in the corps.

I thought about Pomerleau. About Catts. About the mad tango that had left so many dead in Montreal.

I thought about Ajax. To what sick music was he moving? Did he learn it from Pomerleau? Or did he compose the score himself?

In his subconscious, who might Ajax be killing? His daughters? His wife? The babysitter who seduced him and ruined his life?

Birdie jumped onto the bed. I scooped him close. He readjusted, settled, and head-bumped my palm. I stroked him and he started to purr.

Ajax was shopping when Shelly Leal disappeared. Did he have an accomplice? Was it someone at the hospital? If not there, where? Did he have a killing place, as Slidell believed?

Or.

I thought of the home on Sunrise Court. So architecturally right and yet so wrong. Lifeless. Sterile.

I pictured Ajax working crossword puzzles in his bed. Paying bills at his desk. Watching baseball or DVDs from the chartreuse chair. Alone. Always alone. A common pattern with serial killers.

In my mind, I went back through each room. Recalled not a single thing to suggest that Ajax had a life outside his home or the hospital. No woman's robe in the closet. No Post-it on the fridge saying, *Call Tom.* No picture of himself with friends or co-workers. No reminder on a calendar to meet Ira for lunch. Nothing to suggest anyone in Ajax's life cared about him. That he cared about anyone.

No. That wasn't true. He'd kept the three photos. Old photos. Of whom? Had to be his wife and daughters. Was the woman the template for his victims? One of the girls? Why?

No one at Mercy knew Ajax. No one on his street. No one in New Hampshire or West Virginia remembered him.

Again the unsettling thought. *Could we be wrong? Could Ajax be innocent?*

Could we be bullying a man who cut himself off from the world out of self-loathing? A man who had made a hideous mistake and lost everything? A man unable to forgive his own actions? Unwilling to trust himself outside the confines of the workplace or home?

There was no excuse for taking advantage of a child. But had anyone followed up on that? Talked to those involved in the arrest and prosecution? The babysitter would be in her thirties now. Had anyone talked to her?

I would ask Slidell in the morning.

Outside, the rain fell softly. Inside, the annex was dark and still.

My mind refused to clock out.

Over and over, I glanced at the time.

11:20.

12:10.

2:47.

My iPhone woke me from a sound sleep. The room was dim. The digits on the clock said 5:40.

Mama!

Heart banging, I clicked on.

My mother wasn't dead.

Hamet Ajax was.

34

Slidell picked me up with no more greeting than a sour glance. Which was fine.

He handed me a Styrofoam cup with a white plastic cover. The tepid contents bore some vague resemblance to coffee.

As we drove, the horizon bled from black into pearly pink. Trees and buildings took shape, and gray oozed into the spaces between.

The lighter it got, the worse Slidell looked. His lower face was dark with five o'clock shadow; the bags under his eyes were large enough to house small mammals. His outfit was a color-clashing, coffee-stained rumple that stank of cigarettes and sweat.

Slidell briefed me in a voice gravelly from too much smoking and too little sleep.

After collecting his car, Ajax had driven to the hospital. He'd committed to a double shift that day, a practice not out of character. Thirty minutes after arriving, he'd left. Definitely out of character.

Ajax had told his supervisor, Dr. Joan Cauthern, that he was a victim of police harassment. Said he hadn't been home all day and needed to shower and check his house. Assured Cauthern he'd be back by seven.

The surveillance team had followed Ajax from Mercy to Sunrise Court. He pulled into his garage at 5:22. Never left.

When Ajax failed to return as promised, Cauthern began phoning. Tried repeatedly throughout the night. By early morning, she'd grown concerned. Ajax had been perspiring heavily and acting fidgety, behaviors she'd never seen him exhibit. At four A.M., when the ER grew quiet, Cauthern went to his home to see if he was ill.

The surveillance team observed a vehicle pull into Ajax's driveway at 4:20 A.M. A woman got out and rang the bell. Dialed a cellphone. Rang again. Getting no response, the woman shifted to the garage. Appeared to listen with an ear to the door. Walked to the side and peered through a window. Ran toward the cruiser, waving her arms.

The officers approached. The woman appeared agitated. Gave her name as Joan Cauthern. Stated she was Ajax's superior at Mercy Hospital.

Cauthern said a car was running inside the garage. Said she feared Ajax was in it.

Hearing engine sounds, the officers forced open the door. Found an adult male unconscious behind the wheel of a Hyundai Sonata. Tried to resuscitate, but the victim failed to respond. Called for a bus. Called Slidell.

The ambulance was now gone, and the MCME van had taken its place. Larabee's car was there. The CSS truck. A cruiser with bubble lights flashing. A Lexus I assumed belonged to Cauthern. The garage door was up, the overheads on. Ditto every light in the house.

A gurney had been rolled up the drive. On it lay a black body bag, unzipped, ready. Beside it were the same CSS techs who'd worked the site less than twenty-four hours earlier. One held a video camera, the other a Nikon.

Slidell and I got out. The sky had morphed to a foggy gray. The color of Ajax's lonely rooms, I thought.

The air was cool and damp. The frost-coated lawn pulsed red and blue. As Slidell and I crossed it, my insides felt like a lump of granite.

Larabee stood in the space between the Hyundai and the garage wall. Beside him was Joe Hawkins, an investigator with the MCME. On the floor between them was the metal death scene kit. Hawkins was shooting pics.

The driver's door was open. Through it I could see Ajax slumped over the wheel, head twisted to the side, nasal mucus and saliva crusted on one cheek. His hands hung limp at his knees. A pair of tortoiseshell glasses lay on a mat by his feet. The macabre tableau brightened every time Hawkins's flash went off.

"Doc." Slidell's way of announcing our arrival.

Larabee turned, thermometer in one gloved hand. Hawkins kept snapping away. "Detective Slidell. Dr. Brennan. Gotta love a brisk winter dawn."

"What have we got?" Slidell opened his spiral.

"Probable carbon monoxide poisoning."

"The guy offed himself?"

"The first responders found no signs of forced entry in the house or garage. No note. I'm seeing minimal trauma."

"Minimal?"

"Abrasions on the forehead and right ear. Probably caused by the head impacting the wheel."

"Probably?"

"Possibly."

"Meaning suicide."

"I'll know after the autopsy."

Most carbon monoxide deaths are due to accident or suicide. A few are due to foul play. Larabee knew and was being guarded.

"The garage door was down when Cauthern arrived?" Slidell asked.

"So I'm told."

"The car hood wasn't raised, right?"

"Right."

"The vic have any grease on his hands?"

"No."

Slidell scanned the small space where we stood. "No tools lying around."

"I agree, Detective. This doesn't look like an accident."

"Time of death?"

"Based on body temp, I'd put it somewhere between twelve and two this morning. As usual, that's only a rough estimate."

"How long's it take?"

"Death by carbon monoxide poisoning?"

Slidell nodded.

"Not long."

Slidell frowned.

"It requires very little CO to produce lethal levels of carboxyhemoglobin in the body."

The frown continued.

To his credit, Larabee showed no impatience. But he kept it simple. Very simple. "Carboxyhemoglobin disrupts oxygen supply to the cells."

"Gimme a little more than that."

"Okay." Larabee did some editing. "Hemoglobin is a molecule found in the red blood cells. Its job is to circulate oxygen throughout the body. But hemoglobin has a strong affinity for carbon monoxide, CO. If both oxygen and carbon monoxide are present, hemoglobin is much more likely to bind with the CO. When that happens, you get carboxyhemoglobin, which can't do the job."

Larabee didn't go into the fact that hemoglobin has four binding sites to maximize the capture of oxygen from arterial blood flowing from the lungs and to expedite its release into the tissues and organs. That in the presence of both oxygen and carbon monoxide, hemoglobin is two to three hundred times more likely to bind with the latter. That this binding with CO inhibits the release of O_2 molecules found on the hemoglobin's other binding sites. That, as a result, even if blood concentrations of oxygen rise, the O_2 remains bound to the hemoglobin and isn't delivered to the cells. That, as a consequence of oxygen deprivation, the heart goes into tachycardia, increasing the risk of angina, arrhythmia, and pulmonary edema. The brain short-circuits.

That carbon monoxide is very bad shit.

"We're talking how much?" Slidell pressed.

"High blood levels of carboxyhemoglobin can result from air containing only small amounts of CO."

"You breathe the stuff."

"Yes."

I was sure Slidell knew the basics, that he'd worked similar cases in the past. I wondered at his uncharacteristic interest in the physiology of carbon monoxide poisoning.

My brain fired a series of stats on CO blood levels. Of symptoms of toxicity. Bizarre. A stored holdover from some long-ago grad school course. 1 to 3 percent: normal. 7 to 10 percent: normal in smokers. 10 to 20 percent: headache, poor concentration. 30 to 40 percent: severe headache, nausea, vomiting, faintness, lethargy, elevated pulse and breathing rates. 40 to 60 percent: disorientation, weakness, loss of coordination. 60 percent: coma and death.

Slidell sighed. "How 'bout a ballpark?"

"Of?" Larabee had squatted to inspect Ajax's hands.

"How long you last."

"Inhaling air with a carbon monoxide level as low as point two percent can produce carboxyhemoglobin levels exceeding sixty percent in just thirty to forty-five minutes."

"That'll kill ya?"

"That'll kill ya."

Slidell jotted, then gestured with the spiral. "And we got that here?"

"Engine running in an enclosed one-car garage. Door lowered. Windows shut. Definitely." Larabee spoke without looking up. "In as little as five to ten minutes."

"So Ajax was toast soon after he turned the key."

"Assuming he turned the key."

"Assuming that."

"And that he was breathing when he went into the car."

"And that."

"Which I suspect was the case. See this?" Larabee lifted one of Ajax's hands.

Slidell eyeballed it from where he was standing. "That blood-settling thing. Because the arms are hanging down."

"Yes. But I'm talking about the nail beds."

Slidell bent for a closer look. "They're bright pink."

"Yes again. Which suggests he was alive."

I pictured the cherry-red blood and organs Larabee would see when he made his Y incision. The slivers of liver, lung, stomach, kidney, heart, and spleen still cherry red when floating in formalin. Still cherry red when sliced into thin sections and placed on microscope slides.

"Remind me. When does the blood-settling thing start?"

"Livor. Within two hours of death. Peaks in six to eight." Larabee stood. "But it's cold out here. That would slow the process."

"The livor in the fingers. That says no one moved the body, right?"

"Yes."

"And he ain't in rigor." Slidell pronounced it "rigger."

"There's some stiffening in the smaller muscles of the face and neck. But that's it."

"Rigor starts when?"

"In roughly two hours. But low temperatures would slow that, too." Larabee stood. "I'll run a full tox screen."

"Looking for what?"

"Whatever he had in him. People often self-medicate before killing themselves."

"What's the story in the house?"

"According to the first responders, the bed was made, the TV and radio were off, there was a single coffee cup in the sink, clean and upside down."

"No note?"

"No note."

"Nothing to suggest a visitor."

"Not last I heard."

"I'm done with my prelim." Larabee turned to Hawkins. "Joe?"

Hawkins shot a couple more angles, the flash burning Ajax white-hot onto my retinas. Draped over the wheel, he looked like a man dozing, or drunk after a night on the town.

Slidell and I stepped outside. Hawkins positioned the gurney as close to the car as possible. Then he bent and grasped Ajax by the shoulders. Ajax slid free, lifeless and limp. Hawkins pinned the arms to his chest. Larabee caught the legs before the feet hit the ground. Together they transferred him to the body bag.

Flash recall. Maneuvering Pomerleau from her barrel in Vermont with Cheri Karras.

After collecting Ajax's glasses and placing them by his head, Hawkins zipped the bag. Then he rolled the gurney to the van, loaded it, and slammed the doors.

I watched the van disappear. Feeling cold inside and out.

"I want to see what this piece of dog shit's got in his trunk."

I turned. Slidell was pulling on gloves. After yanking the key from the ignition, he circled to the rear of the Hyundai and jammed it into the lock.

The trunk popped with a soft thunk.

An odor floated out. Sweet, acrid.

Familiar.

35

It was our worst nightmare.

And Ryan's big bang.

Jaw clamped, Slidell lifted a Ziploc from a cardboard box holding other Ziplocs and a small plastic tub.

Through the clear side of the bag, I could make out four things. A silver seashell ring. A key on a red cord. A yellow ribbon. A pink ballet slipper.

We all stared. Dejected. Appalled. Angry.

"Whose ribbon?" My voice sounded high and taut.

"It don't matter. This nails the sonofabitch."

Slidell laid down the bag and chose another. It contained vials filled with a dark liquid that looked like blood. A third held hypodermic needles. A fourth had cotton-tipped swabs, a fifth wadded-up tissues.

"What's in the tub?" Larabee asked.

Slidell pried off the lid. A noxious odor slapped our nostrils.

"Bloody hell." Slidell's head jerked sideways.

"Let me see," I said.

Slidell extended his arm. Have at it.

Larabee's breath caught. I think mine did, too.

I saw pale hair floating in muddy brown soup. An unrecognizable mass below.

"It's some kinda body part, right?"

No one had an answer to that.

"Another souvenir?"

Or to that.

"You believing this? All the time the bastard's stonewalling us, he's driving around with this freak show in his car." To Larabee. "Take the body parts. I'll send the rest to the lab."

Larabee nodded.

Yanking off a glove with his teeth, Slidell stormed over to the CSS techs. I couldn't hear his instructions but knew what they were. Bag and tag everything, impound the car, burn the house down looking for more.

As Larabee sealed the plastic tub into an evidence bag, the techs pulled rolls of yellow tape from their truck and began securing the scene. Slidell hurried to his car and threw himself in.

I watched him gun up the street, mobile mashed to one ear.

Larabee decided to examine the tub first. He didn't really need me, still asked that I assist. Said if there was anything requiring an anthropology consult, I could proceed with that while he autopsied Ajax.

I agreed willingly. I was jittery and on edge. Knew the annex would feel cramped and claustrophobic, peopled with the ghosts of five dead girls. Maybe six.

Besides, I had no ride home.

We were at the MCME by eight. After changing into scrubs, I met Larabee in the stinky room. Hawkins was busy doing prelims on Ajax, so we'd decided to proceed unassisted.

As I readied the camera, Larabee set the tub on the counter. I asked the case number, prepared labels, and shot pics. When I set the Nikon aside, Larabee gloved and raised his mask. I did the same. He opened the tub. Same stench. Same hair and shit-brown slop.

I took more photos, then, using a fine mesh strainer, Larabee poured the liquid off into a beaker. Unfolded and spread a green towel in the sink.

When he tipped the strainer, a glob dropped onto the cloth, spongy and slick and covered with hair.

Larabee used a probe to uncurl and lay the glob flat. It was thin in cross section, oval, approximately one inch wide by two inches long.

Larabee tested the glob with a probe. Lifted its tangle of hair.

My mind flashed a series of images. I saw flesh the color of curdled milk. Darkness at the end of each pale strand.

I felt a pang of nausea. Swallowed. "It's scalp."

"Human?" Larabee bent closer. "Could be."

"Not could be." Forcing my voice even. "It is."

Larabee's gaze cut to me. Without a word, he got the handheld magnifier, positioned it, and bent close. "I see what you mean. The hair is bleached."

"It's from Anique Pomerleau."

"You're kidding." Twisting to face me.

"I assisted at the Pomerleau autopsy."

"In Burlington."

I nodded. "Pomerleau had three scalp lesions we couldn't explain."

"Areas of necrosis?"

I shook my head. "The tissue was gone right down to the skull. Each lesion was oval and measured roughly one inch by two."

Above our masks, our eyes held. Larabee's showed bewilderment. Mine undoubtedly showed revulsion.

"What are you saying?"

"I'm saying the killer took"—I struggled for the right word—"specimens from Pomerleau and placed them on his victims."

"The hair in Leal and Estrada's throats?"

I nodded.

"The vials. Christ, he also took blood? Maybe used the Q-tips as swabs to get DNA?"

"I think it's possible."

"Why?"

"I don't know."

Larabee's brows drew together. He started to speak.

At that moment Hawkins's head popped through the door. "Ready," he said quietly.

"Be right there," Larabee said.

A long minute passed.

"Ajax was a doctor. He'd have the skill to draw blood. To incise tissue."

"Yes," I agreed.

"If the liquid in those vials tests positive as human blood, serology should fire it through for DNA sequencing."

"I'll phone Slidell," I said.

"Thanks."

Stripping his mask and gloves, Larabee hurried from the room.

After shooting a final series of photos, I repackaged the slice of scalp and placed it in the cooler. Then I went to my office.

Maybe it was fatigue. Maybe distraction. Slidell showed no reaction to my news. Just asked that I phone when Larabee finished the autopsy. He was at Mercy, talking to Ajax's co-workers.

At three-thirty Larabee came into my office. His scrubs were dark at the underarms and stained with blood. Spatter on one sleeve reminded me of the electric icicles framing my neighbor's front door.

I set aside my report and assumed a listening pose. The boss liked to share detail.

Larabee found no fluid or adhesions in the pleural cavities, no congestion or hemorrhage in the lungs, no infarction in the heart, no ulcer in the stomach, no fibrosis in the liver, no thromboembolism, no varices in the arterial, venous, or lymphatic systems.

Except for minor arteriosclerosis, normal in a man of forty-eight years, Hamet Ajax was in good health. He hadn't eaten all day. Had only coffee in his stomach.

Larabee had observed the telltale cherry-red blood and musculature, as well as marked hyperemia, or blood engorgement, in all tissues. He'd noted hyperemia, edema, and diffuse punctate hemorrhages throughout the cerebral hemispheres of the brain, widespread degeneration of the cortical and nuclear ganglion cells, and symmetric degeneration of the basal ganglia, particularly the nuclei.

"Asphyxia by acute carbon monoxide poisoning."

"Manner?" I asked.

"Tougher call."

"Any hints at something other than suicide?"

"Not really. But I'll wait for tox results before signing it out. I also want to know what they find in that house.

"And now." His elbows winged out as he pushed to his feet, one palm on each knee. "I have a Christmas party to attend."

"Holiday."

"What?"

"Can't forget Hanukkah."

"And Kwanzaa."

With that he was gone.

I passed none of the minutiae on to Slidell. Simply reported that Ajax's death was confirmed as due to carbon monoxide poisoning. And that Larabee would know more when he received toxicology results.

I also called Ryan. As I laid it all out, I could picture him running a hand through his hair.

"So Slidell thinks the souvenirs nail the coffin on Leal, Gower, and Nance. And possession of Pomerleau's DNA ties in Estrada," he said.

"He wasn't chatty, but I'm sure that's his thinking."

"Skinny should be decking the halls. Four solves and bye-bye, Tinker."

"He sounded exhausted."

"What about the others?"

"I don't know."

"It sucks that Slidell can't question Ajax," he observed.

"It does."

"Stand down on my end?"

"I guess so."

"I was out of road anyway."

A long stretch of silence.

"Merry Christmas, Brennan."

"Merry Christmas, Ryan."

I hung up and sat a moment, hand still on the phone. I should have felt pleased. Relieved. Why didn't I?

The others. Koseluk. Donovan. Would they remain open MP cases? Would active investigations continue?

Was someone somewhere searching for the child whose skeleton lay on my shelf?

Annually, over eight hundred thousand people vanish in the United States. At least four years had passed since ME107-10 died. Three since Avery Koseluk went missing. I knew the sad answer.

But Ajax was wearing a tag on his toe. The madness was over.

My eyes drifted to a flyer tacked to my corkboard. Larabee's comment reminded me. I also had invitations.

The UNCC anthropology department's holiday gathering was scheduled that night. Often the venue was a zillion miles out in the country. This year it would take place at a faculty home in Plaza-Midwood. Not far from the annex.

Still, I wasn't in the mood. Rarely am. Hot crowded rooms. Bad sweaters. Merrymakers rosy with eggnog and yuletide beer. It's not the drinking. I've learned to live without alcohol. Small talk over canapés just isn't my strong suit.

Nevertheless, I like my colleagues. Most of the grad students.

I bought a bottle of pinot, put on a red silk blouse, and headed out for some holly jolly.

I should have been ready to party. We finally had our killer. No motive. No explanation how Ajax hooked up with Pomerleau. Why or how he killed her. Why he continued to follow her playbook. Those answers would come later. What mattered was that he'd never strike again.

Still, troubling questions kept me distracted.

I thought of Ryan's words. Had Ajax wanted to be caught? Then why the lawyer? Why the innocent act when finally reeled in?

That one was easy. Ajax was a sociopath. Sociopaths lie. And they do it well.

I recalled the interviews. Ajax had expressed no sympathy for the murdered girls. For a child he had treated.

Ajax killed himself. If he was planning suicide, why promise Cauthern he'd return to the hospital? Had the decision been spur-of-the-moment? Triggered by what?

Ajax was ten miles away when Leal was abducted. How could he be in two places at once? Did he have an accomplice?

When I look back on that Christmas, on those cases, I always remember the moment we opened that trunk. The quavery fluorescents carving our features. The lights strobing blue and red in the cold dawn air. The overnight frost yielding to the warmth of sunlight.

I always wonder—had I voiced my concerns then, might things have gone differently?

I'll never know. I said nothing.

Part III

36

The holidays came and went.

I drove often to Heatherhill Farm. Goose was omnipresent, fluffing Mama's pillows, brushing her hair, setting out clothes and insisting she wear them.

Harry flew in from Texas.

For three days we stayed at a B&B near Marion, the same one where Goose had taken up residence. Our rooms featured four-posters and chintz gone wild.

Harry bought Mama a stuffed zombie doll designed to be pulled apart and disemboweled to vent frustration. And a four-thousand-carat diamond brooch. I got her a cashmere poncho.

Being the center of attention perked Mama up. She twittered about Christmases past. The ones at the beach. The one in Grand Cayman. No mention of the ones she spent in the underworld solo in her room. Or gone.

When we were alone, Mama asked about my cases. I

shared the whole story. Pomerleau, the Corneau farm, the barrel of maple syrup, the horror in Ajax's trunk. I figured the outcome would appeal to her sense of justice.

Mama asked about Ryan's contribution to the tale. I figured that in her mind, we were Orpheus and Eurydice. Maybe Scully and Mulder.

I told her Ryan had spent most of his time searching for Pomerleau's sole surviving victim. She asked where the poor thing was. I said he hadn't found her. She was intrigued, wouldn't let up on the subject until Goose arrived to bully her into a bath.

The boards at the LEC came down. The photos, maps, interview summaries, and reports were packed back into their respective boxes. The conference room reverted to its intended purpose.

Tinker faded off. Rodas disengaged. Barrow moved on to other cold cases.

Slidell went incommunicado. I hadn't a clue what he was doing. Made no effort to learn.

The CMPD held a press conference. Broadcasters went fluently doleful. Headlines howled. Reports told of Ajax's arrest in Oklahoma, of "evidence in his possession linking him to the murders of Shelly Leal, Lizzie Nance, and others," of his death on Sunrise Court. Slidell stayed away. Tinker did humble while deftly exaggerating his role and that of the SBI. I had to agree with Slidell. The guy was an unctuous little prick.

Ryan and I talked often. Almost like old times. Almost. He was back on the job, working as a floater as before, adding his expertise to investigations as needed.

Friday morning, the second day of the New Year, Larabee received the toxicology report. Ajax had a blood carbon monoxide saturation of 68 percent. A level that kills you deader than shit.

Ajax also had chloral hydrate in his system, which showed up only when Larabee requested a second test expanding beyond the opiates, amphetamines, barbiturates, alcohol, and other substances on standard tox screens. Though the drug was a somewhat antiquated choice, in Larabee's opinion, it wasn't significant. As he'd said at the scene, a lot of folks need pharmaceuticals to pull the plug.

There was no record of chloral hydrate withdrawal at the Mercy dispensary, no prescription at any Charlotte pharmacy. Not a big deal. As a physician, Ajax would have had easy access to the drug, often used as a sedative prior to EEG procedures.

More troubling was the fact that no empty pill bottle turned up at the house on Sunrise Court or on Ajax's person. CSS found the kitchen trash container empty, unlike other cans on the premises. A Hefty in the curbside rollout produced nothing that might have held the capsules.

The big shocker came the following Monday.

Larabee caught me in the biovestibule, paper in his hand, puzzled expression on his face.

Kathy Reichs

"Post-holiday credit card bill?" Unwrapping a scarf from my neck.

Larabee thrust the paper at me. I shifted my briefcase and took it.

A quick skim, then the line that mattered. I understood why Larabee hadn't laughed at my joke. "You're kidding."

"I wish."

"The DNA from the lip print isn't a match for Ajax."

Larabee shook his head solemnly.

"Any possibility the jacket was contaminated?"

"They say no way."

"And the samples you sent over were good?"

Larabee just looked at me.

"I saw lip balm in Ajax's medicine cabinet. Maybe—"

"CSS collected it. The lab ran it as a cross test. In case some defense attorney found an expert to say the stuff scrambled the DNA sequencing, or some other junk-science hogwash."

"What about the lip balm itself?"

"Not the same brand."

"So, wait." My mind was struggling to reconstruct the picture we'd so carefully crafted. "Ajax might not be our guy?"

Larabee shrugged with upturned palms. Who knows?

"But he had Leal's ring."

"Nance's shoes. Gower's key."

"What about the blood in Ajax's trunk? The scalp?"

"That's taking longer."

"Have you talked to Slidell?"

"He's on his way over."

An hour passed before Slidell's heels clicked like bullets outside my door. Voices floated from Larabee's office, modulated, no ire or outrage. Ten minutes later, Skinny blustered into my office.

The change was subtle but there. Same ratty brown jacket. Same bad haircut. What?

Slidell ankle-hooked and dragged a chair toward my desk, dropped onto it. When his legs shot forward, I saw a flash of tangerine sock. Some things are permanently set.

"You heard?"

"I did."

Then it struck me. Slidell had lost weight. His face was still saggy, maybe more so than usual. But his belly wasn't hanging as far over his belt. The mustard-yellow shirt was fully tucked.

Slidell's next statement stunned me. "Some shit don't add up."

"What are you saying?"

Slidell's jaw muscles flexed energetically.

"You have doubts about Ajax?"

"He was on Pineville-Matthews Road when Leal was grabbed up on Morningside."

"Yes."

A ten-second pause.

"IT put a name to the user in that chat room for cramps."

"HamLover."

"Yeah. Mona Spleen. Forty-three, lives in Pocatello, Idaho. Belongs to the Pocatello ARC. That stands for Amateur Radio Club."

"Spleen is into ham radios."

"Big-time."

Another, longer pause.

"April 17, 2009. Two-twenty P.M. Ajax got pulled for doing sixty-eight in a fifty-five."

"The afternoon Lizzie Nance disappeared. That doesn't mean—"

"The stop was on I-64, outside Charleston, West Virginia."

"You're just now learning this?"

"I ain't a magician. People been busy tying bows and stuffing socks."

"The ticket gives Ajax an airtight alibi. Why didn't he mention it?"

"The trooper let him off with a warning. No fine, no court. Ajax probably forgot all about it."

"Forgot the trip?"

"The date coincides with his start at Mercy. He maybe had a lot on his mind."

I said nothing.

After another long pause, Slidell said, "I did some follow-up on the kid in Oklahoma."

"The babysitter Ajax molested?"

"Yeah." Repositioning his tie down the middle of his chest. It was black and spotted with something shiny. "The lady's got a jacket going back to juvie."

I kept my face expressionless.

"Three bumps for solicitation since 2006. Off the record, my source says her first pop was the year after Ajax went into the box."

"That may or may not be meaningful."

"Eeyuh."

"So what are you thinking?"

"Maybe the dirtbag ain't our guy."

"Have you shared any of this with Salter?"

Slidell gave a tight shake of his head.

"Why?"

"I'm still working it."

"Doing what?"

"For one thing, taking a hard look at this fuckwad Yoder."

"The CNA at Mercy?"

Slidell nodded.

"Any reason?"

"I don't like the guy."

"That's it?"

"No, that ain't it." Curt. "While you've been caroling and hanging mistletoe, I've been moving back in on the neighbors, the other hospital staff."

"Meaning?"

"Heart-to-hearts all around."

"And?"

"And nothing. The guy lived under a rock."

"Now what?"

"I'm hitting the ones weren't around. Over the river and through the woods. Ho-ho. Pain in the ass."

"Aren't you the Grinch."

"I practice."

"When you've finished the interviews, you'll take it to Salter?"

"Yeah."

"What about Tinker?"

"I'll see that yank-off in hell before I bring him back in."

"Who's on your list?"

"Couple nurses, a doc, a CNA. Probably a waste of time. But could be someone picked up on something."

I looked at the clock. At my stack of unwritten reports. "Let's go." Pulling my purse from the drawer.

Slidell took a breath, caught himself. Nodded and stood.

We got lucky with one RN and the physician. They were day shift.

Both said they'd been stunned by the news reports on Hamet Ajax. Both had worked with him and felt he was a fine doctor. Both expressed sadness at his passing. Neither knew a thing about Ajax's personal life.

The other two were off that day. Alice Hamilton, a

CNA, and Arnie Saranella, an RN.

Slidell was particularly eager to talk to Hamilton. She'd been on duty when Colleen Donovan and Shelly Leal presented at the ER. And Ellis Yoder had hinted that Ajax and Hamilton were friendly.

Slidell had phoned Hamilton repeatedly. Left messages on her mobile, gotten no reply. It didn't predispose him to warm feelings toward the woman.

Hamilton lived on North Dotger, within spitting distance of Mercy Hospital. The street was winding and, in summer, overshaded by trees large enough to form a canopy blocking all sunlight.

Hamilton's wasn't one of the townhomes that had sprouted like toadstools after a rain, progeny of the yuppification of the Elizabeth neighborhood. Her apartment was in an uninspired brick bunker dating to the postwar era. One of four such bunkers, all painted beige in an unsuccessful attempt to discourage algae growth.

On their street sides, the bunkers had paired concrete patios surrounded by metal fences and protected by metal awnings, every one rusted and warped. Each patio was large enough to hold a chair, maybe two if your personal space requirements weren't demanding. Each was accessed by double glass doors gone milky with age. The units above had uncovered balconies. Same square footage. Same cloudy doors.

Slidell and I took the walk, mud-caked and, like the brick, exuberantly green with life, and entered a small lobby with a grimy black-and-white floor. Four mailboxes formed a square on the wall to the left.

Overflow mail lay on the tile, mostly flyers and ads, a few magazines. *Good Housekeeping. O. Car and Driver.*

A. Hamilton was on the box marked 1C. Penned by hand and slipped behind a tiny rectangle of cracked glass.

Slidell pressed the bell. Waited. Pressed again.

No buzz. No voice from the little round speaker.

"Goddammit." Slidell pressed harder, jabbing repeatedly with his thumb.

While waiting, I scanned labels at my feet. The automotive magazine was for Roger Collier, Oprah's monthly for Hamilton. The housekeeping tips were going to Melody Keller.

Slidell rang a fourth time, his anger so palpable that I felt it elbow my ribs.

"Don't have a heart attack," I said.

"Why don't she answer?"

"Maybe she's not home?"

Slidell stared at the mailboxes, narrow-eyed and tight-mouthed.

"What did her supervisor say?"

"She's on some kinda arrangement she don't have to work regular."

"PRN. *Pro re nata.* It's a common arrangement in hospitals. Means the employee's schedule changes a lot and hours aren't guaranteed."

"Whatever."

"Let's move on. Talk to the other nurse."

"Pisses me off Alice goddamn Hamilton don't call me back."

Slidell was on his fifth round of jabbing when my iPhone vibrated in my jacket pocket. I answered.

Larabee had DNA results on the materials from Ajax's trunk.

37

"It was Pomerleau. The blood, the scalp."

"I knew it."

"Some of the Kleenex had saliva."

"Pomerleau?"

"Yes."

My pulse threw in a few extra beats.

"What are you thinking?" Larabee asked when I didn't reply.

"The killer seeded the bodies."

"That's my take."

"With Gower and Nance, he put saliva on tissue and left it in the child's hand."

"But that's iffy. What if it rains? What if the tissue blows away? Animals drag it off?" Larabee was right there with me. "He had to get more sophisticated."

I closed my eyes. Saw a syrupy corpse on a stainless steel table.

"Pomerleau had punctures on her inner elbows," I

said. "The ME in Vermont thought they looked wrong for needle drugs. So did I. And Pomerleau's tox screen came back clean."

"Ajax drew her blood and stored it in vials."

"Or she gave it to him."

"I doubt she gave him hunks of her head."

I spent a moment grinding that down.

"He's smart," I said. "Knows shaft isn't good enough. That root is needed to sequence nuclear DNA."

"You think he scalped her when he killed her?"

"Yes."

A pause. Metal rattled in the background. I figured Larabee was in an autopsy room.

"The killer created a larder." I was thinking out loud. "Hair. Blood. Saliva."

"Probably kept the stuff in a freezer."

"But why go to all that trouble?"

"To deflect suspicion away from himself? In case he got caught?"

"Maybe. Or maybe it was part of the game."

"Which he continued to play after stuffing Pomerleau into a barrel. That happened when?"

"Probably 2009," I said.

"When the action moved here."

An incoming text landed on my phone. "I've got to go."

"Can you tell Slidell?"

"I'm with him now."

I heard a catch in Larabee's breathing. Then, "You're saying killer. Not Ajax. Is that Slidell's thinking?"

I pressed the phone hard to my ear, guilt already gripping my gut. "Yes."

"I thought he'd take my face off this morning when I gave him the news. He didn't. Just sat there."

"He already had doubts."

"Son of a biscuit."

"Something like that."

The text was from Mama. A link to a YouTube video. Seeing Slidell stomping my way, I decided it could wait.

As we drove to Saranella's condo in South End, I relayed Larabee's news. Slidell listened. Shook his head once.

Saranella wasn't home. His roommate, Grinder, had bad hair plugs and a fuck-you demeanor. After some attitude-adjustment tips from Slidell, Grinder shared that Arnie was in Hilton Head and would return the following Monday.

Back in the Taurus, I checked the time: 3:10.

Slidell was growing surly. So was I. We were accomplishing nothing. And the sense of guilt about Ajax was building inside me. Plus, I was starving.

I asked Slidell to drop me back at the MCME.

After easing free of Mrs. Flowers, I got a yogurt from my stash in the refrigerator and a granola bar from the drawer in my desk. Washed the feast down with a Diet Coke. All the food groups.

Then I called Ryan. Got voicemail.

Rodas. He answered. I told him about the DNA reports, the ticket, Ajax's babysitter's arrest record. He responded with more animation than Slidell. A lot more.

When I'd finished, he said, "I've been going over the Gower scene photos."

"At the Hardwick quarry."

"Yeah. Thought if Ajax was there, it would lock in one more piece."

"And?"

"Lots of gawkers but no doc."

"Back to square one?"

"Could be."

I disconnected, impressed. Umpie Rodas would never give up on Nellie Gower.

Ryan called as I was dropping the next-to-last report in my outbox. I briefed him. Then we wove through a maze of speculation similar to the one I'd traveled with Larabee. If not Ajax, who? How did the guy hook up with Pomerleau? Why? Why shift to Charlotte?

"Why plant Pomerleau's DNA on the victims?" Ryan asked after we'd both wound down. "Why not his own? They were a tag team until he killed her."

"Until *someone* killed her."

"Do you think Pomerleau was a willing donor?"

"I don't know."

"Or did the bastard keep her captive to harvest her body fluids?"

Kathy Reichs

I couldn't answer. The thought was too appalling. Even for a monster like Pomerleau.

"Was it simply because he had access to her?" Ryan was throwing theories at the wall to see if one stuck. "Or was Pomerleau specific to his pathology?"

"Not just any donor but Pomerleau personally?"

"Yes."

"In which case she could still be the key. The piece we're failing to understand."

"It's just an idea."

Another pause.

"Is Salter reopening the files?" Ryan asked.

"Slidell's buying himself time." Diplomatic.

"He hasn't told her."

"No."

"What's he doing?"

"Talking to people who knew Ajax. To Oklahoma. Taking a hard look at this nurse's assistant Ellis Yoder."

"Why?"

"Yoder was working on the dates Leal and Donovan went through the ER."

"What do you think?"

"He's got nothing else."

"Gonna be a lot of red faces at the CMPD."

"A lot," I agreed.

It was another takeout evening with Birdie.

We were eating Il Nido spaghetti and channel-surfing when my iPhone sang "Frosty the Snowman."

"Why'd he wash the cup?"

"What?" Slidell's question threw me. His calling at night threw me.

"Ajax. He's heading to the garage to off himself. Why bother with the cup?"

"He was a neat freak."

No reply.

"And he was zoned on chloral hydrate," I added. "People do funny things."

"I'm looking at the CSS photos. There's dirt on the floor inside the back door."

"A lot?"

"Not the point. Why's he clean the cup and the coffeemaker and leave the dirt?"

"He cleaned the coffeemaker?"

"And took out the trash. The grounds were in a plastic bag on top in the can outside."

"What are you saying?"

"I'm saying either a guy's neat or he ain't."

"Maybe he tracked in the dirt when he went to the garbage can, then didn't see it."

"Tracked it from where? The thing sits back-ass to the door."

I heard a series of soft *tick*s, probably photos hitting a blotter.

"Thread." *Tick. Tick.* "Snagged on the backyard hedge."

"What kind of thread?"

No answer.

Now it was the sound of pages turning.

"Purple." I wasn't sure Slidell was talking to me anymore. "Fiber guy says purple wool."

"Were the coffee grounds analyzed?"

More pages.

"Gotta go."

Dead air.

I tossed the phone on the couch. Got up. Began pacing in tight circles. Birdie's head swiveled as he followed my movement.

What was Slidell's purpose in calling? He was disturbed by some findings at the scene on Sunrise Court. Did he have doubts not only about Ajax's involvement in the murders but also about Ajax's own death? Did he suspect it was other than suicide?

Homicide?

We'd probably been wrong about Ajax. Was my crushing sense of guilt about his death unjustified? Had someone killed Ajax and staged it as a suicide?

Who? Why?

Jesus. The same questions I'd been asking myself for weeks.

My phone pinged an incoming text.

Mama.

Did you look at the YouTube video?

Viewing it now.

Right place?

I shifted to the message above. Clicked on the link. The video was titled: *Overland Riders of Northern*

Essex Community College. Spring Bike Hike 2008(3): Over the Passumpsic. The clip was twelve minutes long and had been viewed 18,927 times. Most liked it.

Interested in why the tape had caught Mama's attention, not in its content, I hit the little white triangle. Queen began singing "Bicycle Race." A frozen cyclist started pedaling, not furiously, but with strong, steady thrusts.

A rectangle appeared on the screen, outlined in scrolly white, like a dialogue box in an old silent movie. It framed the words: *Spring Bike Hike 2008.*

The camera zoomed out to show eight more cyclists, all in helmets, windbreakers, and knee-length black spandex shorts. They were moving single file along a two-lane highway. The action was wobbly, captured by a handlebar- or helmet-mounted camera at the rear of the pack.

Mama had never shown an interest in biking. I couldn't fathom why this video appealed to her.

The group passed a post office/general store combo: a gray building with an old red auto seat on the porch and a red plastic kayak affixed to the top of the front overhang.

Another text box announced: *Barnet, Vermont.*

I read the words on the side of the kayak. Suddenly sat straight up.

Pulse humming, I watched the cyclists cross a narrow river on a green metal bridge. Another text box. *Passumpsic River.*

Two minutes of pedaling through mixed hardwood and pine, then a bit of crude editing caught the group on the shoulder, laughing and pointing to a plank nailed to a tree above their heads. On it were four faded blue letters. *ORNE.* It was the weathered sign from the Corneau house.

ORNE. They liked the Corneau sign because what was left matched their club's acronym. Overland Riders of Northern Essex.

As the cause of their amusement registered, a car entered the frame from a driveway to the left of the sign. One silhouette at the wheel, no passenger.

The car lurched to a stop, and a door flew open. A figure shot out and strode toward the cyclists. The camera followed her, now handheld. I couldn't see a face, but body language said the driver was angry.

Another text box materialized. *Hostile Aboriginal!*

The figure turned toward the camera. Shouted and waved both arms.

I went cold to the marrow.

38

I replayed the scene again and again. Froze the image. Studied the features, the body shape, making sure. Hoping I was wrong.

I wasn't.

No point showing the video to Slidell. The face would mean nothing to him.

Not so with Ryan.

Fingers shaking, I sent the link north, then hit callback for the last incoming number. Slidell picked up after two rings.

"Tawny McGee was at the Corneau farm." Circling the room.

A moment of silence as Slidell ran the name through his mental Rolodex. "The kid Pomerleau had in her cellar?"

"Yes." I told him about the video.

"You're sure?"

"I'm sure."

"Jesus freakin' Christ. How'd you stumble onto that?"

"I'll tell you later." *After Mama explains it to me.*

"How does McGee fit in?"

"How the hell would I know?"

"Think she's the big dude the mechanic saw?"

"She's tall."

"Or maybe the big dude was Ajax and we got us a threesome?"

"Or maybe it was some other *dude.*" Churlish, but I didn't like feeling confused. "The DNA on Leal's jacket says our doer is male."

"I need to talk to McGee."

"You think?"

"Can you blow up that frame and print it?" Slidell asked.

"The face will be too blurry. But McGee's mother has a snapshot that's fairly recent. I'll get that."

"I'll put out a BOLO. Have Rodas do the same in Vermont."

"I have a feeling McGee's living under a different name. Ryan dug pretty deep, looking for her."

"How'd she get to Vermont?"

"I don't know. Maybe lean on Luther Dew over at ICE?" I was using the acronym for Immigration and Customs Enforcement.

Slidell snort-laughed. "The mummified-mutt guy?"

I'd helped Dew on a smuggled antiquities case involving Peruvian dogs. Slidell never tired of the canine-corpse jokes. I ignored this one.

"The video shows McGee at the Corneau farm in 2008. I'm not sure when passports became mandatory for travel between the U.S. and Canada. Or what kind of records they kept back then."

"I'll give it a shot first thing in the morning."

"Why wait?" My eyes bounced to the clock: 10:27.

"Good thinking. Calling now will make Dew want to knock himself out."

Three beeps. Slidell was gone.

Crap!

Who to phone first? Mama or Ryan?

Mama decided it. I answered her ring and jumped in before she could speak. "How did you find that video?"

"Sweetheart, good manners dictate a greeting when answering a call."

I drew a deep breath. "Hi, Mama. How are you?"

"I'm well, thank you."

"How did you discover the YouTube video?"

"Is it the farm where that terrible woman was hiding?"

"It is. How did you find it?"

"Oh, my. Do you want the full journey?"

"Just the process."

"It wasn't complicated. But it did require hours and hours of watching tasteless drivel. Some unkind fool actually posted a clip of a reporter having a stroke on-air. And—"

"But how did you find it?"

"There is no need to be brusque, Tempe." Disapproving sniff. "I Googled various combinations of key words, of course. Corneau. Vermont. Hardwick. St. Johnsbury. One link led to another and another. I plowed through endless news stories, viewed interminable images of maple trees and shopping malls and snow-covered campuses. Did you know the mascot for the University of Vermont is a catamount? That's a—"

"Big cat. Go on."

"Eventually, I landed on the second in a series of five YouTube videos documenting a college bicycle trip. St. Johnsbury appeared in the title.

"After watching that clip, which I must say was excruciatingly tedious, I moved on to the third. While I was observing the group posing on the shoulder of a road, my mind filled in the missing letters on the sign above their heads."

"How did you know about the Corneau farm?"

"You spoke of it when you were here." Surprised and mildly condescending. "The bridge. The Passumpsic River. The broken sign."

I remembered Mama's ceaseless questions, didn't recall going into so much detail.

"Is it helpful?"

"More than you can imagine, Mama. You are a virtuoso of the virtual. But I have to hang up now."

"Pour téléphoner, monsieur le détective?" Almost a purr. *"Oui."*

Ryan didn't answer. Which wasn't calming. I was amped. Wanted action. Answers. Resolution.

I tried reading. Couldn't focus. Knowing Ryan would call when he'd viewed the video, I gathered Birdie and went up to bed.

Hours passed. I lay there feeling wired, helpless. Asking myself what I could do. Coming up blank.

Around two, I finally drifted off. More sleep would have helped.

The next day the world spiraled into madness.

Ryan called at seven A.M. I'd been up for almost an hour. Eaten breakfast, fed the cat, read a proposal for a student project. I told him everything.

"McGee was driving a 2001 Chevy Impala," he said. "Tan. Not the F-150 parked in the shed."

"Could you read the plate?"

"No. But it was green, probably Vermont."

"Contact Rodas?"

"Already did. He's requested an enhancement. If that works, he'll run the registration through the DMV."

"Get Tawny's photo from Bernadette Kezerian. Scan it and email it to Rodas, Slidell, and me."

"Done. I'll also contact border control on this side, see if they have any record of McGee crossing into Vermont. Or back into Quebec."

We'd barely disconnected when Slidell showed up at my door. I offered him coffee. He accepted. We settled at the kitchen table. I briefed him on my conversation with Ryan.

"Dew says no can do."

"What do you mean, no can do?"

"As of January 23, 2007, you gotta have a passport to enter the U.S. from Canada."

"That's good. ICE keeps records—"

"You wanna let me finish?"

I settled back, having vowed to be more patient with Slidell.

"That's for airports. The reg didn't kick in for land and sea borders until June 1, 2009."

"Not likely she'd have flown such a short distance."

"No."

"Crap."

"Yeah. But I got this." He pulled a printout from an inside jacket pocket and flipped it onto the table.

I unfolded and read it. A tox report. I looked up, stunned by the implications. "They found chloral hydrate in the coffee grounds?"

"Yeah." He tipped his chin at the paper. "A boatload."

"Ajax was drugged?"

"Doubt he laced his own Joe."

"You think someone sedated him, then put him in the car?"

"Explains the washup on the cup and coffeemaker. The grounds being outside in the trash." Slidell thought a moment. "Kind of an odd choice, eh?"

"Chloral hydrate?"

"Yeah."

"It was found in the victims at Jonestown." I was referring to the 1978 poisoning of more than nine hundred people at the Peoples Temple in Guyana, a massacre orchestrated by a power-mad evangelist, Jim Jones. "Also in Anna Nicole Smith and Marilyn Monroe."

Slidell said nothing.

"Ajax died between midnight and two." My mind was spinning. "There was a cruiser parked at the curb all night. The surveillance team didn't see anyone enter or leave the house until Cauthern showed up at dawn."

"The Ajax property backs up to a walking trail behind Sunrise Court and a couple other dead-enders along that stretch. Whoever capped him probably parked on another cul-de-sac, took the path, then crossed the yard to the kitchen door."

"That could explain the fibers on the hedge. The dirt on the floor."

Our eyes exchanged the same questions. Who? Why?

"You taking it to Salter?" I asked.

"Soon."

I raised my brows in question.

"I want to go at this scumbag Yoder one more time."

"Why is he a scumbag?"

"There's something smells there."

"Not exactly an answer."

"We ask Yoder about Leal and Donovan, the next thing you know, Ajax is dead with a kit in his trunk."

Slidell looked at me a very long moment. "What's your gut? We looking at the same doer?"

"The girls and Ajax?"

Slidell nodded.

"My gut says yes."

"Sonofafriggin' bitch. And we got squat."

"We know our killer is male."

Slidell stared into his cup as if the answer were floating in his coffee. I'd never seen him so discouraged. "Think the guy's a sexual sadist?"

"None of the victims was sexually assaulted." I'd chewed on this a lot. "I think his arousal comes from control, from the ability to manipulate."

"Us or his vics?"

I hadn't looked at it that way. "Both. He's definitely toying with us."

Slidell rose. I walked him to the door.

"How's he do it?" As he stepped outside.

"Do what?"

"Move under the radar and leave us nothing."

I was in the study checking email when the phone rang again. I glanced at the caller ID. *S. Marcus.* Not recognizing the name, I let the call roll to voicemail. Seconds later, I heard the voice of my little catsitter friend, Mary Louise, on the answering machine. She wanted to visit after school. Had something for me.

Sorry, sweetie. Not today. Adding my guilt over Mary Louise to my guilt over Ajax, I turned back to the computer.

Ryan's email attachment had opened. Tawny McGee looked at me from the deck of a boat, breeze lifting her collar and tossing her hair.

"Why?" I whispered. "Why did you go to Pomerleau?"

McGee continued to gaze straight ahead with her empty, still eyes. She was tall and full-breasted. But she didn't flaunt what a lot of women paid big bucks to have. She downplayed it with a modest turtleneck.

I recalled the odd dynamic between the Kezerians. Bernadette's comments. Jake's.

Tawny hated being photographed. Hated being seen naked. Never dated or felt comfortable around men or boys.

Bernadette said her daughter had body-image issues. Jake said she was nuts.

I studied the long limbs, the double-D's, the expressionless face. Wondered what was going on behind the vacant eyes.

From nowhere, another conversation winged into my consciousness.

Ryan's report on Lindahl. He'd said the therapist had hinted that something was off.

As I stared at the woman on my screen, an idea slowly shaped up in my brain. An improbable possibility.

Heart hammering, I reached for the phone.

39

After a grilling, then a brief wait, "Pamela Lindahl."

"My name is Temperance Brennan. We met some years back."

"You work at the medico-legal lab here in Montreal."

"Yes."

"Yet you are calling from North Carolina. The receptionist said you were quite insistent."

"The matter is urgent."

"Go on." With the wariness of a snitch in witness protection.

"It's about Tawny McGee."

"I suspected as much." Sighing. "I will tell you what I told the detective. To discuss a patient without his or her permission would be a serious breach of professional ethics."

No dancing around. No appealing to her sense of justice or fairness. I put one straight in her gut. "Tawny hooked up with Anique Pomerleau."

"I don't understand."

"Yes," I said, "you do. And I don't have time to play games."

"What is it you want?"

"Tawny has androgen insensitivity syndrome, doesn't she?"

No reply.

"The lack of menses at puberty. The height, the large breasts, the abundant head hair."

"You seem confident in your diagnosis. Why call me?"

"I need verification."

"I'm sorry but—"

I fired another zinger. "Tawny may have killed Pomerleau. She may be murdering children."

A deafening quiet came down from Montreal.

"Young girls. Four so far. Maybe six."

"Where?"

"Does that matter?"

"No."

"Well?"

"Her medical status, which I am not confirming, would be relevant for what reason?"

"DNA was recovered from one victim, a fourteen-year-old girl. Amelogenin testing indicated it was left by a male. That finding has pointed the search for her killer in what I now suspect is the wrong direction." I didn't complicate the discussion by mentioning Pomerleau's DNA.

"How does this involve me?"

"I think you know."

"One moment."

I heard movement, guessed Lindahl was closing a door.

"Tawny came to me following an unimaginable ordeal, as you know. I cannot divulge details of our conversations, but five years in that basement left her terribly damaged."

"Fine." For now.

"We dealt with her immediate issues first. As I gained her trust, Tawny opened up, eventually talked of concerns about her body."

Lindahl paused to collect her thoughts. Or to devise a strategy for revealing only what was essential. "Tawny had never menstruated, never grown underarm or pubic hair. The doctors told her it was due to a combination of poor diet and constant stress. Advised that, with time, she would catch up.

"In many ways, she did. Tawny grew tall, grew busty, but other changes never took place. At my suggestion, she agreed to be tested. If I chose the doctor and accompanied her. Which I did." Pause. "What do you know about androgen insensitivity syndrome?"

"The basics. It's a condition that impacts sexual development both prenatally and at puberty. Persons with AIS can't respond to androgens, male sex hormones. I'm sketchy on the underlying genetics."

I regretted the last as soon as the words left my

mouth. I didn't want a lecture. Was anxious to establish only one thing.

"Androgen insensitivity syndrome is caused by mutations in the AR gene, which encodes for proteins called androgen receptors. Androgen receptors allow cells to respond to hormones that direct male sexual development."

"Testosterone." No matter my preference, the lecture was coming down. I wanted to hurry it along.

"And others. Androgens and their receptors function in both males and females. Mutations in the AR gene prevent the androgen receptors from working properly. Depending on the body's level of insensitivity, an affected person's sex characteristics can vary from mostly female to mostly male."

I tapped my nails on the desktop, impatient to get what I needed. To confirm what was keeping my pulse in the stratosphere.

"AIS patients present across a spectrum of severity. Complete androgen insensitivity syndrome, or CAIS, refers to the body's total inability to use androgens. CAIS individuals have the external sex characteristics of a female but abnormally shallow vaginas and sparse or absent pubic and axillary hair. Such individuals lack a uterus, fallopian tubes, and ovaries, and have undescended testes in the abdomen."

"They can't menstruate or become pregnant."

"Correct. A milder form of the syndrome, PAIS, results when the body's tissues are partially sensitive to the effects of androgens. Persons with PAIS—also called Reifenstein syndrome—have normal male or female form, virilized genitalia or a micropenis, internal testes, and sparse to normal androgenic hair."

"With both CAIS and PAIS, the karyotype is 46,XY?" I shot to the core.

"Yes. Though outwardly female, these individuals are genetically male."

"And Tawny McGee?"

"Tawny has complete androgen insensitivity syndrome."

"Meaning she has one X and one Y chromosome in every cell in her body."

"Yes."

My fingers froze. "Who ran the genetic tests on Tawny?"

"A colleague who specializes in such disorders."

"He sequenced her DNA? Has biological samples?"

"To access anything in his possession would require a warrant."

"Of course. May I have the doctor's name?"

She gave it to me. I wrote it down.

"One last question. How did Tawny feel about Anique Pomerleau?"

"Do you really need to ask?" I heard something hard and sad in her voice.

"Thank you, Dr. Lindahl. You've been enormously helpful."

"I can send literature on CAIS if you'd like."

"Thank you."

A hitch in breathing. Then, "Will she be all right?"

I took a moment before responding.

"I don't know," I said softly.

After breaking the connection, I hit another button.

"Yo." Slidell was somewhere with a lot going on around him.

"The killer could be McGee."

"The spit says she's out."

"McGee has a condition that makes her body female, though her genes are male." As complex as Slidell could handle.

Or more so. There was a very long moment of silence.

"Whoa, Doc. You talk bones, what you say always tracks. But this, I don't know."

"What do you mean?" Had Slidell paid me a compliment?

"Bones never lie. But this. This is fucked up."

"Look, it all fits. McGee would know the dates of the Montreal abductions. She loathes Pomerleau, yet was with her at the Corneau farm. She's tall and matches the description of the mechanic."

"Why target kids?"

"Sweet mother of God! Forget the psychoanalysis and find her!"

"You dealt with McGee. Got any thoughts what name she might be using?"

Kathy Reichs

I started to say no. Stopped. "Pomerleau called herself Q. Called McGee D."

"Why?"

"Because she was crazy!" Way too sharp. "Q stood for queen. As in Queen of Hearts. D, I can't remember." I heard a robotic voice page a doctor. "Are you at Mercy?"

"I'm going back at Yoder."

"Forget Yoder. Look for McGee."

Slidell did that noncommittal thing he does in his throat.

"I'm serious. Find her."

"Probable alias. No known addresses. No credit card purchases to check. No bank account. No mobile phone or landline. No highway pass. No social security or tax payments. No paper or cyber trail at all. She might as well be Alice down the fucking rabbit hole."

"You're a detective. Do some detecting."

I disconnected and hit another speed-dial key.

"Ryan."

I told him what I'd learned from Slidell. From Lindahl. My theory about McGee.

"CAIS squares with the Y-STR finding?"

"Yes. And the physician who tested Tawny has her DNA on file." I gave him the name.

"I'll push for a warrant."

"Any progress on the license plate?"

"Not yet."

"Let me know if anything pops."

Hours passed. I paid bills. Took down the tree and decorations. Finished another goddamn report. Repeatedly checked both phones. Of course they were working.

I called Larabee. Mama. Harry.

No one called me.

Birdie spent the day napping or with his red plaid mouse.

I couldn't sit still. Couldn't concentrate. When I got up to move, I didn't know what to do with my arms and legs. Where to look. I glanced at my watch every few minutes.

And the itch was back. The sensation that I was missing something. That my id knew a fact I wasn't receiving yet.

I returned to the files. The bloody, unyielding files. Surely somewhere in that forest of paper, an answer lurked. Proof I was right. Proof I was wrong.

At four, I went to the kitchen for Oreos and milk. Comfort food. When my eye fell on the phone, a tentacle of guilt slipped free about the call I'd had earlier from Mary Louise.

Why not. Throwing on a jacket and scarf, I pocketed my mobile and headed out.

Dark cobalt clouds were skidding across the sky. The air was warm but listless and heavy with moisture. Rain was on the way.

Mary Louise lived only a block up Queens. Her mother answered the door wearing cinnamon sweats that looked cashmere. Her hair was brown, swept up on her head, and secured with a turquoise and silver clip. I introduced myself. She did the same.

Yvonne Marcus could have made an orca feel small. I guessed her weight at close to three hundred pounds. Yet she was beautiful, with amber eyes and skin that had never laid claim to a pore.

"My husband and I appreciate your kindness toward our daughter. She adores your cat."

"And he loves her."

Peering past me, she warbled, "No one looks under the porch!"

I must have shown surprise.

"You think I've lost my mind." Throaty chuckle. "It's from a story Mary Louise loved when she was little. She'd hide, I'd call out, she'd pop up and run to a new hiding place. I know she's much too grown up for such games now." Again the chuckle. "But it's still our secret little thing."

"I came to see if Mary Louise wanted to go for frozen yogurt at Pinkberry."

"But she's with you."

"No." A tickle of unease. "She isn't."

"She said she'd be visiting you after school."

"She called, but I was unavailable today."

"No worries." Warm smile, but a note of uncertainty. "She'll turn up."

"You're sure?"

She shrugged as if to say, "My kid—what a scamp."

Retracing my steps, I pulled out my iPhone. No calls.

No messages on the landline at the annex.

What the hell?

At six I put a frozen pizza in the oven. Yvonne Marcus called as I was taking it out.

"Mary Louise still isn't home, and she's not answering her cell. I was wondering if she'd shown up at your place?"

"I haven't seen her. You've no idea where she might have gone?"

A pause. Too long.

"Mrs. Marcus?"

"Mary Louise and I had a little tiff this morning. Trivial, really. She wanted to wear her hair in this ridiculous upsweep, and I insisted she braid it as usual." The chuckle sounded less genuine than earlier. "Perhaps I just don't want my little girl to grow up."

"Has she done this before?" I glanced at the window. It was now full dark outside.

"The little imp *can* hold a grudge."

"I'm happy to look around Sharon Hall."

"If it's not too much bother. She often goes there to feed the birds."

"It's no bother." Actually, I was glad for the diversion.

One slice of pepperoni and cheese, then I set off. Though I walked the grounds and called out repeatedly, my efforts yielded no sign of Mary Louise.

I phoned the Marcus home. Yvonne thanked me, apologized again. Reassured me there was no need to worry.

And I was back to mute phones and the silence of the annex. To the obstinate dossiers.

To subtle taunting by my subconscious.

Screw the files. I stretched out on the couch in the study. Crossed my ankles. Closed my eyes. Cleared my mind.

What had happened? What had been said? What had I read? Seen? Done?

I allowed facts and images to percolate in my head. Names. Places. Dates.

The files. The conference room boards. Gower. Nance. Estrada. Koseluk. Donovan. Leal.

The old cases in Montreal. Bastien. Violette. McGee.

The more I struggled, the more the subliminal needle lay flat on the gauge.

The interview with the Violettes. With Sabine Pomerleau. With Tawny McGee's parents, Bernadette and Jake Kezerian.

Little blip there.

The photo. The realization that McGee had CAIS.

The conversation with Lindahl.

Blip.

McGee was our perp. Though devastating, I knew it in my soul.

Where was she? Who was she?

I thought of the interviews with Slidell.

Hamet Ajax.

Ellis Yoder.

My higher centers touched something in the murky depths.

What?

Alice Hamilton.

The needle blipped higher.

Come on. Come on.

A dingy apartment on North Dotger.

The needle lifted, dropped as the thing slipped away.

Crap. Crap. Crap.

From nowhere, a comment by Slidell. Alice down the rabbit hole.

A name printed on a magazine. Alice Hamilton.

A name scribbled in a journal in a cellar. Alice Kimberly Hamilton.

The needle fired up and slapped over to the right.

40

Same drill.

I called Slidell. Got rolled to voicemail. Swore. Left a message that I hoped would goose his ass.

I called Ryan. Actually got him. Explained my theory. Asked him to check the evidence log from the house on de Sébastopol. To confirm.

Then I waited. Paced. Was my epiphany due to frustration? To the power of suggestion? A groundless leap triggered by a rabbit-hole quip?

No. I felt it in my soul.

When my cell finally rang, my whole body flinched. "Where the hell are you?" I barked.

A long moment.

"My cruiser." Low and husky.

My agitated brain took a moment to process. Hen Hull. The investigator on the Estrada case.

"Sorry. I was expecting someone else."

"I don't envy the dude."

I was too pumped to conjure a witty reply.

"Took some doing, but I finally located Maria Estrada," Hull said. "Tia's mother. She's in Juárez and has no phone. But there's a cousin living just outside Charlotte, in Rock Hill. I've got some free time, so I'm going there now."

"That's very generous."

"The kid got shafted every step of the way. The family deserves the story firsthand."

"You might want to hold off."

"Hold off?"

"We're thinking it wasn't Ajax."

"You're thinking?"

"It wasn't Ajax. And he didn't kill himself."

I gave an edited version of all that had happened. Felt a cold front coming my way from Wadesboro.

"Ajax's tox results didn't land on Larabee's desk until yesterday." Trying to justify leaving her out of the loop. "And I only talked to McGee's doctor today."

"Uh-huh."

"I should have kept you better informed."

"Yes." Pause. "You really believe McGee is capable of this?"

"The therapist didn't come right out and say it, but she implied that Tawny is very disturbed."

Like Slidell's, Hull's mind went straight to intent. Because homicide demands it. Unlike robbery or fraud, the motive for murder is often unclear.

"Why kill?" she asked.

"I don't know."

Brief pause before Hull spoke again.

"Maybe McGee gets her charge out of dropping Pomerleau again and again."

"If that's the fantasy, why pick young girls?" Quick glance at my watch. Ten minutes had crept by since last I checked.

"Or maybe she's symbolically killing herself. It's a guilt thing. She survived while Pomerleau's other victims died."

Though the same questions had tormented me, at that moment I had no desire to play Freud. I wanted verification. Action.

"Maybe—"

The line beeped to indicate an incoming call. "Hold on." Without waiting for Hull's consent, I clicked over. It was neither Ryan nor Slidell.

Any pretense at calm was now abandoned. "Mary Louise never came home. It's almost eight. Something has to be wrong. Oh my God! You see these things on the news, but oh my God!" Yvonne Marcus was frantic. "I've called everyone I can think of. Her teachers. Her friends. No one has seen her since school dismissal at three-thirty. My husband is out looking, but—"

"Mrs. Marcus—"

"What do I do? Shall I call the police?"

"Does Mary Louise ride a bus?"

"No, no. She attends Myers Park Traditional. It's right up the block, so I allow her to walk."

Directly past Sharon Hall.

I felt the tiny hairs rise on the back of my neck. Sensed my hand gripping the phone too tightly.

"I'm sure she's fine." Controlled. "But just to be safe, phone 911. I'll also make some calls."

"Oh my God!"

"It will be all right."

"I should go out and—"

"No. Stay home. Be there when Mary Louise returns."

As I reconnected with Hull, a terrible medley of images spewed from my neurons.

A gangly girl who loved fashion and hats.

Movement in the shadows of an enormous magnolia.

A photo of myself measuring a skull.

Why hadn't I picked up the phone? Why hadn't I returned the child's call? How could I have been so selfish?

"McGee may have taken another child."

"Are you serious?"

"Mary Louise Marcus left school four hours ago on foot. Still hasn't arrived at her house."

"The kid got any issues?"

"No."

"Not likely a runaway?"

"No."

"She fit the profile?"

"Yes." Fourteen. Fair. Long brown hair center-parted and braided.

I heard Hull suck in a long breath. Then, "If it is

McGee, you think she's taunting us? Snubbing her nose at authority?"

"I think this time it's personal." I swallowed. "And I think I know where she is."

A light drizzle was falling. I had the wipers on high. Not for the rain. To match the cadence of my heart.

I called Slidell. Rolled to voicemail. Of course.

Screw Slidell.

I called the MP division. Got a guy named Zoeller whom I'd heard was a dolt but didn't know personally.

"Yep. Yvonne Marcus. Called twenty minutes ago to report her daughter missing."

"And?"

"Who'd you say this is?"

I explained again.

"The two fought. The kid's probably catching a flick to teach Mama a lesson."

"I think this child could be in danger."

"Aren't they all."

"What did you just say?"

Faux-patient sigh. "The kid's only been out of pocket a few hours. There are regs. We follow every hunch, abuse the system, eventually, it loses its punch."

"I have an address I want you to check."

"Sure." Zoeller could have sounded more bored, but only after a pitcher of tranqs. "I'm outta here, but I'll pass it on."

"When can you activate an AMBER Alert?"

"When an abduction is confirmed and adequate descriptive information has been obtained." Rote.

"And you're starting the process now." Glacial.

"Look, it just came through we got a 10-91 with a 10-33."

A domestic disturbance with an officer down. Shit. Now I'd never get him to help me look for Mary Louise.

"I *will* call you back."

"I'll look forward to that." Zoeller disconnected.

I tried Barrow.

Salter.

Had the whole damn world gone AWOL?

As I barreled up Queens, my mind whirled in search of benign explanations for Mary Louise's nonappearance. Found dozens. All bullshit.

I continued through to Providence, cut right onto Laurel, and shot across Randolph. At Vail, I sat paralyzed, palms damp on the wheel. Left or right? Where? Where would she go?

A horn *brrp*ed behind me.

Dick that he was, Zoeller was correct on one point. A false tip could divert critical resources and personnel up a blind alley.

The horn again. Longer. Less polite.

Decision.

I turned left, fired north, circled the block, then winged into the drive leading to the Mercy ER.

Four blue and whites sat under the portico, angled like guppies at feeding time. Something looked off.

What? The careless parking? No. The cop shooting that Zoeller had mentioned. Of course they'd been abandoned in haste.

An ambulance sat with its back doors open. Two unmarked sedans. Vans from every TV station in town.

Officer down. Dead? The story would be on all channels at eleven, in all morning papers in skyscraper font. But before that, it would appear in cyberspace, attracting every assignment editor not yet clued in. The media would slather all night.

The CMPD would focus on avenging one of its own.

No one would give a rat's ass about my "hunch."

I looked around. Slidell's Taurus was nowhere in sight.

I was on my own.

I slammed the gearshift into park and killed the engine. Sprinted up the walk and through the doors, pulse running faster than my feet.

I expected chaos. EMTs shouting vitals. Doctors bellowing orders. Nurses scurrying for equipment or meds.

Not so. The scene was tense but subdued.

The usual supplicants occupied waiting room chairs. The bleeders, the coughers, the junkies, the drunks.

Uniformed officers stood talking in clumps. Men in dark jackets and loosened ties who I assumed were detectives. I knew none.

A few eyes tracked me as I hurried to the front desk, worried, hard with anger. I spoke to no one. Didn't interrupt their vigil.

When I posed my question, the woman looked up. Maybe surprised. Maybe annoyed. I couldn't tell. She wore glasses that covered half her face. Her name tag said *T. Santos*.

Knowing I had no authority, I flashed my MCME security card. Fast.

Santos bounced a glance off the photo, my features. She was about to speak when a man shuffled over reeking of BO and booze.

"Mr. Harker, you will have to wait your turn."

Harker coughed into a hankie that was stained and wet with phlegm.

Santos pointed Harker to the waiting room. Looked at me and jammed a thumb over her shoulder.

I hurried in the direction indicated, mind scrambling, eyes scanning. Hoping. Fearing. Could Mary Louise actually be here? Where Alice Hamilton claimed her prey? Outside in the backseat of a car? The trunk?

Please, God. No.

My flesh felt tight on my bones. On my lungs. I worked to keep my breathing even.

As out front, the treatment area was relatively calm. A patient sat in a wheelchair by a wall. A CNA went by with a cart, its rubber wheels humming on the tile. Somewhere out of sight, a phone rang.

Staff passed with X-rays, with trays of specimen tubes, with stethoscopes looped sideways around their necks. All in scrubs. All efficient. All indifferent to my presence.

The only crisis was occurring at a curtained cubicle, third in the right-hand row of curtained cubicles. A CMPD uniform stood guard outside. Sounds filtered through the white polyester: taut voices, the rattle of metal, the rhythmic beeping of a machine.

I felt sorrow for the person behind the partition. A man or woman gunned down while helping a distraught wife or girlfriend, maybe her kids. I said a silent prayer.

But I had to find Mary Louise's abductor. Or determine that I was wrong.

Feeling like a trespasser, I began parting fabric, searching for a face.

Behind the first curtain lay a child in a Spider-Man suit, forehead stitched and smeared with blood. A woman with mascara-streaked cheeks held tight to his hand.

Behind the second, a bare-chested man breathed oxygen through a clear plastic mask.

When I neared the third cubicle, the guard raised a palm. Behind him, a hastily positioned cart created a wedge-shaped opening into the enclosure.

As I veered left to cross to the other row, I glanced through the wedge.

Saw equipment. Bloody clothing. Masked doctors and nurses.

The patient on his gurney, face gray, lids closed and translucently blue.

I froze in place.

41

I stood paralyzed. Staring at Beau Tinker.

The death-mask face. The blood-soaked shirt.

Suddenly, the cruisers made sense. Blue and whites, yes. But some SBI, not CMPD.

For a moment I saw only a terrible whiteness. In it, a name in bold black letters.

I'll see that yank-off in hell before I bring him back in.

I took a step toward the guard. He spread his feet and shook his head. Stay back.

Beyond the parted curtain, the doctor's head snapped up. Muffled words came through his mask. "Keep everyone away."

I felt a buzzing inside my skull. Placed a palm on the wall to steady myself.

Was that why Slidell wasn't answering my calls? Where was he? What had he done?

Seconds ticked by.

A moth brushed my hair. Looped back.

I spun.

Ellis Yoder stood behind me. Doughy and freckled. Like some hideous apparition summoned by my fear.

Close. Too close.

I swatted Yoder's hand from my shoulder.

"The gunshot patient in there." Tipping my head toward Tinker. "What's the story?"

"You work with that psycho detective."

"What happened to that man?"

"Tell the jerk to lay off."

"That patient is a field agent with the SBI. How was he shot?"

Yoder just stared.

A hundredth of a second slipped by. A tenth.

I grabbed Yoder's arm, hard. "I know you're a snoop." Vise-gripping the flabby flesh. "What's the word, gossip boy?"

"You people are all nuts." Yoder tried to turn. I yanked him back.

"How. Was. He. Shot?" I hissed.

"You're hurting me."

"Call a nurse." My fingers clamped tighter.

"All I heard is another cop did it."

My mouth went dry. I swallowed.

Another tick of the clock.

Forget Slidell. Mary Louise needs you.

With my free hand, I yanked the picture of Tawny McGee from my pocket and held it up. "Point me to her."

Yoder glanced at the image. "She's not here."

Dear God, I'm right.

"Santos at the front desk says otherwise."

"Santos is clueless what goes on back here."

"You're sure?" Clutching the paper so hard it crumpled.

"I told you—" Whiny.

My nails dug deep into the mushy biceps.

"I'm sure."

I could hear my breath in the quiet of the car. Blood pounding in my ears.

I sat a moment studying the scene. The algae-coated brick. The rusty fences and awnings. The stunted concrete slabs.

Nothing moved but the rain. Which was falling harder now, drumming a tattoo on the car hood and roof.

I got out and scurried under the towering trees. Pushed into the lobby.

Not a single magazine lay on the tile.

Ring her bell? A neighbor's? Think!

No time.

I hurried outside and across the soggy lawn. Threw a leg over the railing and dropped onto the patio. Squatted and put my face to the milky glass.

Light seeped from a hallway running from the back of the apartment, feeble, barely penetrating the gloom. I could make out the silhouettes of a sofa, chair, and TV stenciled in the darkness cramming the room.

I reached up and tried the door. To my surprise, its latch disengaged, and it hopped a few inches across the track. The sound was like thunder cracking in the stillness. I froze.

Wheels whooshed wetly on the street at my back. A dog barked. Its owner whistled and the animal went quiet.

From the apartment's interior, an ocean of silence.

Was Mary Louise in there? Was my quarry? Did her twisted ritual involve some prelude that was buying us time? How long would it last? Was the child already dead?

Wait for Hull? I'd given her the address, but she wasn't here yet.

Move!

Pushing with both palms, I eased the door six inches more. Waited, senses alert to the tiniest nuance. Then, still crouching, I scuttled inside.

Like an animal seeking cover, I darted into a corner. Blinked to adjust my eyes. Listened.

Nothing but the hum of a motor. The hammering of my heart.

I rose and pressed my back to a wall. Slid to the hallway and peeked around the corner.

Two yards ahead, a bathroom, empty and dark. The light was coming from a door on the left.

My adrenaline-stoked brain flashed a rational

thought. I had no weapon. No way to defend myself should she be armed.

Heart banging, I backtracked through the living room and into the kitchen. A window above the sink oozed a fuzzy peach quadrangle onto the porcelain. Streetlight. Odd, but some tangle of cells made note.

The first drawer held towels, the second a jumble of cooking utensils. I cautiously rifled among them.

Bingo. A paring knife.

Ever so gently, I teased it free and set it on the counter.

Carefully digging out my phone, I tried to text Hull.

My fingers refused to obey my cortex. They felt numb. As though deadened by cold or anesthesia.

Shake it off!

Breath in.

Breath out.

I managed to key three words. An address. Hit send. Pocketed the phone. Then, blade angled backward and down, I tiptoe-ran back to the hall.

Light slivered the jamb and across the bottommost edge of the door. Yellow, steady. A low-wattage bulb, not a candle.

Shrinking inside my own skin as much as I could, I began inching forward. Two steps. I paused, straining for signs of another presence.

Only the hum of the refrigerator and the drumbeat of rain.

Three steps.

Three more.

Tightening my grip on the knife, I closed the final two feet. Stepped to the side of the door and pressed my back to the wall.

Every nerve a heated wire, I extended my free arm and pushed with a back-turned palm. No theatrical Hitchcock sound-effect creak. Just a noiseless re-angling of the door on its hinges. A slo-mo reveal of the room. I scanned the contents.

A twin bed, all done up in pink. A dresser with a ballerina princess lamp. A rocker stuffed with animals and dolls. A desk. Above it, a bulletin board layered with photos, news clippings, and memorabilia.

It looked like the room of a teenage girl.

My eyes probed the blackness in the corners and under the dresser and desk. The edges of bed skirt. A door I assumed gave on to a closet.

I listened for breathing. The soft whisper of fabric.

Heard nothing. The room was empty.

My gaze reversed. Swept more slowly. Came to rest on the bulletin board.

My brain did a cerebral cinematic zoom.

My chest tightened.

No! I was mistaken. It was a trick of the meager lighting.

I shook my head. As if that would help.

Front teeth pressing hard on my lower lip, I crossed to the board and stared at the photo.

Anique Pomerleau gazed up from her barrel, eyes

blank, blond hair wrapping her skull like a shroud.

I took an involuntary step backward. Maybe to distance myself from the evil I sensed. Maybe to avoid contaminating the scene.

A box sat dead center on the desktop. Old, carved, the knob on its cover darkened by the touch of many hands. Or the touch of just one.

Careful to avoid contact, I inserted the tip of the knife into the narrow space surrounding the lid. Levered up. Then, fast as lightning, I caught the lid's underside and flipped it free.

The box was full. Too full to disclose what lay in its depths. But one object sent blood surging into my head.

The uppermost item was a ballet slipper. In size and color, a perfect match for the one found in Hamet Ajax's trunk. Lizzie Nance's.

The slipper rested atop two photos. Me in a lab coat measuring a skull. Me entering the annex at Sharon Hall. My home.

My thoughts began racing. Emotions. Fear. Rage. Mostly rage.

Where was Slidell?

Where was Hull?

I closed my eyes. Felt heat at the backs of my lids.

No tears! Get more help! Find Mary Louise!

Using my iPhone, I shot two pics. Then, no longer concerned about stealth, I raced back to the kitchen, set the knife on the counter, yanked off my jacket, and

Kathy Reichs

wrapped it around my hand. Deep breath. I opened the freezer.

Popsicles. Fish sticks. Bagels. Lasagna.

Ziplocs containing hair and flesh. Vials of blood-red ice.

My stomach did something gymnastic. A bitter taste filled my mouth. I pivoted and took two shaky steps. Steadied myself on the sink with a jacket-swaddled hand.

When the nausea passed, I raised my eyes to the window. Saw a rain-blurred distortion of my face.

Beyond the glass, a streetlight, not five feet distant. Power lines crisscrossed its misty glow, casting spiderweb shadows on a patch of gravel below.

On a striped bucket hat with a tassel on top.

42

The shock morphed into a bloodlust of which I would have thought myself incapable. A savage hatred I'd never experienced.

I wanted the bitch.

And I knew where to find her.

The picture in the box.

Was it a mistake? Or a plea to end the insanity? Perhaps bait to lure me into a deadly trap?

I didn't care. I knew she'd gone to find me. I texted Hull again.

At the wheel, minutes after leaving the apartment on Dotger, I winged onto a narrow street shooting behind Sharon Hall. At ten P.M. the block was still as a tomb.

I killed the engine and flew from the car. Rain stung my face as I pounded up a driveway, through a backyard, and onto the grounds.

At the point where I pushed through the hedge,

the townhouses were freestanding brick structures in rows of three. The structures formed two sides of a square. Inside the square was a patch of concrete for parking.

I stopped to catch my breath and do a quick scan. Five cars. Among them a 2001 Chevy Impala. Tan.

She was here!

But where?

The main house was off to my left. Straight ahead, beyond its two wings and back courtyard, was the coach house. Beside it, the annex.

Would she dare bring her malignancy right to my doorstep?

My eyes probed the shadows among the trees and shrubs.

Rain soaked my hair, my jeans. My jacket clung to my shirt like an outer layer of skin.

Circle to the front? Take the brick walk along the back of the property?

Wait for backup? How long?

Fearing a male presence might trigger a full psychotic break in Tawny McGee, I hadn't phoned 911. Had I erred in relying on Hull? Had she gotten my second text giving this address? Was she already here? Could she even take action in this county?

My scalp felt tight and cold, my skin clammy inside my shirt. Not from rain. From adrenaline jolting every system into high.

Screw it.

I was off the block and sprinting. Around the back, down the walk, to a live oak directly opposite the annex.

There was no one in the patio, the side yard, the area where I parked. No one at the coach house.

Flashback.

Movement below a giant magnolia.

Heart banging, I raced to the front lawn.

And saw her beside the tree, brick boundary beyond her.

I reached into my pocket and pulled out the knife.

Go! screamed every cell in my brain stem.

Wait! urged a reasoning part of my cortex.

Panting and sweating, I allowed my higher centers to process. To convert my animal instincts into rational thought.

My breathing slowed. My heart eased its hammering against my ribs. My dilated pupils took in detail.

Her back was to me, so I couldn't see her face. But I could tell she was tall and broad-shouldered. Long neck. Slender legs. High boots.

She held an object in one hand. A larger one lay at her feet.

Above and around her, a tower of leaves gleamed slick as black ice. Here and there, a dull underside looked darkly opaque.

One deep breath. I began zigzagging from tree to tree, placing my feet soundlessly on the wet lawn. Jealously guarding the element of surprise.

When only one live oak stood between us, I tightened my fingers into a death-grip on the knife. Checked my hand.

No trembling. Good.

As my mind tore through options, she squatted and leaned over the thing on the ground. Head movements suggested speech, but no words made it to where I stood.

The thing on the ground changed shape.

She reached out.

The thing twisted, rounded like a sprout in time-lapse video.

Sat up.

White-hot fury sent wasps whining in my brain.

Blowing off caution, I strode forward.

"Alice." Loud. "Or should I say Kim?"

Both heads swiveled at the sound of my voice. One fast, one slow, as though dazed. Or drugged. Two pale ovals pointed my way in the darkness.

"Which is it, Tawny?" Coming in hot on adrenaline. "Did you kill her to steal the name?"

Tawny McGee rose to her full height and regarded me mutely.

"Or did you just like the ring of it? Alice Kimberly Hamilton." The steadiness of my voice surprised me.

"Go away."

"Not a chance."

I took another step. The oval topping the stalk neck

428

took on detail. Eyes. Nose. Mouth. The same face I'd seen framed in mother-of-pearl.

I couldn't read her expression. It might have been surprise. Or fear. Or anger. Or nothing.

"Kim's name was in a journal left at de Sébastopol. It survived the fire that Pomerleau set."

No response.

"Was Kim a fellow captive in the basement? Did Pomerleau or her sidekick murder her?"

Nothing but the patter of rain.

"Or was it you? Did you hunt Kim down and kill her?"

"I would never hurt Kim."

"Where is she?"

"I loved her." A statement about feeling, devoid of feeling.

"Where is she?" Cold.

She might have answered. But in that splinter of silence, Mary Louise whimpered, a sound like the mewing of a kitten.

"Let the child come to me."

"No."

"Now." Diamond-hard.

"I can't."

"Why not?"

"I love her, too."

"You don't know her."

"She won't endure what we did. What Kim did."

"Where is Kim?"

"She died." Flat.

"In the cellar?"

Again, no answer.

"Did you kill Anique Pomerleau?"

"I loved her."

"She tortured you."

Her eyes held, unblinking, wormholes into evil. Or madness. But her jaw slackened as she withdrew into her mind.

Several beats passed.

Sensing an altered vibe, Mary Louise raised her knees and planted her heels.

McGee placed a restraining hand on her head. "Stop. You'll get muddy."

"Let me go." Half pleading, half defiant.

"Soon."

"I don't like you. I want to go home."

"Down." With gentle pressure.

As Mary Louise lay back, a small ragged sob floated on the night.

At the sound, McGee tensed and looked down at the thing in her hand. For a moment my heart stopped beating. Was she holding a weapon? A gun?

I imagined my blade piercing her flesh. Her bone. Crushing through honeycombed marrow. The black cavity filling with blood. I didn't want to stab this woman. But I would. Dear God, I would.

McGee had escalated beyond her previous pattern. Perhaps due to pressure from Slidell. Maybe Ajax. The trigger didn't matter. The fact was, she was spinning out of control.

If armed, would she shoot the person closest to her? The one spoiling her game? Could I act quickly enough? Overcome her before she hurt Mary Louise?

The hollow stare. The disembodied voice. I feared the slightest thing would cause her to snap. Better to stall. To wait for Hull.

Unless McGee made a move.

Unless.

"You're a healer, Tawny. Not a killer."

"I'm a freak."

"No. You're not."

"How would you know?"

"I've spoken with Dr. Lindahl."

"She's useless."

"I've talked to your mother."

"My mother." Whip-crack sharp. "The bitch who never searched for me? The bitch who just moved away to start over?"

"She did search." Emptying my voice of all emotion.

"Not hard enough to find me."

"She—"

"Shut the fuck up about my mother!" The first note of hysteria.

Fast change of tack.

"You helped the girls." I said the names slowly, a mantra meant to calm. "Nellie. Lizzie. Tia. Shelly. You made them pretty. Made sure they wouldn't suffer."

"No one should hurt." Barely a whisper. "No one should die in the dark."

She was like a raft on white water. Lurching and spinning, wildly unstable.

As I groped for the right things to say, my eyes caught a glint in the shadows at two o'clock.

A bat or a bird? Imagined? I couldn't tell. It was there, then gone.

"The child's name is Mary Louise." Trying to personalize.

No response.

"Why have you brought Mary Louise to this place?"

"For you."

"I don't understand."

"You took me out."

"Of the cellar."

"You said I wasn't just a creature in a cage." McGee dropped to her knees and pressed the object that she was clutching to her chest. With her free hand, she stroked Mary Louise's hair. "She will never be a creature in a cage."

I could see two tiny white crescents in the dark recesses above Mary Louise's nose. Knew her eyes were open and wide with fear.

My fingers tightened on the knife. I would do it. I would.

"Where will you put her?" Skimming one foot over the grass. Inching the other forward to meet it.

"Here. In the sun."

"There are dogs." Taking another silent step.

No response as McGee thought about that. Or her next move.

"You must find a safer place," I said.

"Where?" Still caressing the child she would kill.

"No one looks under the porch."

Mary Louise blinked, all panic and heartbeat. I held up a finger. Wait.

"No," McGee said. "No darkness."

The next step brought me to within two yards. "Sun always shines through the slats."

McGee whipped around, startled at my proximity. "Get back!" Shooting upright.

"Let her go."

"No."

Now or never.

"No one looks under the porch!" I shrieked.

Three things happened.

I lunged for McGee.

Mary Louise rolled, then scrambled away on all fours.

A form burst from the shadow of the boundary wall.

Hull and I hit McGee at the same time.

It took thirty seconds to subdue her.

Another ninety to gather Mary Louise.

43

The earth had twirled on its axis fourteen times. Charlotte was enjoying one of those midwinter flukes that make you thankful you live in the South. The sky was an endless blue-gold dome, the temperature somewhere in the low seventies.

Mary Louise chose mango, topped it with strawberry and pineapple chunks, walnuts, raisins, and a thousand gummy things. It was a truly impressive amount of poundage.

We took our frozen yogurt to a small iron table outside the Phillips Place Pinkberry and watched post-holiday shoppers there to score bargains or off-load unwanted gifts. We made a game of guessing what item each might be returning. The kid's ideas were much more inventive than mine.

In the previous two weeks, CSS had spent days tossing the apartment on Dotger. The contents of the freezer were as I suspected. Blood. Scalp. Swabbed saliva. DNA testing showed everything came from Anique Pomerleau.

Chloral hydrate capsules were found in an unmarked vial in a bathroom cabinet. A syringe. A dish and pestle for mixing the powder with water.

Drawstring plastic bags were recovered from a kitchen drawer. Content analysis demonstrated that those remaining in the box were from the same manufacturer and batch as the one McGee had taken to Sharon Hall to asphyxiate Mary Louise.

A purple wool coat was collected from a hook in the bedroom closet. Fiber analysis linked it to the threads snagged on Ajax's backyard hedge.

In addition to Lizzie Nance's other ballet slipper, the box on McGee's desk contained news clippings covering the murders of Gower, Nance, and Estrada, and the disappearance of Donovan. And more pictures of me.

Mary Louise seemed unscathed, more than willing to talk about her ordeal. On her way home from school, she'd stopped by the annex to give me a picture of Birdie she painted in art class. Getting no response to her ringing and knocking, she'd decided to read her book on the patio and wait a short while.

She'd barely settled when a woman appeared, claiming to be my friend. The woman said I'd been taken ill and that I'd asked her to contact Mary Louise about minding Birdie, whom she had in her car. Trusting the woman, who was wearing scrubs and therefore a nurse, Mary Louise went to gather the cat.

Mary Louise remembered sharing apple slices as she and the woman walked to her vehicle; after that, "only swimmy bits from the romp on the lawn." Her words.

Ironically, at the time Mary Louise was being abducted, I'd been two blocks away, at the Marcus home.

Remains of an apple were found in Tawny McGee's Impala. Tox analysis showed portions contained chloral hydrate. The injected slices had been notched at one end.

An old MacBook Pro was dug out from under the car's front seat. Pastori and his IT pals were dissecting it every which way but Sunday.

McGee was charged with two counts of first-degree murder, kidnapping, and a dozen other offenses with regard to Leal and Nance, kidnapping and assault with regard to Mary Louise. Vermont was waiting in the wings with Gower. Deciding what to do about Pomerleau. Quebec was in line with Violette and Bastien. The upside to homicide: no statute of limitations.

McGee was interrogated daily, mostly by Barrow and Rodas. Slidell was on administrative leave, routine in any officer-involved shooting. He watched via remote hookup, smoldering, jotting notes so fiercely that his pencil lead often snapped and went flying.

Tinker—who had been discharged from Mercy and was recovering nicely—and Slidell gave differing accounts of the incident. Both versions and witness statements agreed on core facts.

Tinker had been at the home of Verlene Wryznyk, Slidell's former girlfriend and Tinker's flavor of the month. Tinker wanted to tango, Verlene didn't. She asked him to leave, he wouldn't. Frustrated, Verlene called someone she trusted.

Slidell stormed in breathing fire. Hoping to neutralize Skinny long enough to allow him to cool down, Tinker drew his weapon. The two struggled and the gun discharged. Tinker caught a bullet in the shoulder.

Slidell visited me at the MCME a week after McGee's arrest. God knows why, but he felt compelled to share the true story. After demanding stick-a-needle-in-my-eye confidentiality, he told me that Tinker had shown up drunk and become aggressive, and Verlene had capped him.

I told Slidell he was a sap for taking the hit. Got "Eeyuh" for an answer. Clearly, Skinny was not over Verlene.

McGee waived her right to counsel, even when she was assured that efforts would be made to secure a female attorney. Barrow and Rodas nearly wet themselves with joy.

Along with Slidell, I observed most of the questioning. Throughout, McGee was cool and distant. But her eyes were empty as glass, never connecting with anything or anyone in the room.

McGee admitted to stealing Kim Hamilton's identity. Talked freely of the girl with whom she'd been imprisoned. With whom she'd whispered, naked in the dark.

In 1998, Alice Kimberly Hamilton and four older teens made a clandestine trip from their hometown of Detroit to Toronto for a night of Canadian fun. At that time no passport was required to transit the border, so she carried a birth certificate in one shoe.

The secret trip turned deadly when Hamilton's path crossed that of Pomerleau or Catts/Menard. McGee didn't know why either would have traveled to Ontario. I suspected we never would.

Hoping to keep the sole link to her life out of the hands of her captors, Hamilton hid the birth certificate behind a cell wall, in a gap between the wood and cement. McGee listened to Hamilton's hushed secret, stored the information for possible future advantage.

Hamilton lasted only nineteen months in captivity. McGee had no idea what happened to her body. She was sixteen years old at the time of her death.

Once freed and in therapy, McGee pressed for a visit to the house on de Sébastopol. When Lindahl finally agreed, she went to the basement and dug out Hamilton's carefully concealed ID.

The document proved useful sooner than McGee could have anticipated. After storming from the

Kezerian home in the summer of 2006, she spent a week on the streets and eventually hooked up with a group of girls from the University of Vermont. Drunk or stoned, they offered her a ride south. Passports were still unnecessary for vehicular crossings, so McGee entered the States using Hamilton's birth certificate.

For several months she crashed at one student pad or another in Burlington. Using the money she'd stolen from Bernadette, and the name Alice Hamilton, she enrolled in a quick-trip online course and obtained certification as a CNA1.

McGee had learned of the Corneau farm by overhearing conversations between Pomerleau and Catts/Menard. More info stored for future advantage. In early 2007, using what remained of Bernadette's stash, and perhaps more obtained by the same means, she bought the aged Impala and set out for St. Johnsbury. One can only imagine that first meeting between former predator and prey.

By McGee's account, she and Pomerleau lived together for a while, making maple syrup and playing in the snow. All sins forgiven. One night Pomerleau died in her sleep. Saddened, McGee left Vermont for North Carolina to fulfill a long-standing desire to thank me properly. Thus the clipped photos.

Not sure if she'd flourish in Dixie, and wanting backup options, McGee kept paying the bills on the Corneau property. Pomerleau had explained the scam, the accounts at the Citizens Bank in Burlington. Or, more likely, McGee had extorted the information and stored it for future advantage.

I suspected a far different reality for the time in Vermont. McGee pursuing much darker desires. For payback. For torture. Eventually, for blood. One day we may learn how she overcame her former captor, how she harvested Pomerleau's tissues, how she killed her. Or we may not. That will be up to McGee.

When questioned about Gower, Nance, Leal, and the other girls, McGee switched to abstractions. Talked of angels, of sunlight, of eternal peace and safety. Only then did something remotely human soften her eyes.

When asked why Pomerleau was in a barrel, McGee stared blankly.

When asked about human tissue in her freezer, she stared blankly.

When asked about chloral hydrate, she stared blankly.

When asked about Hamet Ajax, she stared blankly.

Incredibly shrewd or crazy as a loon. I couldn't decide.

"Ready?"

Mary Louise's voice snapped me back to the present. I was wrong about her intake capacity. The kid had cleaned her tub.

"Yes, ma'am," I said, bunching my napkin.

While driving, we discussed the latest project. Mary Louise was creating hats to honor each of the murdered or missing girls. A knitted stocking cap for

Nellie Gower. A chignon-wrapping thing for Lizzie Nance. A seashell affair for Shelly Leal. A cloche with a fleur-de-lis on the band for Violette, an Acadian flag for Bastien. The other designs were still on the board.

Mary Louise knew, of course. The story had dominated the news for over a week. Leal. Nance. Estrada. The CMPD was basking in the warmth of citizen approval. But there was one alteration to the cast of characters. The press conferences hadn't featured Tinker on the dais.

In the glow of generalized goodwill, Henrietta Hull had escaped all censure for acting outside her jurisdiction. Even in her hurry, she'd been smart enough to notify her dispatcher that she needed to go to Mecklenburg on one of her cases to question a potential witness possibly planning to leave the area. She'd also notified the CMPD that she needed to see a person of interest in Charlotte on an out-of-county matter, but would not require local assistance. That seemed to satisfy everybody, and it cut her in for a portion of the credit for subsequent events.

I was asked for interviews. Did them at Salter's request. Journalists wanted to probe my emotions. "How do you feel about these murdered children? How do you feel about catching their killer?" I felt like smacking the mikes into their carefully practiced frowns.

And then the fickle media moved on.

Ryan phoned twice immediately after McGee's

arrest, his voice thick with remorse. My comment about the journal found at de Sébastopol and the possibility of another victim had made him start looking into Kim Hamilton. He'd been working nonstop, pairing hints dropped by Lindahl and the Kezerians with data dug from Canadian border control files, and researching participation in online nursing courses tracing to Vermont. One more day and he'd have zeroed in on McGee. It was why he'd stayed in Montreal.

I told Ryan that he'd done the right thing. That it was the way we worked. Our MO. He said he should have been there for me. Yeah. For me. I tried to believe it, but deep down, I suspected his true regret was at not being part of the final climax scene. And then he stopped calling.

I drove Mary Louise to her door. We hugged, then I watched her all the way into the house. Two weeks, and still the guilt turned me inside out. Perhaps always would.

The next day, I showered, blow-dried my hair, and donned fresh jeans and a white Ella Moss blouse. Hip but not overdone.

I was looking forward to the rendezvous. And dreading it. I hadn't exactly been rescued. But I'd been assisted in a situation I might have bungled alone. I felt grateful. And embarrassed by the need to feel grateful.

At ten past seven, I turned in to the lot outside Good

Food on Montford. My suggestion. The place would be loud enough to shield our words, quiet enough to allow conversation across a table.

Hull was there, seated at a two-top off to one side. Dressed as I was, with careful nonchalance.

On seeing me, Hull waved, palm pink against the deeply pigmented skin covering the rest of her ample form. I wove my way to her.

"How's it going, Merlin?" Her smile was warm and toothy.

Synapse. A flash of white in the darkness. A grunt. Simultaneous hits that blasted air from McGee's lungs and laid her flat.

"Can't complain. And you, Mean Joe?"

"Smooth and in the groove."

Mary Louise had gone off in an ambulance. Tawny McGee had gone to jail. Sitting in the darkness, waiting to tell our story, Hull and I had eased the tension by tagging each other with NFL nicknames. Olsen and Greene, two legendary tackles.

I slid into the vacant chair. Seconds later, a waiter appeared. Sean.

I asked for Perrier. Hull wanted a Bud. While Sean got the drinks, we considered the menu. Which took some time, since the place had a tapas format.

"How's Slidell?" Hull asked when we'd ordered— I'd ordered. Hull had just tossed the menu and rolled her eyes. Which were large and the color of Hershey's syrup.

"Skinny's like the heroine in a bad horror movie," I said.

"Still breathing at the credits."

"Always."

"And Tinker?"

"No idea."

Once all the little dishes arrived, we served ourselves, then turned to developments since last we talked.

"The DNA from the lip print was a match to McGee?" Hull poked at a mussel.

I nodded. "The results came back yesterday. Her face must have brushed Leal's jacket as she was transporting the body."

"No one knows diddly about the hair found in Estrada's throat."

"It's gone?"

"Like the wind."

"Not surprising, given the ineptness of the autopsy report." I helped myself to a meatball. "Plowing through all the surveillance video paid off. Twice they've got what was probably McGee's Impala heading in the direction of I-485."

"The night Leal was left under the overpass."

I nodded again. "They're hoping enhancement will allow them to read the plate."

Hull smiled wryly. "The two-digit match to Ajax was just coincidence."

"And the child seen on Morningside wasn't Leal.

Talk about the world's unluckiest sex offender."

"How about the laptop?" Hull eyed the beef carpaccio, opted for another fried oyster.

"Pure gold. It appears McGee found Nance through chat rooms that answer questions about nursing as a career."

"She'd already moved from Vermont to Charlotte?"

"Looks that way. Five years later, she spotted Leal in the ER. Used the opportunity to tip the kid to the dysmenorrhea forum. Communicated with her there."

We went silent, thinking about the vulnerability of children amid the pitiless anonymity of the Internet.

"Any evidence of contact with Colleen Donovan?" she asked.

"Nothing so far. Donovan was living on the street and may not have had access to a computer."

"She's still in the wind?"

"Yeah."

A few beats passed as we ate.

"So McGee laced Ajax's coffee, then set him up in his car," Hull said. "Why?"

"Slidell's phone calls and visits to the ER and to her apartment must have triggered some sort of paranoid spiral. Knowing the cops suspected Ajax, McGee killed him and planted evidence in his trunk to close the deal."

"Why do you suppose Ajax let her in?"

"Undoubtedly, she'd concocted some plausible story about the ER and when he'd be able to return.

McGee may be deeply disturbed, but she's cunning."

"And clever at hiding the fact that she's psycho."

Not exactly PC, but true.

"McGee used chloral hydrate to subdue her vics. How come the stuff only showed up in Ajax?"

"Mary Louise Marcus had chloral hydrate in her system. The toxicologist found it because he knew to look. Standard drug screens typically test for alcohol, narcotics, sedatives, marijuana, cocaine, amphetamines, and aspirin."

"But we're talking dead kids. No one went beyond standard testing?"

"The girls' bodies weren't found right away. For Gower it was eight days, for Nance fourteen, for Estrada four. Even if you're looking for chloral hydrate, which no one was, decomposition can mask its presence."

Hull's brows dipped in confusion.

"On a gas chromatograph, decomp chemicals will peak higher than chloral hydrate. Even if further testing had been done, it might have been missed."

"You think McGee killed Gower by herself? Or after she hooked up with Pomerleau?"

"Murder was never Pomerleau's style."

Hull dipped her chin and tipped her head. Seriously?

"You know what I mean. Of course it was murder. But in Pomerleau's case, the killing was a by-product of cruelty and deprivation. Not a primary objective."

"Right."

"Anyway, unless McGee tells us, we may never know where she was living when Gower went down. Or if she acted alone."

"Or if Gower was her first."

I'd had the same grim thought.

"Why'd McGee break the pattern of dates and grab Marcus?"

"Same answer. Slidell's probing sent her spiraling out of control."

Hull's chewing slowed as she rolled that around. Then, "I get the dates. She's killing on the anniversaries of abductions or deaths in Montreal. Kids she knew. Maybe kids she saw die. But why the hair, the tissues soaked with saliva? Why plant Pomerleau's DNA on her victims?"

I'd posed that question to Pamela Lindahl during the many hours we'd spent on the phone. Though difficult to assess long-distance, the psychiatrist's tone had suggested agonizing guilt.

I took a moment to organize my thoughts. And have a bite of sweet-corn risotto.

"McGee's therapist is convinced the arousal didn't come from degrading or controlling, as with many serial killers. She feels McGee's psychosis is two-pronged. First, she's reenacting the deaths of the original victims, but killing them quickly and leaving them 'in the sun' to assure that her victims will never suffer as she did."

"That's why the bodies were placed out in the

open, arranged with care and free of trauma or disfigurement."

"Exactly. Second, McGee was seeking revenge on Pomerleau. But at the same time, she was diverting attention from herself, should she ever fall under suspicion."

"So the shrink says she was driven by both love and hate." Dubious. "And an instinct for self-preservation."

"Yes."

"Targets were chosen because they resembled one of Pomerleau's Montreal victims?"

"Probably McGee herself. She was abducted at age twelve."

"McGee made the calls six months out? Checking to see if the cops had anything on Donovan or Estrada?"

"Probably," I said.

Hull bunched and tossed her napkin. Leaned back. Crossed her arms and wagged her head slowly. "Don't sound like enough crazy to me."

I pictured a girl in a trench coat and crooked beret. Felt sorrow clot any response I might have offered.

I knew the drill. So did Hull. McGee's mental competence would be determined by pretrial motions and hearings and judges and lawyers.

Sane. Insane. Either finding would result in Tawny McGee's worst nightmare, one she'd already endured. A life in one type of prison or another.

It had to be.

Even the damaged cannot be allowed to damage.

44

The next morning I drove to Heatherhill Farm. Like the magnolia at Sharon Hall, the azaleas and rhododendron winked both waxy green and dull brown. I imagined the upside-down leaves, startled by the warm spell, turning for instruction from their roots.

River House itself was half in shade and half in bright sun. Its windows also looked confused, undecided between reflecting and ingesting light.

Mama was on the back deck, bundled in a parka and scarf, stretched out on the same chaise she'd occupied Thanksgiving week. As I had then, I paused a moment to study her. Perhaps to fix her image forever in my memory.

She'd lost weight, though the bulky jacket made that appraisal difficult. Her hands were chapped, the treasured hair a bit dull. Still, my mother looked beautiful.

It was a pleasant visit. No rancor. No resentment. I didn't bring up chemo. She didn't correct my manners or dress.

I told Mama about the arrest of Tawny McGee. About the CAIS. About the psychopathology of hatred and love. She called it Pomerleau's legacy of madness.

I thanked Mama for her input. Said the YouTube cycling video had been the big break in the case. Ryan's big bang.

She asked if I'd seen Ryan. I said not for a while. She didn't persist.

Then I told her the good news. The police had located Kim Hamilton's brother, now living in Miami. He was saddened to learn of his sister's death and troubled by not knowing the location of her remains. Mostly, he was comforted by confirmation of a truth he'd always felt in his soul. Kim hadn't turned her back on her family by running away.

At noon Mama and I shared a lunch of avocado salad and grilled chicken breast. At one Goose trundled Mama off for her nap.

That evening I turned in early. As was common since I'd met Umpie Rodas two months earlier, memories bombarded me the instant I closed my eyes. Unbidden apparitions involving bones and corpses and children.

I had no say in the order or arrival times of these sad visitations. Only in their duration. As soon as a reel began to play, I'd shut it down.

For some reason, that night I let my mind roll.

I saw Nellie Gower pedaling her bike, brown hair flying and catching the sun. Tawny McGee tightening the drawstring of a plastic bag under her chin.

Lizzie Nance practicing pliés and arabesques at a ballet bar. McGee closing her lifeless little fingers around a bunched white tissue.

Tia Estrada walking hand in hand with her mother. McGee tucking long blond hairs deep into her throat.

Shelly Leal tapping a keyboard, face radiant in the glow of the screen. McGee arranging her still body on a highway embankment.

I imagined the girls at the moment their worlds halted forever. Did they know death was at hand? Did they ask why?

In addition to the ballet slipper and clippings, McGee's souvenir box had contained a yellow ribbon identical to the one found in Hamet Ajax's trunk. Avery Koseluk's mother didn't recognize the ribbons. Laura Lonergan said they had not belonged to Colleen Donovan. Neither had yielded DNA.

I pictured those ribbons, wondered if they'd once bound the hair of my Jane Doe skeleton. Of another little girl as yet unknown to us. Though we might never learn for certain if there had been other victims, Barrow and Rodas would investigate on the U.S. end, Ryan in Canada.

I saw my Jane Doe, a sad collection of bones labeled ME107-10. Wondered if somewhere a family was searching.

I saw Colleen Donovan. Avery Koseluk. Hoped one day each would enter a police station seeking help.

We'd never know who removed Donovan's name from the list of MPs on the NamUS site. It was back there now. With Koseluk and the scores of others either missing or lying anonymously in morgues or police evidence rooms.

Anique Pomerleau. Tawny McGee. Victims. Monsters. Their childhoods stolen. Their adult games played out with cold-blooded cunning.

It was finished now.

Yet it wasn't.

The next morning I ran two miles. A quick shower, a bout of paper shuffling. Then I began grading lab exercises for the spring-semester course I was teaching at UNCC.

Earlier in the week, my front doorbell had begun sounding like a seagull with adenoid issues. I'd gotten halfway through the stack when a wobbly squawk interrupted.

Curious, I hurried to the door and peered through the peephole.

A spectacularly blue eye peered back.

Startled, I jumped.

Great.

Conscious of my wet hair and baggy yoga pants, I opened the door.

Ryan was wearing jeans, a leather jacket, and a black wool muffler. His cheeks were blotchy red. Probably due to overheating.

For a moment no one spoke. Then we both tried at once.

"This is a surprise," I said.

"I should have phoned," he said.

"You go first," I said.

"Marry me," he said.

"I— What?" That couldn't be right.

"I'm proposing."

"Proposing."

"Marriage."

"Yes."

"It's my first time."

"Yes."

"I'd envisioned a much more romantic pitch."

"Your delivery was clear."

"Shall I practice and try again later?"

"You were fine."

"Or we could do dinner."

"I often eat dinner."

Ryan pulled me close. I put my arms around him and pressed my cheek to his chest. A beat, then I stepped back.

We looked at each other.

"Eight o'clock?" he asked.

"Eight is good," I said.

Then Ryan was gone.

Zombie-like, I went inside. Closed and leaned on the door.

I couldn't say how long I stood taking in the familiar. The known.

Harry's chenille throw on the sofa back. Gran's sweetgrass basket on the rug by the armchair. Mama's silver candlesticks on the mantel.

My gaze fell on an item confiscated at the apartment on Dotger. A child's painting—the one Mary Louise had made of Birdie that she'd wanted to show me.

In my mind, I saw ice-blue eyes. Heard again and again the offer of an altered future.

I thought of endless uncertain possibilities. Of impediments I could neither foresee nor control.

I felt a smile nudge my lips.

Maybe.

Just maybe.

But today I would frame the painting of the white cat playing with the red plaid mouse.

Acknowledgments

As usual, I owe a huge debt of thanks to a whole lot of people.

Bones Never Lie benefited greatly from all those at the Charlotte-Mecklenburg Police Department Homicide/ADW and Cold Case units who shared their time, their memories, and their expertise with me. A special shout-out to Chuck Henson, Dave Philips, and Lisa Mangum.

I am grateful to Mike Bisson, Michael Baden, and Diane Seguin for answering many questions, and to Courtney Reichs for input on hospitals and the nursing profession.

Cheri Byrd and Michelle Skipper provided copious quantities of buoyant enthusiasm. And wine and giggles.

I appreciate the continued support of Chancellor Philip L. Dubois of the University of North Carolina at Charlotte.

Sincere thanks to my agent, Jennifer Rudolph-Walsh, and to my rock star editors, Jennifer Hershey and Susan Sandon.

I also want to acknowledge all those who work so very hard on my behalf. At home in the U.S.: Gina Centrello, Libby McGuire, Kim Hovey, Scott Shannon, Susan Corcoran, Cindy Murray, Kristin Fassler, Cynthia Lasky, and Joey McGarvey. On the other side of the pond: Simon Littlewood, Glenn O'Neill, Georgina Hawtrey-Woore, and Jen Doyle. North of the forty-ninth: Kevin Hanson and Amy Cormier. At William Morris Endeavor Entertainment: Caitlin Moore, Maggie Shapiro, Tracy Fisher, Cathryn Summerhayes, and Raffaella De Angelis.

I appreciate Paul Reichs's insightful comments on the manuscript.

As always, a big *merci* to my readers. It is gratifying that you follow Tempe's adventures, attend my signings and appearances, visit my website (KathyReichs.com), like me on Facebook, and follow me on Twitter (@kathyreichs). You guys dazzle!

If I left anyone out, I apologize. If the book contains errors, I own them.

Chapter 1

"I'm unbound now. My wrists and ankles burn from the straps. My ribs are bruised and there's a lump behind my ear. I don't remember hitting my head."

"I'm lying very still because my whole body aches, like I've been in a wreck. Like the time my brother pushed my bike and I wobbled down the hill and crashed. Mama got mad because I tore my dress. I cried and cried. I think I was eleven. Six years ago? Seven?"

"Where's my family? Why don't they rescue me? Why don't they save me? Is no one missing me? Worried about me? I have only my family. I have no friends. It was just too hard. I'm all alone. So alone."

"How long have I been here? Where is here? The whole world is slipping away. Everything. Everyone."

"Am I awake or asleep? Am I dreaming or is this real. Is it day or night?"

"When they return they will hurt me again."

"Why? Why is this happening to me?"

"I can't hear anything. Nothing at all. No. That's not true. I can hear my heart beating. Blood working inside my ears."

"I can taste something bitter. Probably vomit stuck in my teeth."

"I can smell cement. My own sweat. My dirty hair. I hate when my hair isn't washed."

I'm gonna open my eyes now."

"Got one. The other's crusted shut. Can't see much. Just dark. Walls. Floor. The bed. The chair. It's all blurry, like I'm looking at the room from way down under water."

"I hate the waiting. I know they are coming."

"That's when the pictures take over my brain. I try to block them, but it's no good. Not sure if they're memories or hallucinations."

"I see him. Always in black, his face crazy red and beady with sweat. I try to avoid his eyes. Keep looking at his shoes. Shiny shoes. The candle flame's a little yellow worm dancing on the leather."

"He stands over me, all big and nasty. Thrusts his horrid, smelly face close to mine. I feel his icky breath on my skin. Hear it moving between his skinny little lips."

"He gets mad and yanks me by the hair. His veins go all bulgy and his eyes go wild. He screams and his words sound like they're coming from another planet. Or like I've left my body and I'm listening from far away. Or maybe on a phone with a bad connection."

"I see his hand coming at me, clutching the thing so tight it quivers. I know I'm shaking but I can't feel my body. I'm numb. Or am I dead?"

"No! Not now! Don't let it happen now!"

"I don't hear anything."

"My hands are going all cold and tingly. My scalp is tight. I shouldn't be talking about him. I shouldn't have said he was horrid."

"I don't hear anything but I know what's coming."

"Yes. They're coming."

"My feet are like ice."

"Why is this happening to me? What did I do? I've always tried to be good. Tried to do what Mama said."

"Don't let them kill me! Mama, please don't let them kill me!"

"My muscles are cramping."

"My mind is going all fuzzy."

"I have to stop talking."

Silence, then the click-creak of a door opening. Closing.

Footsteps, unhurried, firm on the floor.

"It's time."

"No!"

"Take your place."

"No!"

"Don't resist me."

"Leave me alone!"

The cadence of frantic breathing.

The thunk of a blow.

"Please don't kill me."

"Do as I say."

Sobbing.

Sound as if dragging.

Moaning. Rhythmic.

"Are you in my hands?"

"Filthy bitch!"

A soft rasp.

The tic of metal snapping into place.
"You will die, slut!"
"Will you answer me now?"
"Whore!"
The drumming of agitated fingers. Scratching.
"Give me what I need!"
"Filthy whore!"
"Yield!"
Pfff! The violent hurling of spit.
"You will not answer?"
Moaning.
"This has only begun."
Click-creak. The furious slam of a door.
Absolute stillness.
Soft sobbing.
"Please don't kill me."
"Please don't kill me."
"Please."
"Kill me."

Chapter 2

The woman's knuckles bulged pale under skin that was cracked and chapped. Using one knobby finger, she depressed a button on the object in the Ziploc.

The room went still.

I sat motionless, the hairs on my neck lifted like grass in a breeze.

The woman's eyes stayed hard on mine. They were green flecked with yellow, and made me think of a cat. A cat that could bide, then pounce with deadly accuracy.

I let the silence stretch. Partly to calm my own nerves. Mostly to encourage the woman to explain the purpose of her visit. And the meaning of the terrible sounds I'd just heard.

The woman remained angled forward in her chair. Tense. Expectant. She was tall, at least six feet, and wore boots, jeans, and a denim shirt with the cuffs rolled up her lower arms. Her hair was dyed the color of the clay at Roland Garros. She'd yanked it into a bun high on her head.

My eyes broke free from the cat-gaze and drifted to the wall at the woman's back. To a framed certificate

463

declaring Temperance Brennan a diplomate of the American Board of Forensic Anthropology. D-ABFA. The exam had been a bitch.

I was alone with my visitor in the one hundred and twenty square feet allocated to the Mecklenburg County Medical Examiner's consulting forensic anthropologist. I'd left the door open. Not sure why. Usually I close it. Something about the woman made me uneasy.

Familiar workplace sounds drifted in from the corridor. A ringing phone. A cooler door whooshing open then clicking shut. A rubber-wheeled gurney rolling toward an autopsy suite.

"I'm sorry." I was pleased that my voice sounded calm. "The receptionist provided your name but I've misplaced my note."

"Strike. Hazel Strike."

That caused a little ping in my brain. What?

"Folks call me Lucky."

I said nothing.

"But I never rely on luck. I work hard at what I do." Though I guessed Strike's age at somewhere north of sixty, her voice was still twenty-something strong. The accent suggested she was probably local.

"And what is it you do, Ms. Strike?"

"Mrs. My husband passed six years back."

"I'm sorry."

"He knew the risk, chose to smoke." Slight lift of one shoulder. "You pay the price."

"What is it you do?" I repeated, wanting to draw Strike back on point.

"Send the dead home."

"I'm afraid I don't understand."

"I match bodies to people gone missing."

"That is the task of law enforcement in conjunction with coroners and medical examiners," I said.

"And you pros nail it every time."

I bit back another priggish response. Strike had a point. Stats I'd read put the number of missing persons in the US at around ninety thousand at any given time, the number of unidentified remains from the last fifty years at more than forty thousand. At last count North Carolina had one hundred and seven UID's.

"How can I help you, Mrs. Strike?"

"Lucky."

"Lucky."

Strike placed the Ziploc beside a bright yellow case file on my blotter. In it was a gray plastic rectangle, roughly one inch wide, two inches long, and a half inch thick. A metal ring at one end suggested dual functions as a recorder and a key chain. A loop of faded denim suggested the device had once hung from the waistband of a pair of jeans.

"Impressive little gizmo," Strike said. "Voice activated. Two gigabyte internal flash memory. Sells for less than a hundred bucks."

The yellow folder called to me. Accusingly. Two months earlier a man had died in his recliner, TV remote clutched in one hand. The previous weekend his mummified corpse had been found by a very unhappy landlord. I needed to wrap this up and get back to my analysis.

But those voices. My pulse was still struggling to get back to normal. I waited.

"The recording lasts almost twenty-three minutes. But the five you heard is plenty to get the drift." Strike gave a tight shake of her head. Which re-angled the bun to an off-center tilt. "Scares the patooty out of you, don't it?"

"The audio is disturbing." An understatement.

"Ya think?"

"Perhaps you should play it for the police."

"I'm playing it for you, doc."

"I believe I heard three voices?" Curiosity was overcoming my reticence to engage. And apprehension.

"That's my take. Two men and the girl."

"What was happening?"

"Don't know."

"Who was speaking?"

"Only got a theory on one."

"And that is?"

"Can we back up a bit?"

I brushed my eyes past my watch. Not as discreetly as I thought.

"Unless you're not 'tasked' with sticking names on the dead." Strike hooked sarcastic finger quotes around the term I'd used moments earlier.

I leaned back and assumed my listening face.

"What do you know about websleuthing?"

So that was it. I vowed to keep my tone patient, but my answers short.

"Websleuths are amateurs competing online to solve cold cases." Wannabe forensic scientists and cops.

Overzealous viewers of *NCIS*, *Cold Case*, *CSI*, and *Bones*. I didn't add that.

Strike's brows drew together over her nose. They were dark and looked wrong with the pale skin and fake carrot hair. She studied me a very long moment before responding.

"Most people die, they get a funeral, a wake, a memorial service. There are eulogies, an obit in the paper. Some get holy cards showing their faces with angels or saints or what not. You're really hot stuff, maybe there's a school or a bridge named in your honor. That's what's supposed to happen. That's how we deal with death. By recognizing a person's achievements in life.

"But what happens when someone just disappears? Poof." Strike curled then exploded her fingers. "A man leaves for work and vanishes? A woman boards a bus and never gets off?"

I started to speak but Strike rolled on.

"And what happens when a body turns up lacking ID? On a roadside, in a pond, bundled in a carpet and stashed in a shed?"

"As I've stated, that is the job of police and medical examiners. At this facility we do everything possible to ensure that all human remains are identified, no matter the circumstances or their condition."

"That might be true here. But you know as well as I do it's a crap shoot elsewhere. A corpse might luck out, be examined for scars, piercings, tattoos, old trauma, get printed and sampled for DNA. A decomp or a skeleton might end up with an expert like you, have its teeth charted, its sex, age, race, and height entered into a database. Another jurisdiction, similar remains might get a quick once-over then storage in a freezer, maybe a back room or basement. A nameless body might be held a few weeks, maybe a few days, then cremated or buried in a potter's field."

"Mrs. Strike—"

"Lost. Murdered. Dumped. Unclaimed. This country's overflowing with the forgotten dead. And somewhere someone's wondering about each and every one of those souls."

"And websleuthing is a way to solve the problem."

"Darn right." Strike shoved her sleeves hard up her arms, as though the cuffs had suddenly grown too tight on her flesh.

"I see."

"Do you? Have you ever visited a websleuthing site?"

"No."

"You know what goes on in those forums?"

Recognizing the question as rhetorical, I offered no response.

"UID's are tagged with cute little nicknames. Princess Doe. The Lady of the Dunes. Tent Girl. Little Miss Panasoffkee. Baby Hope."

The ping exploded into a full-blown synapse.

"You identified Old Bernie," I said.

Old Bernie was a partial skeleton found by hikers in 1974 behind a shelter on the Neusiok Trail in the Croatan National Forest. The remains were sent to the Office of the Chief Medical Examiner, in those days located in Chapel Hill, and were determined to be those of an elderly white male. A New Bern detective assigned to the case had no luck in establishing ID.

For years the skeleton remained in a box in an OCME storeroom. Somewhere along the way it came to be known as Old Bernie, named for New Bern, the town closest to the point of the old man's discovery.

Articles ran at the time Old Bernie turned up – in Raleigh, Charlotte, New Bern and surrounding towns. The case was featured again, with the photo of a facial reconstruction, in the *New Bern Sun Journal* on March 24, 2004, the thirtieth anniversary of the gentleman's discovery. No one ever came forward to claim the bones.

In 2007, a technician at the OCME mentioned the case to me. I agreed to take a look.

I concurred that the remains were those of an edentulous African-American who had died between the ages of sixty-five and eighty. But I took issue with one of my predecessor's key findings, and suggested the victim's nickname be changed from Bernie to Bernice. The pelvic features were clearly those of a female. And the lady had clearly given birth.

I took samples for possible DNA testing, then Old Bernie went back to her cardboard carton in Chapel Hill. The following year, the National Missing and Unidentified Persons System, NamUs, came online. NamUs, a database for unidentified remains, in cop lingo UID's, and missing persons, in cop lingo MP's, is free and available to everyone. I entered case descriptors into the section for UID's. Soon amateur websleuths were swarming like flies.

"Yep," Strike said. "That was me."

"How did you do it?"

"Pure doggedness."

"That's vague."

"I scanned a billion pictures on NamUS and other sites listing MP's. Made a lot of calls, asking about old ladies missing their teeth. Came up blank on both fronts. Then I went off line, pulled up stories in local papers, talked to cops in New Bern and Craven County, the park rangers at Croatan, that kind of thing. Nothing.

"On a hunch I started phoning old folks homes. Found a facility in Havelock had a patient disappear in 1972. Charity Dillard. The administrator reported Dillard missing, but no one really made much effort. The home is close to a boat ramp, so they figured Dillard fell into the lake and drowned. When Old Bernie turned up two years later, no one paid attention because the skeleton was supposed to be that of a man. End of story."

"Until you made the link." I'd heard about the ID through the state ME grapevine.

"Dillard had one living grandson, out in LA. He provided a swab. Your bone samples yielded DNA. Case closed."

"Where is Dillard now?"

"Kid popped for a headstone. Even flew east for the burial."

"Nice job."

"It wasn't right, her gathering dust in a box." Again the shoulder shrug.

I now knew why Strike was sitting in my office.

"You've come about unidentified remains," I said.

"Yes, Ma'am."

I angled two palms in a "go on" gesture.

"Cora Teague. Eighteen-year-old white female. Disappeared up in Avery County three and a half years back."

"Was Teague reported missing?"

"Not officially."

"What does that mean?"

"No one filed an MP report. I found her on a websleuthing site. The family believes she took off on her own."

"You've spoken to the family?"

"I have."

"Is that a common part of websleuthing?"

"Something's happened to this kid and no one's doing dink."

"Have you contacted the local authorities?"

"Eighteen makes her adult. She can come and go as she likes. Blah. Blah. Blah."

"That's true."

Strike jerked a thumb at the Ziploc. "That sound like someone doing as she likes?"

"You think Cora Teague is the girl on that recording?"

Strike gave a slow nod of her head.

"Why bring this to me?"

"I believe you've got parts of Teague stashed here."